# Beyond the Great Dying
# By NS Austin

Author's Note:  Beyond the Great Dying is the second book in a series. I've purposely written each book to be different and to have a definitive ending. If you are interested in more about the characters, particularly regarding the New Washington Enclave Founders, please consider reading the first novel of the Endangered Series, Critically Endangered.

# Contents

## Prelude

*Flying above the snow swept landscape, a bird would take little notice of the two unremarkable buildings below. The only signs of life, a man hauling a sled and a dim glow of lights. The man, trudging over an ice packed path between the two lonely structures, slipped once, almost falling, and stopped to secure his balance. Of course, a bird wouldn't be flying over this desolate place. Above sea level elevation was too high and temperatures too frigid once the sun set. In a mostly empty world where humans had their pick of the best spots, a settlement on the side of Mount Rainier might defy good logic.*

*From one hundred years past, the world had changed in an instant. If only the stubborn nature of man could change so quickly. The people of New Washington needed a forward guard. Someone to watch, wait, and warn the others; to protect their vulnerable enclave from the aggressions of other men. And so, they waited, over half way up the side of a mountain, with weapons from the old world to keep the others safe.*

Manny's prosthetic leg pushed the door open. He turned his body and used the massive pack on his back to keep the door ajar as he maneuvered a loaded sled through the entrance. Wind and storm snow surged through the opening. Dripping ice wads clung to Manny's curly, dark beard from the short hike to the Rainier Station.

Dee jumped up to help. "You could have called me, Manny."

"No need. I had it. I brought our sleeping bags and some storm munchies. The heater in the house isn't for crap. I've made a command decision to hunker down here until this thing passes." Manny reached down to greet Goldie. "How's it hanging, wonder dog?" Goldie's tail wagged in an excited circle as she pressed her head to his hand.

Craig barely looked up from his monitor. His heel was rapidly tapping the floor and only paused when he yelled, "Close the damn door!"

"What's up with him?" Manny said under his breath to Dee.

"They're back, and they brought a friend. A sizeable friend."

Manny's normally open, friendly face drew into a look of concern. He finished pulling the sled into the room and heaved the door against the wind to close it as the roar of an early spring storm engulfed the station. Dropping his pack onto a chair, Manny walked across the room in his stilted one-legged gait, stood behind Craig, and looked over his shoulder at the radar display.

"See it? There's the three UFO's that fly south from Canada in a loop every other month but look what's following them. It's huge."

Holding the back of Greg's chair, Manny leaned in. "Could it be a radar anomaly because of the storm?" Inside a green lit circle on a video display, three tiny circles surrounded a much larger oval-shaped image crawling across the screen.

"That's what I thought at first, but an anomaly isn't going to cruise in formation at the same speed and distance. It isn't a weather shadow. The shape is consistent—oblong and over a kilometer at its longest point. If that's some kind of aircraft, it's the biggest thing I've ever seen. They didn't have anything that big before the Great Dying."

"Are they travelling on the same heading as before?"

"Not exactly. Heading at 295.5 instead of 266."

"Can you overlay their flight pattern from their visit two months ago on the screen?" Manny asked.

"Yeah, give me a moment." Typing madly on his keyboard, Craig entered the date of the last sighting, and a red line appeared on the screen. "I was right, not exactly. They're further west. I'm getting freaked here, Manny. What if they don't make their normal turn and head north away from the enclave? No telling what a ship that size could be carrying. That's why we're stuck on the side of Mount Rainier in the first place, to shoot anything out of the sky that has plans to drop a bomb on our collective heads. I think we have to use the missiles."

"This isn't good." Manny exhaled as he nervously rubbed his head.

"You're a master of understatement," Craig quipped.

Standing on the other side of Craig's back, Dee put her hand on top of Goldie's head, nervously playing with her fur. "I've seen enough. We need to call Jed now."

She threw herself at the old-style, wheeled desk chair and grabbed their only landline as the chair rolled by the phone. "I hope this storm hasn't caused another outage and that Jed can be reached. Land lines aren't the most reliable way to make decisions. It's fifty-fifty whether anyone will pick-up." She dialed Jed's number. After twenty rings and just as she was ready to try the shortwave, Janet answered.

"Hello, this is Air Systems Headquarters, Janet speaking."

"Janet, it's Dee. We have a situation. I need to talk with Jed ASAP. Is he there?"

"He's here, but he's indisposed right now. Is it an emergency?"

"Didn't I just say that? I need to speak to him now!"

"You don't have to be rude, Dee. Let me get him."

Rolling her eyes, Dee shook her head and waited. Goldie was lying next to her on the floor in her normal position, her chin resting on Dee's toes.

"Hello. Jed here. What's up?"

"Jed, the UFO's are back, and there's an additional ship. It's a large one. They're heading directly toward the enclave."

"Dee, they're always heading toward the enclave before they make their turn, and this is about the right time for their regular visits. Let me pull the Rainier feed and take a look."

Dee could hear the subtle clicking of an old-world keyboard through the phone. She turned to study her concerned colleagues still peering at the radar images and trying to determine what manner of foe the images might represent. Placing the phone on speaker so Manny and Craig could listen,

Dee pushed the rolling chair back and forth with her toes, careful not to bother Goldie.

"Oh wow! That is interesting." Jed exclaimed.

"We know. What do we do? It's your call on missile use."

"Let's not get ahead of ourselves, Dee. Is Manny there?"

"Here, Jed," Manny yelled from across the room.

"Can't you try to talk to them?"

Manny moved toward the phone. "Seriously? Would you like me to try landline or the shortwave? This isn't the bridge of the Starship Enterprise. I could ask the enclave to broadcast a radio message, but it will take at least ten minutes for anything to go out over the air. That won't be soon enough. At their current speed, the UFOs will reach the enclave before anyone could receive a message."

Jed was silent and then mumbled to himself, "And we were so close to getting a communication satellite up."

Craig's foot tapping continued unabated. The gale force wind added a symphony to his failed effort at percussion.

Manny, not a particularly patient fellow on a good day, finally blew. "Jed, man, it's your call! Decide. We don't have a lot of time."

"I know, I know. You don't have to remind me. I just never dreamed I would have to decide on missile use. I'm going to change the procedure as soon as this crisis is over. I shouldn't be the one. This is not my area of expertise."

"Nevertheless," Dee added.

"Right. If they don't change their heading south of Lake Chelan like always, fire six missiles. Target one each at the three smaller ships and three at the big one. Then let's pray they are human rather than an alien with some sort of otherworldly shielding technology. Otherwise, lobbing missiles at their ships will probably just piss them off."

Dee's face paled. "Are you sure that's the smart move, Jed? They've been visiting for, well, at least as long as we've had the radar up. They've never been aggressive before."

"You asked for a judgement call, Dee. I have very little information from which to inform a smart decision. The only absolute certainty, the only thing I know without doubt is that it'll take very little to destroy our enclave, and with it, a big part of humanity west of the Rocky Mountains. I don't know who they are, where they come from, if they're human or alien, and most importantly, what they want. What do you recommend, Dee?"

"I don't know," Dee lamented. "Something more than firing missiles at them." She looked over at her colleagues. "Craig, is there any way you can get a visual on the larger object?"

"Sorry, Dee, but we don't have time to get an unmanned drone close enough before they reach the enclave. The only one up right now is in the Yakama Valley."

"I guess we really can't risk it then, but damn it!" She rubbed her eyes with the palm of her hands, interlocked her fingers, rested her chin on top, and stared at the floor. Finally, she sighed, "OK Manny, let's do this."

Manny and Dee rushed back to their work stations to target the UFO's. Dee called out, "I'll take the three smaller ships. You take the big one."

"Roger that," Manny responded. "I hope we aren't wasting missiles. If six can't stop these ships, we've blown through over half of our entire inventory."

Dee shook her head. "I'm not sure it'll matter if this doesn't work. We'll be just as screwed."

"They are reaching the directional change point," Craig yelled. "Wait…." All eyes turned to Craig.

Goldie the station companion dog and workmate whined. Dee was breathing hard. Even though it was colder inside than normal because of the storm, sweat beaded on her forehead.

"Shit, no turn," Craig uttered.

"Give it another minute, Craig," Dee pleaded. Screaming wind outside seemed to increase in intensity as they watched the seconds pass. The northern facing windows shuddered in protest each time a particularly strong gust struck their faces.

"Fire, you have to fire," Jed spoke through the speaker phone, a smidge over a minute later.

They watched the missiles streak to their targets--Dee, Manny, and Craig from the northeast side of Mount Rainier and Jed from his live feed at the science center facility located at what used to be Boeing Field, just south of Seattle.

Impacts could be seen on the radar screens. "Come on. . ." Craig urged. He exhaled and stated flatly, "Impacts had no effect. They haven't changed heading, but they've increased speed to, good lord, over 2600 knots. They'll be at the enclave in no time. Better call Chrystel right now!"

Sensing the stress level of her human companions, Goldie sat up alert. For a moment, before panic sent the Rainier Team into action, the only sounds in the station were Craig's manic foot tapping and the groan of an old building standing against relentless wind.

# 1. Chrystel

Chrystel shifted from foot to foot, bouncing on her toes as she watched the instructor. She absorbed the movements and fluid transitions. "On my count," the instructor intoned in an incongruently soft voice, "Turn to your partner and begin the exercise. One, two, go."

Chrystel turned and grabbed her partner's arms on the outside, as he did the same. The point of this exercise was to use leverage to take your partner to the ground. Since everyone was equally trained and free to use any of the many fighting strategies except kicking and punching, this maneuver was more difficult than it might seem. Her partner today was a 6-foot 4 inch, mountain of muscle. He was quick too.

Chrystel looked left and then aimed for his right side. Planting her foot, she moved lightning fast to take advantage of her lower center of gravity. She pushed toward him while pressing his foot to throw him off balance. Her exercise partner knew the look to the left ruse meant she was coming at his right side. This wasn't his first rodeo. What he hadn't planned for was having to perform the splits in the movement. He had settled into a wide stance to compensate for Chrystel's propensity to use her strong lower body to get under him. As his right foot slid outward, he felt his muscle's shriek. It was already too late when he shifted to counteract Chrystel's maneuver. She was lifting him off the ground.

He landed hard after turning in the air backwards. Not wasting a moment, the young stud lifted himself from packed dirt to demonstrate it didn't hurt. They bowed to each other. "Damn, Chrystel, how do you do that?"

"To start, you were too wide. I simply used your weakness and my strength. It's all up here, Jess." Chrystel pointed to her head. "Don't give up. If you visualize everything before you start, all the moves and countermoves, you'll be throwing me around like a rag doll."

"Yeah, maybe," Chrystel's latest victim said with a pained smile.

The instructor was already leading them in a rigorous exercise regimen. The end of training was a six-mile run up and down as many hills as the instructor could find. Chrystel loved that part. She loved pushing her body past exhaustion, to the place where her mind could separate from the pain in her limbs.

She did her best thinking during those times. Somehow, the mental frustration of being the mayor of an entire enclave with all the competing demands faded away and left a crevice of clarity. In less than two months, there were two viable candidates running against her for mayor, and the election was going to be close. Carlton was a pretty boy with a great smile. Always easy with the right joke, at the right time, people liked him and hovered around like flies on stink. He was a quick study too. She had heard him speak at least four other languages. Word around the enclave was he had helped one of the enclave's premiere engineers solve a particularly daunting problem. Chrystel couldn't comprehend how someone that smart could have so little vision for the future of their enclave. As far as Chrystel could tell, the only thing important to Carlton was Carlton and winning.

Then there was Brodie, a more complicated man to be sure. His platform was to consolidate power inside the enclave and build a stronger defense for wars that he claimed, "Would surely come." He wanted to limit outsider access to only those individuals who could be thoroughly vetted before joining the enclave. Everyone knew that vetting anyone outside the enclave was nearly impossible. There were no records available from which to evaluate "walk-ons," the term they used to describe anyone who wasn't born to the enclave.

Carlton and Brodie were both walk-ons, and Brodie's platform was to shut down people like himself. Brodie had secured his place in New Washington, but in lip serving political fashion, wanted to deny the same opportunity to others. Both men were hitting Chrystel hard on the charge of nepotism. Her grandmother, Karen, had held the mayoral position for several terms. The nepotism label was starting to stick.

The townspeople didn't appear to care that Chrystel had helped steer the enclave through a nightmare of procedural government transitions. Or that, because of her focus on progress, they had maintained their technological edge. She was the granddaughter of one of the founders; ergo, she must be bad.

Chrystel had given everything of herself to the enclave. Never married, she chose not to distract from her goals by marriage or children. It was a lonely existence, but necessary if she was going to lead them to a safer and more prosperous world.

"Hey Chrissy, what's happening in that noggin of yours?"

Chrystel jumped from the intrusion. "You know I hate when you call me that, Thomas."

Running alongside, Thomas matched her pace. He grinned. "Yep, but it never fails to get your attention. I tried Chrystel, but you kept pounding away on the turf. You doing OK?"

"Right as rain, Thomas. What could possibly go wrong?"

"Uh, just about everything." Thomas' nearly bald head was framed in a silver ring. His bronze skin barely registered any moisture. Most clavers thought Thomas was Chrystel's uncle. She had started calling Thomas, Uncle Tom during her childhood. He was always around, and as one of the eight enclave founders, he was like a brother to Chrystel's founder grandparents, Mike and Karen. More nepotism, Chrystel thought sadly.

"Are you thinking about that election?" he asked. Chrystel flashed a glance in his direction, a half-smile plastered to her face. "Chrissy, I warned you a long time ago about politics. Not that you listened to me because you're as stubborn as I was at your age. It isn't any place for someone with real character. It'll eat you up and spit you out unless you can be as ruthless as everyone else. Nearly killed your grandmother. Do your best and then let it go if you don't win. You know I've always wanted to turn the force over to you. If you aren't the mayor, you can take my job. Katie nags me every day to give it up. You're the best person to take my place."

"Keep your voice down, Thomas," Chrystel huffed while controlling her breathing. "Just what I need, more claims that I don't really want to be mayor and that I have a job waiting for me because of my founder family connections."

"Now listen-up! You'd get the job because you've been training since you were a child. I would never consider you unless I believed you could keep our people safe. You're a good leader and the best person for the position. Dammit, just give it some thought. Doing this job, protecting our people, is as important as being the mayor."

Chrystel could tell Thomas was mad. He ran ahead to harass one of the other runners. Ghost the third or fourth or fifth, she couldn't remember which, was right by his side. He always had a dog named Ghost, just like his first dog companion during the change. Chrystel didn't have any doubts Thomas was right about her competence for taking his job. That wasn't the source of her consternation. She wanted to play a role in moving the enclave into the future and serving as enclave mayor was the best way to make that happen.

Chrystel had been following Thomas around since she had been old enough to go to school. Out exploring one day, she saw them, the force, doing drills in the woods. She began sneaking off after classes to watch what the forces were doing each day. At first, she would hide in the bushes, but somehow, Thomas always knew she was there. One day, he looked right at her and headed directly to her hiding spot. She thought about running, but knew he would catch her, so she pretended to be reading one of her books. "Whatcha doing in there, little lady?" he asked.

"Just a nice place to study," she responded, not taking her eyes from the page.

"Hmmm. Your mama know where you are?"

"She doesn't care. She never leaves the house. If I'm home by dinner, she's right as rain."

"That right?" Thomas chuckled. "You ever interested in doing something other than read that book, which is a darn good thing by the way, just let me know. We can teach you some of the stuff we're doing if it's OK with your mom. And you make sure to keep an eye out for rangers. We got dogs all over this place, but the rangers are sneaky."

Chrystel looked directly into his eyes as if she'd been insulted. "I know that! I've got my sling shot with me, and I know how to use it. Those rangers don't stand a chance with me!"

"I bet you're right. They would rue the day they took you on. How come you don't have a dog?"

"Mom says she allergic, but Grandma says it's because she can't stand the voices. I'll let you know tomorrow if I can train to be a soldier."

"Good enough. I'll look forward to it. By the way, my name is Thomas, and what might you be called?"

"My name is Chrystel, spelled with a Y. And I don't like Chris or Chrissy, so please don't call me that."

"I'll do my best to remember. Until tomorrow then." Thomas walked away with full knowledge of Chrystel's parents. Her mother was one of Karen's daughters, the agoraphobic, seer daughter, Amelia. Quite a piece of work that one. The little red-head's dad had died in an accident helping shore up a bridge not long after she was born. Chrissy could most likely use a father figure. Thomas knew Mike, her grandfather had tried, but he and Amelia were estranged over her housebound lifestyle.

Dressed to work out, Chrystel was there the next day twenty minutes early. She was there every day after that when school didn't interfere. Considered a mascot by the men and women on the force at first, she mimicked workout drills and ran after them red faced, huffing and puffing, wherever they went. Chrystel's bright green eyes and a curly, red pony tail that sashayed with her every movement quickly won hearts.

One day, she turned into a real warrior. Chrystel thought it was on her twelfth birthday when she beat a guy a head taller in a wrestling match. Thomas saw Chrystel's potential on her first day of training. Her expression and focus told him all he needed to know. He had seen that same look on her Grandma Karen's face a time or two during their struggles to create the enclave.

Chrystel's mind shifted gears again, back to Brodie. Infuriating Brodie. She couldn't get him out of her mind. He was always looking at her from the corner of his eyes. It wasn't just the normal, "check out my competitor" kind of look. For Pete's sake, he was engaged, and he was gawking at her. Still, she did the same thing to Brodie, clandestinely watching him and hoping he wouldn't catch her. She wanted to know him. God help her, she dreamed about him.

Brodie was a good-looking man, but there were plenty of other good looking eligible men around. Carlton for example, whom she wouldn't touch with a ten-foot pole. It wasn't that. There was something about the way he moved, effortlessly and totally contained, as if he knew where he was and what he wanted at every moment. A confidence that exuded strength, but not arrogance.

Then again, maybe it was her problem with wanting most what she couldn't have. Chrystel hated to admit it, but there was nothing quite as satisfying as taking on a challenge. The more difficult the better. It was both her greatest strength and her most troublesome weakness.

That must be it, Chrystel thought. I want him because he is running against me, and he's taken. She congratulated herself for her ability to pull back the curtain on her own frailties. She smiled to herself, still running hard, realizing it might be better to consider why attaining the impossible was so damn important. Perhaps, she would ponder it during tomorrow's run. For today, her insight might be just enough to stop this self-destructive, time-sucking, school girl crush.

Brodie might be right about his protectionist ideas. There were more than a few rumors that some of their technology had been stolen. The Southern Florida Enclave had popped up with a version of Jed's latest communication device. The only way that was possible was for someone on the inside to steal it. They couldn't afford to get behind technologically. To be behind meant New Washington might be more vulnerable to threats from other enclaves. The eastern enclaves were much larger than New Washington. Technology was the single greatest advantage for a small enclave like theirs.

Chrystel heard buzzing and shook her head to ward off a stinging insect. The buzzing morphed into a low rumble. The other runners were slowing and looking around for the source of the sound. Chrystel stopped in a clearing to survey the area. A bright, gray nose peeked from above the trees in the sky. She stood totally still as a spaceship filled the blue sky overhead. Without a second thought, she turned and started running in the most direct route to the enclave.

Thomas caught up and glanced at his protégé, his mouth slightly open to exhale in a hard run. "Guess they're here then," he whispered. Chrystel and Thomas and a few selected members of the enclave shared a secret, a fearsome secret they'd kept hidden for years to protect the people of New Washington. When the Rainier radar system first went online, it wasn't two weeks before three unexplained aircraft visited Washington. The flight pattern of the aircraft swept across the mountains from Canada toward the enclave and then turned back from whence they came. The missiles systems weren't operational at the time so there was little anyone could do but watch.

Jed, a founder and premiere scientist before the Great Dying, believed the flying ships were not of human origin. Once it became obvious the visits were a regular occurrence, Jed strategically placed drones alongside the flight path to record and collect data. For secrecy's sake, Jed didn't tell anyone of his study and used his personal computer to control the drones. The resulting video of disc shaped objects, which could turn and fly at unheard of speeds, was convincing. They weren't of this world.

He passed the video to Karen, the mayor at the time, and Thomas. They agreed the ships looked like aliens, argued about what to do about otherworldly visitors, and finally decided the best approach was to keep the information hidden.

Her mind whizzing through contingencies while her body found a rhythm in the punishing pace, Chrystel exchanged a grim expression with Thomas. "I don't have any idea what to do about this one. I'm going to need your help, Thomas."

"You've got it, Chrystel. Gotta warn you though, I don't know jack shit about aliens."

## 2. New Washington Historical Notes, Part I

I've decided the best way to tackle New Washington's history is to start. Isn't that always the case? I've been thinking about this project for more than thirty years and have concluded there is no perfect way to organize my thoughts. Every time I create yet another outline, I'm left feeling like I missed the mark. That somehow a factual outline doesn't capture the essence of our struggle for survival. I only know until I put pen to paper, I will be caught in an endless loop of trying to achieve perfection.

I ardently believe that history is always influenced by the culture and outlook of its authors. My outlines reflected that belief. I tried to make my extensive blueprints factual and found there was no texture, no life in the words. Old world high school textbooks were more interesting. I'm scrapping the entire mess. Instead, I will tell our history through a journal with my humble opinions and insights in full display. Perhaps at some point in the future, I'll be able to weave together enough facts and opinion that readers will be able to form their own conclusions.

The reason I'm called upon to write New Washington history is that it's my job. My position in the New Washington Enclave is Official Historian. My unofficial position is Librarian and collector of pre-change information, in all its forms. The unofficial duties consume most of my time. When the world ended in the early part of the 21st Century, humanity left a vast trove of information and literature on comatose computers and servers.

I supervise a team of two individuals who seek out data stores, supply a power source to dead information technology equipment, and then hack into those systems. I could use a team of fifty.

It is painstakingly slow work. We don't have the people-power. To our great fortune, two large corporate data farms were located near our enclave. With the help of my team, one farm was secured and revitalized for our own use before time and decay destroyed any possibility of its recovery. The other farm was already significantly degraded and unsalvageable. We got what we could from prominent websites of the time and transferred that information to a New Washington data farm located north of the science center.

Lest readers believe I have been resting on my laurels, I recently completed a novel to provide a more personal account of what happened during and immediately after the Great Dying. My mother and father, Karen and Mike McCollough, were both original founders of our enclave. They survived the Great Dying and were instrumental in establishing the New Washington Enclave. I used their accounts and the accounts of other founders as the basis for the story. For those who enjoy historical fiction, a book is a better means to communicate the struggle surrounding the near extinction of humanity. It is entitled *Critically Endangered* because that is the category the human species would have been given at the time, if such lists still existed. We are still Endangered, but at this very moment, perhaps not critically.

A few facts are in order here to provide the necessary background. At the beginning of the 21st

Century, almost everyone on earth died in the span of ten days. They died from an unknown malady that began with a stiff neck and quickly progressed to a spiking fever. Once the fever began, victims succumbed to this blight within 24 hours. A brief underwhelming sickness cost more lives than the combined total of all previous natural and manmade cataclysms. Even individuals completely isolated were affected.

No one knows with absolute certainty how many were left on Earth after the Great Dying. There was no way to verify exact numbers because communication in the early days was only possible by short wave radio or face-to-face contact.

Estimates of survivors ranged from 1 in 250,000 to 1 in 300,000, worldwide. In just over a week, global population went from 8 billion to approximately 25,000, spread across the planet. Man's survival had never been so tenuous.

Of the remaining 25,000 human survivors, everyone changed in two distinct ways comprising 60/40 percent of the population. The first set, named Group A of which I'm a part, physically regenerated to young adulthood. Individuals above the age of 18 or so shed their skin, regenerated teeth and regained reproductive capability if it had been lost during the aging process. Everyone in this group became bigger, stronger, and healthier. Some individuals gained heightened, or in some cases, new sense abilities. These included extraordinary night vision, acute olfactory and auditory ability, an ability to sense others from long distance, prescience, and most curiously, the capability to hear dog thoughts from some dogs (more about that later).

Far less is known about the second set, Group B. While Group A appeared to have jumped forward on the evolutionary ladder, Group B may have regressed to an earlier Homo sapiens version. Group B also completed a physical metamorphosis. They increased in size, immensely expanding muscle mass, making them exceedingly strong. They may have lost the ability to verbally communicate. In the early days, interactions between the two groups were often violent. It is not known if Group B humans were aggressive by nature or if the violence was a byproduct of an inability to communicate between the differing humanoid species. It may have been some combination of both.

Regardless, in the intervening years, sightings of Group B have all but stopped. Seven years ago, a self-proclaimed archeologist said he had encountered a settlement of Group B humanoids in Wyoming and barely escaped with his life. He was not a reliable source, for he was known to return from expeditions with large quantities of rare whiskey and beer but very few artifacts. A team was sent to investigate. It is thought Group B's DNA may hold some clues as to what happened to all humans. The only thing the team found was a campsite indicating presence, but not who or how many. Colloquially, most people refer to Type B humanoids as Bigfoots.

Our estimates indicate the global population of Group A has reached to almost one million. Without consistent and reliable communication between groups and individuals, there is no way to know for sure.

The aging process for Group A has also changed. We do not know the outside limits of Group A's lifespan because nearly all originals are still alive. Physical examinations conducted by enclave physicians indicate we age at about one-third the rate of pre-change humans. Our lifespan is likely 230 to 270 years. The leading cause of death in New Washington is accidents, followed by ranger attacks.

By way of explanation, rangers are a new species of dog/wolf/coyote hybrid. Millions of human dog pets were left abandoned after the Great Dying, and they took to the wilderness to hunt and survive. DNA samples of rangers indicate they are about two thirds dog, almost a third wolf, and a dash of coyote. Rangers are highly intelligent, very resilient, often aggressive, pervasive in the Americas, and are no longer considered domesticated.

As of yesterday, the population of the New Washington Enclave is 6,732. There wouldn't be that many except that in 2066, a major earthquake in Southern California destroyed most of what was left of Los Angeles and the surrounding areas. The survivors of the LA Enclave moved north to join ours. It was a godsend, for they brought with them a renowned aeronautical engineer, a rocket scientist, a robotics engineer, and several specialized physicians. Clint Eastwood, a well-known actor and director, was also among the Los Angeles survivors.

No one has conclusively determined what caused the Great Dying. We know that something triggered a catastrophic, rapid evolution of humans, but not the how. In the early years, theories about what generated an almost overnight change to human DNA ran the gamut from aliens to the Russians. Scientists could agree on only one thing—it was unlikely to have been a naturally occurring phenomenon. Nothing in man's pre-change knowledge of biological science could explain why nearly every human being on earth got sick and died in the span of 7-10 days, followed by a consistent set of resulting DNA changes to the two survivor groups.

The general assessment is that this horror was purposeful. That someone or some group implanted a virus, bacteria, or chemical in our environment and then pulled a pre-determined trigger to cause mass devastation on an unimaginable scale. At least, that's what the scientists think. They believe it is important to understand what happened to guard against a second occurrence, even though knowing can never give back the billions who lost their lives.

Scientists have a better idea why dogs can communicate with some people, and it's another reason they believe the Great Dying was manufactured by man. Dogs have nanites in their bloodstream that adhere to cells and are passed from one generation to the next. The mechanism for the dog/human communication is still not known, but it is likely these nanites act as bio-transceivers, allowing dogs to transfer thoughts to people. Not all humans have the capability to hear dogs. Most of the founders did not possess this gift after the change, but nearly all their children do. The dog nanites were clearly designed in a laboratory. Since these nanites appeared at the same time as the change it follows that the near loss of our world was manmade.

We desperately need more people, especially those with pre-change education and training. Originals, as we call those that experienced the change, help educate and inform those who come after.

If an endangered species list still existed, humans would be given top billing compared to the rest of the natural world. Without man sitting in the catbird's seat of predators, wildlife has flourished. Water is clean, the air is fresher, bodies of water are teaming with fish, and fauna has nearly overtaken any evidence that we were once an advanced civilization. In the pre-change world, there were groups of people so intent on saving the planet, they would probably delight in the knowledge that human's no longer hold dominion over earth. Of course, these were people who had access to everything they needed. It's easy to recommend to others that they live a simpler existence. These people never had to experience how difficult life can be for both individuals and communities without reliable communication, a modern hospital, or a ready supply of groceries.

There is hope that new humans can find a more perfect balance between our survival and that of the rest of the planet. The founders knew of the pitfalls of ignoring human impact on the physical world. In our enclave, even though our environmental footprint is relatively microscopic, we consider the long-term effects of any new projects.

For now, what we need most is more people. More people to create a safe and thriving community. We Endure.

Geronimo M.

# 3. They're Here!

The light was almost perfect in Karen's studio, a cozy little building Mike and Manuel had built for her nearly seventy years ago. Well, perfect when it wasn't raining. Encroaching shadows changed her mood and her painting whenever Washington skies leeched rain. This time of the year, she couldn't even count on the hypnotic sound of raindrops tapping the studio's corrugated rooftop. The rain came as misting, dribbling, vapor clouds, clinging to every surface like the spongy moss the dampness created.

In front of her, another outline of Uh Huh was taking form on canvas. She had tried many times to get him just right. Uh Huh, aka Jeff, was one of the two Bigfoots she had encountered right after the change. In her thoughts a lot these days, reading Geronimo's historical fiction book had uprooted Uh Huh memories from their shallow grave. She hummed Moon River to herself, thinking about the first time she had sung it from her jail cell at a ranch in Idaho. Uh Huh, a fellow captive of a very weird post-apocalyptic cult, heard Karen singing and began to say, "Uh Huh," in time to the rhythm, thus the name. No one knew Bigfoots could talk, but Karen heard him.

For the millionth time, she wondered what had happened to him and those like him. No one had seen their kind in many years. Who could blame them for hiding far away from humans like her? They were tormented or slaughtered in the beginning. Even Karen had killed one. To this day, a shudder ran up her spine when she thought about

Jack, her German shepherd, plunging his canines into a Bigfoot's neck to save Karen from an attack.

She wanted to get this painting exactly right. Maybe Type A humans like her would be able to see the intelligence and pain behind the eyes if she could capture Uh Huh's essence.

Karen sighed and asked herself again why that was even important. Then she shrugged and mixed a beautiful, slightly gold-brown for his eyes.

Two of her favorite canines were lounging around the cramped room. They seemed to enjoy the relaxing painting time as much as Karen did. Rocket, an unusual mixture of German shepherd, Cairn terrier and who knows what else, arrayed himself on the back of a loveseat and watched for rabbits and squirrels out the window.

Then there was Sadie, a very special dog, and Tilley's second great grand-pup. Tilley had been there when everyone died. When Karen woke from the sickness, Tilley was loyally waiting by her side on the bed. Even though Sadie looked different than Tilley, Karen knew by the time Sadie was eight-weeks-old where she had inherited her spirit. She was as goofy, smart, loving, and willful as her predecessor.

Sadie might have been even smarter than Tilley. She could talk. Not to Karen, of course. Karen could never hear dog voices in her head like her husband Mike and most of their children. The fact that she couldn't hear them was both a disappointment and a relief. She often thought it would be interesting to hear the emotions behind their antics, but she loved them just the way they were. For Karen, that was enough. Sadie was in her normal position, in the way by Karen's feet, her head laid on her paws.

Rocket growled and yipped. Sadie joined the uproar, springing to the studio door, pressing her nose to the entry with bared teeth to offer a warning. Karen set her paintbrush on a cloth and listened. At first, all she heard was barking and then a low rumbling she could feel. Her heart started beating triple time before her first thought—earthquake! Karen was already moving to the doorframe as the dogs continued to sound an alarm.

Scrambling on shaky legs, she yanked open the studio's only door. During a sizeable Washington earthquake in 2001, Karen had been outside when it happened. Other than a tremendous boom, the earthquake indicator she most remembered was big firs swaying in time to ground movement. *The trees aren't moving.* Glancing inside at a hanging plant near the far corner of the studio, an overgrown philodendron wasn't swinging either. Karen tried to quiet her pounding heart so she could listen to her surroundings. A vibrating roar filled the studio. Another possibility knocked lightly in the back of her mind, and when unanswered, burst through protective walls of normalcy in a gut-tightening wallop. The sound was coming from the sky. "Oh, my God! This could be even worse."

She ran outside, her dogs instinctively surrounding her to keep her safe. Karen turned in a circle scanning the sky. "What the hell is that!!" she screamed as she caught sight of a humongous, oblong, gray airship just to the west. The ship, gliding just under cloud cover, traveled through air with no wings, no rotors, or any sign of engine exhaust, just a foreboding sheen on a smooth gray surface and a pulsating pressure that Karen could feel in her toes. It was heading toward her. Her body quaked in atavistic fear. Karen squinted and blinked from tiny raindrops. She placed her hands over her eyes to shield them and get a better view. Nothing on earth resembled that thing in the sky.

Out of the side of her eyes, Karen could see Mike running from the house, waving his hands, and yelling something Karen couldn't make out over the riotous barking. She was so completely transfixed by the otherworldly object, Mike surprised her when he grabbed her by the waist, pulled her to the ground, and shouted, "Get down!"

Karen fell onto the dirt with a thud, more than a little pissed that Mike had startled her, even as she was frightened senseless by what was undoubtedly an alien ship. He yelled into her ear over the frightened, barking dogs. "Jed just called me. It's the visitors. They've come."

## 4. The Visitors, Town Center

A crowd was gathering in the New Washington Town Square. Gawkers stared spellbound, pointing to the sky and whispering to partners and friends. Two teenaged boys at the edge of the crowd hid their nervousness behind boisterous joking and playful shoving.

The oblong, fat cigar-shaped cylinder shifted upright when it was directly over the town center. Three smaller disc-like crafts surrounded it at an equal distance. A moan erupted from the crowd as watchers expressed both fright and awe. A reflective haze between the larger ship and its escorts remained as the smaller discs glided into position. While moving, the space-convoy emitted a low rumbling whine that could be felt in the ground. Still and silent, the assemblage now hung in the air. Only random lustrous flashes in the space between the objects signaled there was any life at all in the ships above them.

Thomas shouted to Chrystel as he and the other defense forces rounded the last corner to the city center access road. "We need to get these people under cover. Make an announcement, and I'll start herding stragglers back to their homes."

Chrystel nodded as she continued to run and glance to the heavens. Her grandmother loved old science fiction movies. Often, a vintage science fiction flick played in the background during sleepovers with the grandparents. Even though she was never quite as enthused about them as Grandma, Chrystel enjoyed snuggling with Grandma Karen and laughing or screaming in surprise during alien dramas. Looking at the objects in the sky, Chrystel thought artistic creators of old science fiction may have over analyzed the possibilities--these ships were nothing like those imagined in movies.

They didn't resemble spaceships as much as floating geometric objects, unadorned with seams, antennas, doors, lights or ridges. A dull gray, their design was simple: three perfectly crafted discs and a significantly larger, thin shaped ellipse. It was as if these aliens had ripped a page from a geometry book and smiled at simplicity of form. As the UFOs hung in stasis over the town center, a dearth of sound was more chilling than their visual appearance.

Chrystel pushed through the throng of folks grouped in front of Town Hall. They were shouting questions as she went, "What is it, Mayor?"

"What are you going to do?"

"Who is it?"

"Why are they here?"

"Please!" Chrystel responded, "Let me through so I can make an announcement."

Brodie was there. Of all people, Brodie. He saw Chrystel's struggle and moved with alacrity to run interference.

"Come on, folks, make way. Let the mayor through. You won't get any answers until you let her though." He grabbed one man who appeared bent on a confrontation in a bear hug and yelled over his shoulder at Chrystel, "Just keep moving!"

Chrystel knew she could take care of herself. She didn't need Brodie's help. At the same time, the momentum of the crowd shifted when he added his authoritarian voice to hers. The throng started to back away as she slid through the Courthouse doors.

Her clerk, second cousin, and closest friend, Judy, was running from the back office, a microphone in her hand.

"Chrystel, the intercom system is already powered up and ready. Just flip the on-switch when you figure out what you're going to say."

Chrystel gave Judy a return look which said she didn't have the first idea. "Have you heard from Jed?"

"No, but then I haven't been monitoring the radio. You go on and do your thing, whatever that is. I'll try to get him on the line so he can share his vast wisdom with you when you're done. What're we going to do Chrystel? Aliens?! Are you freaking kidding me?"

"I wish I knew, Judy. Please, just hand me that thing."

Chrystel took the microphone from Judy and stepped back out the door to face the waiting, restless, and frightened town.

Brodie was standing just outside. Chrystel nodded some belated thanks as she took a deep breath and began to talk into the microphone from the Assembly Hall steps. "If I could have your attention please." She gave them a moment to quiet. Shuffling and shifting people gradually turned their attention to the mayor. "I know each of you has a million questions. Unfortunately, I don't have the answers you seek. For the last fifty plus years, since our radars went online, the Rainier Station has monitored unidentified flying objects that appear in the skies every sixty days. These objects come from Canada and fly south to Chelan. When they reach Chelan, they turn and head north, and then they disappear from radar visibility in only 100 kilometers."

Dissatisfied murmuring was the response to Chrystel's admission. One man yelled at the top of his lungs, "Why weren't we told?!"

"That's a fair question," Chrystel continued. "We did not share this information for a few reasons. First, there was nothing we could do to stop them, and we had no means to communicate with them. We've tried the shortwave and could not reach them. It was hoped, when we launch the communication satellite, there'll be an opportunity to contact these visitors and determine their purpose. Secondly, they never demonstrated any hostility and never ventured toward the enclave. Finally, as you all know, life in the new world hasn't always been easy. Together we've shared the burden, the struggle, of keeping our little community alive and safe. It was thought that knowledge of the visitors would be one more thing for the populace to worry about.

"If the council made a mistake by not informing the citizens of New Washington, it is a mistake we'll deal with at a better time. As you can all see, the visitors have arrived. Please, for now, return to the safety of your homes. If anyone needs additional help, the defense force is located on the edge of this crowd. Just ask for assistance. For your safety, please go now. I will broadcast an update as soon as I have any information. We endure!"

"We endure," the crowd responded without enthusiasm.

For a minute, the scared inhabitants milled in the center of the enclave shouting, crying, and even a few, laughing. Two families along the perimeter began to move away grudgingly, and like sheep spotting an open gate, the others followed.

Chrystel was back inside the seat of government, such as it was, yelling orders. "Judy, have you got Jed yet?"

"He's on the landline." She shoved the phone into Chrystel's hands.

"What the hell, Jed? No warning? Did you not see them on radar? I thought that was one of the primary missions of the Rainier Station. We've invested so much of our sweat and tears in your defense system, and we didn't even get a warning?"

"We'll have time for recriminations later, Chrystel. I have my prototype microwave vector communication system up, and I'm getting a message. I'm going to go to speaker phone now. Hold on."

Judy was standing near Chrystel, and Brodie was next to her. Chrystel kept the phone to her ear. The sound was distant, and static at pauses gave only brief snatches of words.

"Humans of Washington." Garbled transmissions followed. "....here to help" Another roar of static. "Must meet with Karen Hen ......"

"Jed, can I speak back on your system?"

"I believe so, yes. Let me do a couple of range adjustments and see if that improves the reception. I haven't worked out all of the bugs."

Chrystel shifted her weight from foot to foot, straining to hear through the erratic roar from the phone. The noise quieted. "Humans of Washington. We are the people of Ardinia. We are here to form a partnership. You are in grave danger, but not from us. We must meet with Karen Henry to speak of our proposal. We respectfully request she be present near the park statue to be escorted to a diplomatic meeting in four earth hours. This is very important."

Chrystel didn't hesitate. "Ardinia citizens. This is Chrystel from the New Washington Enclave. I am the leader of our community. I will represent our enclave for this meeting in four hours." Chrystel's heart was beating hard. Brodie and Judy were watching her. Wide eyes returned Chrystel's fixated stare. There was silence from the line.

Three more minutes of silence. Fear was palatable from the earthbound residents. A quick squawking noise made Chrystel jump, and then she heard, "We will meet with you, Chris, but we must also meet with Karen Henry. This is very important."

"Yes, I will meet with you, and I'll have Karen Henry there as well. I look forward to having a discussion with the people of Ardinia."

There were no goodbyes. Chrystel, Jed at his end, Judy, Brodie, and now Thomas who had joined the group waited for another extended period to make sure the Ardinians were gone.

Thomas was laughing. "What else? After everything, now aliens. And they called you Chris!"

His laughter was met with cold stares.

"I'm not sure I see the humor, Thomas," Chrystel retorted.

"What? As far as I can tell things are looking up. Oh, excuse the stupid pun. They didn't immediately wipe us off the face of the earth with an alien death ray. They want to talk. Not real comfortable with the wanting to help business, but you know. I'll go get Karen. And by the way, the folks that weren't in the town center are loading up and heading for the hills. That may be the smart play."

"No, don't worry about Karen right now. And what's up with that anyway? How do they even know of her? And why the hell us? What I want you to do right now is set up a perimeter around the town center. We don't need any freaked-out clavers doing something stupid during our meeting. I'll get Karen on the phone and then do a radio broadcast to the people. And Brodie," Chrystal glanced in his direction, "I appreciated your help outside, but I think you should leave now."

Brodie stood erect, brow raised in his surprise over being dismissed. "Chrystel, I want to stay and give you any assistance I can. I'll do whatever you want me to do that's useful. This is about our enclave now and not an election."

Chrystel studied his sincere hazel eyes. Her first thought was that she didn't need this thorn in her side, and she should send him packing. If she didn't need the help she would. However, Brodie was a very competent man. As was often the case, Chrystel's pragmatic side won the argument.

"All right. Start by collecting my grandmother. And as an additional mission, try to keep Carlton away from here."

Brodie gave her a knowing smirk, turned, and headed out for Grandma's house.

* * *

Fifteen minutes before the stated meeting time, the tableau was set for earth's first interplanetary diplomatic mission. The streets had been swept and residual debris collected from the impromptu alien witness gathering. The town center, a hodge-podge of buildings that had once housed well known big-box stores, sat along the rim of a massive traffic circle.

The interior of the circle was a grassy area named Founders Park. During the short un-rainy season, concerts and plays lifted the spirits of hard-working clavers from that spot. Clint Eastwood and his team of moonlighting actors and musicians, were a favorite of the populace. His troupe originally called The New World Traveling Show, no longer traveled. Word spread quickly regarding the quality of their productions, resulting in profitable performance offers from other enclaves throughout the old United States. Among earth's surviving population, new and different entertainment venues were a highly-sought commodity, the alternative being re-watching hundred-year-old videos. New world peoples craved relevance in the arts, and Clint and his band of merry actors was more than happy to fill that void.

Unfortunately, a successful kidnapping of Clint and three of the troupe's actresses and a subsequent, substantial ransom payment to the Oklahoma City Enclave put the brakes on further travel. The ransom was paid from New Washington's meager coffers. Clint was warned upon his joyous return that next time, he and his bunch would be forced to remain wherever they were illegally held. Clint changed the name of the group to New World Entertainment Productions and decided to stick to the relative safety of Founders Park. The New Washington Enclave welcomed the troupe back with open arms.

Other than grass, a little landscaping, and temporary structures, the only permanent fixture in the park was a haunting, bronze statue of the Founders and their dog companions. Today's alien meet-and-greet was to be held directly in front of their one civic remembrance of humanity's worst moment.

The town center site was chosen not for esthetics, but rather for its central location and a road network that offered easy access. That and the fact that there were already several large buildings to house multiple functions made the town center an ideal setting. New Washington would never reside on a list of quaint little towns. The center's buildings were ungainly big-box stores, refashioned with little attention paid to architectural niceties.

Parking lots that surrounded square, flat, functional structures offered a level space for the enclave's exchange market held Monday through Saturday, all year long. Vendors traded, bartered, and argued over their wares and services in collapsible tents, or on folding tables when the weather was good. The market was as important to the well-being of the residents of New Washington as the Government, arguably much more so at times. Other than some of the enclave's technology, the market was the economic engine that allowed survival of the populace.

The seat of government, the Assembly Hall or Courthouse as some called it, sat on the western edge of the traffic circle. As much as they had worked to change the front façade of the building, it still looked very much like what it once was, a multiplex cinema. Manuel, New Washington's resident artist and architect, had done what he could to spruce it up. In the end, his comment was simply, "A rose in any other form is still a rose, or a multiplex movie place."

At the front of the Assembly Hall, the diplomatic party was ready to make the short trek across the circle into Founder's Park. Chrystal was shaking her head. She had just eavesdropped on Carlton, sitting in the radio broadcast room making an address to the enclave. Carlton's lawful public political announcement appointment, coincided with the alien meeting. Carlton, followed by a furious Brodie, blithely strode into the courthouse an hour before his appointed time, asking for an accommodation to ensure he got his time to "speak with the people". A heated discussion ensued, at least, heated from the Chrystal contingent and Brodie, but Carlton never raised his voice. He parried every argument with a smile or amusing anecdote. He was so poised and charming, it made Chrystel want to retch. She finally agreed to allow him a radio broadcast when he gave his word with a smarmy grin, that he would do his best to keep the people calm. "No nasty political tricks up my sleeves," Carlton said.

What Chrystel heard from Carlton as she walked by on her way out the door was, "I can't understand why the Rainier Station did not provide a warning. It is unconscionable! Is there no end to the mayor's incompetence?"

*Right, no political tricks. I should have known better.* Chrystel had to shake it off. As far as anyone knew, she was about to meet with the first extraterrestrial beings in the history of the world. She, Chrystel with a Y, was representing humanity. There was no way to plan for this one; it gave her goose bumps if she thought about it too directly.

Grandma was beside her. During their preparation, Karen had insisted, "Chrystel, you have to look like you are actually the leader of this rag tag group of unruly humans! Wild, uncombed, red, curly hair in a pony will simply not do. And those clothes. Don't you have anything besides yoga pants and long, single colored t-shirts?"

New Washington clavers didn't "dress." Hard working people living on the far edge of an uncivilized land had no need or time to make the effort. Functional clothing was considered normal, anything beyond that superfluous and snooty. Surprised by her grandmother's strident demands, Chrystel remembered that her amazing grandmother had lived in a different time with different standards.

"I suppose you're right, but I just gotta mention, you don't have a lot of room to talk, Grandma. I haven't seen you in any finery recently. Sweat pants and flip flops aren't exactly haute couture."

Karen laughed and hugged Chrystel. "That's my feisty little granddaughter. Get Mabel over here. She's good with this stuff. And Judy can help," Grandma glanced at herself in the many-stalled courthouse ladies room, "because I'm going to need plenty of help."

"Aren't you frightened, Grandma? Or even a little bit nervous?" Chrystel asked. "I can't help worrying that any alien asking for a meeting with two earth nobodies is up to no good. What can we possibly offer beings that possess the ability to build a spaceship? It makes no sense."

Karen leveled her gaze at Chrystel. *Well, there's that*, she thought to herself. Then again, it could be expected that her granddaughter would have serious doubts. Chrystel's first impulse was most often to question motives. Until her father passed in an accident and her mother checked out of hotel sanity, Chrystel had been a precocious, willful, and bright child, filled with joyful energy. The loss of both parents, one to death and the other to mental illness, had almost overnight changed the person that Chrystel was meant to be. The young woman before her now was filled to the brim with untapped potential, much of it locked away underneath a shell as hard as her name.

She and Mike had helped raise Chrystel, but the loss of trust at such a tender age always left scars. Karen had her own demons that time and love had helped heal, even if now and then, she felt the raised edges of wounds that never completely vanished.

Chrystel had latched on to Karen's chosen profession as mayor. Who could blame her? It provided a measure of control and respect that Chrystel's personal relationships didn't offer, and she was eminently capable. Not that personal relationships were out of the question for Chrystel, but she guarded her heart against the chance of great pain with the same intensity that she did nearly everything else. As the saying goes, only those that you love can hurt you.

Karen believed with every fiber of her being, Chrystel had the strength and the character to someday see the box she'd built for herself, so intricately woven to her mother's self-imposed exile. When that day came, Chrystel would rip through the walls of her fortress and become a force to be reckoned with. Until then, Karen would hold her hand and drag Chrystel, if necessary, to where she needed to go.

"I sometimes forget your generation never experienced the impossible. In mine, dogs learned to talk, my body of its own volition rejuvenated to young adulthood, and I lost everyone I ever loved in a week. Aliens parked over town center, requesting a partnership, doesn't seem such a stretch."

"Grandma, that's not what I mean. Obviously, I heard their radio message, and I can clearly see their ships. I know the impossible is real. My fear is that they could mean us harm."

"Look, baby girl---"

"Grandma, please, there're people around."

"Right, Chrystel," Karen gave her granddaughter a hard look. "I don't believe we have a choice. Should we send them packing? What then?"

Karen drew a deep breath and sighed, her eyes unfocused to a faraway place. "Chrystel, fear and curiosity can reside together in the same place. Both emotions are part of what it means to be human. Without fear, we might run blindly to our deaths, but without our curious natures, what a sad state that would be. Never taking a chance on the unknown, never pressing the limits of known borders to explore, never allowing a stranger into our hearts for fear of betrayal." Karen shook her head, her lips pressed tightly together.

"The most important thing to understand is that we don't control outcomes, only our actions. We must channel fear of the unknown to do our best and encourage our curious natures along the way. Right now, my inquiring mind wants to know why on God's green earth aliens would want to talk to me. And, I've been given the chance to be one of the first humans to meet ET.  Shit, Chrystel, I'm excited!"

Chrystel stared into her grandmother's determined eyes, a sly smile creeping on her face. "Well, when you put it that way. . ."

Over an hour later, after multiple women's voices chattering in a crowded restroom, some yelling, and much cussing from Karen, they were ready.

Grandma was glowing. Her auburn brown hair swept into a chignon with a pearl encrusted comb. A few grey streaks lent maturity to an otherwise, mostly unlined face. The deep blue dress she had chosen for the occasion, perfectly accentuated her still fit body. Head erect, shoulders back, Grandma Karen was transformed.

Chrystel's hair flowed over her shoulders in shimmering waves. She had refused to wear a dress, reminding everyone she had never, ever put one on and would be totally uncomfortable if forced to wear something without legs. She opted instead for a functional white blouse and straight black pants. The ladies agreed, her clear green eyes and flawless skin didn't really need much accessorizing anyway. Where Karen was regal, Chrystel exuded strength.

Mike whistled as they came down the hall. Brodie for his part had a sharp intake of breath when he saw Chrystel, having never seen her with her hair down. Thomas, always the operator, ordered, "We need to get this show on the road. Only ten minutes left to blast off. Sorry, I couldn't help myself. What I meant was everything is ready."

Mike, Thomas, and Brodie dressed in black polos tucked into khaki pants tried to convey some facsimile of a uniformed security force. They followed Chrystel, Karen, and Karen's two dogs. Grandma had refused to partake of this mission without having her dogs by her side. "Don't worry, they're perfectly trained," she reassured Chrystel. "They go with me everywhere." Mike's round-eyed, raised eyebrow expression did little to reduce Chrystel's concern. But Grandma was Grandma, and no one was going to argue with her.

They stood, poised in front of the Founders Statue on an unusually warm, bright, spring day. The witching hour came and went. Sweat beaded on Chrystel's forehead, and curly tendrils of hair plastered to the edge of her face felt like a sticky helmet. Karen fanning herself, watched as the dogs took the opportunity to nap on the grass. Thomas made a couple of attempts at humor, wondering about the veracity of tardy aliens, but the group was too agitated to even admonish him.

Twenty minutes passed. Mike was about to say something about the kink in his neck from looking up when a blinding, blue light shot from the bottom of the cylinder ship to a point in front of Karen. Uncharacteristically, none of the dogs barked. Both canines raised into a sitting position like stone lawn ornaments. Thomas pulled a pistol from the holster strapped under his left side, pointing to the ground. Karen let out an almost inaudible shriek.

They watched wide-eyed and open-mouthed as the blue light expanded until they were bathed in a silent world of shimmering energy. The hair on Brodie's body stood on end, his skin caressed by a tingling sensation. He tried to move to protect Chrystel, just as Mike was trying to do the same for Karen, but his legs felt heavy and lethargic. It was as if a pressure from the haze, now totally encompassing the group, kept him immobile.

Chrystel's fight or flight response kicked into high gear. Adrenaline poured into her veins. Her heartbeat doubled and core temperature rose. She wanted to run as far and as fast as she could away from this eerie sensation licking her skin. Like the rest of her party, she couldn't pick up either foot. It was if her feet had grown roots that had burrowed into the ground. She was left trembling and breathing rapidly from the useless effort.

Karen was the only one who somehow seemed to know that fighting what was happening was pointless. She inhaled the energy surrounding her in total wonderment. She felt like light was entering her pores to embrace her soul. Deep down, in a place she couldn't explain to anyone, it was as if she had known, all along this day would come. Her daughter Amelia would understand. Karen wished she was here to share this feeling. Maybe it would have helped her understand and accept her gift--the seer gift. A place where time and space, without explanation, bent upon itself to reveal pieces of what the future might hold. Karen felt a tugging. She relaxed and let it carry her.

Chrystel felt the same pull and fought against it with all her might. She was ripping into pieces. Her arms and legs went one way, and her head was jolted in another. She was being squeezed and yanked into a spinning vortex. It hurt and yet, it didn't. With a whoosh and a crackle, the spinning stopped. Chrystel was lying on her side on a smooth, metallic floor, moaning. Karen, who was standing next to her, reached down to comfort her granddaughter.

"Chrystel, just breathe deeply, dear. It's OK. We're here. When you have gathered yourself, open your eyes. That was one fucking amazing ride!"

# 5. The Ship

Two aliens and a massive, lavender, spotted creature stared at Karen as she helped Chrystal to her feet. Calming herself with deep breaths, Karen took the time she needed to witness her surroundings. Lighting in the room gave the impression of sunshine without the shadows or the glare. Everything around her was sleek. Unadorned crème colored, pearlescent walls gently met the floor; there were no corners or angles, almost as if the space itself had been poured and molded by a futuristic craftsman and then set into place. The only break in the symmetry was a silvery stand that flattened at its top to reveal some form of computer graphics.

The aliens looked mostly human: two arms, two legs, ten fingers, and the same facial components. However, that's where the similarity ended and swerved in a new direction. Their eyes were expressive, being both larger and rounder, and the pupils reflected a marbled gold. *Was it a trick of nature or was it compassion she saw in the alien's soulful gaze?*

Very close to the average human height, their bodies were thinner. Even with slightly elongated, thin limbs, they didn't appear fragile or weak. A somewhat smaller nose and mouth accentuated penetrating eyes. Both Ardinians had fair, nearly white hair that was pulled to the back. When the larger of the two turned to look at the animal next to him, Karen saw a braided rope of hair, hanging half-way down his/her back. She guessed one was male and one was female. The floor length pale, yellow robes they were wearing, obscured their body shapes.

The creature standing next to the striking aliens was something straight out of Dr. Seuss' nightmares. Its massive chest ended at least four feet from the ground. Pale lavender, close cropped fur was overlaid with dark purple spots, and a short, matching purple-haired mane grew from the beast's thick neck and shoulders. The head jutting forward from a horse-like stalk, held chocolate brown eyes worn on a square, sloping head. Its ears rose straight up, and could have best been described as donkey ears, if a donkey possessed supernatural ear dexterity, making it able to curl them up and down. A thin, two-foot tail, covered in wispy pink hair, reacted to unfolding events like a dog, swishing back and forth with every glance or sound.

Karen couldn't imagine a scenario where Darwin's theory would have created a cartoon animal like the one standing before her. Her dogs were likewise captivated, sitting behind Chrystel and staring with rapt attention at the multi-colored phenomenon. When it pulled its jowls upward showing saber-toothed sized canines, Chrystel jumped. "Could you please control your animal?!" Chrystel huffed.

The larger alien opened a small delicate mouth to speak. "Tilley has been practicing her smile for some time. Perhaps she doesn't have it exactly right. Please, she means to be welcoming. She was very excited about your visit."

"Tilley?" an astounded Karen asked. "I had a dog named Tilley... how?"

"Yes, we know. The henka, a word in in the Ardinian language which means friend, was named in Tilley's honor. Jack was very fond of her. They shared many wonderful adventures."

"But how?"

"Forgive us. You must have many questions. Could we please begin again? I am Shakete, the leader of the Ardinians." As he reached out to shake Karen's hand, he introduced his partner, "And this is my first officer, Maleta. We are very pleased to make your acquaintance."

His hand was barely warm and soft like a child's. Shakete reached for Chrystel's hand next. Chrystel stood erect and backed her body slightly away from the Ardinian. Then recovering, she hesitantly stuck her arm out to meet his grasp.

Shakete's skin began to glow in a barely discernable, shimmery gold color. "I've always desired an opportunity to complete your handshake tradition. It was most satisfying." Karen and Chrystel looked at Shakete with uncomfortable smiles. "Alas, you feel at a disadvantage—is that correct? We know much about you, and you have no information about us. We will now share a traditional Ardinian meal. It is our custom to eat before discussing important matters. If you could follow us, we will inform you of all questions." Karen wondered where they would go next. There weren't any doors in this place.

Shakete turned and glided toward a wall. With a hiss, a door that wasn't visible before, opened to a corridor. Chrystel looked at Karen and shrugged, and Karen returned a "let's go" head nod to Chrystel. They followed Shakete and Maleta, Tilley brought up the rear still "smiling," and Karen's dogs followed Tilley. The corridor walls were the same smooth crème. Karen wanted to reach out and touch its alluring surface, curious if it might hold some clue as to the light that had no discernable source. No sign of doors, Shakete turned, a hiss sounded, and he walked through an entry that hadn't been there a second before.

A table had been set for them. "Please take a seat," Shakete pointed toward the designated chairs. Tilley and the dogs calmly filed in and sat near the wall looking at the human/alien group with happy faces and great anticipation.

Karen had to ask. "Shakete, why are my dogs so docile. Did you do something to them?"

It was Maleta who answered in a soft feminine voice. "Yes and no. Physically they are as they were before they entered our ship. All three of your companions have communication nanites. It allows Tilley to speak with them and sooth their fears. It may appear they are under her thrall, but I guarantee you that is not the case. They are simply happy."

"Normally, happy dogs are moving dogs," Karen returned.

"Well, yes, good point. But when you caress them, they are still. That is what Tilley can do while talking to them. It is much like a physical connection."

Bending his head down as he sat, Shakete looked up at Karen with expressive eyes. "Before we eat, I believe you will not rest until you understand about Tilley. So please, let me explain. We have been observing your world for generations, so we witnessed the dying of your species. Our hearts were broken—we could not stop it. The only thing within our power was to aid those humans left, to help them survive.

"We brought one of your finest animals to our ship and created pairs of dogs you call German shepherds to seed the planet. They have some of the same genetic material as the henka. We also inserted nanites, which provide for mental communication with humans. Over the short term, our efforts were only marginally effective. Many pairs of dogs were unable to bind with humans and were cast out or killed in fear. Some were left to wander alone." Shakete's expression was one of great sadness.

"Do these nanites also communicate to you?" Chrystel asked. She thought she saw some guilt in the set of Shakete's face.

He paused. "Yes, they do. That is how we know of Karen and Tilley. Karen more than anyone else felt the essential nature of the animals we sent as companions, providers, and protectors. Even though Karen could not speak with them, she knew.

"Your grandmother has the gift of prescience. Some call it intuition. Ardinians can make intuitive guesses, but we are not capable of seeing the future without related data. After years of study, it is a gift that we have not been able to replicate in our laboratories. Naturally occurring without explanation, it is a sense that sets humans apart from many other species. All humans have some, but your grandmother and mother possess far more."

Karen scowled, "So am I here so you can study me?"

At this Maleta smiled knowingly with her small mouth. "We have already completed our study, but we are no closer to identifying this ability. No, we have brought you here for a greater purpose. We have watched many humans by way of the dogs. We believe your enclave, with you Karen as its representative, is best suited for bringing the earth together."

"I'm flattered that you have such confidence in me, but I'm afraid we can barely hold our own enclave together, much less the rest of the world. Please explain to me how these nanites work."

Another Ardinian hissed into the room carrying trays of food. Karen stared from Maleta to Shakete, waiting for an answer to her question as a plate of food was placed in front of each person. Shakete finally answered. "We had hoped a delicious meal would place you at ease. I can see now that I was overly optimistic. As much as we have watched and studied, it is still difficult to anticipate human reactions to unusual or stressful situations. I should have been mindful of your need to understand.

"Yes, the nanites. Your brain uses a form of biologically generated energy to think and communicate. One of the functions of these nanites is to decode that energy. They can then send and receive the decoded signals. If you can imagine what you call Wi-Fi, the thoughts are sent in much the same way."

"But I could never hear Jack or Jill like my husband."

"Yes."

"Yes?"

"Biological energy is not identical within your species. Over time, the nanites become better at interpreting signals. It some cases, it takes much longer."

"That means someday I might be able to hear the dogs?"

"Perhaps. Now please, before your food is cold, please eat."

Chrystel had already started. She was famished and only considered the possibility of poisoning for a brief flash before digging-in. A six-mile run and meeting preparation hadn't left a spare moment to eat. The dogs had also been served and were done, completing their meal in just under ninety seconds.

"This is delicious, Shakete," Chrystel commented after swallowing a mouthful of crunchy green things. "What is this stuff?"

For the first time, since the meal started, Shakete brightened, his pale skin glowing gold. "I am honored that you are enjoying our eatings. We have assembled several delicacies from around the galaxy. The protein serving is from the tender flank of a vestigammon. I will show you a rendering of this animal if you wish. The green nuggets are the droppings of this same mammalian type creature and are also rich in protein."

Chrystel choked, holding in the gag reflex, as Shakete continued a narrative about the marvelous vestigammon and its edible parts. Karen pushed the green things around on her plate to appear that she had at least tasted one.

At the end of the meal, the server entered once more and set in front of Karen a clear glass containing fizzing, black, translucent liquid, over ice cubes. Chrystel received a bowl of ice cream with bananas and chocolate sauce. Having just learned that the Ardinians were known to serve animal excrement, Karen politely inquired about the beverage. "And what is this, Shakete?"

"We have prepared favorite earth deserts! Chrystel's is known, I believe from a previous decade, as a banana split. Yours is something we noticed you enjoyed before, during, and after a meal. Which of course, doesn't qualify the drink as a desert, but we understand it is no longer available. Our chef didn't think it was fit for consumption. We convinced her to do it anyway. It's named a diet coke."

Karen thought the voyeur thing was becoming exceedingly creepy. They knew too much about her. But shit-sakes, a diet coke! She drank a small taste, and then savored the cold, bubbly goodness. It brought back so many memories. Her long-lost daughter, Anne, who had died in her arms during the change, sitting next to her on a short beach chair. Karen drinking from the can, watching her son and husband play in the surf. That petulant thirteen-year-old daughter voice nagging her about all the unhealthy chemicals contained in a diet coke. In her mind, Karen reached out and hugged her beautiful, sweet girl, thankful for her concern. It didn't happen that way in real life. In real life, she told her daughter not to worry about it, and Anne got frustrated and stomped off.

Karen was fighting tears. Her beautiful first family, gone so long ago. Even now, a stray memory could strike like a lightning bolt, fast and hard. It didn't happen frequently now, but the impact was nearly always the same. Seeing their faces in her mind set off a cascade of emotions, ending with a mixture of great warmth and great sadness. A few tears slipped out.

Chrystel glanced at her grandmother and asked in a low whisper, "Are you OK, Grandma?"

Karen nodded and fought to regain her composure. Shakete commented. "I hope it was a gentle memory."

Surprised that Shakete understood, Karen gave him a genuine smile. "It was Shakete. Thank you so much for the drink. It brought back a moment I haven't visited in a very long time."

"I believe it is time to discuss important matters." Shakete waited until the plates were cleared from the table and waved one hand. As the room darkened, the walls and ceiling seemed to evaporate, replaced by a panorama of stars so lifelike, Karen felt a chill. It was as if she was swimming in a void, the outside cold seeping into her bones. Mesmerized, Chrystel's green eyes shimmered against the dark space scene, drinking in planets and suns covering every surface.

"As you must have assumed, we are from a planet named Ardinia. It was destroyed in a supernova many thousand years ago. Our race was saved only by the foresight of our ancestors, who had already developed an ability to travel into space. For one-hundred Ardinian years, we built craft to carry our people to safety. When the end was near, we were able to save nearly all of our people."

The walls provided an illusion of traveling to a solar system. Its sun propelled outward in a dizzying display, destroying the circling planets. Chrystel let out a little scream as the blast radiated off the walls with a resounding concussion. The room video momentarily blurred, and then another scene of an armada of space ships took its place. One ship broke away and headed in a different direction.

Shakete continued, "In Ardinia's sector of the galaxy, what humans call the Cygnet terminus, there were no planets considered to be truly habitable. Within 100 light years of Ardinia, we discovered planets that might have sustained life, but none hospitable to our people. After travelling for many years, a great argument occurred among the Ardinian survivors. Weary of living aboard ships, one group of Ardinians was so desperate to find a home, they desired to colonize a world that many others, to include my family, believed was unacceptable.

"For the first time in written Ardinian history, blood was shed over a decision. Believing it was better to settle for an unworthy destination and take their chances, the impatient Ardinians instigated a campaign of force and misinformation to convince Ardinian leaders to keep our people together as one and populate a rocky planet with little water and a thin atmosphere. One of our ships was destroyed during this insurrection.

"My family and our leaders had already agreed to allow this sect of Ardinians to settle on a home of their choosing, but that wasn't enough for them. With valid concerns regarding splitting Ardinian resources, the belligerent Ardinians were determined to force their ill-conceived will on others. As you've learned here on earth, there is a point where too few people can make survival extremely difficult.

"The ship the sect destroyed was home to the Ardinian council. In the nick of time, the council learned of a plot to create chaos and forcibly take control of the armada and safely traveled to another ship before they were lost in an explosion. Ardinian leaders saved themselves, but there wasn't enough time to evacuate over twenty thousand Ardinian souls that lived aboard that doomed ship.

"In all our history, no Ardinian had ever reeked such evil against innocents. Seeing so many of their number killed, Ardinian sentiment immediately turned against the sect. The last mutinous holdouts were gathered together, given one ship and supplies, and sent to the planet they so coveted.

"My forbearers parted ways from the rogue Ardinians on the same day that we watched the remnants of their rebellion hurl toward an unspeakable destiny. It was decided by our scientists, in conjunction with the Ardinian council, that our fleet would travel to another portion of the galaxy where higher concentrations of stars could increase the likelihood of finding a suitable home. Also, my people wanted to settle somewhere far away from the aggressive Ardinian sect, so unlike peaceful Ardinian culture. Our people were placed in stasis, and the armada headed for the further reaches of the galaxy."

Karen asked, "So, you're saying that out of millions of stars and planets in your area of galaxy, there was nowhere else to settle?"

"Yes, but there is a tremendous difference between habitable and hospitable. A planet like your earth is the rarest of all jewels. My ancestors believed they could find another home as beautiful and distinct as Ardinia."

"And, you just dropped off the other Ardinians and ran."

"I certainly wouldn't describe what we did in that manner. Our people are peaceful. If we weren't, rather than giving them a ship and resources, we could have extracted revenge."

"Tomato, tamato." Karen said under her breath. Her mind was playing out the story Shakete had just told. There were so many other possibilities, such as the Ardinian leaders allowed the sect to destroy a ship so that they could quell an uprising. Or, they shorted the sect on supplies, assuming they would not survive, but still allowing Ardinian leaders to claim the moral high ground. Of one thing Karen was certain, there is always two sides to every story. Not that any of that mattered now since this Ardinian saga happened thousands of years ago.

"But, how could you power ships across those vast distances?" Chrystel asked. "I mean, I can't even imagine it."

"Chrystel, I am aware that this information may appear absurd. Please, there will be time to discuss the technological aspects of space travel later. For now, I agree, my ancestors were too optimistic. When we woke from stasis at the intended destination, more than half of our ships were gone. These vessels had been lost to malfunctions and other calamities during the long journey.

"We continued our search and were rewarded for our patience by three acceptable settlement planets. One of them was yours. After studying humans, we concluded your species was too violent to share, and Ardinian ideology would not allow us to take it from you. Of the two remaining planets, we attempted to live on one we named Greet, but it was found to be geologically unstable and dangerous. The last available home was inhabited by a race called the Mermots. They were a highly industrious, peace loving, and homogeneous species. They also lived primarily underground and were happy to allow us a place to live on the surface. For thousands of years we lived fruitful harmonious lives on Trisunium with the Mermots. That was until the long-lost Ardinian sect found us."

"But how did they find you?" Chrystel interjected. "The galaxy is a huge place."

Maleta answered. "Before the civil war among our people, we shared the same history, data systems, education, and culture. Our best guess is they simply reached the same conclusions in terms of a good place to search for a home."

Shakete nodded at Maleta and continued. "Our lost brothers and sisters were no longer like us. The intervening time and the struggles they experienced made them a hard, aggressive, and heartless people. When they found the planet on which we resided with the Mermots, we tried to reason with them and offered space on Trisunium to settle. But it was not to be.

"They no longer called themselves Ardinians. They call themselves the Hunta, an ancient word for 'special ones'. I believe humans have an expression for what they did next; you call it cutting off your nose to spite your head. The Hunta bombarded the planet we offered to share. Before my people and the Mermots were destroyed, we boarded as many as we could on to space vehicles and fled on ships for our lives. We have been running ever since. The Hunta tried to live on Trisunium, a planet they nearly destroyed in their effort to steal it from us, but the environment had radically changed. The atmosphere was too poisoned by radiation.

"And that brings me to why we are here on earth now. Your planet is the last hope. The Hunta will find earth, and they will bring destruction to humans without mercy. They have lost the capacity for compassion. We wish to join with the people of earth to repel their eventual attack. To win the battle to come. We cannot sit by and let them destroy yet one more, one last, oasis of life. This time we must fight. We must fight for our own people, for the Mermots, and for you."

Karen and Chrystel remained silent. The dogs and Tilley looked on in stillness. Shakete and Maleta waited nervously for a response from their human guests. Karen was the first to speak, her face contorted in disgust, "Well, that's just fucking great!"

"Do you believe it to be great?" Maleta asked confused.

Shakete answered. "I believe that response was what humans call sarcasm. Sarcasm is when someone says the opposite of what is actually meant."

"And what is the purpose of that? How does one know the difference?"

"I believe it is in the tone of voice. If they accentuate—"

Chrystel interrupted the developing controversy over sarcasm. "Enough! We're not zoo animals to be discussed like we aren't here. You brought us here to discuss a partnership."

Shakete and Maleta looked at each other, their eyes wide. "Please, beg our pardon. We truly meant no disrespect. We seek understanding, but we exhibited rudeness." Shakete and Maleta bowed their heads.

Chrystel thought it must be an Ardinian gesture of apology. "Forget it. You're forgiven. Now please, the Huntas."

Karen interrupted. "Before you do that, can we review what I just heard. I'm desperately hoping I misunderstood what you've just told us. To begin, your home Ardinia was destroyed a very long time ago. You jumped into space ships and started looking for somewhere else to stay. It took so long to find a place, you had a big family fight. Some of your relatives went one way, and you went another. You are very particular about where you want to live, so when all available lodging was unsuitable on your side of the galaxy, you drove to another. Even Earth's side of the road has slim pickings, but you met the Mermots and bunked with them. Then your crazy relatives, who had shitty luck with their

67

lodgings, followed you to the Mermot's world and destroyed that planet too. You are desperate now. The only room left at the inn, in all of the vast Milky Way, is earth, inhabited by us violent humans. If we don't agree to join with you and the Mermots, we are all dead meat at the hands of your deranged and pissed-off, long-lost family that now call themselves the Hunta. Have I got the story about right?"

Shakete stared at Karen. His look was grim. "I had trouble following some of your colloquialisms, but I believe you have it mostly correct. We would have never chosen this unfortunate set of circumstances. We will never attempt to take your world from you. But, as you say, we are all dead meat if we can't stop the Hunta."

Chrystel asked, "Why do you need us? Your technology is so far superior to human technology, and our numbers so small, I can't imagine what we can add."

Maleta's round eyes searched Shakete's face. Grief associated with their losses was written across the faces of both Ardinians. She spoke in a low clear voice. "Our once proud people has been reduced to only one starship. Orbiting your earth on what we call a metaship is the last of our kind. We were never an aggressive people, so our weaponry is limited. We have the technology, but not the ability to build what we need in enough time to repel the Huntas. Even the Mermots who possess the capability to regenerate a population quickly account for only one hundred thousand lives. The moon where they are now located is adequate for building space vehicles, but it is not an ideal location for the number and type of weapons we will need. Also, the Mermots are not well suited for piloting the space craft that they build. We were hoping you might assist in flying the ships necessary to defend earth."

"How long do we have?" Karen scowled.

Shakete responded. "Our estimates based on what we know about the Hunta is, at most, two to three years. It could be less time, but it is unlikely it would be more. They are not capable of identifying wayfarer points for travelling and are limited to their FTL and transition drives."

"I have no idea what that all that means," Chrystel added. "What I need to know is exactly what you need from us."

For the first time since Karen's recap of the Ardinian's story, Shakete brightened. His face was glowing again. "As Maleta mentioned, the Mermots are temporarily on a moon not far from here building offensive space vehicles. We need humans to learn to fly these space craft and help build and operate terrestrial weaponry from earth. In the near term, we respectfully ask that you allow some of the Mermots access to your world to build and train. We hope that this partnership might lead to a place on your world for our peoples when the war with the Huntas is won."

Chrystel asked, "Other than saving our skin, is there any additional benefit to us included in your proposed partnership?"

"I thought that would be obvious," Shakete smiled shyly. "Shared technology beyond your wildest imagination. If you want, we can help humans become immortal. The Mermots offer a labor force in whatever size or shape is necessary. Is that enough?"

"No one will believe this," Chrystel lamented.

Karen gave an affirmative head shake. "They might if we met the Mermots and brought a team back with us. Can I meet them, Shakete? Get a feel for how to sell this proposal?"

"Great processors think alike, Karen. We were hoping you would travel with us to their current location and get to know the delightful Mermot species."

"How long a trip can I expect?"

"58.6 of your earth days."

Chrystel interrupted again. "Shakete, can we have a moment of privacy to discuss this partnership?"

"Certainly. I will take the Henka too. She understands most of what we say. I sincerely hope you will give our proposal every consideration. It is a matter of life and death for three of this galaxy's most advanced species."

An opening hissed into existence. Chrystel noticed Maleta glance at her with the saddest of smiles before she stepped out of the room.

Karen's dogs stayed. Now that Tilley was gone, they were scurrying around the room and smelling everything. "It appears the dogs are back to normal." At the sound of her voice, Sadie jogged to Karen's side and scooted her head onto her lap for a reassuring pat.

"What do you think, Grandma? Do you trust them? I'd bet they're listening to us right now."

"I wouldn't be surprised if they could read our thoughts, Chrystel. There were times when

Shakete and Maleta looked at each other almost as if they were talking. To your first question, yes and no. I believe what they say as far as it goes. Their technology is so far advanced to ours, I can't help but believe if they had wanted, they could have destroyed what is left of a barely recovering earth or just plopped themselves down in an unpopulated area and taken it for their own. But, and this is a big but, I think there are large gaps in the story. Thousands upon thousands of years' worth of gaps. There's a lot they aren't sharing."

Chrystel nodded agreement. "That's what I thought too. Great processors think alike." Both women giggled at the slightly off idiom usage of the Ardinians. "If what the Ardinians say is true, and these Huntas are headed to earth with the capability to destroy worlds, there is no way to defend ourselves without their help. Convincing the entire world of the coming threat will be our first greatest challenge."

"Agree. Let me do some negotiation with the Ardinians. I know you're the mayor Chrystel, but I've had a lot of years to practice my negotiating skills. This watching earth people via dog communicating nanites has got to stop. To know I've been watched for all of my post-change life is more than a little disconcerting."

"I'm having some trouble getting my arms around this story. Aliens. Galactic travel. Destroyed worlds?"

Karen studied Chrystel. Her granddaughter had seemed unusually quiet since they had entered the ship. Her normal exuberant confidence was hidden behind glassy, shocked eyes and an uncharacteristically quiet demeanor. "You're holding together pretty well, all things considered. It's nuts, but the first apocalypse gave me at least an appreciation for life shattering events. Not to mention the weirdness of talking dogs and visions of the future. I was a hot mess for months. If what the Ardinians say is true, we don't have time to indulge ourselves in 'why me' questions like I did the first go-round. Strap on your big girl pants, Chrystel. We have things to do and an earth to save."

Chrystel stared back at the stubborn old woman glaring into her eyes. She marveled at the fierceness of some women, particularly this one, when their 'lioness protecting their cubs' side revealed itself. What a mass of contradictions. "OK, Grandma. I've got your back."

Karen reached over and hugged her granddaughter. For a tiny moment, Karen was hugging both her lost daughter, Anne, and her bright, scrappy, grandbaby.

As the history of our world goes, yesterday was the single most significant day since the Great Dying. I am a wreck. My mother was taken by aliens. I had promised myself I would finish the next segment of my meandering history this week, and I almost extended my self-imposed deadline until it occurred to me that productive effort might best serve to keep my worry at bay. The reactions and political maneuverings of certain members of our community during this crisis also illustrate how we function in general. I ask for the reader's forbearance if I am unusually emotional. I will use the last couple of days as a template for our "system" of government.

When the founders returned to Washington (after saving my mother Karen from a new-age cult), they had three overarching goals for government: freedom of choice, freedom of speech, and avoidance of megalomaniacs and ruthless dictators. Like all humans of this new world and the old, they simply wanted to be able to live a good life of their choosing and raise their children in relative peace. Those three goals sounded so simple to achieve at the time.

Democracy was the system the founders were born to. As messy as the democratic process had become in their pre-apocalypse experience, the founders still believed it was better than anything else. They agreed that every decision affecting the group would be made by a simple majority vote. So far so good. What this system didn't do was protect against a decision that was too onerous to a single individual. To guard against seriously wounding someone by a group mandate, every person was given one group veto, every two years. It was a free pass for overturning the will of everyone else. Growth of the enclave population and the number of veto passes eventually resulted in the complete breakdown of decision making. With alarming frequency, someone whipped their veto card on the table just before a crucial vote and said, "I can't live with that!" The bill or policy would then be sent back to the council to be shaped and hammered into something that no one could find offensive, which normally meant the issue was dropped entirely.

After the California Enclave merged with ours, veto passes were reduced to only one per lifetime. Since veto power is now an extremely valuable commodity in the enclave, most are careful how they use it, often hoarding their veto powers. In a few cases, these passes have been auctioned to the highest bidder. The council tried to pass a law to prohibit this behavior, but it too was vetoed.

The Defense Force was designed as both a police and military force. To protect against a military takeover and to ensure individual rights, powers of the members of the Defense Force are expressly limited. They must follow our laws when arresting a citizen and rotational juries decide citizen punishment. The Defense Force is under the command of the enclave mayor (elected every five years). Anything above and beyond normal daily business must be confirmed by a democratically elected steering committee. So far, this process has worked. There haven't been any coups or major upheavals, fates that has befallen many other enclaves. The events of the last few days, however, give cause for concern. The following are my observations of the events of the alien visitation and the worrisome impact on our system of government:

On Wednesday, Jessica, one of my assistant librarians, came running in the library, her hair on fire, screaming, "The aliens are here! The aliens are here!" Because she is often prone to hysteria, at first, I didn't believe her. I was in the book vault and took my sweet time to extricate myself from my study. Eventually, curiosity got the better of me.

My eyes squinted from the differing light in the main room. Everyone had vacated the library building and they were standing in clusters outside on the curb, pointing and watching something. The library is not located among the ring of buildings at the city center. We were not considered important enough to warrant one of those esteemed assignments. Instead, we are three blocks down the road.

Candy, my trusted hound, was running back and forth on the sidewalk, excited by the unusual gathering of friendly people. I was almost ready to put her at heel when I glimpsed a cylindrical, space vehicle right itself to a position perpendicular to the horizon over the top of the town center. My first emotion was raw, unabashed fear. "Everyone get inside now!" I screamed. The people I depend on to help me collect and store historical records completely ignored my pleas. Our best hacker turned for a second, gave a half-smile, shook his head at me, and then began strolling down the street to get closer.

I ran inside to call Chrystel before realizing that she, like everyone else, probably already knew that a strange alien spaceship was ready to land in Founder's Park. I had missed the initial arrival, since I was otherwise engaged inside a soundproof vault. Wondering who to call, I stood by the phone looking out of the windows at that thing. It would take at least an hour for the rumor mill to kick into high gear and deliver information to my front door. I tried Jed and got a busy signal. Candy interrupted my useless fretting. She pushed the door open with her nose, ran around the reception/processing desk, and spoke into my mind with a wagging tail, "*Let's go. They're here.*"

"Who's here, Candy?"

"*Them, the ones.*"

I responded more loudly than I intended. "What are you talking about? What 'ones' for heaven's sake?!"

"*The ones.*"

"Good grief, Candy, that isn't an answer." Realizing the only thing left to do was to do it myself, I picked up my walking stick, pulled the library keys from the hook hidden under the counter, and locked the door on the way out. My team had abandoned me. There was no one outside. If they came back while I was out, they could just wait by the door for my return.

The city center was already sealed off by the Defense Force when we arrived. I had hurt myself in an accident when I was young, and it didn't heal properly, so I don't move as fast as I would like.

Henry Talbot was the first Defense Force guard I encountered. Henry is a burly young man with a thick coat of back hair that always creeps out the top of his shirt. I often wondered why he didn't just wear something with a collar. I tapped him on his shoulder to get his attention, avoiding the tangled mass of hair, and he jumped.

"Geronimo. You scared the shit out of me!"

"Sorry about that." I smiled pleasantly. "What's going on, Henry?"

"Not really sure. We were told not to let anyone through for their safety. There are a few rumors that some sort of meeting is planned."

"Really? What kind of meeting?"

"You know, between us and them." He looked to the sky where the space formation was parked.

"As the Enclave Historian, I really should be at any extraterrestrial meeting to document what happens. Please let me through, Henry."

"Sorry, no can do, Geronimo. I would if I could. Thomas gave us very specific orders, no one was to be let in."

"I can't believe this. I'm always forgotten when it comes to important, dare I say momentous, events."

"Hey man, you aren't the first person who feels left out. And if it makes you feel any better, my family loves your library. My son is a reading fool thanks to you. You know, just a thought, Wilson's place is behind the ring, but high enough you could look out the window on the second floor. You should have excellent visibility of the whole area, including Founders Park. I heard that's where the meeting will start."

I nodded thanks and gave him a pat on the shoulder. "Appreciate the idea Henry. Tell your boy I just got my hands on some old comic books I think he would enjoy."

Turning, I whispered to Candy, at my side. "Talk to the other dogs. See what you can find out."

Candy was known as something of a dog gossip. Like people, some dogs are more gregarious than others. She had a talent for getting information from her canine friends. "*OK,*" she whispered back. "*I said the ones are here.*"

"I know you did, sweet friend, but that doesn't make any sense to me. See if you can find out about this meeting with the 'ones'." She wagged her tail and was off on a sleuthing mission. While she was still paying attention, I yelled at her loping profile, "I'll be at Wilson's!"

Wilson's textile and clothing shop was unlocked. The normal announcement tinkle/bell at my entry served to sooth my frazzled nerves. The store was empty. I walked toward the stairs, through isles surrounded by colorful bolts of salvaged cloth from pre-change civilization. Mr. Wilson was already hotfooting-it down the stairs to greet the new arrivals.

"Oh, it's you Geronimo. Come to catch the show I expect." He gave an inward wave and I followed him up to the second floor and into his family's living room. A chair was sitting in front of the window. He pulled another chair next to his. "Have a seat. Want a beer? We may be here awhile."

"Thanks Ted, I'd love one."

"So, what have you heard?" I asked as he handed me a somewhat cold, Big Foot from our enclave's only brewery.

"Not much. Mabel was just by looking for a dress for your mother. She took three of our best pieces. She is one tight-lipped lady--wouldn't tell me shit. If I had to guess, I would say that your mother is involved somehow."

"What? That's nuts. She's retired!"

Ted shrugged and gazed out at Founders Park. "Doesn't seem fair, does it? After everything, an alien invasion. You'd think the big man upstairs would have sent them while we still had billions of people around to protect ourselves."

"No one ever promised fair, Ted. Hey, where's your family?"

"They took off to Debbie's mom's place away from here. We all thought they'd be safer. I had to stay to protect the store and our home. It's all we have."

Settled into our observation post, Ted, having consumed more than a few Big Foots, was asleep by the time the action began. I was chewing my nails when I glanced up to see my mom and dad, my niece, mom's dogs, Thomas, and Brodie, one of the guys running for mayor, heading toward the statue. *What the hell—why Mom and Dad? Why is my family being put in harm's way? I get Chrystel, but seriously, my folks? And what happened to Candy?*

I was worrying a cuticle when a blue hue reflected off the window. Dumbstruck, I watched with a sick feeling in the pit of my stomach as a bluish beam of light expanded and encircled my family. I punched Ted in the shoulder to wake him up. He jumped, looked out the window, and croaked, "Goddamn!"

Candy trotted into the room as I sat helpless, observing, as the meeting group disappeared behind a screen of flashing blue haze. "*Don't worry*," Candy said with conviction. "*The 'ones' protect.*"

"Enough already with the 'ones'," I shouted. I grabbed my walking stick and headed to the melee in the park at a blistering pace, blistering for me anyway. One way or another, I was getting through the established perimeter.

My righteous indignation was wasted since the light tunnel to the sky broke the discipline of the guards. They, along with other sight seers, stood gawking at the perfectly round, swirling wall. A young girl of about five, ran up to the edge and pressed her hand to the blue face as her mother wailed, "Noooo!" Ignoring her mother's plaintive calls, she pushed inward with her fingers laid flat. The wall gave to her touch but didn't break. The girl was smiling as her mother dragged her away from the area. "It didn't hurt mommy. It tickled."

That wall remained until the early the next morning. I wasn't there when it finally blinked out of existence, leaving the greeting party peacefully slumbering on the park grounds. I was sleeping it off after a rowdy night at the Assembly Hall, performing my citizen duties as the wheels of government came off the cart.

Our constitution says the order of succession for mayor is the steering committee head, the last serving mayor, and finally, the Chief of the Defense

Forces. Letitia Bodwell, our committee chairwoman, was missing in action, and Karen and Thomas were behind the blue wall, leaving exactly no one to assume the mantle of leadership. The first hour of the emergency session was spent in fist-pounding, foot-stomping, over the top drama, detailing claims and counter claims concerning what had happened to Letitia. Carlton's loyalists were convinced she had become frightened, took an unscheduled hiatus, and was, therefore, not fit to serve. Those in Chrystel's corner argued darker motives at play. They suggested someone had done something unseemly to circumvent constitutionally guaranteed succession plans. Brodie's friends, which also included Letitia, were mostly quiet from worry over her absence.

Many lifetime veto passes were used during the session. Carlton called for a vote to allow him to serve as temporary mayor because he was the only one left who wanted the position. It was passed and then vetoed. I would like to add here, the number of votes Carlton received didn't bode well for my niece's chances at the next election. The Assistant Chief of the Defense Forces offered herself as an alternative. Once again, passed and vetoed. On and on it went. At 2:30 a.m., two hours after all available coffee had been consumed, the last vote was for our Animal Control Superintendent, more commonly known as the dog and ranger catcher. It is fortunate alcohol is not allowed in the building or the proceedings might have devolved into fist-fights.

Someone I didn't know recommended adjournment after the dog catcher vote and to begin again at eight the next morning. The motion was unanimously approved.

As I wearily stumbled out of the hall, I overheard snatches of a whispered conversation between a man and a woman, but I didn't recognize the voices. It was impossible to isolate who was speaking from the hoard of heads to my front that were like me, making a hasty retreat away from the hallowed halls of government. I am gifted with extraordinary hearing and was certain of what I heard. *"We may have to move on the Defense Force sooner rather than later"* and *"It's high time someone else takes charge"*.

Outside the building, I searched in vain for the source of the villainous comments. I couldn't allow a coup in our enclave, but what could I, a lowly historian do?

Deciding after a good night's sleep that clearer heads might prevail, I took my leave. When Chrystel was miraculously returned the next day, I informed her of a possible plot to gain control of the enclave.  She was as they say, pissed, but so focused on important alien news, discussions of a possible insurrection had to wait. I hope that choice proves to be the correct one.

Sometimes it seems, the more people available to get things done, the less likely it is that anything at all is accomplished.

Geronimo M.

# 7. Fallout

Thomas felt a rock under his cheek and opened one eye. He looked straight ahead from his vantage point on the ground and saw the Founders Statue. *I'm in Founders Park. Why am I lying on the ground in Founders Park? That's right, the alien meeting. The blue blinking wall….* Thomas jumped to his feet and pulled his pistol from the holster. Mike and Brodie unconscious in front of him, Thomas jumped over their bodies, took three quick strides to the statue, and turned so his back wasn't facing possible danger.

An alien creature stood in the middle of the inert, ground hugging, diplomatic party. The purple monstrosity was huge, powerful, and baring its teeth. Preparing to shoot the giant creature, Thomas raised his weapon and aimed.

"Thomas, don't!!" Chrystel screeched as she jumped from the ground. "She's friendly and smiling at you! Tilley, please quit smiling." The henka looked confused and then loosened its jowls to cover its humongous canines. "Lie down, Tilley." The henka complied, lowering its body with a thump to the ground and then let her dark purple tongue slide out of the side of her mouth. "OK, that's better. Now stay.

"All right. Now. Thomas, we're fine. It may take a few minutes for everyone to wake up. They only took Karen and me to the ship. Oh, yeah, and the dogs too. You, Mike, and Brodie caught a nap. We have a lot to do, so let's get everyone up."

Perplexed, Thomas stared at Chrystel and said, "They took the dogs and not me? What's up with that?" Chrystel rolled her eyes and shook her head. Shrugging, Thomas offered Karen a hand to help her stand. A crowd had gathered by the time they were all awake and no longer lying on the grass. Chrystel explained quickly to Brodie and Mike that the alien meeting was over.

Chrystel turned to speak to the gathered town's people. "I know you are all rightfully, very curious. I will make a broadcast within the next couple of hours to let everyone know what happened. I would like the entire Washington Enclave to receive the information first hand, so please, go on about your day. You have nothing to fear from the spaceships still parked above our enclave or from this highly unusual alien version of a dog laying in front of you. Please, allow me a couple of hours of patience, and I will bring you all up to speed."

"What is that hideous thing!" a woman yelled. Tilley looked at the woman with a hurt expression and yanked her purple tongue back into the safety of her big head.

"She's not hideous, just colorful!" Karen responded. "In fact, our talking dogs were made with DNA from her."

Peering at Karen, Chrystel followed her lead. "That's right, she is very, uh, uh, sweet. Please go about your day, and I give you my word, I will tell you everything I know. We need to meet with the council immediately and confer with them before we proceed."

"Can't you tell us anything, Mayor?" another man asked.

Chrystel paused realizing how curious the townspeople must be. "The aliens are looking for a home and have offered us a partnership to take them in. There aren't that many of them. In return, they're willing to share their technology. There's more, but it'll make more sense once I have a chance to talk to the council and gather my thoughts. Can you give me the time?" She smiled at the man.

"OK. But damn, aliens living here?"

"I'll give everyone a full rundown soon."

Geronimo used his cane to push to the front of the crowd with Candy running interference. "Chrystel, I need to speak with you. It's urgent!"

Giving a "follow us" head nod, Chrystel urged the group forward toward the courthouse. "You too, Tilley!" Chrystel barked. Ferociously smiling, Tilley leaped from the ground, wagged her wispy, pink tail, and strutted after Chrystel. Karen's dogs and Candy fell into line behind Tilley while Geronimo whispered into Chrystel's ear regarding a possible coup attempt.

"Are you sure you heard correctly, Geronimo? That someone may make a move on the force?"

"I'm sure, Chrystel. You know I have extraordinary hearing."

"And you couldn't see who it was?"

"No! I tried but there were too many people to be sure."

Chrystel frowned as she walked. "Geronimo, I can't do anything about it now. I need to meet with the council. Wait for me and Thomas after the meeting, and we can discuss options. A coup attempt? Good grief, how many more irons in the fire can we handle?"

"I'll be waiting," Geronimo responded.

Nervously pacing and muttering to himself, Jed was waiting outside the door of the council meeting room when he saw Chrystel and her entourage enter the courthouse. Relieved to see his friends safe and alive, Jed ran to Mike and hugged him. "Thank God you're all OK. The council is meeting now. I tried to convince them to wait a little longer for your return, but Carlton wouldn't hear of it. He said the people's business wouldn't wait."

"Carlton?" Chrystel said, aghast. "What's he doing in a council meeting?"

"I'm not exactly sure other than using your absence as a power play. He somehow maneuvered himself into the position of interim mayor," Jed answered, looking embarrassed that he hadn't been able to stop the political machinations of an unscrupulous Carlton.

Every eye in the room jolted to Chrystel's reddened face as she flung open the door. Half-filled cups, plates, and papers littered the rosewood surface of a priceless antique dining table, painstakingly removed from an old mansion in Tacoma and restored to its original beauty. It was an impractical piece of furniture, but the elaborate table gave the room badly needed gravitas. Letitia's seat was empty. Carlton sat at the head of the table in Chrystel's mayor chair, his wavy blonde hair judiciously tasseled to give just the right flavor of a hard-working and concerned elected official.

Already agitated, Chrystel's face turned to stone when she saw Carlton in her chair. If a voice could cut diamonds, hers would have sliced right through the rosewood table. "What is going on?" she asked, looking directly at Carlton.

He returned a smile as if he didn't have a care in the world. "Obviously, I was approved this morning in the first vote of the day as a temporary mayor. Now that you've returned to your post, I'll step down. If you're interested in the hard work we've engaged in during your absence, I will tell you now."

"I'm not interested. Whatever you decided, those plans are overcome by events. Please remove yourself from the council chamber. I'll prepare an announcement to the town shortly."

Carlton wasn't finished. "I call for a vote to allow Brodie and myself to remain in the chamber. Since the election is less than two months away, we need to be informed of any major decisions."

"You have no standing in this council to call for a vote, Carlton. Leave now so that we can get to that important business." Chrystel noticed council member expressions. They were mixed, and two of Carlton's friends were glaring at her. She didn't need to give them any ammunition. They would spread rumors about her saying she was unreasonable and too emotional. Having heard those rumblings for years about her grandmother, Chrystel pivoted and softened her voice. "You and Brodie can wait outside. As soon as we're done, I'll personally brief you on the situation and any decisions we make. Now, please, time is of the essence."

The two other mayoral candidates waited outside the chamber doors, after being tossed out of the council meeting. Brodie leaned against a wall, his arms folded in front of his chest, while Carlton strutted back and forth in the corridor. Believing the meeting would be over soon, Carlton returned to his post outside by the door. The men eyed each other warily, like two bulls set to begin fighting over a mate.

"You're a real asshole, Carlton." Brodie blurted.

"And you're a naïve country bumpkin, Brodie. So, what?"

"Don't you have any shame? Chrystel leaves to meet with the first aliens to arrive on earth, and you use that momentous occasion to attempt to insert yourself in her place as mayor."

Carlton sighed as if he disdained having to explain himself to a willful child. "I'm most certainly willing to do whatever it takes to lead this enclave. I don't have time to follow behind my redheaded competitor like a dog in heat. If your whole purpose to being here is to bed our illustrious mayor, pull out of the race now and focus on that instead."

His fist clenched, Brodie had to control the heat rushing to his face. He hadn't realized until this very moment how taken he was with Chrystel. So much so, someone else had noticed. Sure, when she was in a room, Brodie felt like his skin was a metal shell, pulled into Chrystel's orbit by an irresistible magnetic force. The same force Chrystel reversed with a quick suspicious glance, repelling him if he ventured too close. Hell, he'd never enjoyed a normal conversation with her. Carlton may have a point though. His tremendous ego had inadvertently cracked the door on an idea Brodie hadn't considered, one that might offer the possibility of an entry into Chrystel's sphere.

"How do you even walk around with that overinflated head on your shoulders, Carlton?" Brodie asked. He was about to say more when the sounds of a meeting breaking up filtered from the council room.

Chrystel, the first to exit. noticed immediately the enraged looks written on the two men's faces and wondered briefly what had happened, but she didn't have time for testosterone-induced posturing. She gave them a streamlined version of the same alien recap she had just provided to the council. Carlton would try to twist the information to his advantage, but Chrystel knew there was little she could do to stop him. "Now, if you'll excuse me, gentlemen, I have to prepare my statement to the people. Could you please withhold the information on the Hunta for a couple of days? There's no reason to scare the populace until we develop a plan to deal with this crisis. I know it's difficult for you to do anything altruistic, Carlton, but give it your best shot." With those words Chrystel turned and hustled away to prepare her remarks and meet with her friends, leaving Brodie and Carlton dumbfounded by the news.

Only Chrystel's inner circle were left in the courthouse. Jed, Karen, Mike, and Geronimo remained as Chrystel finished her public announcement. With dark rings under her eyes, she looked to her closest allies. "I'm beat. I haven't had any sleep in over twenty-four hours. I know you all want to talk about Geronimo's news. If there's a plot to take over the force, it's urgent business. But

I need to clear my head and take some time to process everything. Thomas, gather the people you most trust from the force and see if they know anything. While Karen and I were interrogating aliens, you were napping in the park." She gave Thomas a sly smile.

"I hardly think that's fair, Chrissy. We were loaded for bear to take on them aliens. Not my problem they feared my awesomeness and left me behind." He became serious, "I would like to be able to say I trust every single man or woman on the force, but lately, I've noticed a group that spends an inordinate amount of time together. I passed it off as just a group of good buddies, but now I'm not so sure. I'll keep my ears to the ground and get some of the dogs listening too."

"Speaking of dogs," Chrystel turned to Geronimo. "Could you do the same. Candy always seems able to sniff-out secrets. Put her to work."

"OK, Chrystel, but I don't want her in any danger."

"I know, Geronimo. Don't do that. Just do what you both do normally, only do it a little harder."

"And Grandma," Chrystel added, "You only have two days before you leave. We need to decide who's going with you by tomorrow."

"Already done. Jed recommends I take Manny and Dee from the Rainier Station. Their tour of duty at the station is almost up."

Jed spoke up. "My great nephew Manny is actually the best scientist I have. If he hadn't lost a leg, he would be at the plant now. He hasn't been right since the accident. He needs this trip. Believe me when I say he's brilliant. He won't fail you. Dee is no slouch either."

Chrystel frowned. "I'm a little concerned with your choice, Jed. After all, they didn't warn us about the aliens. Their credibility is in question."

"Give me a break. I've already explained that. The speed with which the aliens approached the enclave only gave us five minutes to react. Even if someone had been around here to answer the phone, it wouldn't have made any difference. Not much anyone could have done in that time. They're the best I have. Also, Chrystel, when you have the time, we really do need to discuss our Rainier warning and response time procedures."

"I agree. Let's sit down tomorrow. Manny and Dee, it is. Don't let them fail us."

"I also want to take Mabel," Karen added.

Chrystel frowned. "I'm not sure I see the sense in that. What does Mabel add?"

"To begin with, she's my oldest and dearest friend. She's calm in the face of danger—the yin to my yang, and I need her with me. I haven't asked her yet, but I'm sure she'll say yes."

"Why not Mike?" Chrystel asked. "He's Mr. Cool in the face of anything."

"We talked about it. . ."

Mike stepped forward and placed his arm over his granddaughter's shoulders. "You need me here, Chrystel. Simple as that." Chrystel shifted and hugged him.

Chrystel's face changed again from serene to steel in the blink of an eye. She rapidly barked more orders. "Everyone get some rest and let's meet again at the grandparents' house at 0600 to have an informal meeting. Don't let anyone see you arriving.

"I know the upcoming election and a possible enclave insurrection is something we can't ignore. But, if what the Ardinians said is real, and we have no reason to believe that it isn't, we can't lose focus on the larger picture. If alien invaders strike earth, we must be prepared to defend ourselves, at all costs. That's a battle that means everything." Grave nods responded in unison to Chrystel's statement.

Dogs paired with their respective masters as they left the courthouse. Tilley jumped up and scrambled to Chrystel's side. "I suppose this means you're coming home with me?" Tilley's response was a henka back-end dance, feet pumping up and down shaking the ground, with a wildly waving pink tail. She tried to lick Chrystel on the hand with her long, ropy, purple tongue.

Chrystel cautioned, "Please refrain from licking, Tilley."

# 8. Home Sweet Home

The high-pitched rover hum died as Chrystel pushed the off button of her battery powered ATV. Her tiny house looked dark and lonely. She had declined an offer of a larger home, near the city center, which was part of the meager payment package for service as mayor. She didn't want the hassle of having to care for a spacious dwelling. Without glancing in the back seat where Tilley sat, she spoke to the henka for the first time since they left the courthouse. "I hope you don't shed. If you do, we'll be up to our eyeballs in henka hair."

The boxy shaped, unremarkable house was perfect for her. Chrystel unlocked the door, flipped the light switch, and stepped inside to her refuge. Wood floors glistened against ultra-sleek, functional furnishings. Not one little thing out of place--no stray papers, no paperclips or other detritus in a bowl or on the counter, nothing. An observer might say the home was staged, and no one lived in this place.

The way she lived was Chrystel's answer to time spent in an obsessive compulsive, agoraphobic household. Her mother's version of obsessive compulsion was of the bag lady persuasion. Anything that came in the doors, never went out. Stacks of papers and magazines collected over years were piled from the walls inward leaving only narrow tunnels for moving about. Anytime her mother would stash some prized, or not so prized possession in her room, Chrystel threw the worthless junk out the window and then took her mother's precious offal to the town refuse center the next day. By the time she was twelve, her mother finally quit trying to store junk in her room.

At ten, Chrystel took it upon herself to clean the home she shared with her mother. After thirty minutes of enduring her mother's plaintive pleas, followed by Amelia's writhing moaning on the floor, Chrystel stopped. During Chrystel's teen years, they reached détente: her room was hers, and the rest of the house was her mother's.

Tilley followed Chrystel inside. She sensed the floors could be scratched and did a henka version of tiptoeing. She set the pads of her mostly dog looking, seven-toed feet on the floor, laying them flush with the wood and pulled in her claws.

Chrystel looked at her. "I can't talk to you. You're going to have to find a way to communicate what you need."

Tilley responded by panting, her purple tongue hanging down several inches.

"Oh, you need water then." She reached in the cabinet for a stainless-steel bowl, filled it with water, and set it on the floor. Before Tilley could reach the dish, Chrystel slid the bowl to a corner, out of direct eyesight.

In her own space, Chrystel demanded order. Upon entering the kitchen, the sight of a dish partially filled with water and probably infected with alien bacteria, would disturb her in ways that were difficult to explain. Chrystel thought it had something to do with being witness to a building mountain of crap in her mother's home. Day by day, the stacks of junk had risen until living a normal life in an unhealthy firetrap became nearly impossible. Seeing a perfect world around her gave Chrystel a measure of peace. The peace and confidence her world would never descend into the same cluttered madness of her mother's.

Tilley didn't drink like a dog. Chrystel watched as she delicately placed her tongue into the water and somehow absorbed every drop of the liquid.

"More?"

Tilley walked to the living area and lay on the floor.

"All righty then, I am going to take a shower. Just hang here until I'm done." Tilley smiled at her back as Chrystel walked down the hall toward the bathroom.

Enjoying the penetrating pummel of hot water on her skin, Chrystel heard something pounding on the bathroom door. She turned off the water to listen. The sound was more like pummeling, as if someone wanted to break through the wood to enter. Jumping out of the shower, she threw on her robe. Slowly turning the glass knob to crack open the door, Chrystel jumped back when Tilley's dark nose poked through the opening.

"What do you want?! Didn't anyone ever teach you how to knock politely? You scared me to death."

Tilley pushed into the small space and flung her head forward and back, signaling, or at least Chrystel thought she was signaling, that something was in the house. Chrystel nodded and whispered, "Follow behind me." Picking up the toilet plunger as a weapon, she crept with her back to the wall down the hall as Tilley followed nonchalantly behind.

Chrystel peered around the corner shocked to see Brodie lounging on the sofa, drinking a Bigfoot.

"What the hell, Brodie! Why are you in my house?!"

Startled, he leaned back in his seat. "Oh, oh, I'm so sorry! I thought Tilley would tell you. I didn't realize you couldn't hear the dogs. Or in this case, a henka. The door was unlocked, and she told me to come in and get comfortable, that she would go get you. She also said to help myself to something to drink."

Chrystal whipped around and gave Tilley a narrow-eyed scowl. A scowl that could easily turn an alien henka to stone. Tilley's henka eyes were as wide and alarmed as Brodie's.

"We'll discuss this later, Tilley. Once again, Brodie, what are you doing here?"

He stood up, now that he was sure Chrystel didn't plan to club him with the plumbing accessory clenched in her hand. "I came to offer a proposal, and I need you to hear me out. I thought it was better to tell you now than wait."

Exhausted, Chrystel's eyes shifted from Tilley's guilty expression to the surprised face of Brodie. "I don't think now is a good time at all. I'm worn out. Couldn't we do this tomorrow?"

"Please, Chrystal. I wouldn't be here now if it wasn't important."

Chrystel's shoulders relaxed. "OK, let me put on some clothes."

A smile lit Brodie's face. "Thanks, and Chrystel, Tilley is very hungry."

"Since you're here, make yourself useful. Find her something to eat. I don't have any idea what a henka might consume."

Chrystel looked at herself in the mirror as she brushed wet hair. *Why is my pulse racing? I do not care about Brodie. I'm over that passing phase. He is nothing to me other than a competing politician. Why is my heart beating so hard?* She sucked in a lungful of air and dressed in her best yoga pants and long tee shirt.

With her most confident walk, Chrystel's bare feet landed in the kitchen where Brodie and Tilley were busy devastating her clean kitchen. Her teeth ground together when she saw the empty cartons and cans left on the counter as she willed herself to ignore the mess.

Digging around in the neatly stacked frozen goods of her freezer, Brodie turned and beamed a genuinely happy smile. "Good grief, Chrystel, I had no idea anyone could be this organized. I heard through the grapevine you were a neat freak, but crap, you've made it into an art. By the way, Tilley eats almost anything. She told me she'll even eat insects if they're large enough." Tilley's jaws were loudly destroying an apple. "She just finished off the bag of apples in your refrigerator. You might need to ask the counsel for special compensation to feed her. I don't think you should have to absorb the extra cost of an alien visitor that eats like a starving grizzly bear."

Chrystel, unable to resist, was removing empty containers off the counter as she began to talk. "I prefer a minimal existence. Order helps me focus, not that it's any of your business, and the Ardinians didn't warn me about Tilley's voracious appetite before they all but demanded that she remain with me. They said she would be helpful, but so far. . ." Tilley's jaws stopped their arduous chomping in mid-stream. She looked back at Chrystel with an utterly hurt expression.

Brodie glanced at Chrystel and whispered. "Tilley understands everything you say, and she's a very emotional creature. Just thought you would want to know."

*Just what I needed. To feel bad about hurting the henka's feelings and disappoint Brodie all at the same time. Not that I should be concerned about what Brodie thinks.* "I'm sorry, Tilley. Really. First, you scared me by trying to break down a door, and then Brodie parked in my living room, unannounced. I didn't mean to hurt your feelings."

Brodie responded. "She said it's OK. She'll try harder to please you."

Chrystel rubbed her eyes. "Brodie, can we talk about why you're here?

"You want to sit or stand in the kitchen?"

"The kitchen is fine."

"I don't think you or I can win the election in a three-way race. Carlton has put together a strong coalition. I propose I run for council chairperson and support you for mayor."

"What's your gambit, Brodie? What do you want from me to get out of the race?"

"Ye of little faith. Nothing, other than a seat at the table. I think we make a good team, and I think we can work together for the good of the enclave. I know we don't agree on everything, but I also know you're willing to listen and consider different points of view. I couldn't beat him if you pulled out of the election. But you can win with me by your side."

"What if Letitia shows up?"

"I wish she would. We're worried sick about her. I'm convinced one of Carlton's cronies did something to her. I couldn't live with myself if I was the reason Carlton was elected mayor. He has another agenda. I'm just not sure right now what it might be. I need to figure that out."

"Hmmm. Do you really think Carlton is responsible for her disappearance?"

"Actually, yes. Her family says she would never simply leave. She always tells them where she's going. On the day of the alien visitation, she told her husband she was heading to the courthouse, and it's only two miles away. She never showed up."

"I'll have Thomas investigate. I might appoint someone else to conduct a special investigation. Brodie, I have to ask, have you heard the rumors about a coup attempt?"

"Yes."

"Yes? That's it?"

"Chrystel, I don't want to talk out of my butt here. It's all rumor right now, and you know how rumors spread like weeds around New Washington. Even if I believe the rumors, that Carlton is at the heart of a coup attempt and Letitia's disappearance, it isn't right to formally accuse anyone without having more information."

"Will you tell me when you have more information?"

"Absolutely."

"I'm going to hold you to that. As far as your proposal, I like what I hear, but part of me is still curious about your motivations." *Carlton may not be the only one with a hidden agenda.* "Can you give me until tomorrow to consider it?"

"Absolutely, again. But don't wait too long. We don't want Carlton to gather anymore momentum than he already has. And I'm not insulted you would question my motives. You should. Instead of a resounding defeat, I get to play a leadership role in our town. Believe it or not, I simply want what's best for our enclave."

"If there is a *'we'*. . ."

"I'm hoping so Chrystel. More than you know." Brodie looked directly into Chrystel's eyes.

Chrystel stared back, wondering what or if that statement meant something more. Her heart started racing again. *Be still, you implacable beating heart.* She needed to take a step back. "I think you need to be going, Brodie."

Brodie nodded and moved to his exit. Before he left, he turned around to speak. "Tomorrow then. We could do great things together." Then he was gone, leaving Chrystel with her heart racing and her cheeks burning.

After sanitizing the kitchen, Chrystel tossed and turned in bed, vainly attempting to dislodge Brodie from her thoughts. So much was at stake now. It sounded absurd, but the fate of the earth might hinge on the focus and dedication of New Washington people and most of all on her. She didn't have the time to be distracted by a man.

Busy trying not to think of Brodie, Chrystel hadn't noticed the henka standing by her bed watching. As she glanced at Tilley's dark eyes, moonlight filtered through the window and reflected off their wet surface. Chrystel had to admit, as weird as Tilley looked, and as powerful, there was something about her that was kind and joyous. She wished she could steal some of those good vibes and use them as effortlessly as Tilley. As if she could read Chrystel's mind, Tilley put one foot on the bed and then another. "Oh, no you don't." Chrystel giggled. "I am not sharing this bed."

With one good heave, the henka's front paws were replaced by her back feet, as she leapt over Chrystel to the other side. The bed shook and tilted from Tilley's girth. "No! No!" Chrystel screamed as she tried to push the henka back.

Tilley twirled around twice and landed with a bed-sagging lurch, her head gently placed on Chrystel's knee. A spark of something travelled from Chrystel's belly to the far reaches of her body, a feeling of closeness that was as foreign to Chrystel as was a talking, purple, cartoon character. No one had ever shared her bed. Chrystel's mother had a time or two before the accident and her subsequent breakdown. During her nights at the grandparents' home, Grandma Karen often climbed into bed next to her and held Chrystel until she went to sleep. Otherwise, Chrystel kept her own counsel in the deep of night.

She looked at the already sleeping henka once more. *You're pathetic, Chrystel*, she told herself. *The only being to ever share my bed is a grape colored alien. Maybe it's time I get some of that curiosity Grandma mentioned.*

## 9. Inner Circle

The founder family meeting was in high gear when Geronimo came rushing through the door of his parents' home. Karen's crew of dogs joined with the various guest dogs to offer Geronimo a welcome. Thomas' dog Ghost was the first to ask, "*Where's Candy?*"

Geronimo put his hand over his mouth, stifling a sob. "She's missing. Oh, my God, my Candy is missing!" Sadie and Rocket began to howl.

Mike poked his head around the corner to the foyer and gazed at the ensuing commotion. Geronimo was unusually disheveled, his hair wild and uncombed. Mud clung to shoes and pant legs. "Karen, come quick," Mike yelled.

Karen entered the foyer and moved quickly to her son. She had never seen Geronimo look so unkempt or upset. He was always fastidious about his appearance. Karen studied his eyes. "What is it?"

Geronimo pursed his lips, trying to keep them from trembling. "I sent Candy out last night to see what she could learn from the other dogs. She never came home. She always comes home! Something's happened to her. Someone has done something to my friend. . ." Geronimo's eyelids lowered, and he raised his head to the ceiling, as if searching to the heavens for an answer.

Grabbing his arm, Karen pulled Geronimo into the dining room. "I am so, so sorry, Geronimo. I know how much you love her. But we don't really know that anything bad has happened to Candy.

Come in and sit with us and tell us the whole story. I'll get you some coffee."

Geronimo allowed his mother to lead him to the last remaining empty chair as she headed to the kitchen for a warm drink. Mike informed the group Candy had gone missing. "Geronimo sent her out to do some sleuthing, and she didn't return."

Thomas said, "Tell us exactly what happened."

"After dinner, last night at home, I told Candy there might be some people that wanted to cause trouble in the enclave. I asked her to check around with some of her dog friends to see if they were hearing any rumors. It was about 6:30 when she left. She often goes out on rounds to visit at about that same time every night. I was worried to death when she wasn't home by midnight. She's never outside by herself that late because she's terrified rangers will trap her. I convinced my neighbor to help me look for her. We traced her whereabouts to Neill Ferguson's place, and then the trail went cold. She didn't turn up this morning."

Tilley was sitting totally still in the corner of the dining room performing her most critical henka mission: listen to everything and help if you can. She curled her jowls to show her teeth in what she hoped was a winning grin. Even though she still couldn't communicate with Chrystel, she knew Geronimo and Mike would understand her missives. "*Tilley can help!*"

Geronimo turned to her. "How?"

"*Tilley very good scent tracker. Also, dog nanites are distinct to each dog body. Give me something of Candy, like bedding, Tilley can follow scent and nanites energy.*"

"Well then, let's get going!" Geronimo almost shouted as he pounded the table.

Chrystel put up her hand up in a "not-yet" gesture. "Before you go, Geronimo, we've made a few family decisions. You weren't here to participate, so please don't whine later that we didn't include you. Mom is going with Mabel and Dee and Manny from the Rainier Station to visit the Mermots and hopefully bring back some Mermot representatives. The Ardinians said the round trip will take about two months."

"Brodie has offered to quit the race, join with me, and run for council chairperson. There was unanimous agreement between all of us here that his offer may be the only way to ensure I win the election. I'm not sure yet whether we can trust him completely, but he seems sincere. We want to make him feel welcome and that he has a seat at the table without sharing too much. I don't think it's a good idea to include him right now in the inner circle. Also, we still don't know if the coup whispers you heard were idle chatter or a real threat. Brodie thinks Carlson is behind the talk, and I tend to agree. I'm truly sorry Candy has gone missing, Geronimo, but we still need to keep our eyes and ears open for warning signs. Do you have any concerns with what I've just said?"

"No, that's all fine, but it doesn't make any sense."

"What doesn't make sense?"

"If Carlton has gained enough support to win the election, what would be the point of a coup? Unless of course, it's a backup plan if he loses the mayoral race. By bringing Brodie to your ticket, we

104

may force his hand. That's if, and it's a big if, Carlton is behind the rumors.  Chrystel, have you given a moment's consideration to letting the people of the enclave decide who they feel is best able to govern without all the political intrigue? I mean like actually trusting our people."

Chrystel's skin color was changing to a shade more akin to her red hair. "Do you really believe that, Geronimo? That Carlton would be best as mayor? That pompous, shallow, power hungry, con artist?"

"Take it down a notch, dear niece. I never said that. I do believe you are far and away the best choice. It's only that the founders started the enclave with a noble idea, to respect all the people and form a fair democracy. I don't believe they ever intended to create a dynasty. Inner circles, power changing and staying within one family, all of it reeks of a ruling family. Royalty. That is exactly why Carlton and Brodie have gained so much traction in this election. Am I right about your intent?" Geronimo glanced around at the founders in the room.  "Did you ever envision that founder families would still be running the enclave a hundred years after the Great Dying?"

Karen, Mike, and Thomas wore thoughtful expressions. Jed and Manuel were nodding their heads in agreement that a ruling family was never intended to be the outcome of the government they created. The twins, Katie and Rachel, looked sad, having argued over the very same issue the day before. As was often the case with identical twins, they landed on an identical conclusion. As hard as it might be, perhaps it was time to consider loosening the reigns and pushing the issue of new blood.

It was Sara, the only medical doctor in the founder group and Jed's wife who spoke first. "Geronimo makes a fair point. We've all dedicated our lives to making our enclave a safe and prosperous community. I think it's probably natural to believe we are the best able to lead our town into the future. If my memory of history serves me, the same thinking led to a feudal system in Europe during earth's Middle Ages. The world is physically much like it was then--walled communities protecting their villages, surrounded by stretches of mostly unpopulated area. In our case, unpopulated stretches are bigger. immense really. The problem is and has always been when power is too tightly held, human nature is for that power to corrupt. And don't get me wrong, Chrystel, I've never believed you are corrupt or your grandmother for that matter. Maybe it's time to consider a changing of the guard. Perhaps this Brodie will be a good candidate to replace you at some point."

"I would just like to add here that if absolute power corrupts absolutely, we've failed miserably." Karen's face was animated as she interjected. "If you call what we have in this wild west town of independent thinkers absolute control, then I'd hate to see what chaos looked like. We've held free and fair elections since there were enough people in the enclave to vote. No one has been coerced to keep us in power. They chose me and then Chrystel because we've set high standards of integrity and fairness and did a damn fine job as well, if I do say so myself."

His thumb cupping his chin and fingers under his nose, Mike was positioned in his normal thinking position. Always the informal leader of the founder group, Mike was respected for his ability to thread the needle when contentious discussions had the potential to turn one founder against another. The founder group waited for his input. "Geronimo and Sara make excellent points, as does Karen.

"Sara mentioned feudal times, I prefer a more recent example of how power can corrupt even in a democracy with free elections. Recall the disgust at representatives in congress of the old United States before the Great Dying. How they stayed in their positions for years, winning election after election, because voters knew who they were, and change is never an easy thing. I think almost everyone in the country had a sense the whole darn thing was rigged and rotten to the core, but they didn't understand collectively how to fix a broken system. The remedy to this dynamic required congress to vote and hand their power to someone else by establishing term limits. I feel certain these elected officials believed their experience and accrued wisdom justified continued service, that and a lust for power meant term limits never happened. Sure, citizens always held true power to throw the bums out, but they rarely used their votes in that manner because status quo is a safer bet.

"The best example in history of a leader who transitioned power peacefully was the first President of the United States, George Washington. He probably wouldn't have won the next term. As I remember the history, he said he was tired and wanted to return to Mount Vernon. But he also believed that stepping down was a symbol to the fledgling democracy that a peaceful transition of power was possible. He chose not to run for President of the country he helped create. I think it's time we followed his lead. Chrystel, maybe you could recommend a change to New Washington's charter to establish term limits and demonstrate your commitment to ensuring enclave leadership is not a family business.

"All that said, we still have a timing problem. If we had six months to watch Brodie or encourage other good candidates, maybe. But we don't. Karen is leaving today. She must convince not just our own people, but people from around the world to join with the Ardinians. Stability of the enclave is essential, all while we keep our eye on the ball of the bigger problem regarding the Hunta. No one said this was gonna be easy," Mike said, a lopsided grin appearing on his face.

All eyes turned back to Chrystel. No longer carrot red, she sat atypically still. "Those are some powerful sentiments, Grandpa. I don't think I've ever heard you string so many words together at one time." The founder group broke into laughter. They all knew Mike as the guy who made do with less when it came to speeches. After the chuckles died, Chrystel gazed fondly at her grandfather and continued. "The only thing I've ever wanted was to do my best for all of you and the enclave. It would've been nice to have had this discussion before I was all in for the mayor's race. But, yes, Grandpa, you're right. I'll give transition of power serious thought and see how we might adjust the charter. Until then though, I still need the help of everyone in this room. I plan to continue in my quest to secure the mayor position in the next election. We need that continuity for now."

Geronimo looked at his sister. "We know Chrystel. We know who you are and your dedication. I've been thinking about the nepotism complaints for a while and was afraid to bring it up. Events have a way of unearthing simmering problems that boil to the surface at the worst possible moments. I would love to stay and talk more, but I have a missing dog. Can I go now?"

"One last thing," said Chrystel. "I plan to appoint a special investigator to find out what has happened to Letitia and now your dog Candy. Thomas will help, but he has his hands full with—"

Geronimo cut her off. "I'll do it."

Chrystel was surprised. "You'll do it? You mean you're willing to investigate these disappearances? I thought you had your plate full at the library."

"I said I'd do it! I have the best network in the enclave. Everyone needs something from me, and I'm nonpolitical. I'll find out who's responsible for these horrendous acts and bring them to justice."

Chrystel looked around the table. Nodding heads indicated general agreement. "All right, you have the job. I don't know if we have anything in the budget to provide compensation for this duty, but I will see if I can—"

"I don't need anything. I just want to find my dog and Letitia. Can I go now, please?"

"Fine. Take Tilley and Thomas. Report back to me what you find."

Karen interrupted as Geronimo pushed his chair out to stand. "One other tiny bit of information I failed to share about the Ardinians." She stopped and looked at her friends with a guilty smile. "They were spying on us with dog nanites. I wish I could explain how they do it. It didn't make a lot of sense to me. Their detailed knowledge of me and other individuals in the enclave are proof positive they most certainly have that technology. During our negotiations, Shakete agreed to stop this practice. Perhaps, I was hasty. They may have been able to determine what happened to Candy. I will ask if they can help. I'm also curious whether they stopped watching. This might be a good test of the strength of their word."

Jed was suddenly animated. "Are you kidding me? A bio-transceiver? One that can send information over long distances? Do you have any idea of the practical applications of such a device? Karen, make sure Dee or Manny learn all they can about this technology. It could mean an evolutionary leap for communication. Since the dogs possess this capability, it's not unreasonable to assume it might be usable within humans. This is perfect."

Karen looked at her watch. "You've got 28 hours to brief your science reps and get them ready with technology priorities."

"I'm on it," Jed replied and jumped from his chair.

"Hold up for a second, Jed," Mike said as he raised his hand. "Are we still a go for the satellite launch in two weeks, and is it possible to send video to the other enclaves when Karen returns? If

110

she brings the Mermots back with her, video is the best way to convince others the threat is real."

Jed stopped and scratched his head in thought. "The satellite launch is still on, but I can't guarantee the outcome. I'd give it an 80% chance of success. As far as video, no problem on sending that data via the satellite, if, of course, the launch is good, and the satellite operates properly once in orbit. The problem would be from the other end, the technical capability to receive the data. It's a tight timeline. Let me give it some thought. Great idea by the way. I'll work on it." Jed raced off.

Karen sarcastically called to Jed's back. "Goodbye to you too. See you in a couple of months." Turning to the room she chuckled and said, "Guess that means we're adjourned."

Geronimo sighed. "This is all just too strange." He waved at Tilley for her to follow him.

Thomas got out of his chair to go along and grabbed Karen's hand before he left. "I probably won't get to talk to you before you journey to strange new worlds. You take care of yourself out there." Thomas stared up at the sky.

"Thanks, Thomas. You too." After a peck on Thomas' cheek, he was gone.

Chrystel hugged her grandmother before she left. "You stay safe, Grandma. I don't know what I'll do without you. Are you going to see my mother before you leave? She'd probably want to know."

"I went yesterday to ask if she was seeing any visions about our trip or the Ardinians or the Mermots or the Hunta. She told me she would sleep on it, and I should stop over today. I'm going there before I depart. I'll miss you Chrystel. Use

Mike, Thomas, and Manuel as much as you need to keep this place together until I get back. Don't do anything I wouldn't do."

Chrystal responded with a wry smile. "That hardly narrows it down, Grandma."

After more hugs, the remainder of the meeting group departed for their respective responsibilities, leaving Karen and Mike with their arms encircling each other. Mike's eyes focused on his beloved wife. So many years together, wonderful years. There were moments when he felt guilty about having Karen as his partner. Guilty that his first family lost their lives to the change, and that loss was the reason Mike found his way to Karen. Guilty knowing that he wouldn't change a thing even if he could.

"What?" Karen asked.

"Do you think we have time for a quickie before you blast into outer space?"

Karen giggled like the young woman she used to be, the same one that still lived inside when Mike looked at her that way. "I believe I can fit that into my schedule. What did you have in mind, old man? And, let's not be too quick."

# 10. Amelia

The flagstone path to Amelia's front stoop was treacherous. Karen looked down to avoid tripping. The walkway no longer served a useful purpose, as weeds and grass growing between intersecting grooves raised the stones haphazardly to a jagged plane. Karen would have chosen dirt or grass skirting the path entirely, but the overgrown yard made an alternative route impossible. From the outside of a cedar covered, modern home, the dwelling appeared like many other aging buildings inhabited by the enclave populace—run down, but still serviceable. After the Great Dying, building new homes had taken a backseat to a host of other more important endeavors. Only recently had a few enterprising New Washingtonians opened a construction cooperative to help replace crumbling residences. Karen thought it was high time. At least, she had thought so until recent events put in question the enclave's priorities for the future.

Two gigantic rhododendrons had reached massive proportions beside the front door. Karen weaved between the branches to find the door knocker. She made a mental note to ask Mike to cut them back as soon as she returned from her trip. Mike was willing to help Amelia with outside tasks, but he never, ever, crossed her threshold. A big red line had been drawn in the sand over twenty years ago. Mike refused to enable Amelia's choice to withdraw from the world. Worried for her always, the final straw was feeling powerless as he watched Chrystel mostly raise herself. He asked, nearly begged, Amelia to let Chrystel live with them if she couldn't, or wouldn't, get some help. Amelia flatly refused. Karen was left to navigate the pain between her husband, daughter, and granddaughter and care for them all. The emotional jujitsu left her drained, knowing despite her best efforts, this family dynamic was entirely screwed-up.

Karen was relieved there was no trash that extended beyond the front entry. Then again, maybe debris extending into the yard would be a good sign. It would mean Amelia had stepped outside to place garbage there, and she hadn't, as far as Karen knew, walked into daylight since her husband died.

Karen pounded on the door. Amelia was never quick to answer. Before she could be convinced the visitor wasn't an intruder, she would stare through the peephole and then move to other windows for a different view. Finally, Amelia yanked the door inward. It hit on something in the way. Karen picked up the sack of groceries she had brought along and slid through the narrow opening. Amelia said, "Hi, Mom. Let's sit in the kitchen. I've cleared a space."

The smell inside was indescribable and assaulted Karen's nose. The odor was some noxious mixture of dust, mildew, and the vermin who had taken up residence. She choked on the gag reflex and steeled herself for a visit with her daughter. Amelia, completely accustomed to the setting, was already sitting by the time Karen snaked through the narrow isles that led to the kitchen of Amelia's nest.

"You want something to drink, Mom?"

"No, sweetheart, I'm fine," Karen answered.

"I was just reading about the 1960's hippie culture. It sounds very interesting. Were you there at the time? Did you ever flirt with joining a commune?"

Karen placed both elbows on the table and rested her head in her hands, her eyes staring into space as she remembered that time. "Nope, I never really thought about joining a commune. I was a too young when communes were in their heyday. What I remember most from those years is the music. Amazing rock music. Music that made you feel the times in your bones. That's one of things missing in our new world. New music that captures our loss and our struggle. Anyway, it was all kind of a romantic notion, hippies and such. My participation consisted mostly of dressing like a hippie and going without a bra. I was a big-time feminist though."

"That doesn't surprise me, Mom. Next time Geronimo stops by, I'll ask him to bring a download of some 60/70s music. How's dad? How's he holding up knowing you will be gone for two months with the aliens?"

"He's worried, but he hides it well. I know he would like to go too, but Chrystel needs him more. He's also worried about you." Karen studied her daughter as Amelia's face reacted to her last statement. She was such a lovely woman. Even though her long dark hair hadn't been brushed in forever, and she was rail thin, Amelia's skin was porcelain perfection. Having rarely stepped into the sun, it was as if she never aged. Her thin, slightly upswept nose, sensuous dark eyes, and still full lips made it impossible to imagine how this extraordinary child could cut herself off from the world.

As a little one, Amelia had always been different than Karen's other children. Sensitive and intuitive, her natural empathy drew others to her. If not for the visions, maybe Amelia could have learned to weather the harshness of the world. When she was three, Amelia began having visions of future events. Mike and Karen didn't recognize the signs. They didn't understand her fear or her anxiety or offer the kind of early intervention that might have made the difference. Karen blamed herself. She should have known. She had visions too. She should have talked to Amelia and helped her to understand.

At six, Amelia ran into the kitchen after napping, her hands pulling at her hair, "Mommy, Geronimo is going to crash. You have to stop him!" Amelia's stark terror hit Karen like a rogue wave. Visions! They couldn't warn Geronimo in time. He was on his bike playing in the woods. As boys will, he and his cluster of friends had created a bike obstacle course from scrounged boards, bricks, and the sweat of their brows. The "course" was as unique as it was deadly. Geronimo's bike slid off a rough plank, suspended over seven feet high, held in place by only a shallow burial in loose dirt, on either side of rocky gully. He recovered, but his left leg had been broken in three places and would never be the same. His limp attested to the courageous stupidity of young boys.

And then there was Amelia's husband. She witnessed that accident too in a vision. Just as Geronimo's accident couldn't be stopped, Amelia didn't reach her husband in time to save him. After that loss, Amelia stopped leaving her home.

Amelia smiled in her innocent, endearing way. "I miss Dad too, Mom. He's welcome to come over any time."

They both knew that would never happen until Amelia agreed to get some treatment or made an honest attempt to free herself from her keep. Karen nodded and grabbed her daughter's hand. "So, did you think about what I asked? Can you see anything in your visions?"

"Yes, I can. I'm not sure what it all means, but you aren't going to like it. Are you sure you want to know?"

"No, I'm not sure. But I also know we improve our survival chances with real clues to the future. We have to use every tool at our disposal and visions have helped me survive in the past."

Amelia pulled her hand away and looked straight ahead as if in a trance. "I see death. I see rats, and I see big explosions. I don't know who is dead. Only blood and gore and piles of blown away guts."

Karen swallowed, and her face paled. "If I don't go with the aliens, did you look to see what will happen if I don't go with the aliens?"

Tears were filling Amelia's large brown eyes. Her voice was resigned. "I see death there too. I don't see the rats anymore, and the background is different. And in this vision, there is nothing left alive."

"So, you're telling me that both ways contain a lot of death, but if I don't go, everyone will die. Is there anything positive you can see from either path?"

"Only that the rats are important. If you go with the Ardinians, I also see Bigfoots in one vision. They're important too. I just don't know how."

In a quiet voice, Karen whispered, "Thank you for trying. I had hoped for something more specific, but I understand. Visions aren't easy to control. I know how sad it makes you to look at these things."

Amelia's face contorted in terror, Karen held her shaking daughter until she was calmed. "I'll be fine, Amelia. Didn't they used to call me nine-lives-Karen? And I want you to think again about talking to someone. I've been told that Jean Clark is a wonderful therapist. Would it help to have Geronimo bring you everything he can find on your condition? There are treatments that work."

Amelia dolefully gazed at her mother. "For agoraphobia, sure. I've read everything on the subject. For visions, not so much."

They had this same conversation, or one like it, every time Karen came to visit. Karen tried to change it up. Sometimes she cajoled, sometimes she begged, and sometimes she got angry. Mike even thought to take Amelia forcibly from her home, but Karen stopped him. She believed they might lose her completely if she was separated from her safe place.

"What about the hoarding?"

"I'm not a hoarder. I just don't go outside to remove anything."

"Uh huh. I don't understand where all this junk comes from. How does it get inside your home if you can't go out?"

"Well, you know. My brothers and sisters care enough to bring me books and old magazines when I ask. That young kid slips the daily Washington Enclave Newspaper in the slot. I read a lot and sometimes read things several times."

"That newspaper isn't even good reading the first time around. We can help take some of this clutter."

Amelia's expression said, "I'm done talking about it".

Karen heaved a resigned sigh. "I'll never believe it's hopeless, Amelia. It's only hopeless if you quit trying. Just think about it."

"I will, Mom. I promise. Have a nice trip. I know you love space stuff. What an experience. But aren't you at all frightened?"

"Frightened? No, not really. From what the Ardinians said, they've been travelling between the stars for thousands of years. This trip is like a grocery run to the neighborhood store. I never thought in my lifetime I would get off this planet into space. I'm over the moon, as they say!"

"Mom, you can do what I do with visions. Have you tried?"

"I have. For some reason, I don't see the future unless I'm under immense stress. I haven't had a vision in years—maybe I'm too old. But who knows, the insights you've given me may kick start my own ability."

It was time to leave. Karen embraced another of her precious daughters. She thought she might have held Amelia too tightly because Amelia gently nudged Karen away. "You'll be back, Mom. I would have seen something if there was going to be a problem. I want to hear everything when you get home!"

## 11. New Washington Historical Notes, Part III

As the Enclave Historian, I'm obviously not as technically sophisticated as our scientists. Technological development has been important to New Washington's survival and a priority during the years since the Great Dying. This is especially true since we have huge infrastructure challenges, and technology has helped us circumvent some of those issues.

I asked Jed if he could spare someone from the science center to prepare a timeline of technology advances, but as always, they were too busy. Jed later agreed to review my writings to ensure I didn't make any egregious errors in the narrative. It is probably better that way anyway. My explanations will be in layman's terms, which are generally more enjoyable to readers. Manuel Hernandez, another of the original founders, gave me some guidance relating to infrastructure.  He conceived and designed most of the New Washington Enclave with the help of my father, Michael McCollough.

The best way to describe our technical world compared with the one that ended 112 years ago would be to say it is a mass of contradictions. In some regards our technology has far surpassed the technology of the early Twenty-first Century. In others, our society makes due with methods and systems practiced during the late 1800's. My mother described it best after returning from a trading mission to the Elkhart Enclave in Indiana. She arrived from Washington on an airship that could travel faster than any modern jet, able to land

and depart on a twenty-by-twenty-foot clearing, but she was ferried to her meeting place by a horse drawn carriage over a gravel road.

The infrastructure the world created before the Great Dying required people to maintain it. Because New Washington has never had enough people, hard choices were made about which of the existing infrastructure resources to save. The founders watched in frustration as bridges, roads, and cell towers fell into ruin. In some cases, like communication satellites, the wherewithal to stop their eventual demise simply didn't exist.

It may be best to assume that most of our technology and infrastructure is an archaic, amalgam of pre-twentieth century methods. It was determined by the founders that the priority for research and development would go to communication, travel, defense, and medicine, in that order. I make no judgement as to whether those priorities were in the best interest of the enclave and its people. A segment of our populace ardently believes the founders had it all wrong, especially regarding defense. Second guessing has become a full-body contact sport in the enclave community. At least, no one argues about climate change anymore.

Here is a down and dirty of all that we have accomplished. New Washington's achievements are quite remarkable, given from where we started. Jed Carter, another founder and our lead scientist, brought an amazing new energy technology with him from the old world. He possessed the plans for building a thorium powered generator and an ultra-storage battery. If not for this technology, humans

122

might not have survived or, at the very least, had an even more difficult go of it. The thorium energy system made it possible for us to power our airships, and, therefore, bypass crumbling roads and unsafe bridges. These thorium systems have also allowed us to heat our homes and generate energy to establish a small industrial base.

Jed demanded that we offer the thorium generator to the rest of the world. He was convinced, and rightfully so, that everyone and not just New Washington needed this technology to survive. He finally relented to pleas from the council that the generator and thorium be sold in trade for other goods. Any enclave that can pony-up something we need, now enjoys this technology, however, New Washington withheld the plans and specifications to build a generator. Jed felt confident the technological know-how to reverse engineer his power source didn't exist. That means the world must rely on us, a constant point of friction with other enclaves.

Battery powered All-Terrain Vehicles or ATVs are the means for most localized travel. They are small and maneuverable and offer travel on or off road. Additionally, New Washington builds a uniquely designed battery powered airship in what was once a flight manufacturing and test facility owned and operated by the Boeing Company. Boeing was one of the old world's preeminent airplane manufactures. Our airships provide individual travel around the world. Unfortunately, because of the danger, we rarely venture beyond known friendly enclaves. The largest of these ships carry our products for trade.

Communication currently is a combination of land line, limited cell phone service, and shortwave radio. None of it is reliable. We are plagued by outages. Our scientists have promised something far superior within the next five years. It has taken over a hundred years of effort to get to this point. Satellites circling the earth, which facilitated communication and navigation before the Great Dying, were inoperable within ten years. In just a few short weeks, the New Washington Enclave will launch the earth's first communication satellite in over a century. We will finally give the world a more reliable communication system. The plan is to share the satellite capability with every enclave interested, for traded goods, of course. Jed is also promising some sort of laser communication system, which I still have difficulty understanding. Suffice it to say, over a medium range (up to 1,000 miles) we will have another reliable means to communicate.

I have been warned that I cannot describe our military related technology. Quite frankly, I am not in the loop enough to know. What I can say is that protective weapons are a mixture of old world technologies and tech that wasn't even on the drawing board before the change. We are very well defended against any large-scale invasion.

In medicine, our greatest achievement has been the development and production of a new antibiotic not available at the time of the change. It might appear, at first glance, that an antibiotic is no big deal since there were numerous types widely available when the world died. As reviled as some of the big pharmaceutical companies were at that time, they served an important function: they kept the drugs flowing. When their production facilities shut their doors for good, we only had three to five years before nearly all medications reached expiration dates, including antibiotics. It is more difficult than you might imagine manufacturing medications with so few workers and only a handful of trained doctors. Sara Lee, a founder and physician, with the help of two veterinarian assistants, accidentally discovered some lake algae that could be dried and purified into a powerful antibiotic. Who knew? Perhaps those deceased pharmaceutical companies were keeping something from the population, after all.

I mentioned earlier that the change resulted in vastly improved health. Pre-change diseases, such as heart disease, cancer, and autoimmune related illnesses, have disappeared. Accidents are the leading cause of death in the New Washington Enclave and the reason antibiotics are so important. The one thing the change didn't cure was addiction. Alcoholism and drug abuse is still a problem. We have a small treatment center, but as in days of old, an addict must want to be cured. We continue to work on the issue.

I have taken it upon myself to insert an additional priority, the retrieval and safeguarding of old-world information. Free people sometimes do that. A free-thinking person can see a need that isn't on a list of priorities and make it their mission. That is what I have done. I created the Historian position and enticed a small group of qualified people to help me. I did all of this with the full knowledge that it was vitally important, and if someone didn't take the initiative, most of our collective human knowledge might have been lost. I am given very little credit for my vision. I take my applause when our scientists visit almost daily to find a technical manual important to their work. Also, I am rewarded when a child visits our archives and leaves with books that they might never have had the chance to read.

I have not mentioned a great deal about infrastructure because there hasn't been remarkable progress in terms of structures, systems, and networks. We make do with old buildings that have been repaired or modified and are in a constant state of fixing broken things. Systems and networks are ad hoc, designed to get us through the next season. Great ideas for infrastructure investments are plentiful, but it takes resources like people and materials in scarce supply. In some ways, it isn't at all that different from the United States before the Great Dying. The problem with infrastructure is always about a sacrifice now for greater utility later.

Geronimo M.

# 12. Celebration

Spontaneous festivity was a cultural norm for New Washington clavers. Karen and her band of travelers were departing for the stars, and the enclave was in full celebration mode. Any excuse to have a day away from the drudgery and toil of this new world was good enough. Travel to an alien world by starship was a far better pretext than most. The exact day and time of the team's departure was never part of Chrystel's public announcements, but in a small town of just over six thousand, formal announcements were often unnecessary if the news was particularly exciting, unusual, or salacious. Word had spread far and wide, from one mouth to another, until over half the town was crowded around the town center. Vendors carted all manner of crafts and wares to the outer circle perimeter. Artisans and farmers alike were stocked and ready for a big day of sales. They would stay open as late as the mayor would allow.

After viewing the crowds, Thomas and the defense force had opted against trying to keep Washingtonians out of the city center, choosing instead to form a smaller perimeter within Founders Park. The cordoned area was still large enough to protect unwary citizens from being whisked away by the blue-flashing, haze tunnel to the sky.

Arranged around the front entrance of the courthouse, the New Washington Enclave Jazz Band was doing its best to play mood music with an ambiance of extraterrestrial travel. The band leader, Phil Ho, had created a greatly scaled back arrangement of Gustav Hoist's, *The Planets*, but the band's rendition was so plodding and sad, one spectator yelled, "Man, that's a real buzz kill!" Realizing he was losing the crowd, Phil signaled to his band to switch to more recognizable music, with a cadence better suited to toe tapping. *Happy Days are Here Again* played as a nearby clump of children joined hands in a circle and started spinning until the first youngster fell to the ground in a fit of giggles.

In the wee morning hours, Clint Eastwood and his acting company had prepared their stage at breakneck speed. Now located at the opposite end of the park from the Founders Statue, they were performing a play written by Clint himself. It depicted alien invaders meeting a new-age Dirty Harry. Clint would later confess, the play wasn't original, but the drama was the best they could do on short notice.

With overcast skies and temperatures hovering in the low 50's, it was an average spring day in the great northwest. Still hanging above the city center after spitting Washingtonians back to earth, the alien spacecraft was already considered an interesting development rather than an ominous presence. Several residents had met and spoken with the alien henka named Tilley. The consensus appeared to be that aliens who travelled with an affable, talking, purple, dog-ish animal couldn't be all that bad. Besides, the Ardinians had picked their enclave. Among all the enclaves in the world, New Washington was special.

A cheer erupted from the crowd as Karen and her group of interstellar voyagers exited the courthouse and walked through the protective ring to a designated loading dock, a spot in Founders Park where a large X had been drawn in grass chalk. Karen waved and smiled at her fellow citizens. Manny, Dee, and Mabel, overtaken with surprise at the enthusiastic sendoff, followed Karen's lead and began to wave and shout to their friends and neighbors.

The Ardinians were late again. The jubilant spectators eventually become bored with waiting and moved along to more entertaining activities. Only family and close friends watched from outside the safe zone.

Manny commented, "I'm not sure what to make of tardy aliens. I always thought they'd be like superhuman perfect, If they're not perfect then--"

In a blinding flash, the conveyance tunnel surrounded them. Manny's eyes enlarged, and his last statement was cut short in a gulp.

Sullen at the necessary absence of his wife and worried over her safety, Mike watched from his outside vantage point. In over a hundred years, he hadn't been away from Karen for more than three days straight. He thought back to how he had found Karen alive after a three-month trek from Prudhoe Bay through the interior of Alaska. How his desperation had grown with every mile of the journey. Not only had he lost his entire family, as he huddled each night in one deserted building after another, he began to lose hope there was anyone left alive on earth.

By the time he'd pulled up to Karen's house in an RV appropriated in Fairbanks, his plan to visit everyone he'd ever known seemed a foolish, sentimental lark designed to keep himself from total surrender to increasingly dark thoughts. Karen had been hiding in her yard. When she'd heard him call her name, Karen had shot out of a clump of bushes where she'd been hiding, while her pack of dogs ran excitedly to the property fence, warning their intent to protect their master. What were the chances, the mathematical odds that in a deserted world he'd find the most complicated, stubborn, bold, and beautiful woman he'd ever known, before or after the change? "Good lord," Mike whispered to himself. "Be safe and come back to me."

* * *

Thomas, Geronimo, and Tilley were huddled in conversation in Chrystel's tiny office when Judy popped her head in the door and announced, "They're gone."

"Thanks, Judy. The folks still partying?" Chrystel asked.

"It's started to drizzle, so looks like things are settling down."

"Appreciate the info. If you could, we have some important matters to discuss."

Judy viewed the serious faces. "Oh, right, sorry about that. Just buzz me if you need me. Oh, that's right, we don't have a buzzer. Just scream down the hall if something comes up."

Chrystel turned back to Geronimo after the door was closed. "So, you followed Candy's scent to Aldrin's Dairy. Then what?"

"Then nothing. We talked with old Jeremy Aldrin. He claimed he hadn't seen Candy. He said he would check with his son when he returned from town."

"Claimed he hadn't seen Candy? Do you have some doubt about that?"

"It's just strange. Tilley followed Candy's scent all through town, no hesitation at all. We get to the Aldrin's, and the last place Tilley scented was on the passenger door of Jeremy's truck ATV, and then she lost the trail. Tilley told Geronimo she can only track nanites energy when a live dog is somewhere in the vicinity. Either Candy isn't alive, or she was taken somewhere else."

"Please don't say that, Thomas." Geronimo shuddered at the thought. "I'm sure Candy wouldn't have gone any further than the dairy. She's too afraid, and there's nothing much past that point except wilderness. Something happened to her there, and we need to find out what. If we do, that information may also provide an answer to Letitia's whereabouts."

Chrystel was drumming her fingers on the desk. "What seems more important to me is why a dog and a council head have gone missing? The timing for Letitia's disappearance and then Candy vanishing while out sleuthing doesn't feel like a coincidence.

"But without a motive, we're just groping in the dark. We can't even be certain the two disappearances are connected. Tell you what, tomorrow I'm going to go over to Aldrin's with Tilley and look around. I'll come up with a good reason for a visit."

Thomas added, "I'll go with you."

131

"No. Let's not spook the Aldrin family unnecessarily. If I find anything amiss or get a bad vibe, we'll identify a cause to bring in Mr. Aldrin for further questioning. It is only a dog right now."

"Only a dog, huh? She is more than a dog to me, Chrystel. Best you not forget that." Geronimo was glaring at his niece.

"Got it, Geronimo. I know what she means to you. What I meant was a missing dog is not legal grounds to pull someone in for questioning. And, Thomas, Tilley is supposed to be a protector. I'll give her a chance to earn her keep by taking her with me when I visit Aldrin."

Tilley had been sitting in a corner listening to the conversation. At Chrystel's mention of allowing her to prove her worth, she jumped up on all four strange paws, head erect, and waved her pink tail until it knocked over a lamp. Tilley's teeth were fully displayed. Chrystel shook her head and rubbed her eyes.

"You'd better get back outside with the forces, Thomas. There's sure to be at least one drunk causing trouble."

"Roger that, Chrystel. Hey, before I go, did you give Brodie an answer about dropping his mayoral run?"

"Not yet. He's going to stop by the house tonight, so I can talk with him."

"Good enough. Let's all rally again tomorrow at the same time so we discuss where to go next. Call your Uncle Tom if you need anything, Chrystel. I mean it." Thomas gave Chrystel his most menacing look.

"Yeah, yeah, yeah. Get going, Thomas."

## 13. Keeping Secrets

*Should she put on some lipstick?* Chrystel was bent over the sink studying her face. She wasn't the type to spend time staring in a mirror attending to her appearance. If she was clean, her hair brushed and pulled back, and her clothes mostly matched, that was good enough. She had tried to stay casual for Brodie's visit. After all, this was a business meeting and nothing more. Still, she had carefully brushed her hair and left it down, waves cascading around her face. And now she was giving some thought to covering her always pink-hued lips with lipstick. Chrystel grabbed the sides of her head, made a face, and yelled at her reflection, "What the hell is wrong with me!"

Tilley, unbidden, was sitting between the toilet and bathtub watching her charge. At Chrystel's outburst, she stood up and made herself ready to protect this strange but adorable human from any threat. Chrystel turned to the henka and asked while pointing to her hair, "Up or down?" Tilley's response was to lower her inordinately massive head to the floor. Chrystel muttered, "Somehow, I knew you would say that."

Both heads swiveled at the sound of the doorbell. Tilley charged out after gaining traction on the tile floor and scrambled down the hall to be the first to guard the entrance. Chrystel admonished from Tilley's backside, "Don't you dare open that door before I get there."

Brodie, at her doorstep, gave Chrystel a heart stopping smile. He continued to look at her as he said, "I know, you shouldn't do that."

"Do what? What are you talking about?"

"Tilley just said she wasn't supposed to open the door anymore, even if it wasn't a stranger."

"Oh, well yes. We, Tilley and I, have been working on some ground rules for living together. When the Ardinians explained all the features of a henka, they never once mentioned obedience. Come on in and sit."

Brodie looked nervous as he got comfortable on Chrystel's sofa. "I hope you have good news for me."

Without asking, she handed him a beer and sat in the very old, but modern for its time, chair facing Brodie. The leather was worn to a crinkled softness. "The answer is of course, yes. It would be foolhardy to turn you down."

"True and excellent!" Brodie reached his beer across to Chrystel, and they clinked bottles. "Now, that we've toasted, I'll announce my withdrawal from the race tomorrow at my allowed political announcement time."

"Are you going to mention that you support me?"

"Thought about that. I think I should be subtler in my approach. I'll tell everyone I believe I can make more of a difference filling Letitia's vacancy. That she was my friend and that I know what she wanted. Over the next few weeks, we can demonstrate how well we work together and use that as a reason to vote our direction. If I announce a capitulation to you, it could backfire. There's enough talk about how the enclave's royal family runs everything. With Karen leading the team to go with the Ardinians, those whispers are in high gear.

We have to make your withdrawal from the race about the stability and continuity of the enclave."

"That word again, royalty. Geronimo mentioned just that terminology recently. I may have become *out of touch,* over the last couple of years. I knew there were concerns about nepotism but didn't realize the extent. Your approach sounds exactly right to me. I was considering the same thing. Brodie, I need you to help keep me grounded--in touch with what the people are actually thinking and feeling."

He smiled and nodded while looking directly into her large, green eyes. "I can do that, Chrystel."

Chrystel was absently rubbing Tilley's mane. The henka, sitting next to Chrystel's chair, closed her eyes in an expression of utter ecstasy, her donkey ears rolled to half-mast. Chrystel glanced away from Brodie to the henka. She paused before asking her next question. "The other night you mentioned your concerns with Carlton and what some of his friends might be planning, but you wouldn't say what or who. Spill the beans, Brodie. Geronimo's dog Candy has also gone missing."

Brodie's winced. "What does Candy have to do with anything?"

"Geronimo sent her out to ask other dogs about treacherous dealings and she vanished."

"Hmmpf. Maybe she stuck her snout into some bad business." Brodie tightened his lips. "First, I can't substantiate anything I tell you. My sources say there are walk-ons being infiltrated into the enclave. These folks are being hidden by Carlton supporters."

"How do you know there are outsiders being hidden, and who gave you the information?"

"Do you know old Trent Williams? Guess he really isn't old, but he looks that way. He walked on a while ago. He isn't very social. Almost a recluse. He set up a homestead outside of the protected area and lives off the grid, but he still trades with some people I know. Trent has seen trappings of campsites at the far edges of the enclave. It concerned him. First, he doesn't want anyone encroaching on what he considers his hunting land, and secondly, he was suspicious when discovering multiple signs of walk-ons and warned my friends.

"That is strange. But how did you connect these walk-ons to Carlton?"

"Trent trades with the Aldrin family, meat for cheese. He said there've been more people coming and going around the dairy than normal. The activity wouldn't have necessarily concerned him except that the last time he went, there was a group of five younger men hanging around outside the barn, and they didn't look happy to see him. Normally, other than a couple of distributors, it's women and children visiting the dairy. He didn't hang around. When Trent was walking out, parallel to the road, he saw Carlton drive up to the dairy in his ATV."

"How would this Trent even be able to identify Carlton if he lives like a recluse?"

"There were two *Carlton for Mayor* placards adhered to both the front and the back of the ATV. Also, Trent gave a detailed physical description to my friends. It sure sounds like Carlton."

"I've seen that ATV, and it does have signs at both ends." Chrystel's mind was spinning while Brodie stared at her. This situation was sounding more serious than she'd hoped. "Did Trent give a description of the young men? Could they be from the enclave rather than from somewhere else?"

"I guess they could be from the enclave. The description he gave of the men was more generic than his recollection of Carlton. My friends couldn't connect the group to anyone they knew. Trent said the men had packs near in a pile and were carrying weapons. Also, they had the look of travelers— dusty boots, worn clothes, hard faces. None of them had dogs. You won't find five people from our enclave in a group without at least one dog."

Fear was snaking up Chrystel's spine. "Another enclave. Maybe Carlton is getting help from another enclave. Could Carlton be a plant?"

Brodie shook his head and scratched his neck. "I've been afraid of this for a long time. It's why I wanted to limit walk-ons."

"Let's assume for a minute that Carlton is bringing people into the enclave and hiding them. Where would he hide them?"

Brodie returned a look of surprise. "There are vacant and crumbling buildings everywhere. They could be hiding in any of a thousand places."

"I suppose you're right." Chrystel thought about mentioning the connection between the dairy and Candy and then stopped herself. Better to take this professional relationship with Brodie slowly. Very slowly. She blew air out of her mouth to remove the wispy hair from her forehead. "I have to think about all you've told me. Would this Trent speak with me?"

"If you could find him, maybe. But you won't find him unless he wants to be found."

"I could send my grandfather, Mike. He loves to hunt. He knows those woods as well as anyone. He might have come across Trent before."

"Good idea. I'll mention to my friends that Mike will be looking for Trent."

"Who are these friends you keep speaking about, Brodie?"

"I would like to say, but they've asked me to keep their confidence. They don't want to get caught in any civil wars in the enclave. What we need to do now is everything in our power to determine what's happening and make sure we stop any illegal takeover attempts."

"I'm not convinced what we have is a takeover attempt, but if it is, there may come a time when your friends have no choice but to choose sides," Chrystel retorted. Brodie tilted his head in a maybe-or-maybe-not gesture while continuing to stare at her. Chrystel blurted out her next question without giving it enough thought. "Why do you look at me that way, Brodie? It's disconcerting."

"You honestly don't know why? Have you looked in a mirror recently? Are you that clueless about men and how they love to look at beautiful women?"

*Dammit, Chrystel thought, I'm sure I'm blushing. Pull yourself together. Heat was rushing to her face, and her heart started that annoying pounding, again.* "Actually, I looked in a mirror just today before you arrived. I'm not sure I see it.

Nevertheless, we need to get something straight. I don't abide engaged men ogling me. I'm glad you find me attractive, but I have no interest in the drama associated with an already committed man."

Brodie's head reeled back, and he released a laugh that started from his belly and poured out of his mouth. "You find it, funny?" Chrystel asked.

"No, no, it's not that," he chuckled. "I'm not really engaged. And, there is something so honest, so straight forward about you, it just makes me want to laugh…in a good way."

Chrystel wasn't smiling. She was too confused to smile. "Your fiancé, Sherry, certainly thinks you're engaged. She has flashed that bling ring at everyone, including me. How can you not be engaged, *really*?"

"Pure theater and zircon. I found that ring in the old dump. Look, Sherry is like a sister to me. Her parents let me live with them when I first came to New Washington. They are in that new religious sect called the Apocolites. They believe you must marry and have kids as soon as possible and endlessly nagged Sherry to find a man. She begged me to help her out. She thought they would get off her back if she was engaged, at least long enough for her to find someone she wanted to marry. I didn't have anything going, so I agreed. At the time, I had no idea how long this pretend engagement was going to take. It's been almost a year and a half, and Sherry still hasn't identified a likely prospect."

Chrystel's chest felt like it was going to explode. All this time, she had thought Brodie was a player.

"Besides, she isn't my type. She's a very sweet woman, but she's more like a sister."

*What did he mean by that? Oh shit, why I am I such a washout at this sort of thing? I'm a smart woman. I should be able to navigate these waters. What's wrong with me?*

Brodie was studying Chrystel again. "I see complete confusion on your face, and you're a pulsating shade of red right now. Don't ever play poker. I was actually hoping we could get to know each other better."

"I'm sure we will. If the elections work out the way we hope, we'll be working together almost daily."

Chagrined, Brodie replied, "That's not what I meant."

"Oh, oh, you mean as in more than professional colleagues."

"Look, what you do with that information is up to you—I'm not going anywhere. I also want our enclave to succeed. Too many folks are depending on us to make good decisions. Let's leave any mutual attraction alone for right now. Just think about it while we focus on doing our jobs. Besides, I still have to find a man for Sherry."

"Who says there's a mutual attraction?" Chrystel nearly shouted.

Brodie sighed. "Not only do I have great hearing, I'm a sensor, and I talk with dogs. I can feel your heartbeat from my chair, and Tilley may have mentioned it."

"That's not fair, Brodie!" Chrystel had recovered enough to giggle while glaring at Tilley. "I have a lot to consider. I think you need to leave now."

Brodie lingered for a minute on Chrystel's doorstep after being hustled out of her home. He could hear Chrystel through the door, stridently talking to Tilley about keeping some things to herself. Dogs and the henka shared at least one thing in common--they couldn't keep secrets. He laughed again, turned, and was on his way home.

## 14. Deer Hunt

The sun was just below the horizon casting early morning pink and peach light across the eastern sky. Mike and Thomas huddled in a small shed assembling hunting gear. The only light in the rustic building was a single bulb hanging on a cord from the ceiling. Pre-dawn dampness clung to every surface. Chrystel had briefed Mike the previous evening about finding and questioning the elusive Trent. Mike enlisted his closest friend, Thomas, to go with him. They wanted to get an early start.

The men had been friends for so long they didn't need to talk. Since their first meeting soon after the change, their membership in an old-world club, called the U.S. Army, had laid the foundation for an enduring friendship. The fact that they had shared many missions and relied on each other for over a century only strengthened that bond. The two men were opposites in any number of ways, but those differences were secondary to complete trust.

Thomas's dog, Ghost, was excited and roamed the corners of the shed for odd smells. Alert and still, Bruno, a German shepherd and Mike's favorite hunter, lay next to the growing pile of necessary items. Mike heard Ghost ask repeatedly, "Ready?"

Thomas asked, "You have all the ammunition you think we'll need?"

"I'm hoping we don't need any, but yeah, I've packed plenty. You never know, a deer might grace our wanderings."

Thomas displayed his pearly whites. "We may not find Trent, but fresh deer meat is sure to make this boondoggle worthwhile." Mike returned a grunt.

Mike and Thomas loaded what they needed, including the dogs, into an ATV and headed for the far eastern edge of the enclave. "What's the plan?" Thomas asked. "Wander around in the forest until we run into someone?"

Mike chuckled. "Naw, even better. I know where a couple of deer stands are located. I say we stake them out, hoping Trent happens along. If not Trent, maybe a nice buck."

"You ever run into Trent out there? I haven't."

"Once. He was a crazy looking fellow. Maybe crazy like a fox. It was obvious he didn't want me out there hunting in what he thought was his turf. He yelled at me to leave. Arguing with him wasn't worth the hassle, so I moved north."

They pulled the ATV under the cover of some short hardwoods. Hiding vehicles under cover wasn't necessary anymore because there weren't any planes or helicopters flying around, and the danger of being spotted from the air was almost nil. It was a habit learned from their days in the Army, and those habits, no matter how outdated, were hard to break. Daylight was filtering through the dense fir canopy towering overhead as they set off on a quarter mile path through the forest to the deer stand.

A shot whizzed by Thomas' ear as they were nearly there. In an instant, both men and dogs dropped to the ground. They crawled on their bellies through the ferns and ground cover away from the shooting to the most massive fir trunk available. A couple more shots peppered their movement, but whoever was shooting didn't have an elevated vantage point, and no one was hit.

Mike breathing hard, sat with his back against the tree, his shotgun held against his chest. "How many you think, Thomas?"

"Not sure. At least two," Thomas said. "Guess that probably means it isn't Trent since he'd be alone. Just like the good old days, huh, Mike?"

"You have a very strange idea of good, Thomas."

Squatting next to Mike, Thomas picked up a fist-sized boulder and threw the granite like a rocket against another tree twenty feet away. Shots pelted the innocent fir Thomas had just assaulted with a rock. Before he ducked back behind protection, Thomas noted a flash from one direction and sound from a second shooter. A barrage of gunfire followed Thomas' movement too late to catch him.

"Well, they know where we are now. And, if they aren't complete idiots, they'll try to flank us. I'm going to get the jump on that. Cover me. Ghost and I will pull back and go around. From the front of our tree, one is at 10 o'clock and another is just to the right of the deer stand at 2. Keep 10 o'clock busy. And whatever you do, don't let Mr. 2'oclock climb up into that stand. On my count," Thomas put up three fingers, then two, and then one.

He signaled to Ghost and ran as Mike started firing. Keeping low, Thomas and Ghost moved quickly, zigzagging through the forest. When he sensed there were enough trees between himself and his attackers to protect his silhouette from becoming a line of sight bullseye, he slowed and studied the landscape. There wasn't anywhere to hide. The surrounding vegetation consisted of Douglas firs, interspersed with ferns and low growth bushes, over rolling terrain. If one of their assailants was doing the same thing, trying to flank Mike's position, he or she would see Thomas. Of course, Thomas would see them too. He would just make damn sure he saw them first.

Thomas signaled to Ghost to scout ahead of him. Her sense of smell, incredible hearing, and diminutive profile would protect her from any humans traipsing through the forest. She would also know to warn him if someone was near. Thomas had spent many hours training this Ghost. Even though he was never able to hear dogs like Mike, if anyone spent enough time with them, it didn't matter. A look or a signal was all they needed. Thomas marveled, not for the first time, how a symbiotic relationship between man and dog, two completely different species, could be so perfectly complimentary. He still missed his first Ghost, the dog that was with him when everything changed. He doubted he would ever have another friend like that again. When she'd died at the ripe old age of seventeen, he'd cried for a week every time he was alone.

Thomas could barely hear the reverberating bangs of rifle and shotgun fire. *Time to turn and move in the assholes' direction*, he thought to himself, *and I'd better hurry*. Mike was an outstanding marksman, and Thomas had confidence in Mike's ability to hold them off. Still, without communication he knew Mike would be starting to sweat. *I wish we'd brought some hand-*

*held radios, so I knew what was going on. We're*
*out of practice with this shit.*

Mike was indeed sweating. He had kept the two bushwhackers pinned down, but so was he. He whispered to Bruno, lying very flat right behind him, "Why didn't we think to bring communication? We need to get serious in a real hurry. Complacency is deadly. Something's afoot." Bruno didn't reply other than to release another throaty growl not meant for Mike.

The guy by the deer stand was making another try to climb the back side of the wood platform affixed to a tree. Mike inhaled slowly and held his breath. He calmed himself, made sure his position was stable, and fired when the man was halfway up the ladder. The climbing man jerked, grunted loudly enough for Mike to hear him, and dropped back to the ground. The other shooter, obviously unhappy about his colleague's untimely demise, was unappreciative of Mike's marksmanship. He or she responded with a volley of rifle fire that came way to close to Mike. Breathing hard, Mike scrambled to cover. "That, was not on my list of enjoyable morning activities, Bruno," he exhaled to his trusty sidekick, still waiting for a command from Mike. The shooting stopped, and the surrounding woods went quiet. *Wonder what that means?* Mike thought. He waited until he caught his breath, rolled to the opposite side of the tree, and peered out, ready to try again to set up a line of sight to keep his adversary pinned down.

Mike gasped. Thomas, his hands up, was being pushed along by guns at his back. A man and a woman were prodding Thomas forward.

Ghost was nowhere in sight. There must have been four of them, two lying in wait.

The woman yelled. "Throw your weapon down and come out with your hands above your head or your friend is dead."

Mike whispered to Bruno. "Hide and stay."

Bruno moaned. "*No, Bruno help.*"

"Obey me!" Mike whispered harshly.

Mike came out slowly to give Bruno a chance to crawl away. Two of the men came over to Mike. As one pointed his weapon at Mike's head, the other patted him down. "Anyone else here with you? A dog maybe?"

"Nope. Just me and the Calvary on their way here now."

"Nice try asshole. Isn't nobody coming to save you," A burly blonde man, with a neck almost as wide as Thomas' thighs, said, "Check the tree, Ted."

"Nothing here," Ted replied. Mike breathed a sigh of relief that Bruno had obeyed his command.

They nudged Mike over to Thomas with a weapon pointed at his head, and the blonde directed them to get on their knees with their hands clasped behind their heads. The blonde was obviously the leader. He was doing all the talking. "How's Joel, Marsha?"

Marsha, a six-foot-two monster of woman with jet black hair and a menacing stare, spit an answer. "He's dead. Must have hit the carotid artery in his neck. He bled out before I could do anything."

Turning to Mike and Thomas, the blonde scolded, "Not very nice. My name is Pete by the way. Feel free to call me Mr. Pete. My preference would be to shoot you both right now, right here in this spot for what you did to our friend Joel, but the bosses wouldn't like it. Pete pulled a walkie-talkie out of his pocket. He waited and smiled at Mike with the phone to his ear.

"Hey, it's Pete. We have two men." He paused. "Let's see, one is about 6'6", maybe 275 to 300, with a black billiard ball head. The other is fit, but not as bulky, a white guy with dark brown hair. Both look old enough to be founders." As he listened to the phone, the blonde man shook his head and uttered, "Uh huh, uh, huh."

Pete looked at Thomas with a smile. "My man says you're probably Thomas, the Chief of the Defense Force. And your buddy here is probably Mike McCullough, the mayor's granddad. That, about right?"

Thomas and Mike glared at Pete. "Well, methinks that's a yes." He spoke again into the walkie-talkie. "Roger that. We'll bring them to you." He latched the radio to his belt and spit tobacco on the ground.

"Lucky for you fine folks that you can help us with our plan. I won't kill you where you kneel. Wouldn't bet on your chances for a long life, but hey, be grateful for the now. Get ___.

Pete's speech was cut short by a bullet that sailed from the back of his head through the front eye socket, splattering blood and brain matter onto his female partner. She was raising her weapon and beginning to turn when another projectile took her down in much the same manner from the side of her face.

Thomas blasted from his position, off the ground at the remaining bad guy. He tackled him before the man could get his rifle up to shoot. Thomas wrenched the weapon out of his hands and pounded the stock of the gun at the man's head while straddling him. The man went still, his head lolling to one side. Thomas pressed his fingers to the man's neck to check for a pulse. The man was out cold, but not dead yet. "Damn, we need to be able to question him later. I hope he doesn't die on us," Thomas whispered.

Not wasting time, Thomas stood quickly to join Mike scanning the trees with his weapon ready, watching for their next nemesis. "I'm over here," a voice called out from behind a nearby tree, the same tree Mike had recently utilized to keep his fanny from being filled with lead. Thomas wondered how anyone had crept up that close. He hadn't heard a thing. *I'm so out of practice, a junior boy scout would get the jump on me.*

"The name is Trent. Put your weapons down on the ground, and I'll come out so we can talk. Your dogs are with me and safe."

Thomas and Mike gave each other incredulous looks, shrugged, and did as Trent suggested. Thomas whispered to Mike, "Seek and ye shall find."

"How the heck did they flank you, Thomas? I thought you were the one doing the flanking."

"Aww man, I've gotten soft or old or both. It truly pisses me off, and I don't want to talk about it. If you supply the beers, maybe later, after I stop blushing in my humiliation, I'll tell you the whole sad story."

A bearded man stepped from behind the tree. Bruno and Ghost ran to their masters, jumping and yipping a greeting as if the whole ordeal had been a fun game. Trent was hidden in a camouflaged outfit made up of fir boughs and organic, native materials. He was tall and lean and powerful looking, even hidden behind the vegetation. As he stepped closer, he shed his head gear and jacket making him now look more human than bush. Dark, intelligent eyes looked out from a bearded face and a shock of wild untamed hair. Trent did not reach out to shake their hands.

The men eyed each other. Mike said, "We were looking for you, Trent. Lucky that you found us at exactly the right time. I'm Mike, and this is Thomas."

"Yep. Some neighbors said you might be searching for me. I've seen you around, Mike. That one day you took my advice and moved on. Says you're no fool. What did you want to talk to me about?"

Thomas answered his question by pointing at the at dead bodies on the ground. "Uh, this."

Trent gave a head nod and an almost imperceptible smile. "Right. I'll tell you what I know. Your dog Ghost found me. I can hear them, the dogs. Smart girl you got. She told me you were in danger. Had to put mine down just recently. Wouldn't mind terribly if you could find me another dog like her."

Thomas gave his best winning grin and deep baritone, ear-pounding laugh. "I think we could manage that, my man. I like the way you handle yourself. But first, I'm all of a sudden worried about a little red-headed mayor that's headed to Aldrin's Dairy. These fuck-nuts mean business, and I don't want her hurt. Just wish I knew exactly what their business was. I say we truss up that sole survivor over there and head to the land of milk without honey, lickety-split. Care to join us?"

Trent stared at Thomas and then Mike. This time, a real smile appeared on his face. "Sure, I can do that. I heard from another neighbor boy she's a very special lady."

Mike checked on the man he shot trying to climb into the dear stand. "Yep, he's gone. We can come back and pick up the dead later. Get the unconscious one loaded and let's go."

## 15. Tilley Speaks

Tilley was perched on the front seat next to Chrystel. The henka was so tall when seated, her head almost reached the plastic roof of the ATV. Tilley thought that today was the best earth day so far. Finally, the woman with the fire hair seemed to be enjoying her company. Of the many henka duties, companionship was the most important. Henkas existed to serve and protect. Her creators thought the best way to ensure a henka could fulfil their responsibilities was to emotionally bond the protected to the protector. Human dogs were the perfect model for her creation.

It was just too bad Chrystel couldn't hear her. Maybe in time—Tilley had so much to say. As it was, Chrystel was yakking on about signals they could use in lieu of thought transfer. Tilley listened and tried to remember Chrystel's invented signals. For all her advantages, Tilley still couldn't remember as well as her two-legged friends.

"OK, again, Tilley. Show me the nod for there is someone near," Chrystel demanded. Tilley shook her head back and forth. "Oh, good lord, no, that's the signal for everything is safe. Shimmy and shake your head like this." Chrystel shook her head like she had just bitten down on something truly nasty. Tilley smiled until her two-inch canines were fully exposed. *This human Chrystel was so funny sometimes.* Tilley tried her best imitation of the head shimmy, and Chrystal laughed as she glanced at Tilley. "Well, we'll just keep working on it. We're almost there. Hang close to me and try to look intimidating. You do have an intimidating side, right?" Tilley continued her predatory smile.

The smell of a bovine presence greeted Chrystel when she pulled in the parking lot. The dairy was a hodge-podge of buildings that was once a vocational college. A converted mechanical shop, a hundred yards to the rear of the facility, housed the dairy cows. Between the cow barn and the sales office fronting the parking lot, at least ten classroom-sized structures allowed the Aldrin family to make cheese and butter and store milk. Chrystel realized as she parked between two other ATV's, there were any number of places to hide walk-ons at the dairy.

To make matters more difficult, at the time of the change, the vocational college was in the middle of a suburban area. The refashioned college, now Aldrin Dairy, resided on the outer fringe of the enclave. The land beyond was new growth forest interspersed with decaying or crumbling homes never reclaimed by clavers. More places to hide.

Before she exited the ATV, Chrystel commented to Tilley, "After we talk with Mr. Aldrin, we may have to leave and sneak around to the back of the property to see what's what. Hang loose, Tilley." Tilley had no idea what "hang loose meant," but returned an affirmative headshake.

Chrystel opened the door to the office and an automated buzz announced their arrival. No one was in the small office or behind the counter. After waiting for a couple of minutes for the buzz to bring someone, Chrystel used the time alone as an excuse to step behind the counter and through an

153

open door to another smaller office behind the counter.

The walls of the office were adorned with white boards--inventories and schedules handwritten across their surfaces. She moved to a cluttered desk in the far corner. Underneath stacks of receipts and invoices, she saw portions of a topographic map. She pushed aside a stack of papers and studied the curving lines. Red X's and circles were drawn across what appeared to be the terrain near where she was now standing. Chrystel wasn't sure what the map displayed, but a tinkle of suspicion crept up her spine. *Could this be a location map for walk-on hiding spots?* She could feel her heart starting to beat faster.

Tilley was standing directly behind Chrystel. "Tilley, quickly, go guard the door. Get in their way if anyone tries to come in. Now!" Tilley moved with an alacrity that was surprising for her size.

Chrystel had never possessed any special gifts like most of the rest of her family. She had excellent hearing, eyesight, and smell, but nothing beyond the normal range of human experience. She couldn't see visions, sense people from far away, or talk to dogs. Her talent was a skill that happened from time to time and was not the result of the change. Chrystel possessed an exceptional visual memory. She needed to take a picture of this map in her mind. Trying not to spill paper on the floor, Chrystel slid the folder stacks to the edges of the desk. Concentrating, she visualized the map and its markings, seeing the contour lines as ridges and hills, and then connected the map features to what she knew. After clarifying the map context, she photographed the markings in her mind.

A thump and the door buzz jolted Chrystel out of her intense focus. She rapidly slid the papers back into position, spreading the stacks as close as possible to their original location. "What the hell is that? Get out of my way!" a frightened Mr. Aldrin bellowed from the other room.

Chrystel slid out of the back office and rushed around the counter. Positioned in front of Mr. Aldrin, Tilley was smiling except, there was something very different about this smile. Her pink tail and donkey ears were standing straight up and not moving. Even more incredibly, the way she was standing appeared to increase her already abundant mass.

"Hello, Mr. Aldrin. No one was around so I checked the office in back in case you were there. I'm sorry if Tilley frightened you."

"I've never seen a beast like that. Animals aren't allowed in the sales area, Mayor. Please remove this creature immediately!" Mr. Aldrin warily studied Tilley as if she was a coiled viper. "And I don't appreciate you sniffing around in my personal area. What are you doing here, anyway?"

Chrystel's pulse was rising in reaction to Mr. Aldrin's menacing posture. *Calm down Chrystel, talk your way out of this.* "Technically, Tilley isn't an animal. She's an ambassador from the planet of Ardinia. Tilley, please come stand next to me." Tilley obeyed as directed but continued to eye Mr. Aldrin as she backed up to flank Chrystel.

"As to why I'm here, as I'm sure you know, I'm running for a second term as mayor. In the next two months, I'll be visiting all the enclave's local businesses to see for myself how things are going. I was hoping to speak with local business leaders personally and ask how we can make the enclave a better place, for you and your business. I know people are curious about the aliens and thought many would enjoy an introduction to one of them." Chrystel gave Aldrin her most sincere "I'm here to help" look.

His narrowed eyes strongly hinted he wasn't buying Chrystel's pitch. "You didn't answer my question about why you were in my personal office."

"Mr. Aldrin, when we came in, no one was here. I thought perhaps you were hard at work in that office. That's all. I apologize for my error in judgement."

"I've got nothing to say to you, Mayor. Your family has never done shit for me. We work our fingers to the bone out here and can barely make a living. Far as I know, this is the first time you've been here since you was a kid. Too little, too late."

Chrystel surprised Mr. Aldrin with her answer. "You're right. I should have spent more time with our people. I've just recently been made aware of my failures in that regard. I believe I got stuck in a bubble where I thought I knew what people were thinking, and I was wrong. But I do care, and I want to know. Win or lose the election for mayor, every person's welfare is important to me. If you would give me just a minute of your time, I would love to hear your ideas on how to improve the enclave."

Mr. Aldrin grunted, and his face softened only a little. "We have problems with sewage. We're too far away from an accessible river to dump the shit. I have four septic systems that can barely handle the volume. I asked for some help, but no one did a damn thing. The enclave population is still growing, and I can't keep increasing my herd without some assistance. As I said, you are too late, Mayor. Maybe if you had done stopped by earlier, things would be different."

"I don't think it's too late, Mr. Aldrin. What do you mean by things would be different?"

Mr. Aldrin's eyes darted back and forth, as if he had been caught in a trap. He scowled at Chrystel, shifting on his feet and trying to formulate an answer. "Young lady, I thought it would be obvious. We don't support you as mayor out here. Carlton is a much better choice. He's going to make sure the little guys like me get a fair break."

"I see. I appreciate your feedback, and I'll consider what we might do to help. Your dairy and the Aldrin family are very important to this community. I'm hopeful that my future actions will convince you that I do care about the little guy. I won't take up any more of your time. If you think of anything else, I'm ready to listen. Have a good day, Mr. Aldrin. Tilley, please, let's go." Mr. Aldrin's eyes followed Chrystel and Tilley out the door.

Chrystel breathed a sigh of relief. "That was unpleasant. Change of plan, Tilley. We need to hightail it back to the courthouse, so I can get that map stored in my mind for Thomas. I have a feeling those annotations on the map are locations for hiding walk-ons." As she was raising her foot to get in the ATV, a man sprung from his hiding place behind another ATV parked next to Chrystel's own. He grabbed her from behind.

Thrusting her hands up under his arms, Chrystel twisted while using the heel of her boot to pound his instep. The man grunted and momentarily loosened his hold. She was already moving with a folded finger punch to the bridge of the man's nose, smacking him with a hard, fast blow in just the right place. He went down like a sack of potatoes.

As he was falling to the ground, another man hiding behind the same ATV, moved to take his place. Chrystel had been trained by Thomas to see everything at once in a fight—the immediate threat and any others on the near horizon. A third person, this one a woman, sprang from another hiding spot across the parking lot and was running in the direction of Tilley's side of Chrystel's vehicle, holding a pistol to her front.

Chrystel screamed, "Get down, Tilley!" She was already stepping over the man on the ground as she yelled, attacking the next assailant rather than retreating. She reached for the approaching man's arm as he was almost to her and yanked him over the unconscious obstacle. As he lost his balance and fell forward, Chrystel thrust her knee at his face. Two blap blaps, rang out. Chrystel's heart sank.

An unearthly, eardrum-quaking sound, poured from Tilley's jaws. It was at a pitch that would be impossible for a human to describe. There was simply no frame of reference. Holding her ears, Chrystel folded to the gravel. The man she had just kneed in the face was likewise grimacing with his hands over his ears. Chrystel did not hear another shot. In fact, she couldn't hear anything as she lay there immobilized, trying to force her legs to move.

Two or three minutes passed until Chrystel felt her left foot respond. She bent her knee. Looking up, a rifle was pointed at her face. Mr. Aldrin was at the other end of the weapon. "Get up," he directed.

Chrystel stood slowly. "Tilley, the alien, is she OK?" she asked Aldrin.

"She was shot, but I think she's alive. If you'll move over here," he pointed his weapon in the direction he wanted Chrystel to head, "once you're tied up, we'll check on her. Don't try nothing." Mr. Aldrin motioned to the man on the ground. "Get up and put some zip ties on the mayor's hands and feet."

The man was wearing a scrambled expression and blood poured from his battered nose. He climbed from his knees to a standing position and dug zip ties out of his pocket. "What in holy hell was that?!"

Mr. Aldrin answered. "Never heard or saw anything like it. If I hadn't been in the office, I would have been on the ground with you. The building must have given my ears some protection. Now, you need to take care of this mess. We made a deal. No one was supposed to get hurt." He shouted to the woman appearing dazed, but now standing. "Check on the purple alien."

The woman cautiously stepped to the gigantic animal between the two ATVs. She squatted and put her hand on Tilley's neck. "She's alive but she doesn't look good. Her blood is purple too."

"Damn it, I told you to get them without shooting. I agreed to help, but not if anyone was gonna get shot!"

Red-faced, the woman yelled back. "What was I supposed to do? That monster was going to get me if I didn't take it down. Did you see the size of its teeth? Shit."

Mr. Aldrin shook his head. "The last thing we need is pissed off aliens. Take them and get to the facility quickly. Do what's needed to stem the flow of blood from the creature, load up, and be gone. I'll call ahead to have the doc ready."

Glaring daggers at Aldrin, Chrystel stood ramrod straight. "Mr. Aldrin, you are going to be very, very sorry for this. If Tilley dies, it will be on your head."

## 16. Back to School

A rumbling, roaring noise from a boxy vehicle drew Chrystel's attention. The unusual conveyance drove from behind a storage building and turned in front of Chrystel and her captors, a mist plume trailing its journey. Chrystel turned to the woman who had shot Tilley and asked, "Is that a gas-powered vehicle? I've never seen one under its own power. Where on earth did you find usable gas?"

A dirty faced woman with limp brown hair scornfully glanced at Chrystel. "Some of us have had to make do with old technology. You can make gas and a lot of other stuff if survival warrants the need. You wouldn't know much about that though, I guess."

Chrystel was roughly herded into the back of what the woman had called a van. Mr. Aldrin and two other men argued about how to lift Tilley and grunted in unison as they executed their agreed upon plan. "Don't hurt her!" Chrystel nervously yelled out. The van shifted from the henka's weight as they set Tilley inside next to Chrystel.

The woman jumped in last and settled next to Tilley. She pulled a feed bag from a pocket and placed the scratchy cloth over Chrystel's head. "I'll keep pressure on the animal's wound, but most of the bleeding has stopped. She's still breathing, and that's a good sign."

Chrystel didn't respond to the woman. Instead, she talked to Tilley trying to comfort her. "I'm here with you, and we're going to OK," Chrystel cooed. "Just hang in there, my friend. We'll be OK."

The sound of the vehicle increased by untold decibels as it sped out of the gravel lot. A van was never intended to travel the terrain they covered over the next half hour. Rutted stretches sent Chrystel sliding across the floor. More than once her teeth clacked together from a particularly large hole or as they plowed over a rock. She winced each time the van lurched, thinking about Tilley and worrying over her injuries. She tried to pay attention to turns and where they might be headed, but it was impossible with her eyes covered. Chrystel only knew they were somewhere outside of the enclave, travelling over roads that hadn't seen any repair since the change.

The woman caged with her in the back of the van didn't speak. Chrystel asked questions about Tilley's welfare and where they were headed, but the only response was, "Just be quiet." The fourth time Chrystel asked, the woman poked a rifle barrel at her head and spat, "Shut the fuck up!"

No longer indignant about her capture, instead Chrystel was eerily calm. Her pulse slowed as she focused on escape and then retribution. She'd trained with the force her whole life. She was an expert in one on one combat, all manner of weapons, tactics, and what Thomas called SEER, or survival, evasion, escape, and resistance. At the time, when Thomas explained why SEER training was important, Chrystel couldn't imagine a scenario when she might need those skills. It was interesting training though, and she enjoyed their survival training in the woods. Right now, she was thanking Uncle Tom for his prescient wisdom.

The van jerked to a stop, and Chrystel heard the driver step out and yell to someone else. Fresh air blew in as the back doors finally opened. The metallic smell of Tilley's blood and being blind as the van pitched and weaved had begun to sicken Chrystel. She offered no resistance when they yanked her out of the source of considerable misery.

Chrystel could see the ground through the bottom of the hood as her female minder pushed her along with the butt of a rifle. The best time to attempt an escape is during transitions, she reminded herself. Pretending to stumble over the pitted concrete, Chrystel forced herself to trip. Throwing her falling body into the legs of her captor, she rolled and hooked her feet around the woman's ankles and then jerked with all her might. The woman cursed as she fell on top of Chrystel. Chrystel had just shaken her hood free when three men joined the melee and pointed their weapons at Chrystel's face.

"Nice try," one of them laughed.

Chrystel sat up and smiled at the freckled, red-headed man who was still chuckling. "Thank you. I was hoping your security might be a little less robust. You never know. Anyway, this woman shot my friend, Tilley. She deserved it."

The woman stood up, dusted herself off, and glowered at Chrystel. "How's about I take over from here." The large red-head said as he motioned the woman away. "Stand up slowly, Mayor."

Chrystel did as ordered and grimaced as she watched a stretcher being loaded with Tilley's big body. "Come on, she'll get good care. Our doctor will see to her. Now move," the freckled man directed.

Chrystel asked, "What's your name? Aw, come on. We're both red-heads. We've probably got a lot in common. You can tell me your name at least."

The red-headed man smiled as he shoved Chrystel forward. "Just move."

They walked through the doors of a decaying, old school. The floorplan was almost identical to a renovated junior high Chrystel had attended in the enclave. The foyer was small, offices flanked one side, cracked and peeling linoleum covered the floor, and a gymnasium entry was flung open across from the offices. Chrystel was counting the number of men and women she saw, and she made a mental inventory of their faces. "The name's Red, by the way. You're a sneaky one, I can tell." He motioned Chrystel through a door to a gymnasium.

*This is an operations center. No doubt now, whoever they are, they're up to no good.* Radios were set on tables, and two women were listening to something from headphones. Another man was eating his lunch on the same table. Cots lined the wall indicating at least twenty people slept here. The radio operators stopped and stared as Chrystel passed with Red nudging her on. Red gestured to a door in the far corner.

He opened it and forced Chrystel in first, then stepped in behind her, and closed the door. Letitia was sitting in the far corner of a long narrow room. She jumped up when she saw Chrystel. "Oh no," Letitia moaned, "Not you too, Chrystel."

"Hush now, ladies. There'll be plenty of time for reunions. Let me explain the rules. You'll be locked in here for the duration. No one will hurt you unless you attempt to escape or hurt one of the guards that brings food and exchanges your sanitation buckets. Should you decide to try an escape, and this is meant for you Chrystel, there are always armed personnel in the gym. There's no way for you to get from here to the other side of the gym without being shot. We do not wish to hurt you and, in fact, have plans that involve your safe return. Are there any questions?"

"Can you cut off these zip ties? They're cutting into my hands."

Red smirked. "Tell you what, I believe there may be a cooling-off period necessary. If you get with the program and don't give us any cause to be concerned, I'll think about it. Anything else?"

"Could you let me know about the status of Tilley?"

"That I can do. When she recovers, she'll join you in the audio-visual room. How's that?"

Chrystel responded in a sultry voice. She looked up at him from the corner of her eyes, tossing her long pony tail to the side. "I would appreciate it, Red."

He paused and studied her. "Another nice try, Mayor. Very sly. Later, ladies."

He turned and left. Chrystel heard a lock click in place on the other side of the door.

"What an insufferable man," Chrystel huffed.

"He's an arrogant, horse's rear end," Letitia agreed. "Are you okay, Chrystel? How did they get you too?"

165

"I'm fine. It's Tilley, the henka, I'm worried about."

"Who is Tilley, and what in the world is a henka?" Letitia's dark hair was plastered to her head as if it hadn't seen any shampoo for some time. Normally an attractive woman, her beautiful and exotic almond eyes were circled by dark, puffy rings. Carved cheekbones and a high forehead over a wide mouth normally gave Letitia an aura of strength. What Chrystel saw now was a Letitia that looked defeated and tired.

"It's a long story. Tilley is an alien companion. The best description I can give is that she looks like a gigantic purple dog, donkey, and tiger mixture."

"You sure you're all right, Chrystel?" Letitia asked.

"I'm serious. You'll see, I hope. She's really very sweet. Let's sit and I'll tell you everything that's happened since you were taken. Then you can fill me in on what you know. We're going to get out of here, Letitia. Thomas will find us if we don't escape first."

Letitia nodded but didn't seem convinced. She pointed to the mattress pad in the corner, and the two women sat and talked in low murmurs. After sharing everything they knew, Chrystel paced back and forth in the elongated, narrow room. There were no windows. Two heater vents at either side of the space were only large enough to allow rodents entry or exit. On the gym side wall, a long metal table was built into the structure, braces to hold equipment were welded to the table. Chrystel's hands were still behind her back so she pulled with her teeth on objects that might serve as a weapon, but their captors had done a fine job of removing anything useful.

"There isn't anything not bolted or welded down." Letitia commented. "I've already checked."

Frustrated, Chrystel lay on the pad on the floor and immediately fell asleep. Letitia watched her, jealous of Chrystel's ability to sleep on demand. Finally, from boredom, Letitia slept too.

Chrystel's eyes sprung open when she heard voices outside the door. She poked Letitia, napping next to her. "What?" Letitia asked startled.

Red's voice could be heard through the door. "Okay, ladies, please stay to the back of the room." He pushed the door open with a weapon and checked to make sure they had followed his instructions. "Stay where you are."

Chrystel was so relieved she wanted to cry when she saw two beefy men carrying Tilley on a stretcher. They hauled her into the room, set her on the floor gently, then turned, and left. Only Red remained at the threshold of their jail. "We have some animal cages, but none are large enough to hold this one. Doc said he thinks she'll be fine, but he knows next to nothing about alien physiology. He got the bullet out and stitched her up. For now, she'll stay with you. And just in case you get any ideas, Chrystel, she is sedated and will remain sedated for her stay with you. Doc said until we have a cage built, we'll hook to fluids again later to keep her hydrated. Any questions?" Chrystel and Letitia gave Red cold looks. "Well I guess not. Cheer up. It's not long until a tasty dinner."

Chrystel waited until all the noise outside the door subsided. She'd seen a flash while the men delivering Tilley were moving into the cell. It looked like one of Tilley's eyes had opened and closed. Rushing to Tilley's side, Chrystel softly rubbed her head against the great beast's mane and donkey ears. The ears responded, unfurling like spring-loaded flags, and this time, both purple companion's eyes sprung open. "I knew it!" Chrystel whispered in excitement. "You were faking it." She smiled into Tilley's kind face. "I was so frightened for you."

Tilley raised her head and smiled at Letitia, who stopped her forward movement and backed quickly into the corner from which she came. "God lord! Chrystel, that thing is going to crush your skull."

"Naw," Chrystel said, holding back an urge to cry. *I can't even remember the last time I felt like crying. This henka has really gotten under my skin.* "That's just her winning smile. Come closer, Letitia. The only danger is if she tries to lick you with her gross tongue. I wonder if sedatives don't work on her, or maybe they aren't strong enough. I just wish I could hear her. I've never had the ability."

Letitia came forward and stood behind Chrystel, just in case. "I can hear the dogs. Is it the same with the henka?"

"I think so. Ask her a question and see if she answers."

"OK, Tilley, how are you feeling?"

Tilley jumped up and shook from her wide head to her wispy pink tail. Eyebrows raised, Letitia said, "She says she feels great, but it was hard to keep still." Tilley pranced around the room and bumped Letitia with her head, nearly knocking her over. "She is glad I can talk to her. She wants to tell you what she learned."

Tilley's tail was waving madly hitting the wall and metal table, making it shake. "Calm down, Tilley. You're making way too much noise," Chrystel urged. Tilley smiled again, raised on her hind legs and placed her front, many-toed paws on Chrystel's shoulders. Her purple tongue poked out like a lightning strike and swished across Chrystel's cheek and nose. "Yuk, no!" Chrystel gasped. "Get down, Tilley. I missed you too."

"Tilley, can you make that sound again, on purpose? The one that caused us to drop to the ground paralyzed?"

Letitia answered the question. "She said certainly. Would you like her to do it now?"

"No, Tilley. Not until I tell you."

Tilley tilted her head listening. She scrambled to her stretcher and dropped on top of the vinyl covered mat. Realizing she was turned in the wrong direction, Tilley sprang up again and plopped on the stretcher in the opposite direction, closing her eyes and lying still. Chrystel heard someone outside the door saying, "Get back. Dinner time."

Still no sign of my dog Candy, and I just heard through the rumor mill Chrystel is missing. I spent the previous evening fretting and crying about my dog.

At this moment, I am in denial. Bad enough to lose man's best friend, but the possibility my niece is missing as well is too horrible to contemplate. I should get up and start looking for Chrystel or, at minimum, verify the accuracy of the rumor, but I feel too overwhelmed to face the worst truth. I know my father, Mike, and Thomas will release the hounds if she is indeed missing. They will leave no stone unturned in their search, and I would just be in the way. Rather than allow myself a descent into hysteria over Chrystel, I will draft a chapter regarding our culture in the hopes that by the time I finish, my self-reliant niece will have reappeared, and all will be well. If this is an immature reaction to catastrophe, I make no excuses. Writing helps me to keep my head on straight. If I spend some time on my history project, perhaps I will be calm enough to be more useful to others once I am done.

Particularly on culture, it is difficult to provide a completely objective accounting. Most of what I write today will be my own personal observations. I did not experience pre-change culture, but I have devoted lengthy study to the issue. Where possible, I will compare the before and the after, with an emphasis on the more familiar, post-change culture of New Washington.

We live in a small town on a mostly empty earth. Except for trade, our contact with other enclaves is minimal. What happens outside of our cloistered society has little impact on our daily lives. The interconnectedness of the world before the change has gone the way of the prehistoric dinosaur. Even though technological advances may soon make restoration of global communication possible, most people in our enclave shrug their shoulders at the suggestion. They don't see what difference it will make in their day-to-day activities.

Perhaps the aliens will change that. There is nothing quite like an outside global threat, such as the Hunta, to energize initiative to create alliances outside the tribe. Of course, I'm only guessing here. We've never had a global threat like the Hunta before in the new world or the old. I suppose the threat of nuclear weapons or global warming in the pre-change world might be some basis of comparison. If that's the case, we don't have a hope or a prayer of rallying the world's meager masses to march in lockstep to defeat a common enemy like the Hunta.

This physical separateness of New Washington has had a profound impact on our culture. Like small groups of peoples that flourished on water locked islands, ours is a segregated petri dish of what can happen in any given society. Not only is outside communication constrained, but also the internal systems in New Washington are fraught with outages and limitations. We have an Internet in the enclave itself, but it is available only on weekends because the administrator has a job during the week as a teacher. Landlines mostly work but are limited by physical proximity to the telephone device.

Due to the scarcity of connecting technology, people talk to each other more in person. We drive around to our neighbors' homes and knock on their doors for no reason other than to say hello. I know the first names of nearly everyone who lives in our enclave. Our communication is richer, deeper. It includes more than just the words on a page, text type messages, or vocal nuances provided over a phone. Real meaning is expressed as much by facial expressions, gestures, and posture as the words themselves. Even though we are geographically separated from the world, our citizens feel more connected to their community than any normal apartment dweller living in the Twenty-first Century. At least, that's what New Washington founders have said.

We have fewer things than pre-change Americans and value those things that we do have more. We are forced to depend on each other and our families. There is no superstore, no huge hospital system, or online shopping to obtain what we need; self-reliance is an imperative. Our connectedness is local, not global. I often wonder if it wouldn't be a wondrous state to have both— personal and worldwide connection. Is it even possible to hold both, or are those two cultural traits diametrically opposed? I only know I wish we could feel connected to our community and the world at the same time.

For all the human closeness in the New Washington Enclave, we have lost ground in other areas. I believe our people have become close-minded and quite superstitious. Without a multitude of conflicting voices, there is always a tendency toward group think. It's just like my mother recounted in her ruminations about the ranch in Critically Endangered, there is a seductive pull to blend in and be accepted by whatever group you find yourself a member. It's as if people would rather agree to cultural norms they feel are wrong than be shamed and excluded. My study of history suggests that societal conforming has always been a part of the human condition. The problem for us in New Washington is the tenfold magnification of closed minds due to our remoteness to the rest of the planet.

Just last week a friend of mine commented that people outside our enclave have nothing to offer; that they will only try to change what we have built. I was horrified. My friend is smart and has a good heart. How could he see the world this way unless he was simply accepting the conclusion of others? I asked him, "Is change always bad?" to which he stumbled for an answer. My youngest sister believes that the Great Dying was only the first phase of the apocalypse. She and her closest friends think humans will undergo another metamorphosis and become apes again. It makes my head hurt to think about her ideas. The only explanation I have is that in her circles it's cool to believe in another near apocalypse.

Frequent shortages have also impacted our culture; shortages of everything from vegetables to lifesaving health care. Five years ago, an unusually wet summer in the Yakima Valley destroyed most of our crops. We couldn't replace what we lost with trade or individual gardens. Many were the clavers that experienced constipation and bleeding gums that year. Also, if you look around, there are too many like me with missing limbs or stilted gaits that couldn't find a doctor to properly attend to their injuries in time or a doctor who possessed the sophistication to repair complicated injuries. We lose triple the number of children at birth than our pre-change world.

Our culture has become one of hoarders, more selfish about what they share, just in case the worst occurs. Sometimes, they hoard even at the expense of their neighbors, never suspecting that if they hadn't stockpiled, everyone would have had enough. This tendency is also part of the human psyche that has been a part of the world since the beginning of time. The plain fact is the pre-change world was far more abundant than the humans of that time fully appreciated.

The meaning of work is different in our society. Work and the addition of able hands is the only way we survive. Everyone must find a productive contribution. We try to give our population options on choosing their professions, but simply creating art or music is not enough. There must be a realistic expectation that labor will contribute to the feeding, housing, or protection of the population— Maslow's Hierarchy as applied to a post-apocalyptic town. Even Clint Eastwood has a side, scrap metal, salvaging business. My library was viewed as suspect by many until I proved its productive worth to scientific endeavors.

Individuals who do not chose to work are scorned and shamed. Hand-outs are not encouraged unless there is a definitive physical or mental shortfall. Even then, with creativity and caring, those folks are provided a means to feel the dignity of participating in their own success. Grace is also allowed for women or men as caretakers of children that have not reached school age. Alcoholics and drug abusers are not enabled. They are offered treatment. If they don't accept treatment, they are left in the wilderness to fend for themselves. I know it sounds cruel, but we simply don't have the luxury of anything less than full buy-in to a work mentality. My sister Amelia survives simply because as a family, we can't bear the thought of losing her. Even though my father has drawn a hard line about enabling Amelia, the McCollough family name is not regarded highly because of that choice.

This approach has been successful. I can't think of anyone within the enclave that doesn't have a job, other than my sister. Productive effort encourages self-esteem, and overall, our citizens have benefitted. Maybe I am drawing parallels or cause and effect that isn't real, but we have almost no crime or suicides in the enclave. Regardless of my accuracy, our culture is work-based to the benefit of individuals and our society.

It is my contention that the most profound change to our culture relates to talking dogs. Before the Great Dying, dogs also played a role in society, but their place in the world was far different. Dogs in modern, pre-change populations were primarily pets, pampered animals that provided comfort and companionship to their owners. Even though some humans treated them as people, they were not accepted in any generalized way as having the brains or the emotion to truly relate to the human species.

That has all changed. We can hear their emotion. What they lack in mental acuity they replace with unflagging loyalty. Dogs have always been helpmates, but the higher-level communication allows a more formidable team.

So how has this changed our culture? Imagine if you will a teenager struggling to find an identity. How much easier is that process made by having a warm, furry being always at your side to share your confidences? A being that loves you unconditionally no matter how insecure or rebellious your actions. Or imagine a husband or wife who has just lost his or her beloved spouse. How much comfort would it be to share your grief with a loving, talking dog? The most incredible and amazing facet of this improved human/dog relationship is that loving another warm, breathing, communicating species does not replace or compete with other human relationships or with God if you are a believer. Nay, we have been given the gift of acceptance and have learned from that gift. If hate begets hate, then surely, love and loyalty expand the human capacity for more of the same.

Dogs in their simple, kindhearted way have shown us our better humanity. The ripple effect of modeling acceptance has had a significant impact on how we treat others. In the future, readers of my version of history may decide I am exaggerating these claims. After all, I didn't live in the pre-change world. Any comparisons should be left to founders. I have spoken with them, and to a man and a woman, they agree with my assessment. My mother Karen is adamant she might not have survived if not for her dogs. She couldn't speak with them, but the German Shepherds she found that possessed thought transfer ability saved her life. My father, who had never had a dog before the change, believes talking canines changed him. His eyes fill with tears held in check when he speaks of Jack, his first conversing, fur-covered friend.

As I write it occurs to me, the reduced crime and suicide rates may be as much canine related as our emphasis on work. Nearly everyone in the enclave has a dog. We are raised with them, and they are an integral part of our lives. Talking dogs have given humans a different perspective on the world and life, and that shift has allowed us to be more connected to everything.

I may be raving. I miss Candy, and I am worried for my niece, Chrystel. I hope some of my insights on our culture will be helpful to those who look back and try to understand why we did some of the things we chose to do. It is always important to have context behind the choices of civilizations. The arrival of aliens may change everything, anyway. This culture, built upon the ashes of an advanced civilization, could be only a flash in time, a quick pause in the unrelenting cycle of the universe. If I am alive a hundred years from now, it will be my pleasure to describe the cultural shifts resulting from the first human and extraterrestrial meeting. For now, I must face my fears, get up from my desk, and find out what happened to my niece, Chrystel. Geronimo M.

## 18. Space, the Final Frontier

"How are you feeling, Karen?" Shakete asked.

"Better now. I should have taken the injection you recommended. Mabel, Manny, and Dee fared much better than me. Some fool like me had to be the test dummy."

Shakete pointed to the viewing window. "What do you think? Everything you imagined?"

The viewing window wasn't a window, but a projection from outside the Ardinian ship made to look like a window. It covered a wall two stories high and nearly as wide. "Before the change, our movie makers did a very fine job of replicating what it would look like in space. But seeing it and being here in it, as they used to say, priceless." Karen turned and smiled at the Ardinian leader. "The travel sickness is a whole different ball game. No way to prepare for that."

"Yes, the transition points result in a metabolic reaction that is hard to anticipate. The Mermots had similar problems, and much worse in some cases, so we developed a treatment to allay the symptoms. I can assume then, you are ready to take the injection before our final transition point?"

"Please! Do you also have to take that medicine, Shakete? I haven't noticed any symptoms from your people."

"No. We have been travelling for a very long time." Shakete looked away in thought.

Karen noticed his expression. She was trying to read this new race and wasn't sure if their facial expressions meant the same thing for them as for humans. For all she knew, they may have practiced human emotional responses to make her team feel at home. "Something else, Shakete? Your face appears troubled."

"It is difficult to know what to share with humans. I have a good deal of trust for you, Karen. Even though you don't know me, we studied several humans to determine who would be best for this mission. And, yes, I recognize now the knowledge of how we studied humans is disconcerting to you. Our species has difficulty determining how humans will react to any given stimulus or new information. You are a predictably, unpredictable species."

Karen rolled her eyes. "Might want to just get to the point, Shakete. If it helps, I already surmised there is a lot you aren't telling us."

"Well, yes. Better now than later. We are a blend of biology and android. Our bodies were created not by natural processes, but rather in our labs. We are specifically made to endure the rigors of space."

"So, you're an android? Your race is androids?" Karen asked incredulously.

"There is not a simple answer. Yes and no. Our bodies are a blend of biology and technology. Our processors are downloaded into these bodies. It is the very same processor with the same emotions, memories, and values as our biological forbearer. To my mind, we are not androids at all, but instead, Ardinians with android enhanced bodies. I was concerned you might have some difficulty, as you say, wrapping your processor around that fact."

"Hmmpf." Karen studied Shakete's face.

"What is the meaning of this *Hmmpf*?" Shakete asked.

"It is something we say when we don't know what else to say and are thinking about it. It's a cue that we need time to think, or the information was unexpected."

"I see. How long will your thinking take?"

Karen breathed in and tilted her head sideways. "Hard to say. For me, not long. I mean really, it makes sense. How else would you have survived out here for so long? For other humans, it may take longer. Might be best to just keep this information to ourselves for now. How about the Mermots? Are they also___?"

"No, completely biological. They are an utterly amazing species."

"So, you keep saying. Methinks thou dost protest too much." Shakete squinted his eyes in confusion. "Never mind, Shakete, it's Shakespeare. I'm ready for that tour you promised. How old are you, anyway?"

"Hmmpf," was Shakete's reply. Karen chuckled in return. "If you will follow me, we can start with our propulsion systems. Manny and Dee are there now speaking with our engine experts."

All Karen could think about was the vastness of everything as they strolled the wide halls of the Ardinians' ship. The vastness of space, the vastness of this ship, and the vastness of Shakete's possible age. The walls were the same lovely, pearlescent color as the shuttle the Ardinians had sent to earth. Like the shuttle, light filled the halls and rooms from an unknown source. The Ardinians they passed all offered a simple greeting. They said, "Greetings," and lifted their right hands with their palms facing the greeted party. Shakete merely nodded an acknowledgement, and Karen began to do the same.

The heart of the ship and the Ardinian gathering place was a spectacular hall. At the center of the domed ceiling was a chandelier made of glass or some facsimile that replicated what Karen had been told was the Ardinian home planetary system. It moved almost imperceptibly as their system had moved eons ago. There was nothing suspending these heavenly bodies from the ceiling. How they stayed in place was a mystery to Karen. The light shimmered from a blue and green replica of Ardinia. Karen could only imagine the beauty of that world and the tremendous loss of the Ardinian people.

Underneath the floating chandelier was a garden. The vegetation, although like earth, was at the same time decidedly different. The colors of the foliage had a purple hue. Maybe that explains the henka, Karen thought. Surrounding the garden was yet another vast space. Shakete explained it was where his people met for ceremonies and recreation. He guided Karen to a wall on the periphery of the hall. A door magically appeared. "If you will please follow, Karen," Shakete gestured.

Finally, something familiar. The elevator was like those found on earth--the same moving sensation, sound, and even buttons on the wall. A tiny buzz pinged when they reached their floor. The doors opened to a room not as aesthetically pleasing as the rest of the ship. Here, tubes, racks, workstations, and a central pulsating core, probably the heart of the Ardinian propulsion system, gave the space a sense of purpose.

Manny, squatting next to a petite female Ardinian, was listening intently as she pointed to different parts of the core. "Wait a damn minute!" Karen blurted. She strode toward Manny and looked more closely at his legs. She had never seen him squat like that. His missing leg wouldn't allow it. Karen peered at him as he quickly stood.

Manny had shaved his beard which took years off his appearance. He smiled from ear to ear, and uncharacteristically, reached over to hug Karen "I've died and gone to heaven," he whispered. "The Ardinians gave me a new biological, android leg. See?" Manny lifted his pant leg. The leg he displayed looked every bit like a biological leg, hair and all. He lifted his other pant leg to show how they matched.

"My God, that's incredible!"

"I know. It has feeling too! It isn't perfect yet, but they tell me it should be in two to three weeks. And now I have the chance to learn about this technology and how it works." Manny pointed to the core. "At least they're trying to explain it to me. It's unlike anything I've ever imagined. I mean, sure, Jed and I talked about some outlandish science within the realm of possibility, but this. . ." Manny shook his head in wonder. "Oh Karen, please meet my escort and a premier Ardinian scientist, Dopa."

The Ardinian bowed her head and reached out for a handshake. "Very pleased to meet you, Dopa," Karen said as she accepted the extended hand. You have made my teammate, Manny, one happy guy."

Dopa did an imitation of an earthly giggle. "I am very pleased with your Manny human. He is most agreeable."

Karen nodded politely. "Give me the big picture, Manny. And take it way down to idiot level."

"OK, I'll try. Dopa stop me if I get it wrong. First, transition points are as I expected, what we call worm holes. Their term is probably better because it doesn't just use the bend in the universe to travel incredible distances, but also, shifts time simultaneously. The propulsion is a matter changing, completely renewable, energy source. I haven't even touched the surface of how that works. When doors appear from nothing, it isn't just a hologram. Matter is reorganized to make the space. The propulsion system works on the same principle, utilizing the energy generated from the reorganization of matter."

Karen held up her hand. "Whoa. Don't even start explaining colliding protons and neutrons. I get the general idea, but anything more, I wouldn't understand anyway. Let me allow that much to sink in. Where is everyone?"

"Not sure about Mabel. She and her guide took off a while ago. They seemed to be getting on quite nicely. Dee is getting an explanation of what we call the information technology infrastructure. I'm not sure that term even touches the surface. We should've brought a doctor with us too. I was awake during my leg replacement surgery, but I don't think I could explain what they did or how they make the replacement leg."

"Shakete, would it be possible to send a doctor to the Delamie later to learn about your medical technology?" Karen asked.

"Of course. Our biological restoration section would enjoy sharing their skills with a human protégé."

Karen glanced at Shakete and back to Manny. "I would like to meet with everyone for dinner." She turned to Shakete, "And, I'm hoping we can discuss a plan, Shakete, with my whole team. I assume you have some specific ideas on how we can protect the earth from the Huntas?"

Shakete studied Karen. "Yes, indeed. We have a special dinner planned tonight, now that you are well enough to enjoy it. We can gather after the celebration to begin implementation discussions."

\* \* \*

Every Ardinian, except for those that prepared and served the meal, attended the gala. Musicians with exotic instruments played native Ardinian songs during dinner as dancers and singers moved in and out of a small stage raised above the center garden. After a glorious meal where the human team assiduously avoided green crunchy things, the Ardinian musicians returned to the stage with human type guitars and an electronic drum. The capstone of the entertainment was a rendition of two Rolling Stones hits, *Time is on My Side* and *You Can't Always Get What You Want.*

Karen had to stifle a laugh at the gyrating Ardinians. The entire assemblage was rocking and rolling. Most of the Ardinians stood and danced near their seats. If it hadn't been so crowded, the joint would have been vibrating. Maleta explained that they had culturally appropriated some human music and that it was meant as a compliment. Apparently, the Rolling Stones was a crowd favorite.

Dee danced with her escort, a handsome Ardinian, and then sang along with the music. Karen was surprised that even Dee knew the words. At the end of the last song, everyone stood and hooted. Who would have guessed the Ardinian gesture of applause was to hoot?

Shakete made a speech welcoming the human team and spoke with authority about a long and rewarding partnership. He signaled Karen and her team to follow him for their meeting at the end of formal festivities. Everyone else stayed to continue to party.

The group strolled along the edge of adorned tables receiving excited, nearly frenetic smiles and greetings from the Ardinians as they passed. Karen asked Shakete, "When was the last time you had a celebration?"

He thought for a moment and answered, "I think it was 72 years ago. Maleta could confirm the date. Since the loss of the Mermots' world, there hasn't been much cause. Our peoples have suffered greatly." Shakete began to glow. By the look on his face, it appeared the gold glowing signaled more than an emotional response for joy.

Karen thought it must also reflect sadness, perhaps even any strong emotion.

"I'm sorry, Shakete. It's something we have in common. I too know what it is like to lose almost everything." Strangely, the brightness of Shakete's skin intensified. He nodded and turned down a wide hallway and whisked the humans into a meeting room that was not there a second before.

Everyone sat except Maleta. Shakete explained she would provide a detailed description of the plan. Maleta turned to the data stand, waved her hand over the top, and another view, this time of Hunta warships, appeared. "The Huntas possess a formidable armada. It includes one destroyer class ship bigger than ours and 65 cruisers large enough to house approximately 900 Huntas and 120 fighter vessels each. Additionally, they have at least 100 shuttles available to travel from space to atmospheric planets. The Hunta spacecraft are all armed.

"We have this capital ship and three shuttles, one of which carried you from earth to our home aboard, Delamie, the name of the ship where you currently reside. When we left our home world, our travel designs were meant for the comfort and survival of our species and not for war. Perhaps that was naiveté, but our risk assessments indicated the chances of stumbling upon an intelligent race as advanced as our own was remote. We did not have the time to create war machines and enough capital ships to house our population. We simply never accounted for the risk that some of our own peace-loving people might become an aggressive branch of the family."

Maleta paused and studied the human expressions in front of her. She found it interesting that human's paled instead of glowed when they felt fear. "Please, I know you must be thinking we have no chance against a force like the Huntas, but that is not the case. Our technology is far superior to the Huntas. This ship, as an example, is shielded in such a way that it is impregnable by their weapons."

Manny blurted out, "Well, that hardly helps us. We can't all fit in this ship, and we would still lose our home world to the Huntas."

"Very true. That is why we need your help and the help of the Mermots. We have almost completed a matter reorganizing weapon that will destroy anything the Hunta brings against us. All we have left to do is complete the research on how to project this weapon into space to destroy their ships."

Manny was shaking his head. "You're saying that right now all you have is a theoretical weapon? That's it? And what help are we in that?"

Maleta looked to Shakete for help. She was obviously losing the audience. Shakete nodded sternly at her and waved Maleta to continue. "Let me start from the beginning of our plan. Our thought is that after destroying the Mermots world and making it uninhabitable, the Huntas will be unwilling to take that approach again. We are doubtful they will attempt to destroy the earth. After all, like us, they need a place to live. Instead, we are convinced they will try to take the earth first from space to defeat us and then with an assault force on the ground to defeat the indigenous population."

Karen added, "When you say defeat the indigenous population that's a euphemism for kill all humans, correct?"

Maleta looked grave and nodded. "Yes, I believe that is the most likely outcome. They may choose to keep some humans as slaves. Either alternative is unacceptable." Maleta plowed on trying to forestall any more interruptions.

"The Mermots are on a moon building cruisers and fighting vessels armed with more conventional weaponry, conventional in terms of lasers, photon blasters, projectiles, and nuclear weapons. The shielding for these vessels will be far superior to Hunta technology. It is the same matter shifting shielding we use on the Delanie. We won't need as many ships as the Huntas to protect the earth, but we need more than we have now and most certainly ships that are weaponized.

"We require two things from earth. First, more men and women to fly these ships and hopefully assist in the leadership of space battles. Secondly, assistance to build and use weapons to protect the earth from a possible ground assault."

Dee spoke, "You do understand that because of the Great Dying, we no longer have any large armies or an air force or a space program or even sightseeing helicopter pilots, right? The number of people left on earth, even slightly trained in the art of flying, is minimal. That's a huge learning curve."

Shakete spoke. "Yes, we understand this fact. But humans are far more adept naturally at the art of battle and flying than either the Mermots or the

Ardinians. Mermots are terrestrial creatures. You will understand when you meet them. And my own race, I am sorry to say, doesn't possess the competitive spirit which translates to successful fighters. Humans are most well-equipped for these tasks. The Mermots, the Ardinians, we are all willing to die for this cause, and die we surely will if called upon to perform aerial battles. With humans in the pilot seats, there is a chance. With the development in time of a matter shifting weapon, a very good chance."

Karen was the first to vocalize what they were all thinking. "Sounds to me like you want humans to fight and die while you hang out in your protected ship. That you are trying to make humans your mercenary army. And aren't the Huntas the same species as you. How is it they can fight, and you can't?"

"If your decision is to reject our partnership, we will leave this grain of space and begin again to search for a habitable world. Many of the Mermots will most likely perish as will you. It is, after all, your planet," Shakete answered firmly. "Without capitalizing on the strengths of each of our peoples, I believe we are destined to fail. And I would like to add this plan requires some of my people and the Mermots to take up arms on earth. We are prepared to die to save the earth, your planet. Finally, the Huntas have experienced great challenges. Both branches of the family have changed in ways that make us less like brothers and more like far distant cousins."

It was Manny's turn to express some reservations. "If I am hearing you correctly, neither the Ardinians nor the Mermots have any idea how to fight a space battle. You know the technology piece, but the strategy and tactics of war is entirely new. Is that correct?"

Shakete looked somewhat chagrined at Manny's comment. "Yes, this would be our first battle."

Dee whispered, "Oh my God."

Karen placed her hand on Dee's arm. "Dee, give him a chance. You were about to say something more, Shakete?"

"Yes. Thank you, Karen. We have studied earth battles extensively in preparation. We have also created simulations from which to practice strategic and tactical skills. Still, we recognize that won't be sufficient. We are hoping there may be an earth survivor with the right qualities that can be called upon to assume the role of commander of our combined forces. And it is also important to note that the Huntas have never encountered a force equal to their own. Their approach to combat is to obliterate a planet and not fight in space or on a terrestrial surface. We are, at least, equally inexperienced."

Karen nudged Mabel. "What are you thinking, Mabel? You haven't said a word."

"I hardly know what to think. I'm just a weary old soul from the hills of Tennessee. Long way from there to here. But since you asked, I'll give you my best attempt at an answer. Poking your head in a hole doesn't save your ass from being shot to hell. Once you pull your head out of the sand, there is only one thing to do. Look around, gather your wits, and do the best you can do. Seems to me that's where we are now."

"Very nicely said, Mabel. So, Shakete, I'm beginning to have some concerns about the infamous Mermots. Got any pictures?"

Shakete and Maleta were nearly shining from the gold on their faces as the result of Karen's question. If they could talk to each other in their minds, it was happening now, while gazing into each other's eyes. Finally, it was Shakete that answered. "I ask for your patience, Karen. And your trust. We will be at the Mermot moon soon."

"Hmmpf," was Karen's only reply.

# 19. She's Gone

The gray skies leaked and spit during the drive from the deer stand to Aldrin's Dairy. When Mike, Thomas, and Trent arrived, the drizzle had taken on a decidedly more enthusiastic demeanor. Heavy drops plopped onto their heads at a quicker and more insistent pace. Mike sped, as much as an ATV could speed, to the dairy only to find the parking lot deserted. He yanked the emergency brake up and jumped out, followed closely by Thomas, Trent, and Mike's dogs.

A sign on the dairy office read *closed*. No explanation was provided. The three men peered in the glass-paned door and saw no one. Twisting the knob, Mike stated, "Locked."

"If you gentlemen will please step aside," Thomas directed. Trent thought Thomas' multi-pocketed jacket might contain tools able to defeat the locking mechanism. Mike knew better. Thomas used his boot as a giant battering ram in a quick flat soled kick to the handle side of the door. The sounds of the wood frame splintering and the crack of the door indicated the lock was truly and utterly defeated. Thomas commented when he saw Trent's surprised expression, "Have I wowed you with my finesse, yet?" Trent merely smiled and shook his head.

"You go left, Mike, I'll go right. Trent, if you could please head to the back of the building in the event there are any rats left to scurry from their holes, it would be much appreciated." Trent grunted an affirmative response and headed around the building. Thomas waited until he was certain Trent was in position, then looked at Mike, and said, "Ready, set, go."

The duo burst into the office, guns at the ready. Mike stood immobile as Thomas headed to the back room behind the counter. The dogs held at the threshold, waiting for Mike to give a signal to enter. He commanded Ghost and Bruno to stay.

Thomas returned shaking his head. "If anyone was here, they're gone now. I don't see Chrystel's vehicle in the lot either. Let's hope she changed her plans."

"Trent, no one is here!" Mike yelled out the front door.

Trent hustled to the front of the small building, weaving around dogs into the sales office. "I've never seen the office close unannounced. Something is not right."

Mike and Thomas looked worried. "All right, let's divide the work. I'll search this building. Mike, you and Trent are the hunters. How about you check around this structure and the parking lot for any tracks or clues. When we're done, we need to search all the dairy buildings, one at a time." Thomas waved his hand at the surrounding area. "I just wish the hell we'd brought a radio. If you see a radio or phone anywhere on the property, someone call Judy at the courthouse and see if she knows anything about Chrystel's whereabouts."

The search didn't take long. Trent found purple liquid residue staining rocks in the gravel lot. Mike grabbed a cloth bag from his ATV and scooped small stones in with the dirt underneath to be tested later. He commented to Trent, "This stuff has a weird smell, almost like blood."

There was no call for Thomas' foot-sized battering ram to enter the other buildings. The remainder of the dairy was unlocked. Establishing a pattern for entering each part of the facility, Mike and Thomas went in first while Trent observed from the opposite exterior side. They found exactly nothing until they jumped into the cheese making area. A man yelped and nearly passed out from stress upon being surprised by Thomas pointing a weapon at his head.

"What are you doing here?" Thomas demanded.

The man holding a pan in both hands said meekly, "Making cheese?" His wide blue eyes stood out in terror against his copper skin. He finally recovered enough to ask a question, "Well, what're you doing here?"

"We're looking for Mr. Aldrin and the mayor. Sorry, I didn't mean to frighten you."

The man was beginning to get angry. "I know you. You're Thomas, the Chief of the Force. Nice way to go looking for someone!"

"Oh wait," Thomas eyed the man, "You're Marcus, right? Our daughters used to play together. Damn, it's been awhile. I didn't recognize you at first." Thomas shouldered his rifle and reached out to shake Marcus' hand. Marcus offered his own in return only after wiping them on the front of the apron he was wearing.

Mike shouldered his own weapon and stepped next to Thomas. "We're genuinely sorry if we frightened you. We were searching the dairy for the mayor, and you appear to be the only person working today."

Marcus rubbed his bald head. "Well, it's been a strange day. You want to tell me what's up?"

Thomas and Mike shared a look. Finally, Thomas decided the truth might be in order. "There's some rumors Aldrin is sneaking in walk-ons that are up to no good. A group of them shot at me and my man Mike. The mayor was headed out here earlier to speak with Mr. Aldrin. We're concerned something happened to her."

"That explains a lot. Now some things are making sense," Marcus said.

"How so?" Thomas asked.

"I've been working out here most of my life. Wasn't too bad until recently. Mr. Aldrin has always been an ass, but lately he's been on a hair trigger. My boys work in the cow barn and mentioned some strange men coming through. I didn't think much of it. Figured Aldrin needed more help and was looking for walk-ons."

"How long has he been acting differently?"

"Maybe a few months. Anyway, two or three hours ago, he came by and told me there was an emergency. That I needed to leave for the day. I was in the middle of a batch of swiss and didn't want to lose it, so I ignored him."

Mike asked, "Do you have a landline?"

Marcus pointed to his left. "Yep, over in that corner."

While Mike was talking on the phone, Trent poked his head in. "I thought maybe something had happened to you all. Me and the dogs have been waiting patiently for someone to remember we were out here."

"Come on in, Trent," Marcus signaled. "Keep the dogs outside to guard."

Mike hung up the phone, his face grim. "Judy said Chrystel has been gone since early this morning, and she can't reach her either. Chrystel told Judy she was headed to Aldrin's, and she was taking the henka with her."

"Do you know anything else that could be helpful? Have you heard anything about where these walk-ons are staying?" Thomas asked Marcus.

"I talked with one of the guys that comes around and asked him where they were sleeping. He said at a school. Does that help?"

"More than you know." Mike responded. "Did they give you a name of the school or say anything else that would give us a clue as to where these walk-ons are from?"

Marcus shook his head, "No, sorry. He did say it was a broken-down school. I just thought it was somewhere outside the enclave."

"Has Carlton been out here much?" Thomas asked.

Marcus looked surprised, "Now that you mention it, yeah. I've seen him a few times. Thought he was just politicking for votes. He is kind of a fish out of water at a dairy--dressed-up, nice shoes, flashy hair style, that sort of thing. Nobody wears that kind of shit around these parts."

Mike was getting antsy. "Thomas, I think someone needs to get back to town and check the maps for old schools. Could you and Trent finish the search and then meet me back at the courthouse?"

"Roger that, Mike. We'll call someone to pick us up."

"We've got to find her, Thomas."

Thomas nodded with a devastated expression. "I know Mike. I love her too. We'll find her!"

* * *

Looking at a map pinned to a wall in the small conference room of the courthouse, Judy and Brodie were searching for school symbols and circled each one they found within a ten-mile radius of the enclave perimeter. Thomas, barking orders into a radio they had moved to a hastily prepared operations center, was coordinating search teams from the force. The normally calm and collected Mike rubbed his head repeatedly while using the landline to enlist the help of his children to help in the search for Chrystel.

All activity stopped when Carlton burst into the room. "I've heard the mayor is missing. Why is it I was not informed?" Carlton looked as always, perfectly coiffed. Khaki pants that might have been starched, a button down pale blue shirt, and tasseled loafers completed the anachronistic ensemble. No one in the enclave wore shoes that could possibly slide off their feet. Carlton's thick blond hair swept over his forehead just so, somehow remaining in place while still appearing as if he hadn't styled his locks. His steady green eyes were both questioning and sincere. Judy thought if Chrystel were here now, she would be gagging into her mouth at Carlton's perfection.

Mike dropped the phone to restrain Thomas, who looked to be ready to provide the beating everyone in the room felt Carlton richly deserved. Thomas hissed, "As if you didn't know, you worthless piece of shit! As soon as we find Chrystel and prove you're behind these kidnappings, we're going to lock you up and throw away the key. Get out of here, NOW!"

"You're mad," Carlton calmly responded. "Why would I kidnap anyone? I can win this election flat out. The founders have been in control so long, they've lost sight of what people want and need. Now, please, as a candidate for mayor, I deserve to be informed as to what is going on. I see you have my competitor assisting with something. Brodie is obviously your preferred mayoral replacement. I simply request the same respect."

"Respect is the one thing you don't deserve," Thomas spat as Mike grabbed his arm.

"We have information that walk-ons are being funneled through Aldrin's Dairy," Mike said. "This morning, Chrystel went out to speak with Mr. Aldrin and vanished. So far, Letitia disappeared at an inopportune time, Geronimo's dog Candy went missing when trying to ferret information from other dogs, and now Chrystel. We also have first person information that you, Carlton, often frequent the dairy. Unless you have some form of milk or cheese fetish, there doesn't appear to be any good reason for you to drag yourself out there a few times a week. You are the only person who has cause to gain from these kidnappings, Carlton."

"Would dating Aldrin's daughter be an adequate reason for frequent visits to the Aldrin home? I have been seeing Aldrin's oldest daughter for three months. And I think a persuasive argument can be made that Brodie has as much to gain as me from these unfortunate disappearances. We need to have a new mayor until Chrystel is found. Obviously, finding her is the priority, so I'll give you two days. If she can't be located, an enclave session must be held to select a temporary mayor." Carlton stared at the hostile faces. "My dog is waiting for me outside. Good day." He turned and walked out, closing the door softly.

Thomas was still angry. He pounded the table with his fist to release pent up frustration. "That guy has one very large set of balls, I'll give him that. Did you see the way he looked at us? Like he didn't have a care in the world. No guilt whatsoever. Either he's a pathological liar, or maybe we've been led down a blind alley. I'm going with liar."

Brodie asked, "I wonder. Is it possible he's telling the truth? Is there something else going on that we've completely missed? It seems the upcoming election has ignited these occurrences, but maybe there's no connection. It is possible the mayoral race is just coincidental timing? Thomas, have you had any luck getting any information from our captive?"

"Not yet. Mike says I have to follow the rules when getting information." Thomas rolled his eyes. "I may have left some music on with the volume cranked-up while we were here working. I'm going to send Judy over with a nice dinner later and have her turn down the sound. Try a good cop, bad cop technique first. If that doesn't yield any fruit, we may be able to deceive him. Clint and his players have agreed to stage a break-in."

Mike smiled slyly. "Keep working on it. And, please, keep following those rules, Thomas. If we want a society that values rights, we can't resort to torture." He glanced at Brodie. "Just out of curiosity, Brodie, where were you this morning?"

"Where I always am that time of day, tending to my hogs."

"Anybody tending them with you?"

"Don't I wish. Nope, just me and my dog."

"Do you talk to them? Could your dog vouch for your whereabouts?"

"Yes, I can talk to the dogs, and I suppose mine would vouch for me if he could tell time or even what day it was."

"Point taken," Mike said.

"Look, Carlton made an excellent argument. I could have as much to gain as him if Chrystel was taken out of the mix, especially if I could pin the kidnappings on him. But I can't. Also, I would never hurt Chrystel. Not for anything."

Mike raised his eyebrows. "Care to expand on that?"

"Not really. I didn't do this. If you don't trust me, send me away right now. But, just know, it won't stop me from trying to find her." Brodie was a tall, well-muscled man. He drew up his over 6 foot 4-inch frame and glared at Mike.

"Okay, Brodie. We need your help. Keep at it. Thomas, how close are you to having your search teams ready to go?"

They will meet us in an hour. Trent really knows the outer fringes. He's going to look at the school locations and prioritize them based his knowledge of the comings and goings of walk-ons. We only have about five hours of daylight left, and so far, we already have twenty different schools to check-out. I had no idea the old world had so many schools."

"My extended family will augment your teams. Geronimo couldn't be dissuaded from helping."

"Roger that, Mike. Time's a wasting," Thomas replied.

\* \* \*

Twenty-three schools were checked in two days, yielding not a trace of the New Washington Mayor. After failing to find Chrystel or the mysterious walk-ons at any of the abandoned schools, search teams switched to grid searches, starting from the area near Aldrin's Dairy and fanning outward. It was frustratingly slow work. There were tens of thousands of degraded buildings where people could hide.

The only available map that listed local schools was dated 1999. Geronimo had searched the library archives and could not find anything more current. No one could be sure that there wasn't another facility in the hinterlands, built sometime after 1999 but before the Great Dying.

In his concern and frustration after the first day of searching, Mike swallowed his pride, drove to his daughter Amelia's home, and knocked on her door for the first time in many years. He knew Karen would be very disappointed in him if didn't inform Amelia that Chrystel was missing. He smiled as he thought "disappointed" might be an inadequate expression for what Karen would be. If he didn't tell Amelia, Karen would in fact, take a major piece of his derriere in recompense for his error in judgement. Also, asking one of his kids to tell Amelia was cowardly. Geronimo had diplomatically informed Mike of that fact when he hinted to his son that "he wouldn't mind" if Geronimo shared Chrystal's situation with Amelia. As Mike waited, he wondered if Amelia's gift could yield some clue as to whether Chrystal was safe.

When Amelia opened the door, after several checks from different windows to be sure it was her father, she was already crying. They stood tensely and looked at one another. It was Mike who reached out first. He had buried his disappointment, his fear for this child under righteous anger over her inability to choose something different. He hadn't realized how much he'd missed this precious daughter. Of all his unusual children, Amelia was the most gentle and sweet. As he held her in his arms, Mike regretted every minute missed by a self-imposed separation from his ethereal daughter, a daughter who had the power to make him feel better by a simple touch to the cheek or delight him by her wonder at the sight of a squirrel playing in a tree. That daughter had been truly and utterly missed. Mike had lived with the gaping wound of her loss for so long, the pain became a part of him, constant and, therefore, unnoticed. They hugged for an eternity.

Amelia invited him in, but Mike stepped inside only as far as the foyer. He still couldn't stomach the mess that was her home, and he had to get back to help. He took Amelia's hand as he explained that Chrystel was, at least for now, gone. Amelia's tears flowed even stronger. She dropped to her knees and held her head as she moaned. Mike wrapped her in his arms, waited, and then tenderly helped her up.

"All is not lost, Amelia. We believe she's safe. And you know how strong she is. If anyone can get themselves out of a situation like this, it's Chrystel."

Amelia gazed up at her father, tears brimming in her eyes and running down her cheeks, as she nodded. She touched Mike's face. "I know, you're right. I just wish there was some way I could help her. I've failed her as a mother." Amelia dropped her head and started sobbing again.

"Maybe you can help her. Use your gift, Amelia. I know it frightens you, but it's who you are. Maybe if you embrace that power instead of trying so hard to hide from it, your issues will subside. I can't know how difficult it is to see what will happen in the future and still sometimes not be able to change it. But, Amelia, that's true for all of us. I stood by and watched as you slid into your reclusive world, knowing the result, and still, I couldn't fix it for you. I've tried. Your mother has tried. Your brothers and sisters have tried."

"I know, Dad. I never blamed you for cutting me off."

Mike released a long, tortured sigh. "Sweetheart, that doesn't stop me from blaming myself. I thought I did the right thing, but right now,

I feel like the world's biggest horse's ass. You might be able to help us find Chrystel, and you might not. You might be able to see where she is, and we still won't find her in time. There are never any guarantees. All we can do is use every resource we own to the best of our ability. That's all we've got."

Amelia had stopped crying. She gazed at her father with a look that Mike hadn't seem from her since she was a child. She was frowning in concentration. It was as if, maybe, this time, something he had said had broken through the shell Amelia had erected to protect herself. "I love you, Amelia. I always have, and I always will." Mike gulped back his own emotion.

"I'm glad, Dad. Me too. I promise I'll try to see where Chrystel might be."

Mike smiled. "I have to get back. If you see anything in your dreams, even if it doesn't make sense, let me know immediately. Does your landline still work?"

"No. I didn't want to ask anyone to fix it."

"I know a guy named Trent. He's sort of a strange fellow, but he told me when he was young living in the Flagstaff Enclave, he helped his father set-up a telephone system. If I send him out here to fix yours, will you let him in?"

"Okay." Chrystel gave a sly smile. "I'll open my door to almost anyone who brings me tea or chocolate. Will you come back, Dad?"

Mike's response was another hug. He inhaled the aroma of his most vulnerable child. "I'll be back. I promise. Hopefully, next time with Chrystel in hand." His hug lasted a long time until his eyes too were filled with tears.

# 20. The Vote

Every seat was taken in the largest theater of the courthouse. Townspeople took to standing along the walls until crowd overflow snaked into the lobby and further into Founders Park. Other than children, almost every resident of New Washington was in attendance to get firsthand information on recent disappearances and vote for a temporary mayor.

Judy, Chrystel's admin assistant, and two council members hefted bulky speakers outside for the umbrella holding attendees in the park. The enclave fire marshal groused to Brodie about the number of people in the courthouse. Brodie nodded effusively in agreement, even though he had no intention of acting on the marshal's complaints. When the drizzle outside morphed into a persistent downpour, the meeting was postponed for an hour while the force gathered and erected tents to protect outside clavers from the rain.

Gary Grimes, one of the committee council members, was drafted to lead the proceedings. Gary, generally a crowd favorite, used humor and a quick wit to encourage an audience to follow his bidding. His red face was surrounded by long white hair and an equally white beard, earning him the nom de plume of Santa. It was hoped Gary's genial continence might forestall an outright riot during contentious discussions.

As the clock neared the witching hour, what had been a low murmur of people talking with their neighbors increased to a voice-filled roar and quieted when important enclave figures stepped onto the stage and took their seats. Santa, wearing a plaid shirt, faded denim, and work boots, strolled to the microphone and said, "Good Evening." Like timework, the audio system shrieked feedback to the audience as many winced or held their ears. Gary glanced offstage to Judy who was already moving to adjust the system. He tapped on the microphone until the sound was magnified without blowback and began again.

"Good Evening, New Washington!"

The crowd responded with, "We Endure."

"Indeed, we do. Welcome to each of you. I am very glad that almost everyone in our community has seen fit to participate in tonight's proceedings. There is nothing more important than our citizens. The best way to ensure the continuity of the New Washington Enclave is for individual voices to play a part in important decisions. Since the founders chartered our democracy, we have always strived to include___"

"Just get on with it!" a man bellowed from the center of the audience. Enthusiastic applause followed his recommendation.

"I can see the natives are restless. In that case, I will skip my twenty-minute introductory speech, cut the political bullshit, and as you have recommended, just get to it." Santa paused and smiled at the crowd as another smattering of applause broke out.

"Here is what we know. Letitia, our council chairperson disappeared during the alien visitation. Candy, Geronimo's dog, disappeared the next night. Two days ago, Mike McCollough and

Thomas, the Chief of our Forces, were shot at in the woods by walk-ons not part of the enclave. That same day, our mayor, Chrystel, the alien visitor, Tilley, along with Mr. Aldrin and his family all went missing near Aldrin's Dairy." Gary paused as the audience noise grew in response to the news.

"Please, please, hold it down so I can continue. We obtained information that unidentified walk-ons might be holding Chrystel and perhaps Letitia and the Aldrin family at an old school. We don't know the motive for this mischief. For the last two days, we've scoured every school within ten miles of the enclave without result. This morning, we began a grid search using our best sensors. Thomas' lovely wife Katie, the founder whose sensor gift helped save our originals after the change, led that effort. Thus far, the sensor search teams haven't found any miscreants hiding in abandoned buildings around the area.

"Thomas and Mike captured one of the men who made an attempt on their lives in the woods. He has been taken into custody and is currently being questioned. The only thing we've learned thus far is that the mysterious walk-ons are probably from the Dakota Territories."

Gary Grimes paused again to allow the people of New Washington to digest the information. "The reason we have called this meeting is that Carlton, one of our mayoral candidates, called for a vote to provide a temporary mayor replacement. It just won't do to go too long without someone in charge.

"What we must do tonight is decide how we will decide and then make a decision. As many of you know, the meeting that was held for this very same reason some days ago became a mess of nominations and vetoes. The council believes this proceeding could end the same way. Our esteemed librarian, Geronimo would like to offer an alternative. Geronimo, could you please step up to the podium."

The crowd began to chant, "Geron-i-mo, Geron-i-mo, Geron-i-mo." As he wound through the throng of people against the wall, Geronimo waved and smiled. Santa gratefully handed the microphone to his replacement and whispered, "Good luck," into Geronimo's ear.

"Thank you, Gary. Good evening to each of you. I believe I have found a legal way to elect an interim mayor. I researched our charter and the discussions surrounding the founders' original decisions. Discussions were often used in the old world to determine the intent of laws. I also believe it can be legally argued that a conversation taking place during the forming of the charter is justification for including those unwritten recommendations in the law. On the fourth page of charter deliberations, the founder Manuel asked, 'What happens if we can't decide because of vetoes?' The founder Rachael responded, 'It's like maybe, we should like probably, just do things the old way. Like just take a vote and like, leave it at that." Geronimo paused for the crowd's laughter at Rachael's pre-change, teenage way of speaking. She and Manuel also sat in the front row. The crowd applauded when they stood up and waved happily at the crowd. They were a very popular and respected family in the enclave.

Geronimo lowered his hand to signal he wanted to continue. "From the written text of the founders' conference, there were no objections to Rachael's input. My recommendation is that we nominate candidates and then take a vote the old way. Before the change, it was normally specified that the first person to get over 50% of the total is the winner. I formally put forward this approach. Do I have any vetoes?"

Geronimo watched patiently as people talked to the neighbors. He waited a full five minutes and sent Judy to see if there were any vetoes from the lobby or outside crowd. When it was confirmed that there was not one veto, a tremendous achievement for the enclave, Geronimo continued. "I believe we have a plan! Judy will be passing around voting slips. Each adult should take one and please share pens and markers because we don't have enough to go around.

"We have nominations for Brodie, Carlton, and Gary already in the hopper. Do I have any other nominations?" For the first time, the rowdy audience became quiet, glancing back and forth for other worthy candidates. Geronimo waited an appropriate time before speaking. "If there are no more nominations from the audience, I would like to nominate one additional contender, my father, Mike McCollough. I know he's a founder, but keep in mind the temporary mayor will serve only for a short time. We're hoping to find Chrystel very soon. In the absolute worst case, it's less than six weeks until the official election. Given that we have an alien situation and now some group infiltrating our enclave, there is no one more qualified, more competent, or more honest than my dad to keep us together during this turbulent time. What do you say, Dad? Will you do it?"

Geronimo shifted and peered at Mike sitting on a chair at the side of the stage. Mike's chagrined expression and head shaking back and forth made his reluctance very clear. "My dad doesn't covet power. He loves his privacy and the ability to stay in the background to pull levers that make things work. He is a humble and responsible man. For that very reason, he is the perfect candidate. Please, Dad."

Mike wearily nodded his head in an OK gesture and shrugged his shoulders. He was embarrassed to be called out in front of the entire enclave. He knew he could do the job. In fact, he knew he was probably the best person to serve temporarily. The time when Karen was mayor provided complete understanding of how the enclave worked. Karen didn't hold back anything and frequently wanted his opinion. Together, they were a strong team. But, he would be the one with his neck out this time, and he wouldn't have her shoulder, or her energy to help him.

"It's settled. Your four candidates are Carlton, Brodie, Gary, and Mike. Let the voting commence. While we're gathering votes, are there any questions for the august group sitting on the stage behind me?"

A woman in the back of the audience stood up, and a microphone was shepherded to her location. "Is it possible the aliens are causing all these problems? I mean, could the alien Tilley have done something horrible with Chrystel? Or is it possible the aliens are mind controlling the walk-ons?"

Brodie grabbed the on-stage microphone from Geronimo. "Absolutely not. Tilley was protecting Chrystel. I witnessed her doing exactly that at Chrystel's home. And as for mind control, the walk-on in custody has made it clear, he is acting of his own accord. Please be assured, the aliens have nothing whatsoever to do with the goings on in the enclave."

The woman mumbled, "I still think it's possible," and then sat down.

The atmosphere in the courthouse was lively. Everyone stayed to wait for the gathering and counting of votes. The council was in a back room tallying the results as quickly as possible. A huge cheer erupted when Santa stepped on the stage with an envelope in his hands.

"If I could have your attention one last time." Gary stuck the microphone under his arm and slowly ripped the end of the envelope. He blew into the paper container for dramatic affect. As he pulled out a sheet of paper, he shook the folded note open and raised his eyebrows at the written results. "The winner, with 84.2% of the vote, is our very own founder and an all-around good guy, Mike McCollough."

Geronimo had pulled a chair up to wait with his father and smiled when Mike's name was announced. Clapping Mike on the shoulder, he said to his dad, "I knew it!"

"Thanks a bunch, Son," Mike returned dourly.

# 21. Satellite

Mike's first official act as temporary mayor was to attend the launch of the communication satellite rocket that Jed had been working toward for most of his post-change life. Mike suspected the aliens could easily populate the outer atmosphere with the necessary hardware to restore global communication. The Ardinians would probably do so upon request, but he didn't want to rain on Jed's parade. It was an amazing achievement, and Jed deserved his day, even if Mike had more than his hands full back at the enclave.

Mike and the town council arrived after a short trip via airship to the launch site, located two miles away from Boeing Field in what was once a giant Walmart parking lot. Jed and his staff had searched high and low for a safe launch location. They needed a site far enough from their precious science center to guarantee its safety from rocket back-blast, but close enough to control the launch from the Boeing Field control tower. If a crumbling Walmart took a hit, no one would shed any tears.

A gaggle of scientists in white coats were already onsite preparing for the launch. Mike shook Jed's hand and then gave him a man hug. "Good to see you, Mike, and thanks for sharing this day. If it weren't for you, I wouldn't be here." Immediately after the change, Mike's calm, reasoned manner had persuaded Jed to join with him in New Washington. Mike had also saved Jed's life by locating him in Oregon after Jed had been shot. Mike and Jed's mutual affection was just another example of an enduring friendship forged through hardship.

"I can't imagine how Geronimo roped you into playing mayor for even a little bit. I wish now I had made it to the vote to see your face when he nominated you." Jed's eyes were smiling when he looked at Mike. "I know how much you enjoy that kind of role."

Mike scowled. "Sometimes Geronimo is so much like his mother it frightens me. He knows exactly what buttons to push to guide me into doing his bidding. But enough about me. We have a lot of catching up we need to go over."

"My thought exactly. I want to hear what's happening with the search for Chrystel and the walk-ons. Also, I have some concerns I need to share."

Mike studied Jed's face and sighed. "Does it ever get easier?"

One of the white-coated scientists joined Mike and Jed and proudly stated, "We're ready. We need to move the group back to the control tower."

Jed grinned and pointed the way, "If you will, Mayor."

It was a beautiful day for what was most likely earth's first space launch in a century. The gathered group oohed and aahed as the rocket completed a perfect lift-off and soared into the nearly cloudless blue sky. Mike pounded Jed on the back when the silver craft was almost out of sight. "Utterly amazing work, buddy!"

The scientists continued to monitor progress until the proper separation of the rocket from the satellite in orbit was confirmed. Jed beamed when the team lead turned to him and said, "I'm getting a link-up with the satellite. Everything's green. It's working!" Mike waited as Jed and his crew congratulated each other for a job well done. The council members shook hands and offered their thanks for the hard work of the science team before shuffling out of the tower to fly back to the enclave.

"I'll be in my office if there're any issues." Jed said. "I can't thank you all enough for your dedication and loyalty to this momentous goal. We did it!" The group cheered one last time, and Mike and Jed headed to the science center and research facility for their talk.

One of the few new buildings in the enclave, the science center was a two-story, sprawling structure, with clean lines and an abundance of glass windows on one side. The other side was dug into the hillside allowing the center to blend with the landscape. Since glass was always in short supply in the enclave, the broad windows lent an air of elegance to an otherwise functional shape. When the founders decided to place a premium on research and development at the expense of more rudimentary needs, Manuel led a group to design and build a modern research facility that would last for generations. Jed's face lit with excitement as he pulled the small battery powered cart into his designated parking space. Mike commented, "After all these years, Jed, your science center still gives you a thrill."

"Guilty as charged," Jed replied, grinning at his friend Mike. The two men strolled through the widened hallways of the research facility, turning into Jed's office. While the science center was designed to be easy on the eyes, Jed's office was functional work space. Everything served a work purpose. Diagram-covered tables and hanging, work flow charts filled the room. Missing from the office were elaborately framed degrees, of which Jed had many, or pictures of Jed shaking hands with dignitaries decorating the walls. He had not thought to save his "I love me" memorabilia when the world ended. Even if he had, Jed would not have felt any of it mattered enough to show it off. To Jed, it was always about the science and what the science could create.

Mike and Jed sat at a small table in the corner of the office under a window. "Any leads on Chrystel?" Jed asked.

"It's been nearly a week and nothing. Thomas believes the walk-ons may have pulled-back to hide when we captured one of them in the woods. The only thing we learned from our prisoner is that he's from the Dakota Territories. Clint's players tricked him into believing they were leading an escape effort, and that they were friends of Mr. Aldrin sent to help. The prisoner went with them willingly. When Clint asked where the school was located, so he could take him there, the prisoner responded, "Hell if I know, don't you?

"The prisoner is a self-described foot soldier. He knows only one thing for certain: three consecutive frigid winters and dry summers in North Dakota had left them desperate. Their leader, a guy named Red, was planning to take, infiltrate, or do something at New Washington with the intent to assume control of our enclave. The prisoner said a group of men had come to his farm and asked him to go along. Since he was worried about surviving the next planting season, he agreed. He also didn't know who within the enclave, other than Aldrin, might be helping the North Dakota aggressors.

"Trent shot and killed the man and woman in the woods that were holding me and Thomas at gunpoint. They might have known more.

"Anyway, as far as the search, you may have heard Katie and the other sensors haven't had any luck. They've scoured a 20-mile radius. My next plan is to borrow your drones. Perhaps, we can identify some activity from the air. You still have the drones we used to find the ranch here, right?"

"Sure, I always knew they might come in handy again. I was going to call you after the launch with the same recommendation." With a wry smile, Jed added, "Even though we didn't actually find the ranch using drones. Rachael's escape saved us from continuing that tedious effort. Let me make a call right now and have someone gather them and perform preventative maintenance. For sentimental reasons, I still have the computers we used to locate Karen at the ranch."

"We'll start using them as soon as I get back. Oh, and on a positive note, I visited Amelia."

"You did? I'm surprised, but happy to hear it."

"I had to tell her about Chrystel."

"Right, or risk your life upon Karen's return."

"Exactly, my friend," Mike grinned. "I'm glad I did. Sometimes, I lose myself in a deep groove of doing the same thing over and over because of righteous conviction, and then I can't find a way to extricate myself. Anyhow, she agreed to use her gift to assist in the search for Chrystel. The first night she tried, she saw Chrystel alive and in a school. Beyond that, she hasn't had any other visions to help determine where the school might be located. The only other thing she saw was violence. Amelia's sight becomes fuzzy when it involves brutality of any sort. Most likely because she finds it difficult to look directly at violence.

"There's only two ways a relatively small group of attackers could take the enclave. The first and easiest is an inside man, someone like Carlton. The only other possible strategy is to strike at the Defense Force and disable or overwhelm them. Without organized protection, New Washington clavers could offer some resistance, but maybe not enough.

"Thomas directed that the force be deployed around the clock in teams at possible avenues of approach. I just wish there were more of them. The men and women of the force are already overworked and tired. We've asked for volunteers and so far, only a handful have signed up. People are simply too busy keeping the enclave running. All these years, we thought our greatest vulnerability would come from the air in the form of a missile or attack air ships. You've done a great job of preparing us for that eventuality, Jed. We never thought it possible an army of ground warriors would travel great distances to try to take our home. The Dakota folks are still out there. We'll find them and Chrystel!"

"Is the grid sensor system we developed fully operational?" Jed asked.

"It is. I'd be far more worried if not for our ability to be warned of anyone entering the enclave's outer boundaries. Until recently, we kept the system off to allow people to travel freely. We don't have that luxury anymore."

"It sounds to me as if you have the situation well in hand, Mike. I have total faith in you and Thomas."

Mike nodded. "Oh, and I sent Trent, the man who saved us in the woods, over to Amelia's house to fix the phone. Trent was living off the grid and appears to be an extremely resourceful individual. He hates to be inside, and Amelia won't go out. I never dreamed he would do more than just fix her land line. When he arrived at her home, he agreed to enter her house, but only if she would step outside to speak with him. She did it! Trent told me she stood on her porch for a couple of minutes until she panicked and started to shake. I know two minutes isn't much, but it's a start. Later, Amelia confided to me Trent was a "broken" man, and she believes she can help him. Trent lost his wife and children and had his own version of a mental breakdown." The irony was not lost on Mike.

"Wow, that's incredible news. Taking on Karen's sometimes role as matchmaker?"

"Hardly. The Amelia-Trent thing was a total accident, but I'm sure as heck going to take credit when Karen returns."

Jed chuckled and then his face turned serious. "My news isn't as heartwarming. Quite the opposite. I'm fairly certain, someone accessed our computers."

"Fairly certain?"

"My IT chief has found footprints of someone hacking our internal system and downloading data."

"How is that possible? Your system isn't on any external network."

"All they'd have to do is physically enter the facility and use one of the numerous available terminals."

"This could be very bad," Mike said as he scratched his head. "Could they get the thorium generator specs or access the missiles at Mount Rainier?"

"No, I've specifically firewalled that data. Only I have access. But, they could get prototype information for my new microwave vector communication radio. Possibly even data about our weapons research or the grid warning system protecting the enclave."

"Jed, is there any possibility it's someone on the inside? Could one of your employees be selling secrets to another enclave?"

"I'd hate to think so, but anything's possible. Perhaps, someone from the outside obtained a facility entry code and hacked through the eye screen. In any event, we've upgraded our physical security and set up an alert for anyone entering the facility at night. Also, my IT guru set a trap for anyone trying to download sensitive information. If they try it again, I think we're prepared. Not much we can do about data that's already been compromised. I'm sorry we weren't on top of the possibility earlier."

"Don't beat yourself up, Jed. We've all gotten a little soft. Those jerks in the woods got the drop on me and Thomas. I just wonder whether your data break-in has something to do with the North Dakota group or something else entirely."

Jed thought about Mike's question. "It does seem too much of a coincidence. First the walk-ons and now a hack into the science center system."

"Maybe," Mike looked away as he thought. "Feels different though. Do you need any help here with security?"

"I always need more help, Mike, just like everyone else shorthanded in the enclave. You and Thomas already have a full plate. If we have any other problems, or we track down a culprit, I'll let you know. It's a wonder I have any hair at all."

"Maybe you should be working on a human cloning program or even robots. I'll take the first models of whatever you come up with." Both men laughed at the thought. "There's something happening. I just can't get my arms around what. If I could determine which events are related, that would help. Alien Hunta aggressors, starving North Dakota farmers, illusive science center hackers. Anything else, Jed?"

"I don't suppose you want to hear about a series of tremors we've picked up along the Juan de Fuca Plate?"

"That would be a definite no!" Mike responded. "An earthquake is all we need right now. Unless you can predict one with any accuracy, I'm not sure there's a darn thing we can do about it. I'll send out a message to remind everyone to be prepared for emergencies. I should have done that anyway with the infiltrators somewhere out in the wilderness. We can also add more days of supply to the enclave emergency stash. Other than that, I think I'll just pretend it won't happen, like everyone else that lives in an earthquake zone."

Jed shrugged. "I'm glad you're in charge, Mike. I know we're in good hands."

"I'm glad you're glad," Mike responded.

## 22. Mermots

Strapped into seats, the humans sat across from Shakete, Maleta, and an Ardinian who controlled the shuttlecraft. A screen above Shakete displayed the immediate space beyond. "Karen, if you watch the left side of the screen, you will see the spacecraft fleet the Mermots have completed. They are very proud of their accomplishments."

There were three lines of space vehicles arrayed by size. The first row was the smallest and most numerous and looked like some form of winged insect. Predatory was the first word that came to mind. There were fewer craft in the middle row and only two looming in the back, even though they were far and away the largest. Karen asked, "How do you get them to just hang there? Is someone in them?"

Maleta answered, "No, they are currently on, but set to very low energy levels. No one is in them. We use a web tractor beam to keep them in place."

Manny whistled as the curved horizon of a desolate, crater-pocked moon came into view. The sun of this star system reflected off the surface in a sparkling sheen, like a dark jewel that only exposes its rare beauty in the light. Maleta spoke. "We will be landing on the dark side. Much like earth's moon, this moon travels around its host planet, but does not rotate. It is extremely cold on the dark side. The Mermots are underground in a temperature-controlled environment."

Karen was surprised by Mabel's reaction. She had taken a risk by bringing Mabel along. Mabel had never shown even a passing interest in anything that was otherworldly. The smile on Mabel's face hinted to a different side of her old friend that Karen had never seen. "Amazing, isn't it?" Karen asked.

Awestruck, Mabel nodded. "You know, Karen, I just never spent any time considering space. There were always too many earthly considerations to give it my attention. Now that I'm here, looking at this. . . I don't have the right words. We're so insignificant. I always knew that, but this," Mabel waved her hand in a large circle, "drives it home."

As the shuttle passed from light to dark, a bright tunnel could be seen on the surface in the distance. They could feel the ship turning and slowing as they moved to the entry point. Then the screen went dark. "I would like to save the rest as a surprise," Shakete said. "The Mermots have arranged a welcoming ceremony. They are most excited to meet you."

Karen looked suspiciously at Shakete. She knew something was up, but all she could do was be patient, not always her best quality.

The shuttle turned and then seemed to hover in place. Karen and the group waited as the pilot focused on a screen and manipulated the controls. A shaking thud indicated they had either hit something or were safely ensconced in a landing apparatus. The whoosh of the door opening signaled the latter.

Shakete went first. Outside the entry, he turned facing Karen and the human group to make the climb down a short ladder. "Follow me please," he said. Karen let the rest of her group go first and was the last out. She plastered a huge smile on her face as she hit the deck and swung around to greet the Mermots.

Her eyes blinked several times from the bright light. Or, maybe the blinking was because of what she saw standing to her front. There had to be a hundred of them. They weren't very big. Then again, it was hard to tell how big the Mermots were, if these were in fact Mermots, since they were crouched on four, long-toed feet. A shudder ran down her spine. She had to stifle an urge to yell, "Rats!". *I'll be damned, Amelia was right when she saw rats in her vision. I must hold tight to her claim that the rats are very important.*

Karen glanced quickly at her human colleagues. Their expressions were a mix of disgust and horror. Only Mabel appeared to take in the scene before her without a visceral response to the Mermots' physical appearance. Dee's face was screwed into a twisted scowl. Looking to Shakete for support, Karen bit her lip and forced another fake smile on her face.

"I believe we need to address the elephant in the air," Shakete began. "The Mermots are a race that evolved underground as scavengers. It was the key to their survival and produced a remarkably resilient species. I warned them that their appearance, like an earth rodent species, might engender an immediate revulsion response. I guarantee you, once you get to know them you will find their appearance, what's the human expression, grows at you."

Dee whispered to Karen, "It might be different if they were cute little chipmunks."

"Shush," Karen cautioned. She heard a tiny squeak, and as one, the Mermots stood balancing on their tails. They were nearly three feet tall. Hundreds of beady eyes assessed the humans with interest. The largest of them scampered forward to Karen. This Mermot rose again and stuck out a clawed hand for a shake. Shakete had obviously shared earth etiquette with his friends.

Without moving its mouth, the Mermot spoke into Karen's mind. "I am honored to meet you and your team, Karen. My name is Rappel, and I am the leader of my clan. The Mermots with me here today are all part of my family. There are two other clans that reside on this moon. We had a game to determine who would receive the privilege of greeting your arrival, and my clan won."

"I am honored to meet you as well, Rappel. Shakete has shared his great esteem for your people." Karen couldn't hear what came next. She thought the Mermots must have the capability to project speech into minds, like earth's dogs, and at the same time could control who heard the thought. The sea of rat like beings parted, and a miniature Mermot came forward carrying several rings on one of its arms.

"This is my favored daughter, Tweet. She begged me to be given the honor of making ceremonial rounds to welcome our human guests." Tweet stood and wrinkled her wet, pink nose. Even though she was smaller than the other Mermots, her shape and physical characteristics were identical. Her body near the tail was wider and rounder than her chest. Tweet's face was pointed to the nose and almost hairless. Rounded ears residing on the sides of her head stood mostly erect. Other than the stomach and face, the remainder of Tweets body was covered in flat, shiny, dark gray hair. In a high, sing song voice, Tweet hummed a delightful melody.

Somehow, she maintained the background music while speaking to Karen. "May your years be fruitful and filled with fellowship. May your bowl always be filled with the ground's bountiful harvest. May your nights be warm and your partners amorous. These things we hope for you." Tweet fully extended her arms, reaching up to place one of the neckless-like gifts over Karen's head. Fully extended, Tweet's hands reached only as high as Karen's neck, so Karen bent from the waist and dropped her head to accept the gift.

"Thank you, Tweet, for the wonderful song and well wishes. Your gift is beautiful. What materials did you use to make this?"

Tweet's face quivered in what Karen hoped was excitement, rather than displeasure at her question. "I am very pleased you find the gift to your satisfaction. We were unable to use the natural elements of our home planet as our world has been destroyed. We used instead, minerals from this lifeless and hostile moon."

Tweet's father gave her a stern rat look, and she returned an even more significant stare. "My father indicates I have been impolite, but I only speak the truth, which is our way."

"No, Tweet, you were not impolite. Human's generally find truthfulness refreshing." Karen fondled the chain around her neck. It was nearly a half inch thick. Gold, silver, and bronze filaments were braided into an intricate and unique pattern. "Your gift is lovely, truly."

"Thank you." Tweet crinkled her whiskers and proceeded to gift the rest of the humans, repeating the well-wishes phrase to each. When she was done, she scampered off in the same direction from which she came. Rappel spoke again into their minds. "If you will please follow me, I will now lead a tour of our facility."

The group maneuvered around the Ardinian shuttle further into a rock-walled cavern. The temperature in the gigantic room was uncomfortably cool. When Dee began to shiver, Shakete noticed and asked one of the Mermots for a blanket. "The Mermots are accustomed to living underground and prefer cooler temperatures. Their metabolisms run very high, and that helps to keep them warm."

Rappel pointed at the foreboding insect looking ships ahead. Mermots were climbing over them with tools and test equipment at a startlingly rapid pace. "These are the attack ships. They carry a crew of two and are extremely maneuverable. When fully armed, they can easily defeat the Huntas' guard vessels. Also, the Ardinian shielding technology is far superior to the Huntas'.

Manny asked, "Have you had an opportunity to test these systems against the Hunta equivalent?"

Rappel stared at Manny. The almost black eyes showed little humor. "No, of course not. We have conducted simulations that provide a high level of confidence."

"Have you conducted any physical tests of these awesome and deadly looking craft?"

Karen thought she saw sadness in Rappel. But then, she wasn't entirely sure she could read the Mermots any better than she could intuit the expression on a rat's face. "Regretfully, no. Mermot equilibrium makes rapid movements in flight nearly unbearable. The Ardinians have created medications that provide some relief, but it isn't enough to extinguish the nausea and dizziness that accompanies what would be necessary to truly test these ships. It is for that very reason we were hoping with all our hearts for a partnership with your race. The Huntas must be destroyed!"

Rappel twitched for a few more moments and then settled. "Excuse me for my outburst. It is a matter of great emotion for our people. Our home was destroyed by those savages. If we could defeat them alone, we would try. From everything the Ardinians have shared about your race, we believe Mermots can build most things approximately five times faster than humans. This productivity is the result of our unique evolution as underground excavators. If you are curious, I can share with you the secrets of our adaptations at the proper time. You will see for yourself as we manufacture. Your race is much more adapted to flight. If we build them, and you fly them, it is a winning team."

Rappel continued, "If you look around at the walls and the passageways in this facility, the rock was carved by my people. We secrete a chemical that allows us to dig through the densest materials. Our hands are uniquely suited for heavy manipulation and the finest detail. Our engineering prowess was renown on our planet. I believe even

Shakete would admit that the Ardinians have learned a trick or two from Mermots."

Shakete nodded and smiled. Manny surprised Karen with his enthusiasm. "I am very impressed at your biology. It's as if you have taken the very best in terms of survivable assets and added mechanical capability and intelligence to the mix. More than impressed, I am astounded. I hope we can learn from you."

"Of course, that is as my people have hoped. Shakete has also explained your relationship to an animal on earth called the dog. Not that we compare ourselves to this simpler being, but rather, a comparison of a relationship built upon mutual benefit. We hope given experience with our race, our appearance will create a feeling of trust and not revulsion."

Dee added. "I know with absolute certainty humans can use all the productive hands they can get. You have no idea of our struggles."

"In fact, I have some idea. My clan folk are extremely unhappy with habitation on this inhospitable moon. If you will follow me, please, I would like to show you the large ship chamber."

Rappel seemed to have a little more pep in his step, Karen thought to herself. As always, Shakete was strolling right by her side. "You were right, Shakete. There is something very charming about the Mermots. Hard to put my finger on exactly why. And, I understand now, why you were elusive when speaking about them. Their appearance will add complexity to the mission of selling their presence on earth. I'm going to have to give the problem some thought."

"I knew you would see it, Karen," he replied in a matter of fact way. "I have total confidence in your ability, as you say, to sell it."

"By the way, it's elephant in the room and grows on you, not at you. If you wish to persist in using English idioms, I might as well help you out."

Shakete broke into an Ardinian laugh. It was an elongated ha, ha, ha. "I can't seem to stop. These language nuances are so interesting. It's one of the many reasons I found myself drawn to you. You use them frequently."

Karen nearly stopped in her tracks when Shakete mentioned being drawn to her. Was he flirting, Karen asked herself. At that moment, the herd of Mermots, Ardinians, and Homo sapiens reached a large window that looked out over a massive chamber. A spacecraft filled the space. "Please view our most impressive achievement," Rappel motioned.

"Notice the area is open to space. This is to allow the vessel some degree of weightlessness and, additionally, allows our crews to move the ship outside once it's completed. Without breathable atmosphere, our technicians must work fully suited. They wear gravitational boots so they don't drift outside. This is the third destroyer class ship in production. You may have seen the other two completed versions during your journey to this moon."

Mermots moved over and around the ship, industriously remaking the ship exterior at an astounding pace. Their hind legs were booted, but the foreclaws merely gloved. As they worked, it was like a maestro conducting a rehearsed and professional orchestra. Each Mermot knew their part, entering the arrangement at exactly the right time. Karen mumbled, "Who is the conductor?"

Rappel responded. "The clan leader of course. He is inside the ship on a terminal, watching progress and directing his relatives."

"Through a mind meld or something?" Karen asked.

"Yes, that would be one description. What are your questions?" Dee and Manny had a thousand. Mabel and Karen watched as Rappel answered each of them as succinctly as possible. As the scientists finally appeared to be overwhelmed with information, their queries slowed.

"We have festivities planned for this evening. A meal, storytelling, and then Mermot games. We hope you will chose to participate. Mermots love games. It is our custom to include guests."

Karen answered for the group. "We would love to. You've just hit on three things humans also enjoy!"

# 23. Earthbound

The entire human contingent sat among several Mermots and an Ardinian pilot on the bridge of a brand-spanking-new, capital destroyer spaceship heading to Earth. In the final meeting on the Mermot moon three weeks prior, everyone agreed; now was the best time to reposition completed destroyers to the human planet. Since the destroyer class ships were designed expressly to protect earth from Hunta aggression, far better the spaceships loitered around the destination planet. This craft and another like it would remain in orbit above earth and be piloted by an Ardinian and a small staff until humans could be trained to augment crews. Two destroyer class ships fully loaded with attack fighters, twelve space-to-ground shuttles, and the Ardinians' very own Delamie travelled with the armada to its destination.

"We still don't have a name for this ship," the Ardinian pilot, Jesa, mentioned to Manny. "Rappel suggested the Mermots would consider it a great honor if humans named the first capital destroyer class ship in the fleet."

Manny's eyes blazed as he answered. "I've always wanted to be aboard the Starship Enterprise. What do you think?"

Dee scowled. "Oh, come on. How uncreative is that? Give me something better."

"Yeah, well, it's a trademark from old earth culture. I think it has a nice ring to it, and it's easy to remember. What do you think, Karen? You love old science fiction."

Karen was ready to answer when the pilot's control panel blinked red, signaling another ship had been detected. Her fingers flying over a three-dimensional screen, Jesa ignored the human discussion about ship names. "Oh, my," Jesa whispered. As if talking to himself, he stated, "Scanning now to verify readings." He turned to Manny in the copilot's chair. "I am detecting two ships. I must contact the Delamie immediately."

The relaxed atmosphere on the ship's bridge took an immediate U-turn. Serious looks replaced happy human faces as they watched Jesa work.

"Delamie control, this is pilot Jesa. Have your sensors identified a threat near star system A332? My readings indicate FTL bearing in our direction. What do we do?" Ten seconds of silence elapsed on the spacecraft's bridge as heart beats surged waiting for a response from the Delamie.

"Jesa, this is the Delamie. Yes, our sensors have identified two Hunta type cruisers. They are most likely scout ships. We are conferencing now for a decision on whether to run or turn and attempt destruction of these ships."

"They will never make it to the transition point in time to stop us. The prudent course is to avoid contact with the Hunta until we are fully prepared for a battle!" Jesa replied, his skin color changing from crème to a shimmering gold.

"Jesa, we understand the options. We are weighing probabilities now. Please calm yourself and consider engaging the Conflict Artificial Intelligence. Shakete has requested an opinion from the humans. He wants to know what they think is the best course of action. Please open a channel so that they may participate in the decision process."

Manny was on his knees by the pilot's station looking at the screen. "Before we provide any advice, please answer a couple of questions. What capabilities do the Huntas possess to follow us once we enter the transition point? Also, what is the likelihood they will find the Mermot moon if we simply leave?"

"Manny, this is the Delamie. Our assessment is that once we enter the transition point, the Hunta will be unable to follow. They do not possess capacitors to travel through the points. However, once we depart in that manner, the Hunta will gain greater knowledge of earth's possible location. It may bring them to your world sooner than we hoped. The probability that we would accidentally run into Hunta in space is so unlikely, we believe they must have intelligence about the location of the Mermot facility. We do not know how that is possible."

Everyone remained quiet for a moment to contemplate this latest information. Soon the voice from the Delamie continued. "We can communicate the Huntas' proximity to the Mermot moon. To hide from Hunta sensor screens, moon-based Mermots must close the open ship bay at considerable effort. It will stop production until we can be certain they are no longer in danger."

Manny responded. "If the Huntas have good intelligence, it may not matter. They could find the Mermots and destroy the moon anyway."

"Affirmative."

Manny turned to look at Karen and Dee and saw the same resoluteness he felt, Karen nodded in agreement. Even Mabel's frightened face communicated a sense that there was only one viable choice. It was impossible to read the Mermots on the bridge. Tweet's whiskers were shivering madly, which could mean nearly anything. Manny answered for the human team. "It's a no brainer, or no processor as Shakete would say. We can't take the chance that the Huntas will destroy the Mermot production facility, much less cause the loss of thousands of Mermot lives. If the Huntas find earth too soon, we're doomed. What's the hold up? We must turn and face the Huntas."

Shakete's voice came through the communication device. "The Delamie has no weapons and cannot provide any significant battle assistance. Ardinian pilots manning the capital destroyer ships are untrained in tactical use of weapon systems, and no one is trained to fly the attack fighters aboard."

"But you mentioned a Conflict Artificial Intelligence. Is this AI knowledgeable in the art of space war? And if that's the case, won't the AI be capable of deploying weapons in a battle?"

"Affirmative to both questions, Manny."

"Again, then what's the problem?"

"The Conflict AI has been tested only in simulation. We have made many assumptions regarding Hunta capabilities and tactics. If we calculated poorly, the result might be catastrophic."

"Catastrophic how? I thought your shielding technology was impenetrable. Oh wait, let me guess, the shields haven't been tested either."

There was silence from the Delamie. Finally, "We have greater confidence in the shield; an 88.2% probability they will function as expected."

"So much for perfect knowledge by an alien species," Manny mumbled. The earth team was beginning to understand clearly why they had been approached for a partnership. The Ardinians were unable to make decisions without a conference, the Mermots couldn't fly, and neither race seemed at all willing to take a risk to win.

"Still, I don't believe we have a choice," Manny said. "If we don't destroy the Hunta ships now, the odds for our success defeating them later are greatly reduced. Not to mention yet another horrible slaughter of Mermots. Those remaining on the moon have little means to protect themselves. We must attack."

"I agree," Karen chimed in.

Shakete responded. "Affirmative, Manny. Can you provide any assistance to the pilot and the AI?"

"I've played more than my share of simulations, what we call video games. Jed, our premier scientist, is quite the competitor. And Dee is better than me on some things. How long will it take to be in range of the Huntas?"

"18.3 earth hours, if the Hunta ships continue at their present heading and speed. We do not expect they would fail to attempt our destruction. Can you become acquainted with our systems in that amount of time? The conflict AI can operate in an assisted mode."

"I've been acquainting myself with your systems since I came aboard. I have a good processor. Eighteen hours is helpful though.

Chatting time is over folks. We need to get going. Jesa, please engage the conflict AI."

"Roger, Manny."

"Minerva reporting for duty, Captain Manny," said a very feminine voice projecting her words throughout the bridge.

Karen began to laugh so loudly every member of the bridge crew turned to stare. She thrust her hands and arms up, wondering why everyone else didn't get the joke. "Minerva, get it—the goddess of wisdom and war? This has to be Shakete's doing," Karen said, trying to control more laughter,

Minerva didn't get the joke either. "Given the cumulative knowledge of this crew regarding battles of any sort, I think Minerva is quite an appropriate name."

# 24. Enterprise

"Delamie, Trisun, this is the Enterprise. Are you ready to move to your positions?" Since Manny had become the battlegroup leader, everyone agreed he had naming dibs on the ship he would pilot. The other capital spacecraft was christened quickly by the Mermots aboard. They chose Trisun instead of Trisunium, a shortened version of the name of their destroyed world. Manny couldn't believe he would lead a fleet of starships into battle, that is if two ships with weapons could be considered a fleet. In only five weeks, he had gone from a one-legged, bitter man residing in a remote outpost, perched on the side of Mount Rainier to this moment. Manny was sweating. His bravado earlier had faded into a nervous, fidgety energy.

"Minerva, systems check?"

"All systems are go, as they were an hour ago when you last inquired."

"Dee, how is it within the realm of possibility that an untested AI named Minerva could have already learned sarcasm?" Manny asked.

"Don't know and don't care. I'm still trying to wrap my arms around my new official position as ship weapons coordinator. Talk about the blind leading the blind. I'm nervous as shit, Manny."

"No need for nervousness. You did far better than the Ardinians and the Mermots in weapons simulations. As it turns out, the long, dark nights we spent at the Rainier Station playing Warship was a fruitful endeavor. It must have been karma on a cosmic scale. Besides, you have a sarcastic AI right by your side."

"Yes, better at simulations, but good enough in real life, who knows? I always believed I was destined for greater things and wanted more responsibility. I just wish there could have been some interim steps before being thrust into the role of savior of many lives."

"Get serious now, Dee. Are you ready to go?"

"Affirmative."

Manny was quiet and checked one last time at their position relative to the Hunta ships. He gave the thumbs up to Karen who was strapped into a seat next to Rappel to the rear of the deck. Ship seats were specially designed with a hole at the back bottom, just the correct size for a Mermot tail. Mabel had left the bridge to assist in the medical bay in the event of injuries

"Delamie, Trisun, go on my mark. Now." Manny ordered.

The two destroyer ships increased speed. Even with gravity assist, Manny strained to keep his focus as G-forces placed pressure on his skeletal mass. The Delamie headed away from the immediate battle area to their position in reserve to collect survivor pods. If the battle went bad, the Delamie would pick up any survivors and make a run for it to warn the moon-locked Mermots. The Enterprise and Trisun travelled at maximum speed to pass over and under two Hunta ships.

"I see missiles inbound. They're targeting Trisun. We're about to see if our shields are as good as advertised. Target Hunta Ship One with rail guns as we pass and then missiles at their stern once we complete the pass," Manny directed.

Minerva cautioned Manny. "Normal procedure would be to respond by targeting missiles first at greater range."

"I hear you, Minerva. Before we waste missiles, I want to get a sense of their capabilities."

Minerva made a huffing sound and then continued. "Trisun's shields are holding without degradation. The shield's matter reorganizing properties is leaving a residual particulate around the Trisun. I believe, in earth's language, the particles are best explained as a dust cloud. The cloud is growing denser with every missile. Targeting Hunta Ship One with rail guns, now."

Firing several pound slugs of heavy metal at a rate of over 100 rounds per second, rail guns bombarded Hunta defenses. The Hunta shield glowed a bright white as rounds struck attempting to penetrate the barrier.

Dee watched her view screen as they passed over Hunta One. The dark, menacing Hunta spaceship was covered with external features. It was nearly impossible to determine what protrusions were important to target. Minerva must have sensed Dee's struggle. A diagram of a Hunta Ship with arrows and names popped up in the corner of Dee's screen. "Oh, that helps. Thanks, Minerva. Also, please advise of Hunta shield viability at regular intervals. And, if possible, can you advise as to the Hunta shield technology?"

"Yes, Dee. Hunta shields were degraded by only 5% from the rail gun barrage. My sensor readings indicate the Hunta shield is not of a compartmentalized structure. In other words, there are not areas which will fail separately. Specific targeting is not advisable. Destructive mass over a short duration is the most advantageous approach. I have no data as to the exact scientific nature of the shield construct."

"Turning in 85 seconds. Please be prepared for additional G-Forces into the turn. In English, hold on!" Manny, advised.

Rappel grabbed Karen's arm as they were turning. She studied his pointed face and thought Rappel might be on the verge of puking. His hand was so strong Karen nudged his fingers and grimaced, trying to let him know he was hurting her. Rappel loosened his grip, but he didn't let go.

Minerva's calm voice filled the space. "Reaching optimal position for missile launch in 20 seconds."

"Fire at will when you reach that location," Dee responded.

"Missiles aloft."

Everyone quit breathing as they waited for the missile impact on Hunta One. Seconds passed. "I'm not sure what happened," Dee nearly shouted. "I have no missile readings. And, the Hunta vessel didn't respond with counter measures to eliminate missiles. Minerva, were the missiles fired?" Dee asked in a panic.

"We have a problem," Minerva announced in a reposeful manner. "Our shield is operating so efficiently, it also neutralized our outbound missiles. You will notice the dust cloud gathering around the Enterprise. That debris represents what is left of the

22 missiles we just launched. Please stand by while I recalibrate."

Manny breathed slowly to calm his pounding heart. "Trisun, this is the Enterprise. Please give status update."

There was a pause waiting for the message to reach Trisun and for the Enterprise to receive the ship's response. Space distances caused message delays, even during close fights like the one ongoing now. After twenty seconds, Trisun responded, "Shields are holding, but I am rapidly losing visibility from collected space dust. I have switched to sensor mode which is still operational."

"Sweep around to port of Hunta Two and hit them with laser cannons and rail fire," Manny ordered. "Minerva is recalibrating shields now. The matter reorganizing shield decimated our outbound missiles. Will advise when recalibration is complete. Until then, don't waste your missiles."

Another time delay occurred and then Trisun responded, "Roger, Enterprise. Beginning sweep now."

Dee yelled out. "Hunta One and Two are deploying laser cannons at Trisun. The cannons are having no effect on Trisun shields, but there's a shit storm of dust. Hunta Two shields at 60%; the lasers are working on Hunta shields. Minerva, target Hunta Two with more laser cannons."

"Roger, Dee. Deploying now. Hunta Two shield is down to 35% and holding. Lasers will not be enough."

Manny's frustration was building. "Minerva, how goes those calibration efforts? We need those missiles, sooner rather than later."

242

"Calibration will require 4 hours, 52 minutes and 32 seconds from my mark, now."

"Shit. What are my other options, Minerva? What we have right now is a no win, stand-off."

"Actually, that is an incorrect assumption. At the current rate of particulate collection, as Dee said, a building shit storm, our visual acuity will be zero in two minutes and sensor capability will follow within ten minutes."

"How do we get rid of the dust, Minerva?" Manny pleaded. "I'm looking for options, not just information!"

"I am pleased you requested my higher processor functions. The only way to rid shields of collected matter is to inactivate them. Unfortunately, dropping shields will also make our vessel vulnerable to Hunta rail guns and missiles."

Jesa, who sat at the co-pilot seat, chimed in, "Hunta One turning and increasing speed, heading toward Delamie."

Dee anxiously disclosed, "Hunta Two is throwing everything they have at Trisun. If I had to guess, I'd say they want to blind us."

"Minerva, your best guess on Hunta strategy, please," Manny asked.

"I believe Dee is correct. They have deduced our technical issue. Hunta One intends to create dust around the Delamie. Once we are all blinded, the Huntas can simply wait until we drop our shields and then destroy us or continue to the Mermot moon unfettered. Neither is a satisfactory conclusion to this skirmish."

"Minerva, are we faster than the Hunta ships?" Manny asked.

"Yes, Manny. By my calculations, our ship can obtain 22.62% more acceleration."

"Set course to run at full speed from Hunta One, Minerva."

"If I may inquire, Manny, what would be the purpose of running now?

"They'll chase us thinking they have the advantage, correct?"

"I would assume so. Huntas will always press the advantage."

"Minerva, I need enough distance from the Hunta ship to drop shields and destroy them before we're completely blind. If I want to launch missiles, how long will our shields be down.?

"Only three seconds for the missiles to pass and another 180 seconds to regenerate the shield."

"Three minutes and three seconds of vulnerability. That's more than I'd like. Minerva, please advise concerning two items. First, our accuracy at counter measures to defend against inbound missiles and secondly, the ship's hull specifications and its ability to withstand direct hits without the shield. In total, your assessment of our survivability if we drop our shields."

"Manny, that would be very bad indeed. This ship was built on the premise that our shield was impenetrable. I believe that has born itself out in this conflict. The hull is not significantly reinforced. We can close sections of the ship to compartmentalize losses, but if our propulsion system is lost, so are our shields. We will not survive without shields. The effectiveness of missile counter measures is dependent on the number of launches and the distance of the enemy. At closer range, the probability of total protection is less than 5%."

"We are going to have an extended talk about ship redundancy upon our return. Until then, I have the beginnings of a plan. Dee, Trisun still has their full missile compliment, is that correct?" asked Manny.

"Yep, Trisun never had a chance to use their missiles. If you're thinking what I'm thinking, we only have six minutes before Trisun is completely blinded."

"One last question, Minerva. Can we fire missiles at full speed?"

"Affirmative, Manny."

"At last, one bit of good news. Trisun, this is Enterprise. Be prepared to engage engines at full, heading at 360887 on my command." Manny described his run and gun tactic. The success of his plan would be highly dependent upon perfect timing, good shooting, and Hunta confusion over their unconventional strategy. That last part, keeping the Hunta guessing, shouldn't be too difficult since thus far, nothing had gone as planned. Decisions on what to do next had been seat of the pants, gut instincts for Manny and his crew. Ironically, Manny thought, his lack of experience and absence of any real training made his actions less predictable.

After speaking with the Delamie and sharing the newest strategy, Shakete was unconvinced of the wisdom of such a risky approach. Defense was the first fallback of Ardinians. Everything about the design of this supposed battleship reeked of minds trying to protect themselves rather than engage and destroy an enemy. Manny ended the conversation with the Ardinian mothership by saying, "You put me in charge, and we don't have time to argue. I will implement this plan now. Enterprise out." As he gave the next order, Manny wondered if on multiple levels, this battle might be his first and last. "Trisun, engage."

Manny glanced at Dee. She was hunched over the weapons display peering intently at the screen. "Not as easy as the Ardinians made it sound, is it?" Manny asked.

"You think?" Dee spat back without looking up.

Minerva spoke, "I will automatically drop shields when we reach optimal distance from Hunta One. As you can see, the particulate build-up is trapped in our shield and will surround the ship until the shield is dropped. Trisun will likewise drop shields to fire missiles when the distance from their pursuer is at the greatest advantage. The missile launch will occur almost simultaneously. Thus far, it appears the Huntas are responding as expected. I must remind you, we will be viewing the outcome of Trisun's actions in the past. In other words, since they will be further away, the light we see will have occurred seconds before. I cannot be certain of outcomes or Hunta responses as they occur."

Manny knew enough about science and the speed of light to understand Minerva's comment concerning viewing events in the past. Rubbing his hands over his face, Manny felt a slight tremble in his fingers. *Real space battles, real lives in jeopardy, this isn't any video game.*

The bridge of the Enterprise was quiet and subdued as they waited. Dee was wishing right now that she had passed on Jed's offer to accompany the space team. In the beginning, to be in the first group of humans to travel through space was quite exciting. She never anticipated a real space battle. Her excitement had been replaced quickly with a sinking feeling of dread. Dee tried to breathe slowly to control the fear. Fear that their ship could be blown to bits by a thermonuclear missile, her lifeless body or what was left of it, hurtling into space for an eternity.

Karen's thoughts were only of her family. She had been with Mike for so long. How would he survive without her? And her precious daughter, Amelia. What would become of her if Karen wasn't around to protect her? And her granddaughter, Chrystel and her dogs—what about them? They all needed her. Karen consoled herself by remembering one simple fact, far better that I'm lost then they are lost to me. They will be fine. She was startled out of her reverie by Minerva.

"Shields dropped. Seventy-two missiles launched at Hunta One. Hunta One has responded with forty-eight return missiles. 175 seconds to shield redeployment," Minerva reminded the bridge.

"Trisun status?" Manny asked.

"Thirty seconds to Trisun shield drop. 167 seconds to Enterprise shield redeployment"

Dee directed, "Minerva, begin deploying missile counter measures as soon as Hunta missiles are in range."

"Yes, Dee, I know. Please be prepared to interpret battle damage tallies for the pilot and crew. Trisun shield dropped and missiles away. 137 seconds to Enterprise shield redeployment."

Jesa had been deathly still and glowing gold most of the battle. As if paralyzed, he sat at his copilot location and spoke for the first time. "I understand now. A defense is important, even essential. But without an effective offense in battle, you may still die. Defense alone cannot win!"

Before anyone could respond to his random comment, Minerva was updating status. "Countermeasures deployed. 62 seconds to Enterprise shield redeployment. Hunta One deploying missile counter measures."

In torment, Rappel moaned into everyone's mind as he waited for this to all be over.

"18 Hunta missiles destroyed, 30 remaining. 20 Enterprise missiles destroyed, 52 remaining. 40 seconds to Enterprise shield redeployment. 85 seconds to Trisun shield redeployment.

Dee wanted to pull her hair out. This was like a slow-motion moving train barreling down the tracks, and she was tied to the tracks. The seconds crept forward. There was nothing to do but wait and keep her fists and toes clenched in anticipation.

"43 Hunta missiles destroyed, 5 remaining. 58 Enterprise missiles destroyed, 14 remaining. 15 seconds to shield redeployment. 44 Hunta missiles destroyed, 45, 47—2 seconds to shield redeployment." They felt one missile strike as the ship lurched. Sparks flew from Manny's pilot station, and the forward video screen went dark.

"Damage report!" Manny yelled.

"One missile strike. It hit the life support section, and I sealed that compartment. The missile damaged food stocks and water recyclers. All critical systems are up, and shields have deployed!" said an excited Minerva.

Manny asked, "Status of Hunta One?"

"Three missiles hit Hunta One, and their shields are down. Their propulsion systems are still operational. Moving closer to the target. I'll deploy all laser cannons and rail guns once we are within range. "Dee," Minerva said. "Your targeting assistance now would be most appreciated."

"Trisun status, Minerva?" Manny inquired.

"Trisun reporting three missiles strikes and significantly more damage. They have limited propulsion. The pursuing Hunta Two ship was also hit. It is drifting without power, but not completely destroyed."

"We'll have to turn back and help them out once we finish with Hunta One," Manny responded.

Now that Hunta One's shields were down, Dee and Minerva directed fire at critical systems and weapons ports. A huge explosion in the aft end of the ship started a chain reaction until the entire vessel became a fire ball, exploding in cascading flames.

The deck of the Enterprise erupted in cheers as did the Ardinians watching on view screens from the Delamie. The Ardinian cheers were technically loud, enthusiastic hoots, but the effect was the same.

"Minerva, take me back to Trisun and let's clean up this mess," a relieved Manny commanded.

"Gladly, Manny."

## 25. Hunta

They sipped warm drinks in the meeting room on board the Delamie. Shakete and Maleta represented the Ardinians while Manny, Dee, and Karen sat in as the human contingent. Only Tweet attended for the Mermots. Her father Rappel, still sick as a dog after the space battle, was resting in the sickbay. After the Enterprise swooped in to aid Trisun with the other Hunta vessel, Shakete sent an urgent message to Manny asking him to delay destruction of the Hunta ship. Shakete wanted an opportunity to convince the Huntas to surrender. He needed to understand why the Hunta were in this sector of space. If given a chance to interrogate Hunta survivors, Shakete hoped to learn whether the Hunta knew of the Mermot moon.

Worn faces waited for Shakete to start. Spent, Manny rubbed his eyes. The emotions of battle were much like those of a professional sports team during the final game of a tournament, except; the adrenaline high went stratospherically higher when your life was on the line. From anxious nervousness to focused determination to controlled panic and back again, Manny had never felt anything that even closely approximated the time he spent commanding the fleet. Even the moment of joy when he realized they had vanquished the evil Hunta threat thrust a heart-pounding, mega-rush of sensation through his system. Now, bone tired, he still wanted or needed to relive the battle.

Manny once asked Thomas what it was like when he fought in the Army during the pre-change world. Like many young men and women who wanted to test their mettle, Manny couldn't contain his curiosity. He had no idea when asking how deep the question plunged into Thomas' very being.

Thomas thought before answering, his eyes wandering. "Like nothing else on earth. Now, some people write about the pain and the grief, the fear, and there's plenty of that, especially when you lose your brothers and sisters. But there's another side that warriors don't like to tell. Best description I can think of is that at times, the heat of battle is an adrenaline surge like no drug can replicate. It can become an intensity addiction. Just like a drug, you against the bad guy, your life on the line. I think that's why some fellows turn to a life of crime. Danger as an addiction. Nothing else like that high for sure."

"But how do you do it?" Manny asked. "How do you get good at handling the pressure?"

"Some people never do. They short circuit like a power surge the wiring can't handle. For those of us that figure it out, I guess it's training, experience, the ability to hold the reigns on fear to act, and some undefined quality that's simply who we are from birth. Manny, an interesting fact; studies after the wars in Iraq and Afghanistan showed that folks who completed multiple wartime deployments were less likely to suffer PTSD symptoms than the guys and gals who had completed only one. Probably a chicken and the egg thing. Those who could were selected to do it again. What makes a good warrior is likely some combination of training, experience, inherent ability, intensity addiction, loyalty to comrades, a true belief in your purpose, or even the cycle of the moon. I believe the mix is different for each person and every situation. No one can say with certainty. Anyone that says they know for sure would be lying. You have to find your own place, where who you are and what you believe, drives your actions."

Manny wanted to be truly good at something. He loved science, but the experience today as a starship captain felt like a thirsty man taking his first cool drink. As he was contemplating how he could continue in this role, Shakete began to speak. "I thought it instructive to share my conversation with the Hunta Captain. It will provide some context for our dealings with them in the future." Shakete waved his hand to activate a video display covering one sun emitting wall.

While the video was on pause waiting for Shakete to begin the recording, a still picture of the Hunta Captain filled the screen. He appeared to be leaning into the room, as if a slender restraint was the only thing preventing this glowering monster from stepping into the meeting area and killing them all. Karen thought Shakete might have allowed the captain's hideous countenance to remain a beat longer than necessary to allow the full impact of their enemy. If that was his intent, Shakete had succeeded magnificently in terrifying the crowd. Dee winced at the sight of the Hunta, and Tweet's whiskers trembled on her pointed snout.

The Hunta creature did not appear in any way physically like his Ardinian cousins, other than large, round eyes. His neck and body, seemingly

252

made of granite, were broad and muscled. The smooth perfect skin of Ardinians was replaced by a gray, nearly scaly texture. His face was larger, or at least looked that way. Instead of blonde hair like the Ardinians, the Hunta's forehead was ridged, growing to a horny growth at the top of his head. The most disconcerting feature of an overall repulsive continence was the color of his eyes. Bright yellow iris streaked with red veins bulged from plump eyeballs.

Karen sighed, "Not a pretty picture. Are you sure you're related to this race, Shakete?"

"Yes, in fact, I believe this Hunta specimen is a far distant grandnephew. They look more like original Ardinians than I do. It was my branch of the family over the millennia that enhanced our bodies to a more satisfying and survivable platform. It is not, however, their appearance that should concern you. Please listen to his words." Shakete waved his hand again to begin the recording of their conversation.

They were speaking in a different language. Hoots and clicks were punctuated by raspy, harsh word sounds. An English language translation appeared at the bottom of the viewing screen.

"So, it is you, Uncle. Shakete, the great betrayer and coward of my ancestors. The one who felt himself a god and left my family for dead on the planet of Marta. How dare you look upon my eyes. Does your guilt not haunt you?"

"That's ancient history, my nephew. And even if you cannot believe me, I did not leave your family for dead. I begged them to make the journey with me. Be that as it may, you have a choice. Your ship is critically disabled. I am willing to give you refuge if you come peacefully and share all information on Hunta plans."

The Captain spit at the screen. "I am not like you, Uncle. I would never betray my people. But our plan is very simple. I will share it with you. We will hunt you and your kind to the end of the universe and destroy you. Our suffering is your suffering. You will be made to share every degradation of your cousins. And then, we will take everything that is rightfully ours."

"Nephew, there is no need to take. I can give you and my cousins a new life. Why must you destroy everything you touch? What do you gain? Bury your hate and bring prosperity to your people, finally."

"We have prosperity and power. We also have courage, unlike you Shakete and your vermin associates. We will never be duped into allowing you an advantage. You are a false god and deserve a place in the oceans of fire."

"We will destroy your ship and everyone aboard if you do not comply," Shakete sadly responded.

"More threats from a false prophet. Do you have the courage, Uncle, to perform the honorable death? Have you regrown male reproduction sacks? Or will you run and leave us to die as you have in the past?"

"One last chance, Captain. Help yourself and your people."

"Never!" the Captain spit another wet loogie as the screen went blank. The sound of Shakete's voice continued in the background recording.

"Manny," Shakete said quietly. "We have no option but to destroy this vessel. If they can make repairs, the Hunta will begin again on their mission. We do not possess the military capability to take and hold their ship. Without a professional boarding force, I have no choice but to recommend their death."

"Roger, Shakete. I agree. This is another example of how good intentions, like not wishing to force acquiesce, can tie your hands."

"Manny, if you please, my mental state is not conducive to another human lecture."

"Understand, Shakete. Enterprise will comply."

The meeting room was quiet as the attendees absorbed the Hunta message and their own actions in the aftermath. Karen glanced at Shakete during the recording. He seemed to shrink in on himself from the Captain's curses and accusations. She wondered what had happened between him and his ancestors. Shakete had left out the part that he was there and a decision maker when the rift between the Ardinians occurred. *Good grief, how old is Shakete?!* As with most arguments, the truth probably lay somewhere between Shakete's account and that of the Huntas. It didn't matter now. The Huntas were aggressive and would take without mercy whatever the Ardinians touched. Shakete was right about that much. Still, why had Shakete touched the earth? Were humans only a means to an end for Shakete and the Ardinians? Karen's gut told her no, but her head was screaming, "Be wary."

Manny started speaking. "We can talk about the technical failures that occurred during our skirmish later. The AI informed me shield recalibration is complete. Outbound missiles will pass through the field. As soon as I return to Enterprise, we will conduct a test. Minerva is also studying the dust collection problem to attempt a mitigating procedure that does not include dropping our shields. My immediate concerns are twofold: how to facilitate Trisun repairs and actions necessary to protect the Mermot moon if more Huntas return."

Maleta answered, "We are investigating to determine how the Huntas found us. The probability that we accidentally came upon them is infinitesimally small. The Huntas have no means to communicate across space. Hunta leadership will wait until they are sure their first scout team will not return and then send another. It will be months before other Hunta ships reach the moon. The Trisun still has limited propulsion. I recommend we send it back to the Mermot moon for repair. After it is fully operational, Trisun can remain to protect the moon."

"So many assumptions. How do you know the Huntas cannot communicate across space? Can you be sure the Huntas' main body isn't near? And more importantly, if they had a means to determine where the moon is located, how do you know they can't use the same method or intelligence to find earth!" Dee blurted.

Maleta began to glow. "Shakete?"

"Dee, as you say, this is not our first festival."

"Rodeo," Karen added. "You say, not our first rodeo."

"Ah, yes, that's it. As I was saying, the Huntas have been chasing us since before your species became an item on earth. We have come upon them, or they upon us, many times. At first, we escaped by running to the nearest transition point. During one of my early visits to earth, I learned of a human named Sun Tzu and the book, *The Art of War*. My curiosity was aroused, and I began a study of his concepts. Sun Tzu's genius made me aware of the absolute need to know more about our enemy, the Hunta. We began a game of cat and mouse. We sought out contact with them and then hid to study their reaction and techniques. As Sun Tzu famously said, 'Rouse him and learn the principle of his activity or inactivity. Force him to reveal himself, so as to find out his vulnerable spots.' We know more about the Huntas than it would seem from our first conflict. And this battle helped us to know more."

Karen stifled a laugh. "I'm not sure I'm comforted to know you have been studying Sun Tzu, Shakete. There are too many implications to name. So, why didn't you know of the particulate build-up on the shields? And it appears you're clueless how the Huntas gained knowledge of the Mermot facility."

"I said we know more than it might appear. I did not state I was all knowing. I am pleased with the outcome and the insights revealed from our first weaponized, Hunta encounter. But, we have much more to accomplish. To learn. The Delamie and the Enterprise should continue to earth as planned as quickly as possible. The Mermots are resilient, and the protection provided by the Trisun will ensure their survival."

Again, Karen was left with the feeling that Shakete had plans, within strategies, within plans. How does a mere mortal human, even one nearing her 200th birthday, compete with an android assisted alien that was older by far than she could even imagine? She had to go with what she felt because there was no way to outthink him. Even though Karen sensed Shakete left out more than he shared, something deep inside said this alien was worthy of her trust. If only she could determine why.

"I agree, Shakete. We have a lot to do, and it's clear you need us as much as we need you. If there is nothing else, I would like to take a well-deserved nap. After all, I am only an old, biological earth woman."

## 26. Schoolhouse

There seemed no way to exit this maddening closet of a room. Chrystel fumed as two jailers entered, one to change the waste bucket and bring food and one armed, pointing his weapon at her face. The door was never left open for any longer than necessary to enter or exit. A third guard stood watch outside their cage, locking it from the outside when the other guards were inside.

Chrystel's plan to use Tilley's tranquilizing bellow to escape never materialized. They took Tilley away three days ago to place her in an outdoor cage. Chrystel's stomach heaved as she watched helplessly while the guards tied Tilley with chains and encased her head in a fabricated metal muzzle.

Her mental state deteriorating rapidly, Letitia was no help. She rarely talked other than to mumble incoherently to herself. Chrystel had begged Letitia to stand up and move around, which only served to agitate Letitia further until she began to weep. Chrystel's first impulse, panic, was closely followed by an uncharitable urge to shake Letitia until she stopped crying. Instead, Chrystel pleaded, "Please stop crying, Letitia. It isn't a productive use of your energy." To which, Letitia became both petulant and weepy.

Vaguely aware that her response to Letitia's fear was as unproductive as Letitia's wails, Chrystel resolved to be more patient. Letitia's reaction to adversity opened the wound of her mother's wholly over-the-top, emotional outpourings. Each time

Chrystel had tried to convince Amelia to leave the house, even for a minute, her mother would shake and moan. If Chrystel persisted, tears and tantrums followed. It was all too pathetic and destressing to deal with, so instead, she walked away. Chrystel dealt with Letitia in much the same way, ignoring Letitia's emotions when they reached a crescendo. Dysfunctional? Absolutely, Chrystel silently acknowledged.

Chrystel heard a clink, the signal the lock on the door was opening. Someone was coming. She readied herself in case this time they made a mistake. Red and another armed guard stepped inside the cramped room. Waving his hand in front of his face, Red winced. "Whew, you ladies are ripe. If you're good girls, I'll try to get you out for a shower. Depends on how you behave, and I'm speaking to you Chrystel. Move over to that corner and put your face in the crack," Red pointed.

Glaring at Red for a moment, Chrystel did as asked. He came from behind, grabbed her hands and locked handcuffs into place. "No zip ties for you, young lady. Now, stay still while I secure your feet. If you move, my buddy over there has a club." Red bent, roughly shoved Chrystel's legs closer together, and placed shackles around her ankles. "We found these at a decrepit jail. Knew they would come in handy. Those legs of yours are weapons. Can't be too careful, can we? Now move."

"Why are you doing this?" Chrystel asked as she turned. "What do you hope to accomplish? Talk to me, Red. I'm sure we can work something out."

He smiled. "Yes, indeed we can. Good to know you're in a cooperative mood. Now move!"

Red nudged Chrystel along through the gym with a bony elbow. Six people sitting around tables covered with communications equipment stared at Chrystel as if she was the monster. Led down one hallway and then another, she inconspicuously watched for other doors and escape routes during the short walk. She took tiny steps pretending the ankle chains were more of a hindrance than they were.

"Sit," Red pointed. Two chairs on either side of a metal desk that nearly filled the small room. "What we have here is a proof of life situation. Your grandad is on the line. Don't get any ideas about telling him anything he doesn't already know. I have my trusty Glock by my side." Red patted the holster slung under his left arm.

Red engaged the microphone. "She's here." He held the mic in his hand and reached across to place it under Chrystel's chin.

"Chrystel are you okay? Did they hurt you?" Mike's concerned voice bleated.

"I'm fine, Grandpa. Letitia and Tilley are here too. Letitia is physically all right."

"Did they hurt you?" he asked again.

Chrystel had not taken her eyes from Red's. She refused to break his gaze.

"No, Grandpa, I'm fine. Really. Letitia is having a breakdown, and Tilley was carted off somewhere outside the school, so I can't be sure of her condition."

Shaking his head, Red withdrew the mic as Mike continued to talk. "Don't worry, Chrystel. We'll get you out of there!"

"I will contact you again, soon," Red said tersely and placed the microphone back in the holder. Maintaining the staring contest with Chrystel, he stood and like a shot, backhanded her across her face. Her head whipped back at the impact. "I told you to keep your mouth shut."

The humiliation was worse than the slap, but still, Chrystel kept her gaze on Red. There was something about him. Something familiar. Something in his eyes and how he tilted his head slightly when he talked. He reminded her of someone, but who? *He reminds me of Carlton. Not the way he looks, but the way he moves and his speech cadence.*

Red signaled to the guard in the hall. "Take her back to the cell."

"Wait! Can you just show me that Tilley's in no danger? Please, I'll cooperate. She's important to me."

"She's fine," Red said dismissively.

"Please. What I can offer you is my help with Thomas. He won't swallow any exchange without making a play. I've worked with him my whole life, I guarantee it. I know how to deal with him to ensure no one gets hurt." Chrystel could hear Mike on the radio, urgently asking if anyone was still there.

Red assessed Chrystel. "Maybe. . . Oh, what the hell. Jerry, walk her by the purple creature's cage before you put her back. And Chrystel, it's dangerous to make promises to me you don't keep."

"I believe you, Red." She bobbed her head in understanding.

Chrystel and the guard turned left outside the small room taking a different route through the silent halls to a cafeteria style kitchen. More of Red's people were working, preparing the next meal. *Perfect*, Chrystel thought. As she was rounding a stainless-steel, food preparation table, Chrystel fell and rolled out of the guard's sight, sliding under the cover of the metal surface.

"Don't even think of trying to trip me," the guard yelled. He bent hastily on one knee, pointing his weapon at a prone Chrystel. "Now, get up slowly and march. If you try anything else, we'll turn around and go back to your cage."

"Sorry, I tripped. These shackles aren't easy. I want to see Tilley. I'll be good, I promise," she said, smiling sincerely.

Scowling, the guard gestured for Chrystel to move through a set of doors at the back of the kitchen. Old style freezers flanked a hall on one side, with humming refrigerators on the other. Straight ahead, the sun was shining through windows of an exterior exit.

Chrystel waited while the guard drew the exterior door open, revealing a loading ramp. As her escort followed Chrystel to the outside, she hit him with a roundhouse swing to the side of his head using her cuffed hands as a club. Surprised, he shook his head once. Before the guard could respond, she hit him again, this time with a powerful swing up and under his jaw.

The guard's teeth clacked together in a porcelain crunch. Grunting, Chrystel hurled the full weight of her body to land a punishing blow to the bridge of the guard's nose. Clearly disoriented, he was still struggling to remain standing. Leaping into the air, Chrystel pounded the top of his head with the heels of her clasped hands, using downward inertia to increase force. The guard wobbled and fell to the ground.

"That should do it," Chrystel whispered to herself. Before searching the guard for keys to unlock her restrains, she surveyed the surrounding area to ensure no one was coming.

Grandma Karen had once mentioned that being short in a pre-change world presented any number of difficulties. Key among them was a one-size-fits-all mentality. Grandma's belief held that the single benefit to being vertically challenged was leg room on airplane flights. Chrystel realized immediately the handcuffs used by Red were loose, probably made to fit larger men. She had tested the slack in the cuffs while trying to talk to Mike. When Chrystel fell in the cafeteria kitchen under the table, out of view for just a moment, she quickly pulled her hands down under her butt and legs, and then drew her feet through her cuffed hands. It hurt, but it worked. Her Houdini-like move allowed Chrystel's hands to be in front of her body where she needed them. Good thing the guard wasn't an observant soul.

*Speaking of the guard*, Chrystel felt for a pulse. She found the restraint keys and freed herself. Pulling an M4 off the guard's shoulder, Chrystel released the magazine to check for rounds. *A full load, yeah!* Chrystel hit Jerry again with the butt of the weapon. It wouldn't be a good thing if he regained consciousness anytime soon. *I hope he lives, but if he doesn't, he has only himself to blame.*

Chrystel needed to free Letitia. Tilley was her only hope to make that happen. Jumping off the side of the dock, Chrystel followed the edge of the building scanning the school exterior for cages. She had picked the right direction. Several filled, wire enclosures lined the edge of a square, cinderblock out building.

Chrystel dashed the fifty yards across a pitted road and hid her profile between two caged dogs. The captive animals were making a racket like a troop of racoons had attempted a theft of their dinner. "Tilley, if you're here, please make them stop!" Chrystel waited. Silence. "She's here," Chrystel smiled.

She slid in front of the cages to the largest of them. Tilley grinned at her. Next to Tilley in another cage, Candy, Geronimo's dog, was wagging her tail and doing a happy dance. "Well, there you are. You're coming with, too. Geronimo will owe me a thousand favors."

Calmly whispering to the animals as she searched for keys, Chrystel realized some moron had left a key suspended by paperclip at the top center of each cage. "Why bother?" she asked a grinning purple monster.

"Tilley, if any of these animals will help, point them out. I don't want them if they are loyal to someone at the school." Chrystel couldn't understand why the dogs were caged. In the enclave, they stayed with people. Perhaps they were captured New Washington dogs like Candy. Red and his crew might have been concerned the dogs would leak information to clavers about their location. At this very moment, Chrystel wished with all her heart she could hear dogs and question them.

Tilley jumped out of her captivity and mewled, rubbing her gigantic head on Chrystel's thigh. "We'll have time for hellos later, and I love you too." Chrystel said. Tilley nodded and trotted to three other cages, pointing her nose at the cage to demonstrate which dogs to take.

Earlier, Chrystel counted at least twenty people at the school, spread through the classrooms and facilities. There were most likely more. Thomas was right when he said a plan was only as good as the first shot. After that, Murphy's Law and improvisation reigned king.

Armed with an M4 and a fully loaded 30-round clip, an alien anomaly, and 4 working dogs, Chrystel's mind was madly churning for a tactical advantage. If not for Letitia, the dust wouldn't have had a chance to settle as she and her companions slipped into the forest beyond. Chrystel couldn't leave Letitia to her own devices; her mental toolbox appeared to be missing a few screws. She had to take Letitia along.

Tilley stared at Chrystel after she explained her best plan and told Tilley to pass it to the other dogs. "Hey," Chrystel smirked noticing Tilley's confused expression, "It's the best I got. I got you out, didn't I?"

On Chrystel's go command, they charged across the cracked pavement to the school. Chrystel traced her earlier movements, hugging the exterior wall to the loading dock. To prevent any school folk outside from causing trouble, two dogs split from the group and headed in a different direction.

Tilley burst through the cafeteria exit in the lead, moved swiftly to the kitchen, and screamed. From this point, Chrystel guessed they had only four or five minutes of unconsciousness to get through the kitchen, down the halls to the gym, release Letitia, and skedaddle.

Chrystel, Candy, and one other dog paused outside on the dock, waiting for Tilley's scream to do its work. Holding her hands tightly over fabric-stuffed ears, she counted to five. The missing bottom half of her shirt exposed a bare midriff. Tilley's canines were used to create ear protection, a testament to the utility of teeth in multiple tasks beyond chewing. Unhappy that a piece of cotton was still lodged behind one tooth, Tilley was willing to overlook the discomfort to protect her charge.

Not one kitchen worker was left standing after Tilley's scream. Chrystel, Candy, and another faithful mutt ran through the scullery. Tilley, already moving, scrambled around a corner sliding on kitchen linoleum flooring and into the hallway headed to the gym. So far so good, Chrystel thought, as she breathed through the sprint following Tilley. A pink tail standing fully aloft, and unfurled donkey ears were visible as Tilley screeched to a halt. Leaning against a corner, she peeked around to check for more people. This was the point where Chrystel's directions to Tilley ended. It was Chrystel's turn to lead. Tilley waved her tail left and then right, the agreed upon signal for all clear.

Chrystel sprinted past Tilley. They pounded past an empty classroom, around one more turn, and straight ahead to the gymnasium entry. Their luck was holding. The wide gym doors were shut. A chrome bar mechanism made an awful metallic thunk as Chrystel pushed against it, held the door a crack, and waved Tilley through. She allowed the weight of the door to pull it shut and crouched to cover her ears. Chrystel completed another five-count hoping Tilley's scream did not reach Letitia.

At five, Chrystel pushed the opening bar with her shoulder and barreled into the gym. The only living creature left standing was Chrystel's trusty sidekick, Tilley, her canines glistening in a beautiful smile. Chrystel didn't stop to admire Tilley's work. As she ran by comatose radio operators, she yanked headphones off a man slumped on a table and grabbed another set hanging over an unmanned short wave. With four long strides, Chrystel came to a halt at the threshold to the schoolhouse jail. She used her rifle again, savagely thrusting the butt against a second-market hasp that secured the door. Two quick hits and the frame side gave way.

Huddled in a corner, Letitia was alert but looked on the edge of reason. Her eyes darted to Chrystel and around the room, as she tried to make sense of the abrupt intrusion. Chrystel shouted, "Get up now and come with us. I'll give you three seconds to make a decision, or we're leaving without you."

Letitia blinked several times and then jumped to her feet. Chrystel hadn't really planned to leave Letitia, but her time locked up with the council chairwoman convinced Chrystel that shocking the poor woman into obedient action was the best first approach. It worked. Shoving one of the headphones into Letitia's hands, Chrystel directed, "Put it on and stay behind me."

Tilley and two other dogs were standing guard at the gymnasium door, energetically pacing and waiting for a command to move. Chrystel crossed the gym with Letitia at her heels and looked out into the school foyer. Light from a sunny day lit the atrium style area. It was clear to the exit. Waving for the crew to follow, Chrystel blasted through the gym doors, attempting one last mad dash out of the school.

"What the hell?!" a female voice shouted from an adjacent hallway. Chrystel barely slowed. She glanced toward the voice and saw Red and a woman jogging in her direction. Raising his hand gun, Red looked straight into her eyes. In Chrystel's mind, time took a hiatus. Everything slowed. One of the mutts, sensing an intruder, had already darted down the hallway of its own accord. As Red was readying a two-handed stance, the brave dog went from a flat, charging blur to sailing in the air, front legs extended and ready. The dog reached maximum velocity at the point of impact with Red, and at the same moment, Red pulled the trigger.

Of all the rotten timing, Letitia chose that very instant to be courageous. She threw herself at Chrystel to push her to the ground. As they were falling together in a macabre dance, Chrystel saw and then heard a splat as a bullet went in Letitia's eye and whizzed out the back of her head. Another high shot buzzed overhead and shattered a glass case on the back wall. Letitia's dead weight fell on top of Chrystel just as Tilley expelled a roar.

Chrystel mouthed a silent moan. The fall had taken her breath, but the moan was for Letitia. She was gone. Tilley's snout was already pushing at Letitia to move her off the companion. Heart racing, Chrystel coughed, finally able to take air, and rolled out from under Letitia's body.

She felt for a pulse. Nothing. Time was almost out. The people in the cafeteria would be rousing soon and the school folk in the gym quickly after that. They had to go now. If not for the woman with Red, who had stupidly yelled out and given away their presence, it might be Chrystel and not Letitia sprawled in the hall. A brave woman and a brave dog had both risked their lives to keep someone else safe. The dog and Chrystel would walk away. Letitia would not. Chrystel laid her hand on Letitia's forehead. Candy yipped an encouraging "*come on*" sound. The Alien and two dogs were already circling at the exit doors. Chrystel took one last look to be sure Red and the woman were unconscious, stood, bared her teeth, and ran.

Calling to the outside guard dogs as they sprinted over a potholed, uneven parking lot to the woods, the last two furry beasts came running and joined them. Together, the unlikely crew charged into the forest.

While Chrystel had been releasing the caged animals, she had also studied the terrain and formulated an escape plan. There was only a single access road to the school from which to flee. If she stole an unguarded ATV, the group occupying the school would catch her. They had more people and more ATVs. But, if she ran into the sheltered arms of a forest, her kidnappers would be on her turf. Chrystel knew they would never, ever catch her in the woods.

Chrystel sailed over a log and deftly chose her strides in the undergrowth. One of Thomas' favorite training regimens was what he called *a run in the woods*. He elaborated further, "Some people like a walk in the park, but I prefer to run free in the wilderness. Ladies and gentlemen, there is nothing quite like the sting of a back-whipping branch against your face." He would laugh that deep base, window shaking laugh. "Besides, if you can run fast without hurting yourself through the brush, you can run anywhere. Anyone who beats me back, gets a Bigfoot, on me."

From the instant Thomas issued that first challenge, Chrystel resolved to get a free beer. In the beginning, she huffed and puffed, fell over stuff, came back scraped and bruised, only to try again the next time. When she was twenty-five, she and Thomas had emerged from the trees side by side, racing to the finish line. Neither looked at their competitor. They used everything they had left to win, steeling themselves against the pain of eight hard miles in the woods. It was a photo finish. Unfortunately, there was no one at the finish line to take a photo. They argued for years about who had won that race. On the evening of his loss, Thomas finally relented and said the race was close enough, and he owed Chrystel a beer. Chrystel didn't think the sprint was close. Her foot was at the finish first.

After that event, one of Chrystel's greatest joys was running like the wind through the trees. She could imagine herself like a breeze, lifting and sailing around obstacles, increasing speed with every open conduit. Her eyes somehow scanning the ground at eye level, while simultaneously leaping and twisting at just the right instant.

A very courageous woman had died to save her. Chrystel didn't know where she was in the forest or in which direction she was running. Still, she looked gleefully back at Tilley when a lavender mass of strangeness trotted near her side to say hello.

Chrystel hadn't heard anyone following them since the first hour. The far-off barking of pursuing dogs and a human shouting were the only signs the school people had made chase. Tilley paused at one point when she heard the dogs, raising her massive head in the direction of the sounds. She stood staring, her eyes soulful. Chrystel thought Tilley had warned the other dogs to move away, but it was impossible to be sure. Chrystel only knew they hadn't heard anyone since.

When light turned to dusk, and Chrystel could see the final vestiges of day, she knew they were headed west. Just as she had hoped.

## 27. Who are They?

Temperatures dropped precipitously as the dark surrounded Chrystel and her fellow escapees. Treading over another long-abandoned homestead, barely visible from nature's relentless encroachment, Chrystel reached her energy limit for running in the forest. The structure was most likely a family farm of unknown specifics. Surrounding chain link fencing, partially standing and buried in the ground spoke to enclosed animals once contained on the property.

The only thing left that hadn't caved in on itself was a rock fireplace. Rooting around in the ruins of shattered lives for anything useful, Chrystel found a hard-sided, polymer-based suitcase buried under a rotten, insect infused mattress. She yelled when she pried it open. Synthetic garments inside had handily weathered the intervening hundred years. As Chrystel was rifling through the clothes for protection from the elements, she mused to her dog companions, "You know, plastic really is forever."

She gathered dry debris to burn in the fireplace after assessing the trade-off. On one hand, it would keep them warm and discourage wolves and rangers. On the other, smoke was a dead giveaway to any night prowling, two-legged creatures. Exhausted and cold, Chrystel gave in to her bodily needs. Anything was possible, but it seemed unlikely Red and his minions could have tracked them this far.

Chrystel shook off lingering doubt. In her bones, she knew they were alone in this place. Only the wail and rustle of roaming wildlife existed.

As she snuggled against her friends for the night in front of a small fire, an unexpected swell of peace and safety rippled through her synapses. Was it Tilley's touch doing that "thing" again, Chrystel wondered? Or maybe, the culmination of an intense day, and the realization she had escaped and survived against long odds. Or even, some instinctive wild part of her humanness that found unrestrained joy in besting her pursuers, now able to sleep under the stars beside her tribe.

Her last thought before weariness took her was of Letitia. Guilt, because she had left her and couldn't save her to share this peace. Letitia, who whined and cried during the entirety of her captivity, was brave when it meant something. The inconsistency was knocking loudly on Chrystel's world view. Dismissing Letitia's emotional displays as weakness, she had been impatient and unkind, and still, Letitia had reached out to protect her. How could emotional fragility and strength reside together in one living being?

For an instant, Chrystel considered that perhaps the same was true of herself. She had buried feelings of uncertainty and loneliness, covering doubts with constant movement—different sides of the same coin. Maybe, outward signs of emotion weren't always about weakness any more than keeping them inside made you strong. The world Chrystel had built for herself, the one where she didn't count on anyone else to care about her fears, was teetering under the weight of Letitia's unexpected valor.

Chrystel could feel the tears sliding down her cheeks. She pulled Tilley close and sobbed into her warm, maned neck.

*  *  *

Chrystel woke surrounded by fur balls. They needed to get moving. She pushed Candy's head off her legs, stood, and stretched with her arms to the sky, expelling a morning sigh. Tilley was up and waiting, three rabbits at her feet.

"Well, I'll be. You've been a busy girl." As Tilley smiled, Chrystel noticed the piece of fabric caught between her teeth. "Come here, let me help you with that."

Rabbits consumed, fabric extracted, synthetic, running-wear encasing Chrystel's limbs, they set off in search of water first and then home. They would keep a stiff pace without running. Chrystel wanted to save her energy for emergencies. The emergency part didn't take long.

Lionheart, the short-haired brindle dog Chrystel named after his valiant effort to take out Red, heard someone coming first. He brayed just once, alerting the home team. Chrystel halted in her tracks and listened. The unmistakable high-pitched whizzing of an ATV gave notice someone was coming. She breathed, "Down," to her pack.

Chrystel peered through fern stalks. An ATV loaded with three men and one woman passed only 50 yards to their front, travelling over a double grooved weeded path. The faces she could see didn't resemble anyone from the school. At the

275

wheel, a stocky, dark-haired fellow in a man bun was laughing at something.

She stood when the ATV rounded a bend out of sight. "This is a decision point," Chrystel stated. Her crew, spread around the bushes and firs, turned alert eyes in her direction. She knew they didn't understand everything she was saying, but it felt good to be able to talk to someone. Anyway, Tilley passed any important decisions to the dogs.

"There's too much activity outside the enclave. Something's happening. We could follow that ATV and see what's up, or we could head home fast and warn the others. Try to get some help and let them know we're safe." Four pairs of dog eyes and one alien creature continued to stare. "You're waiting on me for a decision, aren't you?" Candy and Lionheart wagged their tails.

"Maybe it's high time I count on someone else, quit trying to go it alone. I mean, you guys haven't let me down." Lionheart whined. "Home it is then. What do you say, team?" Tilley shook her head in the affirmative, which of course, she always did.

They stayed in the woods, walking parallel to the ATV access path, heading north to the enclave. Making good time, the group hid only one other time while another full ATV passed, this time going in the opposite direction. It was almost dark by the time Chrystel recognized a dilapidated warehouse on the southern tip of New Washington.

I have always detested history books where the author has an obvious personal bias about events but pretends that his or her ideas regarding the time are facts and not opinion. Really, how is it possible to know for certain why history unfolded in the manner that it did. Admittedly, it is easier in retrospect to gage a patchwork of actions, reactions, crisis, and personalities to ascertain the underlying causes for this war or that war. Writing history is an art, not a perfect science. And like beauty, history is in the eye of the beholder, just as a good war is the war that was won when recounted by the winner.

Determining where exactly the fulcrum of cascading events rests precisely is too often an exercise in futility. We want to know. To know is to perhaps exercise some control over the next series of events that sends us swirling in the vortex of change. I would suggest individual decision points and their outcomes may not matter, but rather, what matters is the tempo of the tide and an ability to correctly identify patterns indicating a turning point is on the horizon. To be ready, as much as humans are able, to navigate rough seas because we clearly see the storm looming. For the helmsperson, preparedness and astute judgement can help, but actual control is nearly always an illusion.

The New Washington Enclave is moving inexorably and with quickening speed toward great change. The alien arrival, just as the Great Dying a hundred years ago, is an obvious sign that the shit is filtering through the fan. If you measure our enclave against a yardstick of other enclaves, New Washington has been wildly successful. We have survived and are crawling past the stage of a small, close knit community isolated from the rest of the world. Whether that is good or bad is not relevant. More meaningful is that our relative prosperity is the very thing that invites others to covet what we have built and attempt to take some for themselves.

This is one of those turning point patterns of which I was speaking: the guy with the goods can expect resistance. Like water equalizing when two receptacles coincide, humans will attempt to take from those that have more if they believe themselves unable to get what they need or want by other means. Fair, not fair, it doesn't matter. What matters is the knowledge that any group that does well economically can expect those with less to offer resistance.

North Dakota. Of all the places. North Dakota people are trying to take some of our stuff. Maybe even all our stuff. Mike and Thomas captured a man in the woods who says he is from North Dakota. A chatty but unsophisticated fellow, the prisoner painted a picture of desperation in the North Dakota Enclave. Harsh winters, drought, and then a blight that destroyed most of their crops. They overconsumed their animal herds to compensate for lost crops, and when the drought went on for a third year, North Dakotans weren't left with many alternatives.

I get the takeover attempt to some extent. North Dakota is terribly cold and flat and in some places barren. Before the change, the Dakotas saw a resurgence of prosperity because of oil fracking, but we no longer need the oil.

Everyone in my family believes Carlton is working with the insurgents. I go back and forth on the truth of this assertion. He has been living in New Washington for over twenty years. If he is helping the North Dakota aggressors, it doesn't seem possible he came to our enclave with the foresight of drought and desperation. Carlton still maintains he was born in Wyoming, and as always, there is no way to verify the truthfulness of his claims.

My father stopped by this morning after attending an enclave council meeting. I think he wanted to bounce plans off me, but he comes at those discussions obliquely. Accustomed to presenting a strong, confident example to me and my brothers, my dad struggles to admit doubt. He started the conversation with news of Amelia, as if I don't visit her frequently. I pretended befitting interest.

Dad sat relaxed in my favorite armchair, his legs spread wide, leaning to one side with an elbow on the arm, his hand rubbing the space next to his eyes. He was neat and well-groomed, but the bags under his eyes gave notice of stress. For only a moment, I felt guilt at my ambush, forcing him to accept the mayoral position. I may not have fully appreciated the toll it would take on my father with my mother gone. The guilt lasted only long enough to remind myself I wanted this man at the helm.

"Amelia stayed outside in the yard for a full hour yesterday. I gave her a small rose bush and helped her put it in the ground. She began to shake as we finished replacing dirt around the roots, and I had to help her back inside. Regardless, it's real progress." As an afterthought, my dad added wistfully, "Karen will be overjoyed when she returns."

I didn't tell him about my last Amelia visit to give her some new books. She answered the door almost immediately. Her hair was combed and tied in a loose, upswept style. Her smile was wide. "Trent, we have a visitor," Amelia called out. Busy working on something under the sink, Trent jumped up, rubbed his hands on a cloth hanging from his belt, and reached to shake my hand. "Good to see you, Geronimo."

I nodded and said, "Likewise." Trent's hair had been transformed as well. Someone had cut it back to a shoulder length style, like an overgrown bush pruned only part way as a starting point. His beard, no longer completely obscuring his face, revealed even features and a patrician nose, giving him the appearance of an educated man rather than a vagabond.

We had a nice visit. As I said my goodbyes, Amelia handed me a stack of books. "Here are a few books I borrowed from the library, Geronimo. They are way past the return date."

"No problem, Sis. I think we can forgive the fines." I hugged her. My heart was filled with a warmth that travelled quickly to my headstrong tear ducts. After zipping the urge to hug her too long, which I knew made Amelia uncomfortable, I was on my way.

I asked Dad the next question to get the ball rolling for what I believed was the real purpose of his visit. "What does Amelia see about Chrystel? Anything?"

"That's interesting. Amelia said Chrystel is no longer at the school. She is running with animals."

"Wonderful news! What a relief. Chrystel will find her way back, on that you can hang your hat! Why do you say it's interesting?"

"Because this Red from North Dakota is still orchestrating a prisoner swap."

"A swap for what?"

"What else, the generator specs. He also wants weapons and the plans for Jed's new microwave communication system."

"The fact that he knows about the new communicator confirms Red has allies on the inside," I replied.

"Uh huh. And there's more. We've been using drones to find Chrystel and discovered more than expected. We know the location of the school in Amelia's visions. There were twenty or so folks at that location. Far worse, there appears to be a base of operations near Olympia."

"That's not good. A base? How many?"

"We estimate at least 300 to 400 people and two pieces of artillery."

"Shit!"

"Shit indeed. We also spotted someone, that could be Chrystel and some dogs, heading north approaching the enclave. Whoever it is, they're moving under cover. Amelia has never been wrong. I'm nearly certain it must be Chrystel. Thomas sent out a couple of force members to intercept the group and bring them in. If it's Chrystel, she should be back by tonight."

"That's great news about Chrystel. I knew she would get herself home! But, if technology for trade was all they wanted, why would these people stage a fighting force near?"

"Exactly. Thomas thinks the kidnappings were a diversion to keep us occupied with a hostage exchange while they stage an attack from the south."

"But, we have an armed perimeter."

"We do. Won't help with artillery. Also, if there're sympathizers within the enclave, a few well-placed explosions could make a ground defense of the enclave more difficult."

"What does Thomas think? I asked.

"He thinks we should, and I quote, 'Send a missile right down their collective throats.'"

"What do you think?" I asked, knowing full well the answer was the most likely cause of my father's dark, circled eyes.

"I think we could use another 400 able hands in the enclave. If we're going to build a real army and space force to protect earth from the Hunta, we need more people. New Washington could easily take them in and anyone else left behind in the North Dakota Territories. In fact, I'd been considering a plan to encourage more walk-ons rather than less. If we want to grow, it involves some risks. Risks that can be mitigated if we're smart. I just don't know how to reach these phantom North Dakotans. I offered Red an amnesty deal and was rebuked—he laughed. We don't have much time to find a channel to the folks beneath the leader and convince them this war they are starting serves no purpose other than getting themselves killed."

"What does the council think?"

"They mostly agree with Thomas. Brodie believes we should take a hard stance to discourage future incursions. As mayor, it's ultimately my decision whether to pull the trigger on a missile from the Rainier Station. We only have two left until we're resupplied by the Ardinian technology they've promised. We used all the others in a fruitless attempt to down the Ardinian spacecraft."

"Couldn't you broadcast an all hands message over the shortwave. Go around Red and any leaders directly to the people? Or, perhaps, we could set up another ruse like the one we used on the prisoner, only this time play Carlton."

"We could. But what do you think will happen when Red gets wind of our broadcast? He will send his people scurrying or even move up an attack. We'll lose our advantage to stop them with a well-placed missile. And fooling Carlton, that's another matter. He's one cool cucumber and very smart. If we use that play, and Carlton has been telling the truth all along that he isn't part of this conspiracy, we waste time and sacrifice the initiative."

I was still puzzled. "I just don't get the why now question. If Carlton is in on it, why not wait and see if he's elected mayor?"

"Yeah, why now? My guess, when Brodie pulled out of a three-way race, Carlton thought Chrystel would win. The North Dakota folks have probably been around for a while, waiting to back up Carlton after he was elected. Since an easy takeover probably wasn't going to happen, they're going with a hard Plan B, an armed invasion."

We sat in silence pondering the options until a hazy notion began to form behind my eyes. "Are you sure no inside sympathizers know about the drones or our knowledge of their base?"

"As sure as I can be. We kept that info very close hold. Jed, Thomas and the guy operating the drone computers are the only ones who know."

I commented, "So they don't know that we know about an attack."

My dad shifted in his chair, as his eyes scanned the floor, a sign the gears in his head were forming an idea. There was an identical smile to my own when he glanced up at me, and our eyes locked. "Carlton can talk to dogs, right?" I asked hoping for that last bit or reassurance.

"Yes, I've seen him with that old hound. No doubt."

"How long do we have?"

"No later than tonight. We have to make our move, one way or the other."

"I'll bet Carlton can be fooled by dogs! Can you get Thomas over here ASAP to add some operational flesh to the bones of an idea?" I asked. "I have just the right dog in mind."

Together, my father, his best friend and I cobbled together a plan. Immediate execution was a necessity. If our strategy didn't work, we'd still have time to blow them to kingdom come with missiles.

I am sitting at my desk now, nervously awaiting word on how the plan is unfolding. My dad promised an update as soon as he was able. Once the first shot is fired, everything can change—best laid plans aside.

Oh, and great news. Amelia's vision was correct. The team Mike sent in the hope of finding Chrystel located my niece with the alien and four hounds on the southern border of the enclave. They were found in the nick of time, only a half mile from the armed perimeter system. Chrystel might not have known the grid was on and walked right into deadly electrical current.

The fact that Chrystel had collected four canines during her capture is curious since she has never been a dog lover. One of those canines was my very own beloved pal, Candy. I have Candy's favorite meal, baked salmon (well actually salmon of any preparation to include raw), prepared and waiting for her arrival. I owe my niece a huge debt for getting herself back to the enclave safely and for bringing my trusted friend with her. Funny, I never had a doubt Chrystel would find a way to free herself and return.

As a summary of my winding turning point chapter, it seems we Washingtonians are left with a tragic, age-old choice. With only the belief of an imminent attack, if we mercilessly destroy 400+ Dakota lives by missile to protect our enclave and 6,000 New Washington residents, will history view us as coldhearted, brutal aggressors? When the Americans dropped atomic bombs on Hiroshima and Nagasaki to save millions of their own and the enemy in future battles, was the act a horror of unprecedented proportions—absolutely. Just as the killing of the unwitting North Dakota people, in a sparsely populated world would be an unimaginable tragedy. Consider this: the Dakotans now lingering in Olympia represent a larger percentage of the earth's population than the combined population of Hiroshima and Nagasaki at the time of the atomic bomb.

History often describes aggression of one people against another as bad, as merely a two-dimensional struggle. If many lives are lost, particularly when superior weapons are involved, historians can make claim the aggression is unwarranted. Sometimes, they would be correct. Often though, as in our situation, the decision to cause great harm to protect your own are hard and complicated and must be overlaid with a contextual framework. History is never so simple as it seems.

My father is a good man. He has chosen a riskier but more humane solution, which is why he is the right man for the job. I pray we aren't remembered as fools for the effort.

Geronimo M.

# 29. New Tricks on an Old Dog

A gray bearded dog lounged on his side, enjoying the last bit of warm sun from the day. This was his spot, in all weather, good or bad. Here, he could watch the road for his master's return. A soft pad provided by his master cushioned his thinning frame from the hard wood underneath. During a short nap, his closed eyes twitching, the dog dreamt he was running ahead of his master's side and keeping a watchful eye for any danger. Ready always to protect. The master called to him, and his eyes sprang open.

It wasn't the master. An unknown man and a dog stood in his territory at the door. The old dog growled and then forced his stiff body from the ground. With the awareness to know he could do nothing but threaten, he dipped his head and a low rumble began in his throat. The man smiled. "Hey, dog. Just here to see Carlton. Got some shoes of his to return."

Demonstrating respect for a geriatric canine, the young, female dog with the man, flattened her ears and wagged her body in a submissive posture. She approached in a crouch to smell his feet and, if invited, lick his mouth.

Carlton arrived at the door. "Tim Ye. What brings you around?"

"Evening, Carlton. Hope I didn't interrupt anything. I have those shoes you wanted repaired and ready for you."

"Since when do you deliver, Tim?" Carlton asked.

"Well, I heard rumors something was up. You know, of course, the mayor was kidnapped. My cousin on the Defense Force says everyone is on high alert. I just thought I would deliver what I had ready and get paid for what I could in the event things take a bad turn." Tim pointed to a bag full of shoes behind him. "People forget to come back to the store to collect repaired shoes. When they forget, I don't get paid. If you want me to wait or don't have the money, I understand," Tim smiled sheepishly.

Carlton studied Tim and then shook his head. "Sure, Tim. Come on in, and I'll scrounge up some cash."

"Appreciate it, Carlton," Tim said as the screen door was held open for him to enter.

The old dog on the porch wasn't talkative, but the young female couldn't keep her excitement in check. "Old dog help protect enclave? We go join others. Defend home."

The heads of the old dog and the young female swiveled in unison to watch a gaggle of other dogs trotting down the road. Tim Ye's dog signaled to them with three short barks and sent a message. "Go to protect?" she asked.

Mike's shepherd, Bruno, the alpha of the pack, paused to answer, his head and tail raised high in anticipation. "All dogs help! Be ready to protect. No save Chrystel. Traitors caged!" Bruno turned and trotted with his posse as they continued past Carlton's home.

Old dog swung his snout to face the young female, "When you go?"

"Soon," the young female answered.

Tim Ye's return prevented further dog conversation. "Thanks again, Carlton," Tim called as he waved goodbye. He hefted the bag of shoes and boots over his shoulder, gestured for his canine to follow, and rapidly walked away from Carlton's house. Carlton waited outside his home until Tim was out of sight and whispered to his oldest and dearest friend, "What do you think that was all about?"

The old dog, who hadn't had a chance to resume his resting position, looked longingly at his master. "They go protect enclave. To defend."

Carlton became very still. "When? Did they say when?"

"Soon!" the old dog nearly shouted into Carlton's mind. "Traitors caged. No save Chrystel."

"What does that mean? What did they mean by 'no save Chrystel'?" Carlton urged.

Old dog tilted his head in a confused expression. He could not answer the master. Dogs grasped the literal meaning of words, but nuance and conceptual reasoning was a bridge too far. Stymied, Carlton tried a different question. "Did Mr. Ye's dog say, 'no save Chrystel'?"

Old dog was happy. This time he knew the answer. "No, they go to protect enclave. Other dogs passing on road speak. Other dogs talk of Chrystel."

Carlton, not one for emotional outbursts, narrowed his eyes and clenched his jaw in reaction. "I've got work to do, Buddy. You stay out here and warn me if you see anyone coming. People or dogs."

Carlton slid a panel set in a wall up and out of the way. Lifting a boxy telephone receiver from the hidden space behind the opening, he pressed the on button, and waited for a light sequence to indicate the phone was ready to transmit. The design was unique, even though the scientific basis for the phone was the result of a clandestine purchase from one of Jed's scientists.

Carlton thought about how close they were as a chirping noise bleated in his ear. He had served as a one man wrecking crew in the enclave: cajoling the locals to his side, stealing and buying technology, winning influence, and all without a shred of suspicion until recently. I've come too far--I can't lose it all now, he thought as he prepared himself for the final fight. He didn't like thinking of the lives that might be lost, but he knew lost lives were a necessary cost if he wanted to win.

"What's up, Bro?" Red answered.

"We've got problems. I think Washington clavers know about our forces in Olympia. And I don't think they believe you will follow through on a hostage exchange."

"Did Chrystel make it back to the enclave? Could she have seen our base on her way home?"

"I don't know. Possibly. She's smarter and more capable than I expected. Regardless of the how, it's important now that we keep the initiative. I need you to contact Margo. Tell her to be ready to fire the artillery in 90 minutes. I'll need that long to finish my work here and get to safety. The troops should start moving to their positions outside the enclave ASAP."

"It will take at least a half hour for the main body to move out," Red reminded Carlton. "They're ready, but not that ready. We weren't scheduled to move until tomorrow."

"Got it, but sooner is better than later. I want them close after we've used all the artillery ammunition and ready to press the advantage. You and your folks must move out now. Intercept the main body to reinforce their attack."

"What do you want me to do about the prisoner exchange without prisoners? I talked to Mike, and we are on for daybreak tomorrow morning. He may or may not know Chrystel escaped."

"Don't do anything. By that time, it'll all be over."

"Roger, Carlton. Anything else you want me to pass to our sister?"

"Good hunting."

"Good luck to you too, Brother. Time to kick some arrogant, self-righteous butt."

"Roger that. I'll signal for the attack to begin when I'm out of the enclave."

Carlton readied his gear and placed the sophisticated phone into an inside pocket of his jacket. This next part was sad but another necessity. He stepped out to his old dog lying on the porch, waiting and guarding as he was commanded. Carlton sat down next to his friend and gently stuck his fingers in the soft fur of his ruff. He stroked his old dog. "I need you to go in the house. I wish I could take you along to guard the enclave, but I'm afraid your old joints won't cooperate. Wait for me here. I'll be gone longer than normal, and I've left you some food and water.

Don't worry if you can't hold your business. We can clean up later."

The old dog gazed in Carlton's eyes with complete acceptance. He lifted his weary body and waddled on wooden legs into the house. Somberly watching the infirm dog, Carlton experienced a moment of apprehension with the recognition this attack could go wrong. Not that he believed it would fail, but there was always a slim chance. It was some consolation knowing the dog-crazy people in the enclave would care for his old dog if the worst happened.

As Carlton jumped into his ATV, two observers watched from a distance. "He's taken the bait or dog bone in this case." The man grinned into the mic. "Carlton is on the move, and we're ready to follow."

# 30. Timing is Everything

Mark Little, a member of New Washington's Force, leaned low against a rusted truck that had long ago been abandoned to the elements. He really, really wanted to smoke one of the hand-rolled cigarettes he carried in his pocket, but that would give away his position. The skies were a mixture of pink and swirling blues as the sun descended over the horizon. The day had been mostly clear without the annoying drizzle common to spring in Washington. Observing his surroundings, as if he were merely enjoying the pleasant weather, Mark debated whether to linger longer.

Born and raised in New Washington, Mark knew there was something cooking the minute he received the call from his force supervisor. He was told to report immediately to his post. In and of itself, recalls weren't that unusual, but the timing and orders he received at his arrival were extremely odd. His watch captain had said, "No one can leave their post. All force members will be assigned a four-man team and remain with that team at all times until notified otherwise."

Using the excuse that he needed to take a whizz, Mark had slipped away from his team. He'd been given a mission by Carlton that he couldn't complete if he was chained to a team of loyal force members. Getting away to arm the timer on an explosive device, already concealed near the Force Operations Center, seemed almost impossible. Mark huddled lower next to the oxidized hulk to wait until full dark. He could hear the soft murmuring of another four-person team somewhere to his right.

Mark allowed rage over the loss of his sister to strengthen his resolve. No way was it fair that she had been left to bleed to death after a vicious ranger attack. They, the rulers of the enclave, had sent his twin into the forest to collect mushrooms without proper protection. They knew it was unsafe, yet no one cared. If you weren't one of the privileged ones, you got shit, dangerous work. When Carlton became mayor, he would change all that. He promised to look after every citizen, regardless of parentage. Mark had become a willing Carlton follower not long after his sister passed. It was time for change in the enclave, no matter what it took to make that happen.

Mark worked himself into a lather and was ready. Sprinting from his cover, he ran to the next feature where he could hide, heading in the direction of the Operations Center. Carefully moving from one concealed location to another, he was in the open when a bullet thunked into the ground by his feet. He glanced in the direction of the shooter and was blinded by a piercing light. "Drop your weapon, now!" a woman's voice commanded from behind the light. "You are under arrest for conspiracy to commit treasonous acts."

Crestfallen and realizing too late he'd fallen into a trap by leaving his team, Mark dropped his weapon. The enclave rulers knew friends of Carlton on the force would attempt to leave their team. It was the only way to flush them out. *How stupid can I be?*

* * *

Tall, curvy, with an angular face, Margo drove her command ATV on the sidewalk, checking one last time the preparedness of her troops before they set off to the enclave. Together, 450 souls didn't look like all that many against an enclave of 6,000 people. Not for the first time, she questioned the wisdom of her brothers' plan to assume control of New Washington to assure their place in the new world. Both of her older brothers were smart and cagey, polished on the outside, but streetfighter wily underneath. Unbridled confidence was also part of the package, perhaps dangerously so.

Margo hoped the artillery they had found and restored would create enough damage and confusion to overwhelm a superior force. It might if they continued to hold the element of surprise and inside sympathizers did the jobs they were convinced to complete. The recent guidance to move out immediately ahead of schedule only reinforced her concerns that this attack was a fool's errand. She tried to convince Red when he called that it would be better to pull back and wait for a more advantageous time or give it up altogether. Margo recommended they start their own enclave in southern Washington or even Oregon. Of her two brothers, Red the middle child, was the least persuadable. He'd yelled at her, "Just do your job, Margo!"

Even Carlton, normally more reasonable, had responded with anger when she pleaded with him to reconsider. He was too invested in a farcical plan they had hatched at their family home some 30 years prior. Life in North Dakota after the Great

Dying was more than just hard. It was backbreaking, thankless effort. For every step forward, the territories took two steps back. Margo still remembered her handsome brother Carlton, sitting outside on the front porch, his face alive and exuberant, as he said, "What if we could steal New Washington?"

Somewhere along the way, in his prodigious effort to win the enclave, Carlton had lost the ability to see anything except the prize. So much potential in a remarkable man, warped by pride and wanting to be right.

Carlton had set off to New Washington with the thought he could legally gain control of the enclave by winning an election. It just so happened that three years of bad crops in North Dakota and starving winters coincided with Carlton's ascendance as a prominent mayoral candidate. Margo and Red were told to gather an army and head west. Since many Dakotans were ready to leave and seek a more temperate climate anyway, the timing was perfect. Nearly everyone joined.

If not for loyalty to family, she would order everyone to stand down immediately. Margo heard radio static crackling from the open back of a gas-powered truck. "They shouldn't be on the radio now!" she huffed out loud. Braking the ATV, Margo flew out and sprinted to the truck. Six sets of frightened eyes stared up at her reddened face. A man was speaking to them from the radio.

"Please lay down your weapons. We offer refuge to anyone from the North Dakota Territories who chooses to join us. I know your lives have been hard. We've had hard days and hard years here too. But it doesn't have to end like this. This planet and our community needs each person, alive and willing to contribute. We don't need to lose any more. Haven't we lost enough? I'm an original. If there's one thing I know, one thing I learned from that devastated world, it's that we are more prosperous and likely to survive if we don't waste our blood, sweat, and tears trying to kill each other! There is enough for everyone. Power is the only reason for this attack, and for most of you listening, that power won't be to your benefit. Instead, you will lose family and friends in a pointless effort to take something I offer for nothing. All we need in New Washington is your commitment to starting a new life here.

"We welcome your help to move forward in this great world we've inherited. Have hope, have faith, join us. Please, I implore you, drop your weapons, and no one will be harmed."

"Who is it?" Margo asked.

A skinny, black-haired kid answered. "He says he's the temporary mayor of the New Washington Enclave."

Margo, blank faced, nodded. "Get moving." She thumped the back of the truck as it began to pull forward. One last duty and she would join the main body. She had to make sure the artillery crew was set and ready.

She drove as fast as the ATV would travel to the forward site of the big guns. Busy making last minute preparations, the artillery chief for this part of the mission, wasn't happy to see Margo swing in. A broad-backed woman with close cropped hair was standing behind a kid with a computer talking

297

in his ear and barely looked up to acknowledge Margo's presence. "Margo, I don't have time. We have three more minutes before first shots fired. All critical targets are programmed, the guns have been calibrated and checked, and gunners and ammunition loaders are ready."

"Would you mind if I stayed and watched, at least until you start?" Margo asked. "It would give me some peace of mind before I lead the assault."

"You're the boss," she responded. "Get some hearing protection for Margo. And Margo, stay beyond this table," she ordered and pointed to a safe viewing location.

Margo smirked. The woman commanding the artillery section was a bossy bitch, but she was good at what she did. She was one of the two originals left alive in the Dakota Territory after the Great Dying. Given the population of the state at the time, two people surviving the sickness was like drawing a straight flush in just five cards. She and her partner searched the surrounding states for other survivors. They found Margo's great grandfather, Mathias, and his mate, Sylvie, wandering destitute in northern Colorado. Two other originals came later from South Dakota.

It helped that this founder's pre-change profession was as an Artillery Master Sergeant in the North Dakota National Guard. She had located artillery weapons at a deserted Army installation and managed their restoration for enclave protection. Getting them to Washington was a feat in and of itself. Finding and revitalizing ammunition was another challenge. But the Paladin 155mm self-propelled howitzers, parked and ready to disperse high impact rounds, were a sight to behold—lethal and deadly.

Activity surrounding the artillery reached a crescendo. One crew chief, one gunner, and one ammunition loader piled into the back compartment of the tracked vehicle. Huddled with the computer operation, the two drivers in front of Margo laughed over some inside joke. The firing platform on the Paladin chassis whined as it moved to aim at pre-plotted, enclave targets. The crew chief gave the thumbs up. Margo could feel the concussion as massive rounds leapt from the barrels. She jumped at intervals, newly startled from the thunderous sound.

The first sign that something had gone wrong was when Margo witnessed the founder artillery expert running in the direction of the computer operator and drivers. The woman's body lurched in a forward arc, like someone had whacked her on the back with a baseball bat. Her mouth a screaming grimace, she face-planted to the dirt. Margo yanked the hearing protection off her head. The artillery had stopped firing. The only sound now was the popping of automatic weapon fire from individual weapons. It seemed to be coming from every direction.

The computer operator was draped askew over his computer. The drivers, earlier talking and laughing, were motionless next to him in the dirt. Margo, completely in the open, dropped to the ground and positioned her M4 to shoot any assailants. The attackers were there somewhere, but she couldn't see them. Bile in the back of

Margo's throat pulsed with the hard beat of her heart.

Armed men and women sprang from several directions and descended directly to the open artillery compartments. Margo took aim, but before she could fire, she felt a presence behind her. Glancing back, a gigantic man with the barrel of his weapon pointed at her head cautioned, "Push your weapon away slowly. Don't try anything fancy or otherwise. That would be very bad for your health."

Margo pulled the sling off her shoulder and scooted the weapon on the ground as far away as she could. She placed her hands in the air and got on her knees. She didn't turn. While keeping an eye on Margo, Thomas crouched, scooped the M4, and slung it over his left shoulder in one fluid motion. Looking straight ahead and keeping her eyes averted from the giant pointing a weapon at her head, she said, "I give up. I want to join you, just like your mayor said."

"Would have been better for you had you not already fired those Paladins at the enclave. Dammit! We were five minutes too late."

As the co-opted artillery crews were rousted from the safety of the firing compartments, Margo watched, resigned and helpless. It was obvious the big man, someone else had called Thomas, was pissed. Lining up the Dakota survivors, he shouted, "Which one of you dumb shits is in charge?"

Margo didn't hesitate. "I am."

"Should have guessed. Answer me one question right now, and I'll consider your asylum request. What route is your convoy taking?'

"Are you going to kill them?" Margo asked.

"Not if we can help it. If that's what we wanted to do, we woulda, coulda, maybe shoulda rained a missile down on your asses. Answer the damned question."

"They are heading north on the old I-5."

Thomas beamed. "Just as I thought. I love it when a plan comes mostly together." He yelled at one of his team to get on the radio and confirm the convoy route. Eyeing Margo as they were a waiting for confirmation the message was received, Thomas asked her, "What in holy hell did you think you would accomplish by this?"

Margo shook her head back and forth and thought of any number of responses. Not one of them made any sense.

A burly, thick necked soldier hustled over after finishing his call. "Thomas, I just talked to Bravo Team. When they stopped the main convoy with an ambush, nearly all the North Dakota folks surrendered. Guess their leader never showed up, and they didn't know what else to do. Only two KIAs and five injured. None ours. Oh, and yeah, the team Mike sent to look for Chrystel found her!"

"Outstanding! That woman can smell action from miles away." Thomas gestured to Margo, "I'm assuming you be the bugged-out leader?"

"No. Not really. I was never a leader. Just a loving sister following orders."

\* \* \*

Carlton waited flat on his belly until he saw the day crew file out of the power plant. Obviously engrossed in office gossip or planning their next fishing trip, a couple of workers remained behind. *Just shut up and get moving. If they don't get going soon, I'll have to take matters into my own hands.* Carlton pinched his nose and sighed. As the brains behind the plan, he shouldn't have to be the one to take care of the plant. One of the men he'd convinced to be a collaborator had crapped out on him. When he called to give him a time to arm the explosive, the chicken shit said, "Man, Carlton, I'm real sorry, but I've changed my mind."

"What does that mean?"

"Am I speaking in tongues? It means, I changed my mind. I won't blow up the damn power plant!"

Carlton knew he could convince the man. This wasn't the first time he'd gone wobbly. He would only need to remind him of the important place he would have in the enclave once Carlton was in charge. He would kiss his ass and compliment the crude jerk until he changed his mind, again, but Carlton didn't have that kind of time. The power plant was essential. When the lights went out, the grid around the enclave went down too. By now, it was surely armed.

"Can I at least count on you to keep silent until this is all over? Everything will be forgiven if you just keep quiet."

"Mum's the word. Won't say a thing. If I did, they'd probably arrest me for contributing to a conspiracy."

"I knew I could count on you. All I need is the entry code."

Carlton scowled again just thinking about having to gravel to an idiot. He was rolling around in his mind how he might dislodge the two guys shucking and jiving outside the plant when they hastily set off in ATVs.

Wasting not another breath, Carlton sprinted to the plant front entry, his weapon drawn. He knew there was only one person on duty as a night custodian and where she would be. Carlton's mind-changing coconspirator was a construction worker who had placed a bomb behind drywall when he was called to fix damage from a leaking roof. *Take care of the night manager, cut through the drywall, and then set the timer. Easy. Would have been easier in the good old days, when you could arm a device using only a cellphone. When I'm mayor, we'll have reliable cellphones.*

He entered the lock code on the front entryway. The foyer was completely dark. Carlton held his weapon ready, slithered past the reception area, and turned into the right hallway. The night custodian would be in the control room, the last door on the left. Drawing a deep cleansing breath, he hesitated at the door. Rumor had it she spent most of her shift sleeping. Carlton hoped so. It would be far better if he wasn't required to gaze into her eyes before pulling the trigger.

Ever so gently, Carlton pulled the handle and then let loose, kicking the door open and springing into the space, his weapon forward. "What?" he uttered. "I'm looking for the custodian."

The twins, Rachael and Katie, founders and wives of Thomas and Manuel, greeted Carlton with raised shotguns, ready to blow his head from his shoulders. A soothing hum from control panels along two walls in the otherwise spacious room failed to allay Carlton's shock at finding gun-toting originals instead of a slumbering night shift employee. Incensed, Carlton asked, "What're you doing here?" His gun hand was trembling.

Rachael, always the first twin to speak, made Carlton's options very clear. "Seriously, Carlton? Why are we here? Let me break this down for you since you're understandably surprised. There are two of us and just one pitiful you. Should you attempt to fire at a twin, please rest assured the other twin will drop you in your tracks. Should you attempt to flee, we will both shoot you in the back. Katie is still a tremendous runner, and even if we should miss, which we won't, she will chase you down and kill you."

"Thank you, Rachael, for your vote of confidence." Katie responded.

"You're welcome, sister. Now as I was saying, this dog don't hunt. Drop your weapon!"

Carlton's eyes furtively flickered from one twin to the next. Reading his body language, Rachel narrowed her eyes and readied her trigger finger.

"All right, calm down! I'm laying my weapon on the ground. Relax, I don't want to die. Don't shoot!" Carlton said. He was bent halfway to the floor when he jerked upwards without releasing the gun. Two body shots hit him before he could complete his move.

"Well, like, that was totally stupid, Carlton," Rachael grunted. "Katie, call in medical support. I'll try to stem the flow of blood. We need to know where the bomb is located. Damn, what a moron. Was I like not clear in explaining his choices?"

"No, Sis, you were very articulate."

## 31. Homecoming

Karen, her team, Maleta, and the two Mermot representatives, Rappel and Tweet, flew through the blue, shimmering tunnel to Founders Park. Only momentarily confused, Karen was ready to dash home as soon as the haze cleared. Shakete had argued they should get a good night's rest and wait for morning to return, but Karen and crew would not hear of a delay. Home was a draw that didn't need a night's sleep.

It was raining, the downpour soaking them in seconds when the tunnel evaporated. "What the hell?" Karen gasped. Cautiously treading forward, she stared over the edge of hole at least ten yards in diameter filled with muddy water. "Check this out!" Karen yelled to her crew.

Mabel peered over the edge at the strange depression and commented, "For heaven's sake, are they building a swimming pool in Founders Park?"

"That's no swimming pool. That looks like a bomb crater. What the hell happened while we were gone?" Karen asked. Her gut flipped at the notion a large piece of ordnance had landed in the middle of Founders Park. Examining the area looking for clues as to the genesis of the park's new water feature, another crater, appearing as a shadow near the circular perimeter road, indicated a second explosion. Of bad signs, bomb craters were the mother of all unwelcome omens.

Manny leaned out over the edge of the hole staring at the muddy-sided pit. "If someone inadvertently fell in something like this, they'd have a hard time crawling out.".

Maleta, who had no real understanding of wet soil, inquired politely, "Is it poisonous?"

Dee tried to stifle laughter. "I know this isn't funny, but what a welcome. Maybe Shakete was right. Everything looks better in the morning." The dirty look Karen gave Dee prevented a chuckle from escaping through her lips.

Whiskers twitching, Rappel examined the dark earth and vegetation, turning 360 degrees to fully capture the towering trees and the scent of life all around him. He passed a gleeful thought to his special daughter, Tweet. "This is a wonderful place for a new home!"

The group of weary travelers, skirted the hole, walking around the edge to the courthouse, careful not to miss other bomb created divots. The New Washington seat of government sported large sheets of front-facing windows. Glass windows were intact at the spacefarer's departure but were now covered with wood and plastic. "Yep, a bomb," Dee whistled. "Lucky, they only hit the front lawn. What the heck happened while we were gone?"

Judy was hunched over a desk almost asleep and jerked awake when the door opened. It took a moment to process the faces of the dripping bundles entering the courthouse. It took another few seconds to make sense of the pale, slender Ardinian and mostly upright, rat creatures. "Aliens!" Judy blurted as her mouth took the lead over her brain. "Oops, didn't mean anything negative by that. Thank the lord you're back!" she yelled as she raced to Karen and Mabel to hug them. "We were all worried sick when you didn't arrive on time. Oh, and by golly, you're all wet. I'll get some towels. By the way Karen, Mike's in the mayor's office. That's why I'm here. A clerk is always around when the boss is in."

"Why's he in the mayor's office in the middle of the night?" Karen shouted at Judy's departing back.

Judy turned and gave Karen a lopsided grin. "Because he's the mayor right now."

"Huh?" Karen's mouth hung open. Maleta and the Mermots were behaving like little ducklings, following along behind Karen's every step as if she was the mother duck. "Okay, guys. I know you feel uncomfortable with your new surroundings, but I need you to hang here for a minute while I go talk to my husband. Judy will take care of you guys until I get back. She may even have some coffee to offer."

Maleta purred. "I love earth coffee. And Karen, Tweet and I are not guys."

"Wonderful. I'll explain the guy comment later." Charging through the building before Maleta could offer further comment, Karen was in a hurry to see Mike. His trusty hound, Bruno, was lounging against a wall keeping his master company and smelled Karen first. Like a bullet, he streaked out of the office on the hunt for the home woman. Bruno tried not to jump on her, but his excitement overwhelmed better judgement, as was often the case in dogs. He whined and wagged, while circling Karen, prancing in happiness. "Shush, Bruno. I want to surprise him."

Poking her head into the brightly lit, bare walled office, Karen commented, "Whatcha doing, handsome?"

As always, Mike was so focused on his task, it took a few beats for his mind to transition and realize someone was talking to him. He shot out of his seat when he finally looked up to see Karen. Their bodies met in an embrace. They kissed and gazed into each other's eyes before the water works commenced in earnest.

Mike was wiping away the tears and said in a broken voice, "You have no idea how worried I was. You're almost a week late. Late or not, I'm glad you're home." He hugged Karen again, nearly cutting off her ability to breathe.

"We ran into a bit of difficulty. I'll explain later. What on earth is up with the bomb craters in Founders Park?"

"155 artillery shells."

"Who?"

"Carlton and his North Dakota disciples."

"Why haven't you filled the holes. Someone could break their neck."

"My plate's been rather full of late."

"Judy said you're now the mayor? Where is Chrystel? Is she hurt? Is anyone else hurt? Are they still out there and able to cause harm? Why are you still here in the middle of the night?"

Mike placed his finger gently on Karen's lip. "You know I'm an introvert and need a moment to gather my thoughts before I answer questions. An interrogation doesn't make it easier for me."

Karen's shoulders relaxed. "I know, old man. I missed you too." She hugged him again, her nostrils filling with his scent. She thought about her own brush with death during the Hunta space battle and decided to wait awhile before sharing her space exploits.

It took almost forty years to discover a successful communication approach, one that allowed this thoughtful man to adequately express himself. Even now, when Karen was excited, she failed miserably at following her own hard-earned experience. "Let me start again, Mike. What went well while we were gone?"

Mike eyes held a glint of humor as he started. "The best news is that we were able to stop a takeover attempt. As we guessed, Carlton was leading a well-orchestrated effort to assume control of the enclave. What we didn't know is that he had rallied others from the North Dakota Territories to assist in an attack. Using our drones, we saw the existence of his army, if you could call it an army, and proactively changed the dynamics of the conflict. Four hundred and twenty-three of his followers surrendered.

"Part of Carlton's scheme was to kidnap important enclave officials, including Chrystel and Letitia. They planned a prisoner swap to obtain technology and as a diversion from their primary purpose—an attack. Chrystel escaped and returned on her own, almost bumping into Thomas' forces on the old I-5. Letitia wasn't so fortunate. She was shot and killed by a North Dakotan during the escape.

"Finally, our daughter Amelia has a boyfriend. She is making progress toward freedom from her home".

Karen barely knew how to respond to that last bit of news. "You make it all sound so easy, yet I know it wasn't." Karen wanted to pursue more information on this boyfriend of Amelia's but stopped herself. She could find out tomorrow on her own. "I'm so thankful Amelia may have found a way out of her self-imposed cage. What are your challenges, right now?"

"We have a tent city on the outskirts of town, filled with the Dakota folks. I promised them a life or, at least, the chance of one. I'm trying to feed them and locate homes with clavers willing to take them in. A segregated ghetto in the enclave would be the worst way to integrate Dakotans into New Washington. They are mostly good people put in a bad situation. Carlton's brother, Red, killed Letitia. He is incarcerated in the city jail awaiting trial. Carlton will also need to be tried, but he's still in a bad way recovering in the medical center after being shot by the twins, Rachael and Katie. We have some time on that one. Also, we identified several traitors in the enclave. What do we do with inside traitors, Karen? Just exile them or something worse? I'm still struggling with that issue."

Mike stopped, his eyes crinkling at the corners, and in his most sincere way observed his wife. "Have I told you how much I missed you?"

"You did mention it. I'm afraid I have much more to add to your plate. Is this mayor position permanent?"

"God, no! Chrystel needed a couple of days to pull herself together. She's called every morning to say she's ready. Tomorrow, I'll tell her okay. But, that doesn't mean I'll shirk my responsibility to our Dakota guests.

"Of course. Are you ready to meet the aliens?"

"Do I have a choice?"

Karen laughed. "No, you don't. Follow me." Karen had at least a thousand more questions, but they could wait. She grabbed Mike's hand and led him down the hall.

Maleta, sitting on a wheeled desk chair, sipped coffee and listened carefully to Judy, who appeared to be taking her ears off. "Maleta, this is my husband and temporary mayor, Mike McCollough."

Maleta stood and thrust her hand forward to have it shaken. "It's an honor to meet you, Mike McCollough."

Before Mike could return a greeting, Karen asked, panicked, "Where are the Mermots, Maleta?"

"They wanted to go outside and get some fresh air. It's been many years since they have enjoyed the freedom to roam on terra forma."

Karen attempted to hide her horror. Visions of a drunk claver shooting Rappel or Tweet because they were mistaken for some terrible rat beast entered her china shop brain like a crazed bull. "Shit!" was her only exclaim as she ran to the door and outside into the pouring rain, searching the darkness for any sign of them.

Mike offered, "I'll get a flashlight and help you search."

"Wait, wait, there they are," Karen pointed from the courthouse steps. Karen squished through sodden grass to the bomb crater. At least it used to be crater. Tweet and Rappel, covered in mud, rain plastering their fur flat to their round bodies, were packing dirt by scurrying back and forth at a dizzying pace. The hole was nearly filled. Quivering, Rappel and Tweet rose to acknowledge Karen.

"How did you do that in fifteen minutes?! How is it even possible?" Karen exclaimed. "You're shivering. Why don't you come inside?"

Tweets singsong voice burst into Karen's mind. "No Karen, we are joyous. We are joyous to be on your world and to be useful." A haunting melody with words from an unheard-of language filled Karen's and Mike's senses. Tweet's eyes closed as she swayed during the singing.

"What's the song about, Tweet?

"It's about a clan that was lost in a storm and how they finally found their way home."

Mike studied the Mermots, looked at the filled hole, and back to the Mermots. "How many of you did you say would be arriving? And, exactly how soon can you get them here? We've got plenty for you to do here on earth."

## 32. First Times

The roar of a finely aged vacuum cleaner sent the canines scurrying. Only Tilley, from her roost on the sofa, watched Chrystel toil. Chrystel scowled at her. "Make yourself useful. Pick up these toys lying about. After I'm done, it's bath time for dirty dogs and aliens." Tilley's eyes went wide, and her ears furled. Her last experience with a bath had been most unpleasant.

Tilley did her best to clandestinely slide off the couch to hide, but she heard knocking over the din of noise created by the cleaning machine. She moved instead to the door to alert Chrystel a guest had arrived. "You have to go outside?" Chrystel yelled over the racket. She pulled the vacuum upright and flicked the off switch. "Oh, there's someone at the door. Thank you, Tilley, for allowing me to answer," Chrystel sarcastically remarked.

Brodie stood nervously on her stoop, a bottle of wine in one hand and spring tulips in the other. "I know I should have called first, but I badly wanted to see you."

At the sight of Brodie, Chrystel's body involuntarily flooded with warmth. *Why does he have that effect on me*, she questioned for the hundredth time. "You're right, you should have called. I'm deep in the middle of trying to save myself from drowning in fur. You brought wine, and I have some things to discuss, so I'll take a break. Come on in."

Brodie grinned as he released the wine and flowers to Chrystel who turned and immediately headed to the kitchen. Tilley, offering a henka greeting, raised a many toed paw in Brodie's direction and then set it delicately on the floor. "Good to see you too, Tilley," Brodie replied.

Chrystel listened to Brodie's one-way conversation with Tilley while digging through cabinets for a proper flower receptacle. Sighing to herself at the woeful state of her social life, she couldn't remember the last time anyone had brought her flowers.

Presently, Chrystel was the caregiver for two additional dogs, she named Curly and Moe. The shy mutts greeted Brodie after removing themselves from their napping locations. What choice did she have? They helped her escape from the school in her time of need, and they needed a roof over their heads. Thomas was impressed with Lionheart when he'd heard of the dog's courage during Chrystel's escape and encouraged Chrystel to give him to Trent. Releasing Lionheart to Trent's care was harder than she had expected.

Pouring wine into goblets, Chrystel looked up when Brodie blurted from the living area, "I have good news. I'm no longer engaged."

"That so?" Chrystel said as she handed Brodie his wine. Chrystel sat and waited for further explanation.

"Sherry's family took in a North Dakota boy. I wouldn't say it was love at first sight, but Sherry wanted to drop me like a hot potato."

"I'm sure that's a relief to you, Brodie."

"It is, and I'm happy for her. Happy for me too."

Ignoring the breakup newsflash, Chrystel moved on to another subject. "I've been thinking,

314

the election is next week. Since we are the only candidates left for mayor and council chairperson, I believe we can rest easy that we'll be elected. My grandfather has quite a following and will get a bevy of write-in votes, but he wouldn't take the job if offered. I don't believe I'm being presumptuous by suggesting we might as well get started. I'm back in the saddle tomorrow."

Brodie didn't want to talk business just yet. Chrystel had batted away his engagement news in a nanosecond. Maybe he was wrong about her feelings for him. He was incredibly frustrated about how to reach this unique woman. He reminded himself that forcing something wasn't going to work. She would decide one way or another if she wanted him in her life. *Take your time, Brodie.* "I'll be in first thing tomorrow morning, and as much as you need in the future. Tonight, I was hoping you could tell me what happened during the kidnapping and your escape. That is, if you want to talk about it. Letitia was a friend. It's important to me to know what happened to her."

Chrystel's face morphed from professional to reflective and then sad. As he waited, Brodie was certain she was going to send him packing. After a long pause, she spoke while looking at a point on the floor. "I was heading to the Dairy with Tilley."

Two hours and two bottles of wine later, Chrystel was leaning on Brodie, her legs propped on a sofa table, unable to remember what she was just about to say. "Ah, I think I've had too much to drink. Maybe we could start a little later tomorrow."

Brodie's arm was holding Chrystel's weight and had stayed in place since Chrystel's voice

315

broke during the telling of Letitia's bravery. He casually touched her hair and wound a red curl around his finger. Needles woke in Brodie's blood deprived hand, a hand that had lingered too long in an unnatural position. Chrystel looked up at him with such vulnerability, he felt like a fist had vice-gripped his heart. "I truly appreciate that you listened to me. When I came back, everyone wanted the shortened version of the story. They care, but there were necessary, immediate actions to take. You're the only one who asked. I feel better from saying it out loud. I'm truly grateful."

Brodie thought he should thank her too. Thank Chrystel for sharing Letitia's last moments. He went in for a kiss instead. Surprised and tentative at first, Chrystel responded by pressing against his chest, her body warm, soft, pliable. She parted her lips to his need, exploring the sensation. Finally, able to move his leaden arm, Brodie cradled her neck with one hand, while the other moved over her strong back and down toward her ample behind.

Chrystel, pulled back slightly, breathless, searching for his eyes. "We shouldn't do this."

"Why not?" Brodie croaked hoarsely.

"The first time shouldn't be when I'm drunk."

"It's better that way. Trust me on this. Takes away any annoying awkwardness."

Chrystel continued to stare at Brodie. Her face had transformed from excited pink to beet red. "Wait, first time?" Brodie asked. "First time as in 'first time'?"

Chrystel pulled back further, clutching huge hunks of red hair in her fists and bent as she spoke. "I know! It's so embarrassing."

"Nothing to be embarrassed about. I'm simply surprised," Brodie said while trying to recover the blood that had poured into his extremities.

"I can't explain why. It wasn't as if I was saving myself for the perfect man or had any moral objections. My focus was always elsewhere, and I can be prickly. I scared off most men before it happened. And then I was mayor, and starting a relationship became even harder. . ."

*Pansy asses. This gorgeous, sexy, smart and inexplicable package, and no one possessed the wherewithal to stick with it? I won't be similarly deterred.* "I have an idea. Let's drink big glasses of water to avoid a hangover, go to bed, and just cuddle. If you feel like resuming this moment in the morning, we'll be sober. If not, we've shared a night together and no harm, no foul. You can think about it more. As I told you before you were kidnapped, I'm not going anywhere."

Chrystel grabbed him and hugged his broad, up to snuff shoulders, nearly changing her mind. "That means a lot, Brodie. Tilley won't be happy about giving up her space in bed, but she'll live."

Curious, Tilley watched everything about the human mating process from a far corner of the room and whispered to Brodie. "I will gladly give my space to make Chrystel happy. It is, as it should be."

# 33. Join us

Karen turned to Mike. "I still don't think I should be the one to make this announcement. Chrystel's beautiful face will drive young men and women in droves to our enclave. My old mug is hardly camera friendly."

"We've talked about this ad nauseam, Karen. A mature, stately messenger is what we need right now."

"Then why don't you get in front of the camera? You were, after all, temporary mayor when the aliens made landfall." Karen half-smiled.

"This again? Seriously? The Ardinians chose you. An outstanding choice, if I say so myself. You'll be great. You look beautiful, by the way."

Karen rubbed her hands together and smirked as she shook her head. "Well, shit. I guess I'm as ready as I'm ever going to be. How about Maleta and the Mermots?"

"They're waiting with bated breath for you in the studio," Mike said as he offered Karen his hand to cajole her forward. "Why the nerves, Karen? In all our years, this is a side of you I've never seen before."

"Nothing has ever been this important," she stated, drawing a game face from a lifetime of piled cards.

Karen strode into the studio. A lifelike hologram background provided by the Ardinians, displayed an appealing northwest scene of snowcapped mountains and towering fir trees. The cylindrical Ardinian shuttle was featured prominently in the hologram, its smooth gray form clearly visible against a deep blue sky. Maleta had worn her best Ardinian robes. Shimmering red weave contrasted against her gold glowing skin. Karen realized when she saw her, how important this plea to humanity must be to Maleta as well—the skin color change to gold, an obvious tell of Ardinian high emotion.

The Mermots were as cute as you could make rat-like alien lifeforms. To prevent accidents in the form of mistaken identity, it was agreed that Mermots should always wear some form of human clothing. The thinking went that clothes-clad Mermots would be easier for Washingtonians to distinguish from say, a misshapen deer or monster raccoon. The Mermots preferred to go about their work au natural, but were persuaded early in their earth introduction the first time a scared claver took a potshot at one of their clan. Their preference was to wear only a shirt. Today, in honor of the occasion, Rappel dressed in a grey suit tailored expressly for his unusual dimensions. Tweet, by far the more appealing of the two, was resplendent in a peach dress.

If Mermots could smile, which they couldn't, Tweet's happy countenance would have won the hearts and minds of all prospective viewers. Shakete was right about the positive qualities of the Mermot species. In their every interaction, Mermots endeared themselves to humans. It wasn't just how fast they completed difficult projects, although that alone was impressive for the always short-handed enclave. More than that, their enthusiasm was infectious. No job was too big or too complicated, and no favor was unworthy of consideration.

Exalting in play like work, Mermots joined human games whenever asked. They didn't want or need anyone to provide for them, and they had built their own community underneath the earth while gathering food from local sources. Mermots loved with abandon, particularly, the green gem known as earth.

"Come and stand behind me, Tweet," Karen smiled. The cameraman counted, "Three, two, one, action!"

Karen looked directly into the camera. "Good day fellow citizens of Earth. My name is Karen Henry McCollough. I am one of nine founders of the New Washington Enclave and a survivor of the Great Dying. Today, I bring extraordinary news and hope for the future. Four months ago, my enclave made first contact with life from another planet."

Karen told of her trip to the Mermot moon and the conflict with the viscous Hunta species, all accompanied by videos and pictures on the background hologram. Her last words were a plea. "I can understand if anyone listening has doubts about my truthfulness. In your shoes, I might as well. This is no trick or sleight of hand. Everything I've described to you is the whole and utter truth.

"Our fragile world is in grave danger. The Ardinians and Mermots have arrived to help, but they need us as much as we need them. We must find the willing, those of you that see a higher purpose in our existence. Those of you that wish to put aside the relative safety of your homes to join us to protect our world and our people.

"We need pilots. Anyone who has ever flown anything is welcome. Even those who have only a passion or interest to learn are welcome. We need engineers and workers to help build weapons. We need tradespeople. We will need farmers to feed those that join.

"We understand how important each of you are to your communities. If you are like us, every person is vitally important, but please also understand, none of it will matter if we don't protect our world from the coming invasion by the Hunta.

"We are opening our doors at great risk to ourselves. Just recently, another enclave tried to invade New Washington. Instead of punishing them after we prevented their attack, we welcomed them into our homes. Our very survival demands an open door, a forgiving heart, and a steely eyed view of the way ahead.

"Join us. If you can make your way here, a welcome mat awaits your arrival. If you can't, send a message, and we will send airships to pick you up. Our sacrifice will be shared sacrifice. Our reward, our very existence, will be a shared reward. "The motto of New Washington, since a handful of survivors laid claim to this piece of ground, is 'We endure.' That motto served us well when it took everything we had to scratch out an existence. Today is different. We must do far more than merely endure. We have come too far to go silently into the night. Today, I propose a new motto, 'For Earth!'

"Join us!"

"That's a wrap!" the cameraman shouted. Karen and the other participants were still.

"Do you think it sounded hokey? Do you think they'll believe us, believe me?"

Maleta answered. "No, Karen, it wasn't hokey, if I fully comprehend the meaning of that word, hokey. I was inspired. I would join you if I wasn't already here."

Karen laughed and hugged her. "I hope you're right Maleta. I guess we'll find out."

Tweet broke into song. She was still singing as they filed out to the courthouse corridor and the waiting throng of friends and family. After handshakes and back slapping, a small group headed to a conference room to continue the grueling work of preparing the enclave for a quadrupling of their population.

Chrystel, returned from captivity to her mayoral duties, led the discussions. "So where do we stand on barracks and renovated homes?"

Rappel whiskers raised and lowered. "My dear mayor. We have completed 40 buildings that will house 120 people each. We currently have a work stoppage while waiting for more concrete. We have used the opportunity to clear more ruined homes from their foundations. Approximately 41% of those foundations are safe and usable so that we can build upon them. Once we have concrete, it will take two weeks to finish the last 10 barracks, and then we will start on the homes.

Chrystel and the rest of the planning committee were dumbfounded. "Already, 40 buildings complete. How?" she asked.

"Mermots have begun accelerated breeding. This ability has been very helpful to our species. Our children, born in litters of 12 to 15, can assist almost immediately. We started procreation processes when we knew of travel to earth. Our females are delivering new children to our clan daily. I hope this will not be a problem."

"I suppose not. That's very interesting, though. How is it you didn't overpopulate your world?"

"When the Mermot population reaches the limit of our resources, egg production stops. Females can also will eggs to be eliminated during the breeding cycle. You needn't be worried that we will be a drain on necessary materials."

"No, not at all, just curious."

Brodie, the new council chairperson, chimed in. "What challenges are you experiencing besides concrete, Rappel?"

"Water and sewage. If there were underground aquifers, we could dig to them as a water source. I have my best foreman working the problem, and I'm sure she will resolve the water source issue satisfactorily. Also, furniture production is lagging. We have sent a team of Mermots to assist the human production facility with wood and materials. They were very happy regarding this assistance."

"Thank you, Rappel. Your news is more positive than I expected. How can we help?"

Rappel paused, "I can't think of anything now, but I will pass any requests through Tweet if a route of greater productivity presents itself."

Chrystel turned to Manny next. "How goes the effort to build and outfit a flight training facility?"

"Much better than we expected. The Mermots provided the manpower, or I guess we might call it Mermot power, to shore up an old Boeing hanger. It's mostly done. Flight simulators have been arriving from the Ardinian ship as quickly as they can be fabricated. All told, we should have 30 units available by week's end. That's a good start."

"Has anyone tested their efficacy? Whether the simulators actually train someone to fly a fighter space vehicle?"

Manny ran his hand through his hair. "A tricky situation. No one knows how to fly them. Me and Dee are the guinea pigs. We're using the simulators and will be the first team in a cockpit to see if the simulator training worked."

Chrystel asked, "That's awfully risky, isn't it? We need you both as managers and leaders once we have more people join us. Isn't there anyone else who could do the test flight?"

"Recommendations?" Dee asked ruefully.

"Point taken," Chrystel nodded. "What about Margo from North Dakota. I heard she flew a crop duster in the territories."

Manny answered. "She's hanging with us and training on the simulators too. Smart lady, I think. Anyway, that's a grand total of three."

"Well, if you think of any way to mitigate the risk, do it. Moving on to security, Thomas, what do you have?"

"I have a goat rope. Since we're opening our doors to everyone, I'm not sure what to secure. The Ardinians gave Jed a prototype ray gun." Thomas laughed. "It's a high beam laser that's good for close in fighting or long range to take out something from the air. Just depends on the setting. Cool as hell. They'll come in extremely handy for the good guys, but also any bad actors that managed to steal one. Jed is going to produce a limited number for now, and we'll keep them in the hands of our most trusted lieutenants. Other than that, our vulnerabilities are limitless. Until we take in whoever is going to join us and determine who is truly onboard, I'm not sure what else we can do."

"How about guards on important infrastructure and research facilities."

"Of course, already had facility security programmed. I have another idea though, I would like to discuss with you in that regard and would prefer to brief you one-on-one."

"Thomas, if you can't trust everyone in this room, we're doomed before we start," Chrystel said, with the greatest respect for Thomas' instincts.

He looked around at the meeting participants, eyeing each one. "I suppose you're right, Chrystel, but it goes against my instincts to share too freely. I think we should place our weapons manufacturing somewhere else. And when I say somewhere else, I'm speaking in another state, away from prying eyes. Somewhere we can keep secret. Maybe even Idaho at the old ranch. It had plenty of space and was isolated.

"Just because we're keeping the inn open, doesn't mean we need to be stupid. Weapons are always the biggest target for theft and destruction. We could send a handful of New Washington natives and Mermots to this undisclosed location. Why put all our eggs in one basket, especially eggs that go boom?"

Manny spoke up. "That's an excellent idea, Thomas."

"Yeah, well, us warrior thugs tend to consider the worst of people in our planning."

"There might be even more logistical problems with a distant facility, but the idea is sound. I say we take a vote," Brodie added in his capacity as chairperson. "All in favor."

"Aye," came a resounding reply. Just at that moment, an excited Judy burst through the door. "You aren't going to believe this. We're getting calls from all over the world, Madrid, Cairo, Tokyo, Mexico City, Hawaii, Peking, Hamburg. Small cities too. So many messages we can't keep up. There is even a Russian who said he was an original and the General in charge of the Russian Air Force! A fighter pilot original from Alabama is on his way now. It's way more than we ever imagined."

"And so, it begins," Thomas mumbled. "Let's finish that vote and get to work."

Brodie hung back in the conference room with Chrystel after everyone left. He watched her gather her notes and try to ignore him. She slyly glanced in his direction, her eyes smiling even though her mouth didn't follow. "What?" she asked.

"I was just waiting to ask what you might be interested in for dinner. I know you don't want me leering at you when you're in mayor mode. I'm not sure how we can continue to keep "us" a secret or even why it's necessary."

"Hmmm, dinner. Could you pick something up at the Farelli's on the way home?" New Washington's restaurants couldn't be compared to pre-change eating establishments. Families with a bent toward food preparation, served one or two offerings at mealtimes from their homes. Dining-in amounted to a seat around their kitchen table, but take-out remained take-out. Chrystel's mouth

326

watered thinking about the Farelli's linguini and clams, one their most common meals. It seemed like she hadn't eaten in days.

"Tonight, is spaghetti and meatballs night. No clams," Brodie reminded.

"Darn, you're right. Spaghetti's still good."

"You're going to simply ignore my last statement about secrecy, aren't you?"

Chrystel chuckled. "That was my plan."

"Even though there's that extra little bit of excitement involved with sneaking around, I'm not feeling I need it right now. You?"

At last, the smile had reached her mouth. "No Brodie, I won't be tricked into talking about our excitement here."

"Can't blame a guy for trying. Spaghetti it is then. Meatballs and further discussions later."

"You are a very bad boy," Chrystel answered in a sultry voice.

## 34. Mothers and Daughters

Guilt over not seeing her mother had reached a zenith. Feelings of dereliction had gone from an irritating itch to a nagging doubt and were in the third stage of daughter angst, staging a full-scale squatting protest with Chrystel's every unengaged moment. If Chrystel's mind wasn't fully focused on something, anything else, her mother's face would pop, unbidden, into her thoughts. Her grandparents had assured her, Amelia was better. Chrystel wanted to believe them, but fear that Amelia's recovery was only an apparition had kept her away. Fear that she would be pulled again into her mother's web of neediness, only to be trapped in the sticky strands of maternal longing and obligation.

"Can you pick up some potatoes?" was the first phrase that came to mind when Chrystel thought of her mother. She was six when her father passed. Before that day, her mother was like most moms; loving, nurturing, a place where Chrystel was always safe. Every night, Amelia read Chrystel stories of fantastic places and amazing creatures. She tucked Chrystel into bed with a mantra about bedbugs before a session of hugs and kisses. Dad would burst through the door after work yelling, "Where's my red-headed welcoming committee," to which, Chrystel launched herself at him from whatever hiding spot she had selected that day. What could be more perfect? Two loving parents, and Chrystel was the center of their world.

Inexplicably for a six-year-old, one afternoon she came home from school, and both parents were gone. One forever and another possessed by a stranger, a woman who looked like her mother, but wasn't. This woman haunted their home in a dream of unimaginable pain. Pain a little girl could never hope to understand.

It was the potato incident that changed Chrystel and not the death of the parents she knew. Dusk nearing, Grandpa and Grandma had dropped her home after celebrating Chrystel's twelfth birthday. All Chrystel's many cousins were invited. The party was wonderful. Chrystel sneaked in, hoping to avoid her mom's questions about the birthday party Amelia had, as always, refused to attend. "Chrystel, is that you?" her mom's childlike voice called from the kitchen.

"I've made you dinner and a cake!"

*Great. I'm stuffed to the brim with ice cream and cake, and I must eat again so my mom won't feel left out.* Chrystel plodded to the kitchen. Amelia turned to her and smiled sweetly.

"I just need you to go over to the neighbors and pick up some potatoes. Can you pick up some potatoes for me, dear?"

"It's almost dark, and the Johnson's are two miles away. I don't need potatoes."

"Fried chicken isn't the same without mashed potatoes." Amelia argued.

"Mom, its fine."

"But, I was looking so forward to it though."

And there it was. This dinner wasn't about Chrystel or her birthday or what she wanted or needed. Chrystel was the fetch-it gal, enabling her mother to stay burrowed in her hole. *Screw it*, or a twelve-year-old equivalent was Chrystel's only thought. Chrystel's face reddened as she said, "I feel sick."

Heading to her room, Chrystel could hear her mother's sobs. She shut the bedroom door to dampen the sound. Shaking in rage, she placed her hands over her ears. *She doesn't care about me. She wants me to feel sorry for her, so I'll do whatever she wants. I'm sick of being manipulated, and I'm sick of making excuses for her. From this day forward, I will not be used. I can do everything myself. I don't need her. I will not let her hurt me again.*

On an intellectual level, Chrystel now understood the reasons for her mother's mental disease. She and Grandma Karen had talked about it often enough. But where her grandma had never given up hope that Amelia would someday break the curse that plagued her, Chrystel managed only distant empathy for her mother's plight. Forgiveness would only happen when Amelia made the effort to break the confining spell that held her. Everyone said, the effort had been made, not for Chrystel, but because of a new man named Trent.

When Chrystel murmured something to that effect to Karen, her grandmother had scowled and grabbed Chrystel's shoulders, "Chrystel, I know you suffered too. You felt betrayed and abandoned, and it was never your fault. A child should never have to be the parent. But dear child, change happens, when and only when, someone is ready to move on. Your mother is finally ready. I'm glad Trent came into her life and was the spark that lit the fire.

I hope someday you can forgive her too, when you're ready. There really is another Amelia living somewhere inside her. I knew that other Amelia once, and so did you when you were little."

"Way to go, Grandma, throw it back at me," Chrystel responded, her mouth pulled in a frown.

"Dear Chrystel, I know you know what I meant. Just give her a chance. People can change. One day at a time."

When Chrystel looked at the open front door of her mother's house, her first instinct screamed something was terribly wrong. Shadows from the rapidly encroaching evening lay like ominous specters over the entry. Jumping from the ATV, heart beating in her chest, Chrystel took stock of the area for any threat. Tilley was urgently trying to communicate that they were behind the house, but as always, Chrystel could not hear her.

Lionheart pounded around the corner, a dog smile on his face as he loped the last few yards to welcome Chrystel and Tilley. He almost knocked Chrystel on her rear when he pushed his body against her legs, his tail pounding her front, all while whining for reciprocal attention. "Lionheart! My good boy," She attempted to pat his head and ears, but Lionheart was so energetically squirming and circling, Chrystel couldn't land a good scratch.

Lionheart calmed when Amelia appeared out of the ensuing darkness from the side yard. His arm protectively encircling her mother, Trent matched Amelia's slow gait, allowing her to lean against his chest. He yelled to Chrystel, "We might have overdone it today. Follow us in please."

Amelia glanced at her daughter and tried to smile. In a breathless whisper, she exhaled, "Please, follow."

Trent flipped light switches as he entered the house and shepherded Amelia to the kitchen. Guided to a chair, she dropped to a seat, still breathing rapidly in the almost throes of a full panic attack. Chrystel entered the kitchen with Tilley and Lionheart, surprised by the lack of clutter. The house wasn't neat as a pin like her own, but the stacks of books and magazines were miraculously missing. There was room to move, sit, and cook a meal. The air filled with the smell of cinnamon and vanilla, and a fresh plate of cookies sat on the table.

"Please sit, Chrissy. Would you like something to drink?" Amelia squeaked out through breaths that were beginning to slow.

"Sure, I could use a beer if you have one. I'll get it." Chrystel stood and moved to Trent first, shaking his hand. "Hi Trent. I've heard a lot about you, but we haven't had the chance to be properly introduced."

"Well, I feel like I know you. Everyone in your family is so proud of you. They talk about you all the time. Glad you stopped by. Your mother has been hoping for a visit."

Chrystel nodded, tried a smile, and then busied herself getting a beer.

"Give your mom a few minutes. We were working on keeping the door open and being outside when it's dark. It wasn't quite dark, but close enough. She did great tonight. We were out there for over a half hour." Trent beamed at Amelia who returned a look that was so endearing, Chrystel's heart felt that warm twang she got when she was touched with something of beauty.

"Whew, I'm feeling better. Have a cookie, Chrystel. I know you love oatmeal."

Chrystel consumed one slowly and then three more in quick succession. When she was picking the last crumbs off the table with her finger to eat them too, Amelia came up behind her, placing her hands on Chrystel's shoulders and her chin on Chrystel's head. "I am so glad you came. I wanted you to see how much progress I've made. And I've missed you more than you know."

Chrystel's face broke. Her eyes filled with tears, and she nearly gagged trying to rein in a flood of emotion. "I've missed you too, Mom," she returned in a wobbly voice. After taking a few moments to recover, Chrystel repacked her baggage and went on to a different subject. "Have you guys heard about everything happening in the enclave? Exciting times."

Trent answered. "Me and your family mostly keep Amelia up to date. We listened to the announcement from Karen this afternoon on the shortwave. They said there was video too, but we didn't know how to make that work. I worry about repercussions for the enclave by allowing anyone in, even while I understand the absolute need."

Amelia, leaning back in her seat at the table, was looking off to the side as if listening to something other than Trent. "What is it, Mom?"

She smiled. "Nothing really. Your purple friend was just telling me you have a boyfriend. Who is it? I'd love to meet him."

"Tilley!!" Chrystel screeched. Her head whipped around like a demon possessed victim needing a speedy exorcism. "You know I've asked you to refrain from sharing my personal life. It is mine to share."

Tilley's large, round eyes and furled ears appeared fully repentant. Trent and Amelia were both laughing. "Oh, don't worry, dear. Mom and Dad already told me. I believe the cat's out of the bag. I thought you might share it first, so I didn't say anything. Hard to keep love a secret for too long." Amelia glanced at Trent.

"Awww, crap." Chrystel joined in the laughter. "And I believed we were so discreet. By the way, hearing the animals, or in this case an alien, isn't bothering you?"

"It's wonderful, actually. They are so funny and cheerful. I've missed a lot." Amelia reached across the table and grabbed Chrystel's hand. "I've missed too much, especially you. And, I plan to make up for it, if you'll give me the chance."

"I'm here, Mom. One day at a time." Chrystel withdrew her hand. "Speaking of my boyfriend, I'd better get going. He promised to pick up dinner, and it's probably getting cold."

"Well, you have a wonderful dinner, although after a plate of cookies, I'm not sure how hungry you could be. But then, you always had a voracious appetite. Stop by anytime Chrystel, and next time, bring your boyfriend too if you want. If you let me know in advance, I'll make a nice meal. My door is always open." Amelia chuckled, "Well, sometimes we shut it when Trent lets me."

Chrystel gave her mother a hug. The first she could remember since childhood. "I'll be back, Mom."

Trent saw Chrystel to the door. She looked him hard in the eyes and said, "Thank you, Trent."

He seemed to understand the larger meaning. "Just come back and see your mom. That's thanks enough."

# 35. Pilot Wannabes

Manny waited on the Boeing Airfield tarmac with Dee and Margo. Mike had interviewed Margo for a position at the airfield when she had begged him for a chance to prove herself. As a small plane pilot, Margo had at least some experience with aviation. Mike had come away from Margo's interview with a strong belief that she was sincere and very capable. He'd directed the airfield to take her, even though she'd been involved in the North Dakota conspiracy. Manny and Dee had reservations, but Mike's word was golden and thus far, Margo had proven to be dedicated to their mission.

A transport airship vented its powerful exhaust as it hovered over the runway readying for landing, the steady roar of thrust hurling dust in all directions. Jed's airships, powered by a lightweight thorium generator, made possible a flight propulsion design much like pre-change Harrier aircraft; they could lift and land almost vertically. Where Harriers were simultaneously sleek and destructive, the new world version was of a boxy, tubular construction, two stunted wing sets sprouting from its sides. Unlike Harriers, the only danger of these new age air contraptions was to birds accidentally crossing their path.

The airship turned 90 degrees, made one last high whining blast, and sat down gently on six balloon-like tires that inflated at the last possible moment. A waiting crew hastily rolled a three-step platform under the plane's body as the forward door slid open to release the craft's passengers: volunteer pilots, and others wanting to help defend earth from the Hunta. The pilot exited first, saw Manny, and jogged to his location to provide an out-brief of the mission.

"You don't look any worse for wear. I'm assuming since I don't see any bullet holes in the fuselage, everything went well," Manny said as he shook the pilot's hand and grabbed his arm.

Before answering, the pilot checked out Margo and turned to face the rag tag group of volunteers gathering by the airship. "We picked up fourteen from eastern Europe and ten from Norway. We couldn't land in Germany because the group in Bonn was so large, I was afraid their plan was to overrun us and take the ship. It might've been okay, but I was unwilling to take the chance. Someone needs to get on the horn and explain that we won't land if there's a riotous crowd waiting."

Dee added. "We've been spreading that word, but I'll pass the information to Tweet to make sure enclave headquarters reinforces crowd control in the nightly worldwide broadcasts"

"Better go gather them up," Margo hinted, nodding at the confused and lost looking volunteers.

The Russian was the last person to depart the plane. He stooped as he came through the open door as if his height prevented a normal exit. He was tall, but not appreciably so. His face impassive, he loitered on the steps momentarily to take in the sights.

The unorganized group of twenty-four men and women huddled in clumps, most likely formed by a common language. The new recruits pointed and talked as they took in their new environment. The airfield was a hive of activity. ATV locomotives pulled train carts, full and sometimes overflowing with all manner of supplies and materials on the tarmac. The blur of a Mermot scampering to the aircraft to service it for its next mission caused the greatest sensation and drew surprised reactions from the newbies. New Washington natives had grown accustomed to the movement speed of Mermots. It was unnaturally eerie at first and later reassuring once the realization of speed as the ultimate workhorse took hold, particularly, since the Mermots had established themselves as friends.

Another Mermot joined the welcoming committee and volunteers to interpret into their respective languages. He zoomed between Manny and Dee, stopped on a dime, and then raised his rat like head, balancing on his fat body and thick tail. Twitching whiskers and a voice in their heads said an enthusiastic, "Hello, my friends." He was wearing engineer overalls and a fedora which got a discreet chuckle from Margo.

The foreigners had heard rumors about the aliens, but most had not seen the video portion of Karen's plea. Only the Russian, firmly rooted in his stance, remained insolently unafraid. The rest of the group backed up nonchalantly and tried to hide their immediate rat revulsion responses. One blond haired, blue eyed young man expelled what sounded like a curse in his native tongue.

The Mermot interpreter was not offended by their reactions. Leading with a short narrative about his people and how they had evolved to the pinnacle of a cooperative, industrious and peaceful race, the greetings came next. The Mermot waved to Manny, indicating he could begin his portion of the greetings. "Welcome to each of you and a special acknowledgment to General Tanislov of the old Russian Air Force." Manny looked directly at the general, "Your presence here will be a great contribution to our mission." Standing erect, the general folded his arms in front of his chest and stoically nodded.

"I'm Manny, the lead trainer and facilitator for creating a space force to protect earth. Now, if I could see a show of hands for those of you that understand English." About half the group raised hands. "Wonderful. That's more than some groups we've welcomed. My Mermot translator is sending thoughts to those of you who do not have a good grasp of English. Thoughts you will hear in your mind and understand. As best I can explain this ability, Mermots receive thoughts before they are transcribed to language and then send those impressions by a biological energy mechanism into another mind. Your brain actually forms the transmissions into your language."

A slender, dark haired woman poked her hand in the air. "Can they hear thoughts we wish to keep to ourselves?" she asked. There was a smattering of nervous laughter to her question. Manny told a bold face lie each time this question was raised. "Yes, they can hear personal thoughts as well." Eyes darted, and positions shifted as the volunteers considered the implication of mind readers. The Russian even registered a look of discomfort at the prospect Mermots were the ultimate lie detector machines. The blond man cursed again.

"Please, don't worry about that for now. We have food and drink in the hanger and a welcome celebration waiting. I'm sure you're all looking forward to finding a home here and getting started on our critical work and training."

Dee, Margo, and the Mermot led the group to the hanger while Manny stayed to give the pilot the next mission coordinates. "Rest and refresh your crew. Take what time you need, but no more than eight hours."

The pilot returned a smirk, "Roger, Manny. That Russian dude is interesting. He likes to strut."

"Geronimo pulled some information about him from an old archive. Victor Tanislov, Russian Air Force, General, fighter pilot, Afghanistan war hero, and an original. He matches the picture we found in the archives. I know the old U.S.A. wasn't on great terms with Russia when the world came apart by the seams, but that was then, and this is now. From what I read about him, he earned that strut. We can use someone like him on our side."

"I hear ya. For earth, then." The pilot was cackling at what he considered a silly motto as he left to gather his crew.

Watching him leave, Manny wondered how long they could keep secret that Mermots couldn't read minds. Their ability originated somewhere between where a thought was formed and sent to a language center to be communicated. At least, that's what Tweet had explained. The Mermots might be lying too, just to make humans feel more comfortable. Regardless, it was better to keep joiners on their toes. If they thought someone could read minds, it might prevent some minds from making bad decisions.

As Manny covered the airfield to find Jed, he thought again about the Russian, Victor. Manny had no reason to distrust someone simply because he was Russian. As far as Manny knew, Victor was the first Russian he'd ever met. His concerns were more selfish. That Victor would be better qualified to fly a destroyer class ship or lead the space force fleet they were building. He couldn't let his personal desires overcome pragmatic, real life needs. If Victor was more qualified, which he most certainly was in some areas, then so be it. Manny could still serve somewhere in the space force and keep flying. They would need more than one destroyer captain.

Entering Jed's office, after pausing to knock on the frame of an open door, Manny cleared his throat to get Jed's attention. Jed was hunched, squinting at a monitor, probably examining complicated scientific data. "How goes it, my man, Manny," Jed said, welcoming the intrusion.

"Hey, Jed. Going good. You need glasses or something? I see you squinting."

"Naw, my eyes are tired. Shakete asked me to add a fresh look to the Ardinian effort to project a matter reorganizing bomb into space. The science is remarkable. I've spent the past few days studying the theory to have any hope of offering something valuable to the discussion. I would have never thought to go in this direction for energy. Anti-matter certainly, but not this. Am I boring you, Manny?"

"No, not at all. My mind is simply elsewhere on more worldly matters. I can't seem to get rid of a growing apprehension about our security. Last night, 35 people from Florida showed up unannounced. They strolled across Airfield Two without a challenge. This morning, we found one of our guard dogs, shot."

"Oh, no. Where?"

"Near the laser weapons facility."

"That's not good. Did you talk to Thomas?"

"I did. He came up and looked around. There wasn't any indication of a break-in, and two people worked all night in the facility. There's no way anyone could sneak in and out of the building. It feels like I'm missing something, though. I don't know, maybe I'm just spooked. While we were aboard the Ardinians' ship, Karen told me about her daughter's premonition, that there would be bloodshed. Everyone keeps saying Amelia is never wrong."

"That's true about Amelia. But who's to say the course of the future is set? If you have forewarning, perhaps it's possible to bend the curve of events. What point would prescience serve if there was nothing that could be fixed or changed? I chose to believe that our enhanced abilities, the ones we gained during the change, were not some random occurrence, and that they came as part of some greater purpose."

"Wow, Jed. You've never gone all mystical on me. I'm surprised."

Jed chuckled. "Yeah, I'd better watch what I say, or I'll damage my reputation as a hard core, fact-based, scientist. Sometime, when we have the time, we can have a philosophical discussion about randomness versus patterns over a Bigfoot. For now, there's plenty of utilitarian reasons to feel vulnerable. This open-door policy, by its very nature, makes us susceptible to sabotage. If we're to protect ourselves from the Hunta, it's a risk we must take, and all we can do is be vigilant. The laser facility will be moving soon anyway, so it won't be our problem. We'll keep four laser systems to protect the airfield, facilities and barracks."

"I hadn't heard about a plan to move the laser production facility. Where to?"

"I don't know. I was only told, 'A place where it'll be safe'."

Manny frowned, blowing air through his lips. "Okay? Strange that it's being kept secret, but then lately, yeah, I get the purpose for keeping secrets. With all the walk-ons, we need to be careful."

"Any problems with the pilot training?"

"We haven't officially started. First, we must interview each candidate and then conduct written tests to determine competency and aptitude. The final piece is a tryout in the simulator. Oh, and lest we forget, before any actual training, Dee and I must take a ride in a fighter ship to validate that the simulators prepare pilots for flight. Nothing like a test of two people who have never flown anything, much less an attack spacecraft, to prove the worth of simulators."

"From what I understand, onboard computers do most of the flying. Since no one will be shooting at you, you'll be fine."

"That's what I keep telling myself. Anyway, there are so many applicants and more every day.

Some won't be chosen, or they'll have to settle for second string. It might be difficult for candidates to hear rejection. Especially since they've left their home and travelled long distances to join us."

"I believe if you make them feel like they're part of something important, which they are, hurt feelings won't last long," Jed offered. "Let's all hope we don't have to place second stringers into action too soon."

"Roger that. By the way, the Russian general showed up with the last group."

Jed smiled. "Really? What's he look like?"

"Arrogant, capable, reserved, and maybe a son of a bitch. If I had to create a mental picture of a Russian general, I would have drawn him. I'll let you get back to your work, Jed. I've used up more time than I can afford."

"Anytime," Jed said to Manny's back, already hurrying out of the door.

# 36. Get this Train Moving!

Converted to a processing center, one hanger at Boeing Field was filled with men and women wishing to join the cause. They had walked, driven, and flown to New Washington, some over great distances, when Karen's call for help beamed around the world. Lines formed outside the hanger, wrapping around the steel framed structure and snaking along a runway. Skies were threatening rain, but thus far, the weather had held, and the long line of candidates waited patiently for their turn.

Margo stared at a young man from Louisiana sitting across from her. He couldn't be much more than nineteen. An underdeveloped goatee and long, skinny arms and legs hinted that he hadn't progressed to full manhood. Dark brown eyes, even cocoa skin, and a disarming smile lingered on Margo with a keen intensity. The flight candidate, round robin interview process had grown tedious. Still, Margo couldn't help but smile at the excited earnestness of the young folks who had left their enclave to be here and give the process their best shot.

"So, what experience do you have with flight?"

"No in the cockpit experience, but I have a game that's like a flight simulator. I'm the highest scoring fighter pilot in the Baton Rouge Enclave," he exclaimed proudly.

"Well that's good. Tell me about your education. Did you go to school?"

"Mostly."

"Mostly? Can you expand upon that?"

"I went to school when I didn't have to help out my dad."

"Can you read and write?"

"Not long novels or anything, but good enough to read equipment manuals and fix farm equipment. That's my dad's business."

"Fixing things is a skill that always comes in handy. How are you at math?"

"Pretty good. Is that important?" he asked hesitantly.

"Not necessarily, but it's important to have a basic understanding of math concepts."

"Well, I have a basic understanding," he drawled in the old-time notes of a southerner.

"Do you know how to drive?"

A huge grin covered his face. "Everything, I can drive anything and everything from tractors to cranes to ATVs."

"That's great experience. So why are you here? Why did you decide to join?"

As if she had just asked the most ridiculous question in the universe, the young man replied, "Because you need me. I'm good at everything. Our whole world is depending on people like me."

Margo smiled. "You're absolutely right. You've passed to the next phase, the written test."

"Thank you, ma'am. That's all I can ask." He confidently shook Margo's hand and moved to the testing line.

She wrote on his interview form, "Who knows. Might be a good engineer or may be everything he thinks he is. Loyal would be my estimate. If he can pass a written test, the simulator will tell the tale.

"Next," Margo shouted.

They had interviewed nearly half of the almost 10,000 arrivals. The stream of incoming joiners was finally tapering to a trickle. Margo was lucky today because she had English speakers only and didn't need an interpreter. The interview process went quicker that way. Written testing was bogged down since non-native speakers couldn't read the test. Brodie had translated some into Spanish, French, and German but there were languages, such as Bulgarian where translation was impossible. Manny suggested to be fair, they skip the reading test altogether and only give an equation-based math test. A decision would be made that night.

From the corner of her eyes, Margo glanced again at Manny. The big Russian was at his table for an interview. Impressed that the general hadn't made a big deal of waiting in line for his turn, Margo gave him extra points for patience and aplomb. Given his background, an interview wasn't necessary, but Manny was adamant it would be a chance to find out more about the general's motivations and read between the lines.

Margo shuddered every time she thought about the nightmarish Hunta. How in the world would a Louisiana video gamer and a North Dakota crop duster like her ever have a chance against a race of vicious, hideous aliens? The Ardinians said they might have two years. Only two years and they were already on week three without the first trainee stepping inside a simulator. The only exceptions: her and the Dee-Manny team. They had to pick up the pace of pilot training, or the battle to protect earth would be doomed to failure, just as doomed as Margo's recent experience with her brother's idiotic plan to takeover New Washington.

Margo watched the clock plod to 3:00 p.m., the normal daily stop to interviews. She wouldn't sit idly by this time, not while someone else made nonsensical decisions, even when those decisions were made with good intentions. Manny's fairness mandate was great when you didn't have a horde of aliens breathing down your neck. Margo worked herself up to a frustrated lather until it was time to gather with the team and talk about progress.

Margo marched toward Manny, her fists clenched, ready for her first battle in the war for their world. The Russian, his grey hair styled in a pompadour, was standing beside Manny and saw Margo coming. The visage of an angry woman steaming full speed ahead was apparently a sight common to all countries, no matter their culture. Victor backed away slightly to allow Manny the pleasure of this encounter.

"I need to talk to you now Manny, and it can't wait."

"Okay, Margo." Manny waved them away from the Russian.

"What's up?"

"This isn't working. Doing everything consecutively is too slow. We need to identify anyone who has ever flown anything, throw them in a simulator and get them trained so that they can train others. You need to decentralize the management of this process, split it up with people to manage different operational functions. We need to identify some Mermots to help with interviews, ASAP."

Dee had strolled close enough to hear, but not so close that she would be in Margo's back-blast. Appearing totally uncomfortable, Manny asked with tight lips, "Anything else, Margo?"

"That's just a start. I probably shouldn't have come at you like this, but I can't just sit back and be a good little girl when there's so much on the line. I know you're doing your best, Manny—your heart is always in the right place, but success depends on the ability to trust the people around you and let go of some responsibility. That is, if you want to get it done."

"Uh, Margo, when you talk about trust, is it possible you have conveniently forgotten that you lobbed some fucking artillery at the enclave?!"

"No, I haven't forgotten! That's exactly why I'm standing here yelling at you now. I knew in my gut that attack was a catastrophically ignorant decision, and I did nothing! I counted on my brothers to think it through and change course. That approach was an obvious screw-up!"

Margo's feet were spread, her hands planted on her hips. Red faced, she'd made himself larger like a puffer fish. They glared at each other.

"That Russian standing there," Margo pointed, "is he a qualified pilot? Can he train?"

Everyone turned to look at Victor. "Yes, miss?"

"Call me, Margo."

"Margo, yes, I have spent my life devoted to aerospace. I have flown Russian fighter jets and led the Russian Aerospace Forces. Many times, my duties included training Russian proxies and our own pilots."

"And why did you come here?"

"To be part of this important mission." He smiled wistfully, "And, since a young boy, my dream was to go to space. The opportunity never came in Russia. Now, I will have that chance."

"Good enough for me." She pivoted back to Manny. "So far, we have the general here, a fighter pilot from Mobile, two commercial pilots, and a handful of others that have private aviation training. Come on, Manny, let go!"

Manny was doing his best not to become defensive. He felt blindsided and attacked even while he knew Margo was right. The first sign that Manny might someday be a great leader was when his Adams apple bobbed as he swallowed his pride. "Margo, you have some excellent ideas. I wish you could have come to me before in private to express these concerns, but well, I understand now why it's so important. Tomorrow we were supposed to go to the Ardinian ship to do the first test flight. Rather than go with me and Dee, why don't you stay here and reorganize this mess. Use Victor to help. Talk to Tweet about getting some more Mermots to help. If you can do it better, I'm in."

The fact that Margo had just been handed the keys to the kingdom and the responsibility that went with it took wind from her billowing sails. Now, they were all looking to her. Margo bit her lip and smiled uneasily, "Stay on the ship with the Ardinians for two days, and I think I can work something out. And thank you, Manny."

"No need to thank me. If you can get people trained quicker, we all benefit. Just make sure you don't let anyone attack us while we're gone and stay far away from artillery pieces. I will fill you in on current threats before we go." Manny strolled nonchalantly from the hanger, thinking the whole time, *Yes! Now I can focus on commanding a destroyer class ship or the fleet!*

Margo fidgeted in place as she considered the best place to start this organizational transformation from bureaucratic nose picking to streamlined efficiency. For an instant, she thought about how close she had come to sending her North Dakota boys and girls to a slaughter and resolved never to be in that position again. Buoyed, she directed, "Well, what are we waiting for, Victor. Follow me."

# 37. Maiden Voyage

Beyond the moon and a tiny fraction of the way to Mars, the Delamie floated in space preparing for the first test flight of wasp attack ships. Dee and Manny, guided by an Ardinian called the master of suits, were in the final throes of donning space attire for their maiden voyage.

Only the Ardinians would think to make spacesuits in a shimmering, pale, buttercup-yellow hue. The suit master reassured the novice pilots that wasps were fully pressurized, but spacesuits guaranteed survivability in the event of an unanticipated glitch. Dee commented low to Manny, "In other words, if this turns into a shit show, they might have some chance of recovering our buttercup asses in space."

The wasp, named by Dee in honor of the craft's bug like appearance, sat idly parked in front of a cadre of other wasps. Six ground level openings were evenly spaced across the forward edge of an immense and well-lit launch platform, aboard the Delamie.

Test pilots, or test dummies as Manny often referred to himself and Dee, were advised that the closed openings led to tubes from which wasps were launched. Five craft per tube allowed 30 wasps to be expelled rapidly. After launching a full contingent of 30 ships, it would take another three minutes to assemble and regurgitate the next batch. Since the launch platform was pressurized during operations, launch tubes, with doors on the entry and exit sides, served as the point of access into space.

Manny wondered how it would be possible to reenter the ship quickly if a battle went poorly, and they were fleeing for their lives, when Shakete waved to him, his thumb in the air. They were a go for the test flight. Although beautiful, the sleek suits, boots, gloves and headgear made normal gravity assisted walking awkward. They stumbled to the wasp and climbed into the cockpit. Manny sat in front as the primary pilot and Dee behind him as an assistant and navigator.

Manny could hear Dee breathing heavily. The communication devices in their helmets picked up every minute sound. "You might want to turn down your communicator, Dee. I can't think from listening to your heaving breaths."

"I'm nervous! Give me a minute to figure out how," Dee responded. Green and blue control symbols on the inside left of her faceplate beckoned for manipulation. Simulator training provided information on most Ardinian icons, different from human versions, but Dee was overwhelmed by the multitude of menu symbols. "I see the controls. They're on the inside of my headgear, but I can't determine an interface protocol. Holy hell! Manny, please add spacesuit operation to the growing list of pilot training subjects."

"Roger that, Dee. Try a verbal command."

"Why not? Spacesuit, lower communication volume."

"Yes, Dee," a sultry, female voice responded. "Is the volume more comfortable now?"

"Yowza, they have upgraded the AI's voice," Manny crowed. "That alluring voice may become a little too distracting. Volume is better, though. How're you doing Dee? Are you ready for this?"

"At this point, I simply want to get the flight over with."

"All right. You strapped in?"

"Strapped and terrified."

"Ship, enter ejection chamber one."

"Affirmative, Manny," the AI cooed, throwing Dee and Manny back in their seats accelerating to tube one. The tube had barely opened when the wasp completed a ground maneuver into the rounded tunnel and came to a stop like a last-minute decision not to game a yellow light. Dee and Manny were thrown painfully forward into restraining straps, whipped back again, finally settling in jell cushioned seats.

"Uh, AI. That movement was a bit too jerky for human bodies. You might want to slow it down next time." There was silence from the AI for several seconds.

"My name is not AI. Please call me Tammy. The purpose of the rapid deployment is to overwhelm the enemy with firepower. To meet the three-minute deployment objective, wasps must move to the staging area quickly."

"I understand, Tammy. Today however, there is no enemy. Just keep it in mind."

"I will, Manny. You may want to hang on to your hoods during ejection. The thrust will be exponentially greater than my merely fast tube entry."

Dee commented. "Did Shakete do something to the AI? Tammy, the phrase is 'Hang on to your hats.'"

"But, you aren't wearing hats. I will add that information to my language database. This human language is significantly illogical."

The banter with Tammy was having a calming effect on Dee. She was beginning to like this sexy sounding AI. "I'm ready, Manny. Daylight is burning."

"But, there isn't any daylight," an even more confounded Tammy responded.

"Tammy, eject the wasp," Manny ordered.

Neither Manny or Dee heard Tammy's affirmative response. Their bodies were pressed against the gel seats. This time, what little fat was on their faces, also moved of its own accord away from the G-forces. The ten second burn felt like it had lasted for minutes. When Tammy finally let up on the throttle, they were well away from the Ardinian Ship.

Manny had collected himself enough to ask the question utmost in his mind. "Uh, Tammy is there a good reason for launching us like a bullet out of the ship?"

"A bullet? I'm not sure, let me check my data. Ah, yes, Manny our velocity was appreciably faster than an earth bullet. I believe I did warn you to hang on to your hood hats. Shakete asked that I demonstrate the most cutting edge, I hope that's the right term, capabilities of the wasp."

"Tammy, we truly appreciate learning about the ship. Unfortunately, there is a limit to the stresses our bodies can withstand without injury."

"Manny, Dee, I will initiate a scan to check for injuries and assess your inferior biology. Please, relax and enjoy the ride." The AI was gone again.

"Did she just say, relax and enjoy the ride? Dee asked.

"That's what I heard. She's right though. Look at those stars. They're magnificent."

Dee was pointing out star systems and ruminating about the sight of Jupiter's rings when Manny interrupted. "Are we drifting? It feels like it to me. Tammy?"

When there was no response, Dee chimed in. "Tammy, where did you go?" Silence. "Houston, we have a problem. Manny, I'm going to contact the Delamie and see if they know what's going on."

"Delamie, this is the wasp test flight. Our AI, Tammy, seems to have gone missing. Can you assist? Over."

"Wasp test flight, this is the Delamie. The AI has gone missing? Did I read you correctly?"

"Affirmative Delamie. Tammy said she was going to conduct a biological scan, and we can no longer contact her. Can you assist, please? Oops, over."

"Test flight, give me three human minutes for consultation. Over."

"Just don't leave us, too!"

Dee tried several times to call Tammy as the minutes passed. "Test flight, this is the Delamie. I have been informed a biological scanner has not yet been installed on the wasp. Tammy may be caught in an informational loop, searching for something that does not exist. Since Tammy serves as an intelligent systems interface and flight assistant, navigation, weapons and life support systems remain completely functional. We recommend you transition to manual pilot, the green button next to the pilot lever. Once it is engaged, other controls will appear. We suggest you spend time testing the ship, and we will download data to notify Tammy of the missing application. That should wake her up. Out."

"Should?!" Dee and Manny said in unison.

"We should've known, Dee. For all their science, the Ardinians suffer from some form of technological Alzheimer's. They are amazing one moment and the next, dust clouds blind your ship. I'm going to manual now. We came out here to learn to fly. No time like the present."

"Here's hoping the mechanical features of the wasp were completely installed. Manny, try a heading at 356882. There's some space junk out there we can target and shoot with lasers."

"Now, we're talking!" Manny applied moderate thrust and turned in the direction of the junk. They could feel G-forces but nothing like the harrowing seconds upon launch. Manny was yelling "Ye Haw," as he flipped and dove, turned and rose, swooping near the floating space objects. "Targeting now. Keep us level, Dee. You can have the first shot."

"Roger, Manny, firing now." A flash of light speared the dark of space, hitting the target head on and sending smaller bits of space junk in all directions.

"My turn. I'm going to pick up the speed so hang on to your hood." Manny used the reverse lever, sped with the aft end first, and then reversed thrust causing the ship to flip over so it was pointed in the opposite direction. He leaned on the thrust control heavier than the last round, swinging up and back, targeting another floating rock. "Locked on target. Firing now." Once again, it was a direct hit.

Manny was giddy, and Dee was laughing with him. "I don't know that I've ever had more fun. This thing is more maneuverable than I ever imagined. Other than the software glitch, call me impressed." They continued targeting practice until the space junk was so small there was nothing left to target. Manny asked Dee, "What now?"

"Deploy the shield and fly into the debris field. Not too fast though."

"Roger, shield engaged. Here we go."

The only clue the shield was up was when they hit the granular bits of what had recently been rocks, and the clouded mass parted and disappeared around the wasp. "Looks like they have the dust issue resolved. If we had someone else out here to play with, we could give the shield a thorough test."

"Test flight, this is the Delamie. The script we sent Tammy didn't knock her off task. We'll need to download and overwrite her, which will take some time. What are your impressions regarding ship systems in a manual setting?"

Manny responded, "Outstanding! Awesome maneuverability, easy targeting, and the shield works as originally advertised. I think the simulator performed admirably in preparing us for flight in a wasp. Other than Tammy issues, I would call this test a resounding success. How long will it take to rewrite the intransigent AI?"

"We were confident of success. The Tammy situation is a bit more complex. We wanted her to have the flexibility to respond to changing dynamics in a battle. The adaptation latitude we allowed in her protocols may have resulted in more adaptation than is advisable."

Manny asked, "What does that mean to us?"

"We believe when Tammy didn't find a biological scanning system, she began to write her own. She was obviously distraught that she might have damaged you and felt an imperative to ensure your safety. The timing is inconvenient, but her intent was worthy. She may resist all attempts to be overwritten until she has finished her project."

"And?"

"And, you must manually fly the ship through to mission completion."

"That won't be a problem. I feel comfortable navigating back to the ship and entering an access tube." Manny's confidence was tarnished when his encouraging statement was met with prolonged silence.

"Never a good sign when the Ardinians quit talking, is it?" Dee asked. She couldn't see the irked eye roll Manny gave as a response, since she was sitting behind him. It wasn't meant for her anyway.

"Test flight, this is Delamie. We've agreed the best course of action is to fly the wasp to Earth and land at your airfield. Margo has suggested to Shakete it would be nice to have a few wasps for familiarization located at your facility."

As the navigator, Dee chimed in, "Isn't reentering earth's atmosphere riskier for newbies than simply landing on the Delamie?"

"No."

"No? This is ridiculous. Please explain."

"While you have been on your test flight, we conducted our own tests. The landing platform tubes performed superbly in jettisoning wasp craft. Reentry is problematic. The vacuum tractor we created to assist in rapid redeployment is, I am looking for a good human word, crushing material. They require recalibration. Unless you would like to remain in the wasp for an additional twenty-eight hours and twelve minutes, our suggestion is you head to earth. The onboard oxygen load, including your suits, will deplete in twenty-five hours."

"In other words, if we want to live, we head to earth?!" Dee quipped back at the Delamie.

"Yes, that is another way to express your current situation. We trust in your ability to overcome adversity. Having monitored your flight responses, we are confident in your success and stand ready to assist whenever possible. Delamie Out."

It was the earthlings' turn to be stunned into silence. Dee rocked back in her chair and moaned. If she weren't fully suited, she might also have dropped her head into her hands and rubbed her eyes in total frustration. Manny muttered every curse word he knew, including heretofore new and original curse word combinations.

Finally, Manny shouted, "Screw it. For earth!"

"For earth!" Dee giggled. "Plotting a course now. Huh, Manny, did you practice earth landings in the simulator?"

"Twice, burned up the first time. You?"

"Three times. I was one for three in successful landings."

"On the glass, half full meter, if we make it through this, battles with the Hunta won't be nearly as daunting."

"Roger that. Manny, I'm going to get on the horn to warn Rainier and Boeing field not to shoot us down. I don't trust the Ardinians to complete the loop on that coordination. Margo and the Mermots can help scrape our carcasses off the pavement if we overshoot our mark."

\* \* \*

"Pucker factor engaged. Beginning descent to earth's atmosphere."

"Easy as she goes, Dee."

When the Ardinian ship spat out the wasp, their location was just outside the moon's gravity well. It was a quick four-hour trip back to earth. Settling easily into orbit, Dee watched the navigation controls until a bleep signaled the reentry start point to land in Washington.

The friction from the ship against earth's atmosphere started as a mild bump accompanied by a low roar. Manny could see the flicker of ignited oxygen at the front of the ship just before a flexible, silver shield automatically sloped over the curved pilot's window. As they spiraled away from the upper atmosphere and deeper into oxygen rich air, the bumping, sparks and roar increased with every second.

"How are we doing, Dee?"

"On course. Exterior temperatures are as expected."

* * *

Popping out of the launch tube had been intense but burning into the earth's atmosphere felt like the ultimate test of faith. Dee's eyes alternated between monitoring the temperature readings and blinking back tears that truly wanted a venue for release. The tears never came. She thought it might be because her tear ducts were compressed into her head, just as every other bone in her body was crushed against the downward pressure.

"Dee, keep calling temperature. Stay with me. It won't last much longer." Manny's voice sounded like he was talking with his teeth clenched together. The fervor of the rattling, bumping ride notched up again as if in response to Manny's demand.

"Tempperatuure, norrmall range," Dee said, her teeth clacking in rhythm with the ship. "I feel like I'm hot, though."

CRACK! Dee gulped and yelled, "Shit! What was that?" Her thundering heart hit the gear for overdrive.

"Look at the gauge, Dee, now!"

"The exterior temperature is spiking. Something happened to one of the shields. Damn it. What can we do?"

"I will level off some. Wait for it. Temperature?"

"Still rising. At this rate, I don't think we'll make it, Manny."

Manny felt the ship lurching underneath him. "What if we deploy the matter reorganizing shield. It might dissipate some of the heat."

"It might also reorganize our matter. I didn't see anything in the simulators to indicate that our shield could be used to protect us from atmospheric impacts." Two successive jolts buffeted the wasp. "Nothing in simulator training recommended that shield. But temperatures are almost critical. Try it and God help us."

The bumping was no longer sporadic. The ship was a bucking bull. "Ready to deploy weapons shield."

"DO NOT touch that button!" Tammy's formerly demure voice reverberated through the cabin. "What is wrong with you two? Do you want to get us all killed? I am deploying secondary heat seals now."

"Tammy's back," Dee gratefully whispered.

"With a vengeance," Manny answered.

"Temperatures are now stable. Whew, that was close." Tammy soothed. The difference in sound was almost immediate. Even though the Wasp still rattled, the startling jolts diminished.

"The secondary heat seals are essential for planetary entry. Once they are in place, you may descend through the atmosphere rapidly without worry. So that I can better understand human rationality, could you please provide information on why you chose a suboptimal approach?"

Dee answered. "There was nothing about secondary heat seals in simulator training. We didn't know."

"I see. The seals were an add-on. The simulator specifications must be out of date. I offer my services once we land to ensure they match current wasp capabilities." Before Manny could make excuses to a sexy voiced, disappearing, fickle AI, Tammy continued. "Manny, your respiration is beyond normal ranges. Please breath slowly and think restful thoughts. I will ensure we arrive at our destination safely. And Dee, I would recommend you loosen your jaw. You may feel neck pain later without proper relaxation."

"Should we call you Doctor Tammy, now?" Dee asked and tried not to laugh.

"I am not a doctor, Dee, but I appreciate your confidence in my advice."

* * *

Manny saw the airfield first. He had convinced Tammy he could do the last part of the flight and didn't need her assistance to land. It was a mystery where Tammy had learned the earthly expression "Hmmpf". Dee pointed to the men and women clinging to the roofs of the pilots' barracks to catch a firsthand view of the wasp. There was so many of them. Throngs holding signs like *For Earth* and *Welcome Back*, lined the grassy embankments on the periphery of the airfield. "I don't think I've ever seen that many people in one place in my life!" Dee excitedly babbled.

"Margo's been busy. Would have been a sad sight for all if our ship looked more like a toasted marshmallow, but since we have an enthused audience, I should probably give them a show." Manny zoomed past the spectators, pushed the Wasp nearly perpendicular to the ground, flipped the craft in a tight circle, and then hovered over the landing strip before landing. They set down like a feather wafting to the pavement. "Manny, next time, how about a warning. I don't want to greet the adoring fans with puke on my shirt."

"We did it, Dee!"

"Yes, we did."

Tammy interrupted their revelry. "I will wait here for your return. If I might mention, I greatly enjoy interaction with other intelligent beings. Please feel free to visit or upload me to your network for further assistance. Anytime. I'll be waiting. All you have to do is___"

"Roger, Tammy," Manny said as he unlatched his harness, flipped the switch to open the hatch, and jumped out of the cabin. Dee was hugging his back, almost pushing him forward to make her own quick exit.

Margo, Victor, the Mermot translator, and five other people Manny and Dee didn't know rushed across the tarmac to great them. "Congratulations!" Margo shouted as she stepped forward. "You're here with the wasp, safe and sound. I trust the test flight went well."

Manny answered, "I suppose that depends on your definition of 'went well.' We'll explain later. I'm exhausted and hungry. Food and drink first, then why don't you show me what you've done, Margo?

Sorry, our mission didn't last quite two days. I didn't give you the time you asked,"

"No problem. We completed most of the reorganization within the first twenty-four hours. We're fine tuning now,"

A buffet meal of sandwiches and fruit had been placed onto a cloth covered, foldable table in the hanger. Urns on one end held water and cold tea for the assembled group. Fresh faces, sitting at long tables filling the space, were already inhaling their lunch. They stood and cheered when Dee and Manny came through the door. Flabbergasted, Manny asked, "Who are these people? Some look familiar."

Victor took the lead. "These are our pilots in training. We may add a few later, but we consider them the first string. The most qualified candidates, even now, are working in the simulators. The simulators will be in use twenty-four hours a day on a rotational schedule. Speaking of that, I need to get back to them. I look very forward to hearing about the test flight, this evening." Victor nodded at Margo and left.

"Wow, Margo. I don't know how you did it," Manny said while moving to the buffet plates.

"I didn't do it alone. Victor is a marvelous administrator. And I haven't slept since you left."

"Good to hear it. Not the not sleeping part." Manny was piling meat and cheese onto large slices of bread before he spoke again. He turned to study Margo, a loaded plate and drink filling his hands. "I'm sorry about the artillery cracks earlier. We've got a lot to tell you about. There were some glitches as the Ardinians like to refer to major snafus, but I think this is all going to work."

Today's narrative isn't technically history, but it will be someday. The speed of change in the New Washington Enclave demands a thorough accounting of current events.

Where to begin—justice, technology, Mermots, politics, family? I was just reading about polling in pre-change civilizations. It went something like this: if a person or group couldn't decide which way the wind was blowing through investigation, research, and good judgement, a poll of strangers was undertaken to advise that person or group on what to think. Many of these polls lacked any semblance of a scientific sampling regimen, but it didn't matter. Agencies requesting polls tended to use whatever polling data most closely aligned with their original ideas anyway. The point it seems was to provide cover for decisions, another name for collective irresponsibility. Although interesting and perhaps a bit sad, this information has little to do with my writings. I just thought it might be fun, if I had access to a group of strangers, to take a poll on what readers would most like to know about our history.

I choose justice to begin. The New Washington Enclave values life and able hands. This orientation is one born of need as much as any moral or religious foundations. We assume, quite rightly, every person is necessary to contribute to our collective survival. Our laws and punishments reflect those underpinnings.

Under normal circumstances, the framework of judicial sentences includes work penance (a term of work to be served at a remote farm in the Yakima Valley), monetary fines, often paid with property, and the most severe penalty, lifetime enclave banishment. The death penalty can be imposed only when a panel of citizens decides the offending individual is too dangerous to be allowed to live among civilized society, in our enclave or another. In one-hundred years, the death penalty has only been imposed once. Bad Bob, as he became known in the enclave, raped and killed three adolescent girls. It was an unspeakable, heinous, tragedy. Almost everyone agreed, evil of that kind required the ultimate sentence.

The Enclave doesn't have a prison or the manpower to support one. A tiny short-term jail, mostly used to house unruly drunks for an evening, sits behind the courthouse and is currently filled with five prisoners: Carlton, Red, and three North Dakota sympathizers. Another temporary jail holds fifteen more New Washington natives who were thought to aid Carlton in his unlawful quest.

The difficulty of finding appropriate sentences for their deeds is compounded by my father's mayoral pardon of all North Dakota natives, except for Carlton and Red. How is it fair to allow North Dakota territory folk to wander free in the enclave and then punish our own as accomplices? Red killed Letitia so that decision will be more straight forward. The sentencing of the remainder is even now causing two camps of thought to solidify division among the enclave populace. One group is very vocal in their desire to set a precedent by banishing all North Dakota persons and their sympathizers. The other camp, of which I am a part, believes banishment would only create a new enemy.

I don't know how we will navigate these divisive matters, only that we will. I leave it to the wise judgement of a panel of citizens to make those decisions. History can decide if we acted with enlightened and judicious hearts. I will most likely write about it later.

On to more engaging subjects, the Mermots! I have been captivated by Mermots, especially the winsome and charming Tweet. She came to my library soon after her arrival. Wearing an adorable Hawaiian shirt, lacy gathered skirt, and a fresh flower taped to her round ear, she waited patiently in line. Tweet is fast becoming a fashion leader amongst her peers.

When it was her turn, she said in a sweet, girlish voice, "Mr. Geronimo. I would be most pleased if you could see fit to help me understand humans." She posed the question in a manner that endeared her to me immediately. "To do that, I think I must have knowledge of not just what I see around me, but also of your history, so that I may appreciate how you arrived here.

"As the primary Mermot ambassador, my job is as a form of interpreter. Mermots love stories. If I can explain your race through your stories, I will achieve greater success with my people. I have been told you are this enclave's preeminent historian. Dare I suggest, the world's most influential historian?"

I was left unable to speak. Her sincerity and clear-eyed perspective, totally refreshing. So what if she looked as endearing as Minnie Mouse, and she was buttering me up to enlist my support. I was charmed.

"Where would you like to begin?" I pulled a written copy of Critically Endangered from under the counter and slid it to her. "This is a history of the Great Dying in story form, authored primarily by me. I highly recommend it as a start."

"Thank you, Mr. Geronimo. I will read the book straight away. Also, if you could give me access to your archives, I can begin my study."

"You can call me just, Geronimo. Everyone else does." I stepped from behind the counter and placed a hand on her shoulder to show my solidarity with her people. "Follow me."

Tweet and I have become fast friends. She is intelligent, thoughtful and at times, has shown an unexpected edginess. She stops by most evenings to study, and I stay to facilitate her progress. Often, she will come to me with a historical question that we ponder into the wee morning hours. To say that we are intellectual soulmates would not be an exaggeration. Tweet offers me the chance to bounce ideas and thoughts against another being with like interests. If I could be so bold, our partnership benefits both humans and Mermots. Together, Tweet and I have found many human-Mermot parallels in our long and storied histories. The story songs of Mermots she sings to me inhabit my dreams.

Chrystel has also come to rely on Tweet. I visited the courthouse recently to find out how the trials were progressing and volunteer my services as a jurist, even though I don't have the time. When I poked my head into Chrystel's office to say hello, she and Tweet were arduously reviewing a list of Mermot tasks. They looked up at the same time, Tweet modeling the identical expression worn on Chrystel's face. "Hey, Geronimo," Chrystel welcomed. "Tweet and I are going over work requirements for Mermots.

"Tweet tells me you've been spending time together investigating earth's history. Tweet's a godsend. I'm not sure we could feed and house our additional population without her assistance."

Tweet demurred, "It has been my pleasure to be useful. Your managerial skills make all things possible. I learn new things from the mayor each day."

Sitting silently inside the door in her normal position, Tilley offered her take on the state of Mermot-human relations, "Isn't Tweet cute?"

Smitten by Mermots. Washingtonians are smitten by Mermots. Not a day passes when someone doesn't sing their praises. There are even rumors that in honor of our alien guests, some have taken to keeping earth rats as pets. I find that possibility disgusting since rats, unlike Mermots, are dirty scavengers, but I can at least sympathize with a change in attitude regarding their appearance. When I found a rat in my garage waste receptacle, I was not nearly as horrified as I might have been before our Mermot friends arrived.

If there is a dark side to Mermots and our partnership, it has yet to reveal itself. Let's all hope that what you see is what you get. Given the depth of acceptance and our new bond with an alien species, we are quite vulnerable to any change in fortunes.

Next up in my flighty dialog, technology. Jed's satellite technology and his microwave vector phones are making wireless communication a reality. Finally, we are recouping some of humanity's lost communication synergy. The Internet is up and available to all! I have over a hundred new emails in my account waiting to be read. My mother warned me that email was both a blessing and a curse. For now, I am leaning heavily on a blessing.

I know the Ardinians shared some weapons technology with the airfield but not much about the scope. As I said in an earlier chapter, I am not in that loop. Besides, weapons frighten me. They have also promised manufacturing printers as soon they have completed a full complement of flight simulators. They are like pre-change 3D printers but far better, at least that's what I've been told. I am excited to see what they do.

I've saved the best news for last. The Ardinians are sharing their medical technology. I will finally get my gimpy leg fixed. Sara and Katie are on the Ardinian ship now learning how to use Ardinian medical techniques and will return to earth with the equipment and knowledge to fix all types of injuries. Manny's new leg leaves little doubt that I'm in for a wondrous event. The thought of improved mobility makes me quiver in anticipation.

The Ardinians cautioned that technology changes people and the culture that supports their society. They have much more technology to share, but for our own good, they desire a methodical approach to upgrading earth. I suppose that's for the best, but most of us are extremely impatient. Since it's not our choice, we will wait.

Family. My sister Amelia and her daughter Chrystel are both in love. I am extremely happy for them and not because I ever felt them unworthy of loving and being loved. More, that they are both so unique, finding a perfect match for their special qualities was never intended as an easy feat.

Brodie and Chrystel are almost always together. Their passion is obvious. When they are in the same room together, their eyes seek each other out like the smart missiles stored at Rainier. Their flame burns bright. I hope for my niece's sake the heat doesn't result in a super nova.

My sister and Trent are the other side of that coin. They are a cozy fire on a cold night. Older and wiser, they share a passion springing from a joining of souls. Solicitous of each other to a fault, they laugh at the other's bad jokes and move in an uncommon synchronicity. Funny how the loss of love can enable unmatched appreciation when love rolls around the second time. Being around the two of them is to discard unnecessary weight. I can peacefully sit in Amelia's sunlit kitchen, absorb their light, and then leave hopeful and renewed.

I'm not at all sure why this journal of events has become so sentimental. Perhaps, I want to hold fast to all the goodness and joy that surrounds me at this single point in time. Candy is by my side again, I'm going to have my leg fixed, my family is contented, and I have a new friend in Tweet. Even the alien situation, if you discount the Huntas, has been a win-win for our enclave. Why is it then that I have this nagging feeling destruction awaits just around the next corner? Is this the burden my sister Amelia must carry? I sincerely hope I am not acquiring any of her prescient abilities. I might have to switch from history to future prognostications.

I have one more subject to cover, and I am suddenly maudlin and uninterested in the always contentious issue of politics. I will make this discussion brief. Chrystel won the election for mayor by a substantial margin. The election was rather anticlimactic since Chrystel was the only person left on the ballet after Carlton was arrested for treason. Isn't that often the way of life? That thing or event which consumed a great deal of your time and emotional angst, in hindsight, wasn't a big deal at all. Instead, something else, something you never saw coming, whacks you in the back of the head so hard spots swirl in your peripheral vision for weeks.

My father received a good number of write-ins, which made him scowl. It wasn't a week after Chrystel started her new term that the grousing about nepotism began anew. Even after she made an announcement that she will only serve for two years, some were not satisfied. I have come to understand no matter what a person does or how righteous their intentions, someone is going to bitch.

Geronimo M.

# 39. The Spy

Rain seeped from fir boughs enough to be irritating. Just when it seemed the spring rain had stopped, a fat blob plunked on his head. He normally enjoyed the solitude of a trek to the meeting point, but today was different. Lost in an intractable web of thoughts, he watched his feet as he avoided roots and skirted nature's cull.

He was in too deep. He had started this journey with the certainty of a youthful quest, certain of his own good nature and the truth of his goals. The values imparted by his family and handlers were his values. He was a loyal man.

He was still a loyal man, but those loyalties were so divided, he no longer knew how to sift through the pieces and make the puzzle fit. The people of New Washington had welcomed him, an unknown walk-on, to their enclave. They had given him a home and a job. They had offered their hands in friendship and treated him as one of their own. He had tried to pretend that he was a Washingtonian, that he was one of them while keeping a piece of himself apart. Over twenty years, the wall of deception he had erected, the one constructed to tell bold lies to friends and neighbors, was torn away, brick by brick, until there was nothing left but regret.

The people of New Washington weren't any different than the people he had known in his birth enclave. They were honest and hardworking, doing their very best to make a good life for their families and community. His birth enclave, known as the Capital Enclave, located near the ruins of the

Pentagon in Northern Virginia, survived and thrived in much the same way. If there was any difference between New Washington and Capitol, it was simply one of attitude inherited from geography and a residual memory of what had come before the Great Dying.

His enclave had chafed at the notion that people from some northwestern backwoods near the Canadian border had dared to name their enclave, New Washington. As if these unsophisticated westerners had intentionally usurped a once great symbol of a once great nation. The Capital Enclave believed the name Washington was their birthright. This outlook was further encouraged by an unfortunate coincidence of surviving founders: The Vice President, one Senator, the head of the CIA, and a four-star general, all convinced they were endowed with the power vested by a defunct, United States Government.

In the beginning, his birth enclave assumed their rightful position was as heir to the property that constituted the fifty states, sending messages to other young enclaves with suggestions for consolidating power under their tutelage. To the receiving enclaves, these suggestions sounded all too much like directives. They knew Capital had no means to enforce any consolidation and ignored all requests, pleas, and directives. Only three enclaves, Albany, Boston, and Baltimore threw in their lot to make Capital the most populated of the North American enclaves. In typical New Washington fashion, Karen had sent back a reply that New Washington was willing to trade but made a joke of any notion of remote rule. She offered instead to share successful development strategies with the burgeoning Capital Enclave.

Because New Washington, once again by coincidence, had the technological goods and had stolen the Washington namesake, it was the western Washington version upon which Capital focused its ire. The ex-CIA head cooked up a covert plan to create instability in New Washington, steal their technology, and peaceably take what was rightfully theirs.

The terrain was steeper here, and the man's breathing deepened to compensate for the extra exertion. He noticed a great horned owl sleeping on a tree branch, unconcerned with his temporary existence on a lower plane. Maybe he could inhale some of the great bird's reputed wisdom, wisdom to extricate himself from the pile of excrement upon which he now found himself.

Waking from a bad dream right after the North Dakota attack, he panicked. What was home? With his birth family or his new family? His only certainty was an urgent need lodged in his gut—the need to protect the people of New Washington. Pushed from a well-worn path by an outside threat, he hardened his resolve to find an answer.

If he could use the same techniques that he'd been trained in, perhaps he could turn the tables, find a place where his old masters backed off because he gave a plausible explanation to wait, reaping bigger gains by their patience. Even better, a ruse that could dissuade them permanently from implementing the solution they envisioned. Most importantly, he wanted to achieve this peace without revealing his identity or his own traitorous deeds.

He played again in his mind the reactions of his New Washington friends if he came clean. Could they forgive him if warned them in time? Would he be imprisoned with that asshole Carlton and later be banished from what was now his true home? They were a forgiving people on a whole, but he wasn't sure the love of his life could be that magnanimous.

Nope. He would make sure this all came out right. Full of himself and his importance, he remembered how willing he was to assume this mission. What a joke. What a horrible, horrible joke. He consoled himself that a man of only twenty years, his age when he left Capital, didn't know jack shit about the real world. How many young men and women like him were filled with the dreams and aspirations of powerful people, only to approach the goalpost suddenly aware they'd been seduced?

He stopped and released a primal scream. The owl opened its eyes, spread its wings, and soared away. The last road to old Enumclaw wasn't too far now.

A backdrop of Mount Rainier rose from the foothills, dwarfing the crumbling edifices of what had once been a hardscrabble, western, railroad town. Early 1900's storefronts competed with dead gas stations and convenience stores. His destination was the Enumclaw Fire Station, a brick building that had ably passed the test of time. If Mount Rainier ever blew its top, this place would be forever wiped from the map.

He walked over the remains of blacktop and turned right at the last major intersection. He knew someone would be waiting. As a sensor, he had felt their presence during the long slog up to the Enumclaw plateau. Pausing outside the fire station garage, he peered into the shadows, watching for movement. The huge doors were long gone, leaving gaping holes to reveal the oxidizing fire trucks, pointing outward ready to respond to all emergencies.

"Anyone here?" he called.

Harvetta peeked around the back of a truck. She smiled tentatively. "Is that you?"

"Well, I'll be damned," he murmured as he ran to her, crushed her with a hug, while lifting and spinning in a circle. He knew the minute he saw her the game was just made harder. Harvetta knew what made him tick.

"I wasn't sure I'd ever see you again, buddy. When I was selected for the meet this time, I was ecstatic."

"Is there a reason they sent you?" he asked and tenderly flicked away one of her tears.

"Oh, you know. This alien thing, everyone joining New Washington, new technology. The list is endless. They're nervous as hell and wanted me to make sure you were still good. Are you still good? You look amazing by the way. . .more centered and happier than I remember."

He changed the subject. "Before we get on to business, tell me about you and my family."

Harvetta nodded and motioned him over to a concrete bench sitting outside the station. "Before I forget, I have a letter to you from your mom and dad." She pulled a folded envelope from a pocket and handed it to him. "They miss you. I do too."

He wondered if her statement was genuine or the first attempt to lure a stray sheep back into the fold. Harvetta had the beginnings of a gray steak sprouting from a widow's peak. Her ice blue eyes just as blue and penetrating as the last time she'd inspected him before saying goodbye. She was a sister, mother, friend all rolled into one. A pang of guilt stabbed his chest.

"Where to begin? I have a son named Devon. He just turned fourteen. He was such a cute boy, but he's recently been possessed by a hormonal devil." She laughed at the thought. "Your sister has four kids now, three girls and one boy. You may have known that though."

"No, I didn't. I don't get any information on my family other than assurances they are well. Did you happen to bring any pictures?"

"No, sorry. They thought it might interfere with the mission. I'm not sure why. Doesn't make sense to me, but I've quit asking questions like that. What about you, any kids?"

"No."

"Why not? We always wanted for you to blend in, establish yourself."

He was uncomfortable with the question. How to answer? He needed to keep it real and not make her suspicious. "Harvetta, it would be just one more person to lie to. I couldn't fathom deceiving my own child. That's why."

The edges of her mouth turned down. "Yeah, I get that. Is there at least someone special in your life?"

He couldn't hold the smile that lit his face. "I do have someone special. That's probably why I seemed happy and centered. She means the world to me."

"I'm glad for you, really. You haven't shared with her, have you?"

"God, no. So how are Mom and Dad?"

"Good, they're good, really." Harvetta elongated the last word.

He let it pass. Her response was too casual. Maybe she's suspicious. "I've brought information on the new weaponry. I couldn't get a picture of the laser weapons, so I drew one. They are producing them at a rapid pace, and some of the guards carry them. They are small enough to hide and still deadly to personnel and aircraft. The Rainier station will be restocked with missiles provided by the Ardinians. I don't know when. Twenty alien spaceships, called wasps, are now stationed at the airfield. They are armed with lasers, energy blasters, and a rail gun. If they can get off the ground, anything you plan will be thwarted."

"Okay. That's useful intel. What about the power grid? Have you found a way to disable it?"

"The airfield and enclave just completed a redundancy effort. I can't disable the power grid to have an immediate impact by myself. I need to know who else was inserted into the pilot program to help. That way I can assign Capital clandestine assets to critical nodes. Any word on a timeline?"

"Not yet." Harvetta stood and strolled back into the station, reappearing with a palm sized, square box in her hand. She handed it to him. "Keep this. We used the technology you stole to develop a phone. It's completely encrypted. Someone will notify you of the timeline as needed. Just have your plan in place, and we'll identify helpers in time to make it work."

"Hey, if you're bouncing signals from the New Washington satellite, they'll see it."

"No, they won't. We've got it covered," she stated flatly.

His face remained impassive, keeping a tight hold on growing desperation. "Harvetta, do they really know what they're getting themselves into? The Ardinian ship is orbiting earth as we speak, ready to do who knows what to anyone who makes a go at New Washington. They could take out Capital with one shot. Wouldn't it make more sense to wait until I can smuggle out equal weaponry, or better yet, wait two years until I control the enclave after the mayor relinquishes her position, allowing me to lead them to a consolidation with Capital?"

"You may be right, but it doesn't matter. The new magistrate won't change his mind. He's not exactly a compromising sort. Do you think the aliens can really do that?"

He had to be convincing here. He knew the Ardinian philosophy probably wouldn't allow for a god-like smiting of a bundle of humans. "Harvetta, their technology is so far beyond ours, it defies an easy explanation. You can't even begin to imagine Ardinian power. Of course, they can do that."

She became still. "I'll try to persuade them to wait, but I don't believe it'll make a difference. They've convinced themselves the Ardinians will see Capital as the better warriors to lead earth against the Huntas, that all they need is an opportunity to negotiate directly with the Ardinians."

"I need to talk to my father. He can make them see reason."

"That wouldn't be a good idea."

His eyes narrowed. He grabbed her shoulders, barely restrained, wanting to shake her until she told the truth. "What the hell is going on? We always planned to do this without killing a bunch of people needlessly. What's changed, and what's happened to my dad?!"

She withdrew in shock at his aggression. "I would say your birth enclave isn't the only thing that's changed. I never expected this of you." Then her face cracked into a look very close to despair. "Look, Whitley is the new magistrate. He's convinced everyone in the chamber that if we don't move soon, it won't happen. New Washington will be too strong. And, they've lost faith in your ability to win an election for mayor."

"And my father?"

"He's in jail. He spoke out too forcefully. They're jailing everyone who objects too loudly."

"In other words, everything I was told before I left for this mission has changed."

Harvetta slumped, her head swinging back and forth. "I was also told to tell you that if you didn't hang in and see this through to the end, your whole family, mom and dad, sister, her kids and me and my family would die." Harvetta's lips trembled.

"Fuck me!!" he cried, as he pounded the concrete bench with his fists.

Harvetta released a sob. He pulled her into his chest and asked one more question. "And if Capital fails. What would happen then?"

"Same result, we all die."

"Those sons of bitches. I should have seen this coming."

"A lot has changed in twenty years to include the fact I'm not much of a spy anymore. They lost me when they said I would die if I didn't do their bidding."

He stayed to get all the information he could from Harvetta now that she was more forthcoming. "Where's my dad jailed?"

"At a holding facility at the old Ft. McNair. It isn't heavily guarded, but enough so that getting him out wouldn't be easy."

"Is there any way to reach you?"

"They'll be watching me," Harvetta sighed. "It's crazy, like the Gestapo has assumed control of Capital They don't trust anyone. Let me think about it. If I can figure out something, I'll call you on that box."

"Any possibility you and my family, other than my father, can make a run for it?"

"I can try. If we do, I'll try to get word to you, somehow."

"Are they coming to pick you up?"

"I have an ATV parked outside of town. I'll drive until I'm out of Rainier radar range. Then they'll pick me up in an airship."

Trying to console her, he told her not to worry. He would find a way.

"Stay safe," she said as she hugged him one last time. As Harvetta pulled away, her face said she didn't believe he had any hope of protecting both New Washington and the people he loved in Capital.

After drinking a quart of water, he set off. Just on the outskirts of Enumclaw, he released another, top of the lungs, plaintive howl. This time, there was no owl near to hear him.

# 40. Kindness or Cruelty

He yanked the knots of his boots loose, pulled them off, and placed them onto the welcome mat. The dogs were already barking an exuberant welcome from the other side of the door. Chrystel's mutts spilled onto the stoop, greeted him, and began an age-old dog introduction ritual with Rusty. Tilley's manners were more refined. She rubbed Brodie's hand with her maned head and then waited while the dogs had time to scent-examine the stranger canine fully.

Simmering onions and garlic smells filtered through the air to Brodie's nose. Chrystel must be cooking, he thought. He wondered what occasion had precipitated her unusual foray into the kitchen.

"Just a second. Don't come in just yet, I have a surprise!"

One eyebrow shot up, and he looked quizzically at Tilley, "What's up?"

"I can't explain. She would be mad if I gave away the secret, and I don't understand the surprise anyway."

Chrystel looked around the corner from the kitchen and jumped out, her arms flung wide, "Ta da! Surprise!"

Her red hair was loose, wild curls flowing in every direction. She wore a starched, white chef's apron and nothing else. "It's naked cooking night!" her green eyes glinted.

Both of Brodie's eyebrows raised. "I've never heard of naked cooking night, but it certainly makes an excellent first impression."

Chrystel completed a pirouette and giggled. "Geronimo gave me this old book called, *How to Keep the Fire Lit*. It was mostly funny, but the whole idea of naked cooking got me jazzed."

"May Geronimo live long and prosper," Brodie responded.

She strolled to the spellbound Brodie and kissed him. He placed his hands around her waist and slid them along her back feeling the swell of her hips. Chrystel backed away. "So, part of this whole naked cooking thing is that you can look but not touch until after we eat. It's a way to savor the flavors and the relationship."

"Are you kidding me? How can I eat when you look like that?" he said hoarsely.

"Who's that?" Chrystel pointed, when she noticed the black and white, long haired dog panting near Brodie's side.

Brodie glanced at Rusty as if he had forgotten he was even there, which he had. "That's Rusty. My dog. I brought him with me when I came to the enclave. He's been staying with my ex-fiancé's family. I was hoping since I'm here all the time that maybe you could consider taking in one more. He's well trained and no trouble."

Chrystel stooped to meet Rusty. She let him smell her hand before scratching behind his ears. He gave her a lick on her palm to show his appreciation. "You look like a good doggie, Rusty. Loads of fur, but what the heck. Now that we've jerry-rigged the vacuum cleaner so Tilley can push it, one more won't matter." Brodie heard Chrystel's wooing of Rusty as a voice in a far distance place. He studied her graceful but sturdy shoulders and perfect skin. Heart seizing, Brodie winced. In his mind, he could see the knife he wielded and the pain he might bring to them both.

She stood, "Of course, he can stay here, Brodie. I'm confused why you never mentioned him. I always wondered why someone who could talk to dogs didn't have one of his own."

"I don't know. I didn't want to overwhelm you with too much at first. Rusty kept pleading with me to bring him along when I visited. I thought he would be happier staying at Sherry's folks home, but lately, I think he was getting depressed."

"Aww. I'm glad you came clean. Listen, I'm going to throw on some clothes. I'm feeling weird standing at an open door naked. I can change back to my cooking outfit during cleanup." She gave Brodie an alluring smile. He watched her every step as she sauntered down the hall, her backside every bit as appealing as her front. Taut muscles and curves moved with the fluidity of a jungle cat. She was a marvel of nature, he mused.

Brodie slid the door closed with his foot and sat at the table. He should probably check on whatever it was Chrystel was making, but he needed a moment. He hung his head in his hands. So much for coming clean. He had worked himself up to truth telling on his way home. To enlist her help, even if the mess he was in wasn't her responsibility. Convince her that what they had was real. That he had followed the wrong road for too long. Beg her forgiveness. And then he saw her, a restrained, buttoned up woman who literally let her hair down for him. How could he do that to her? How could he not?

Brodie was quiet during dinner.
Complementing the food, he smiled at appropriate times and listened to Chrystel's funny stories and frustrating moments as mayor. She cautiously eyed him. "Brodie, is something bothering you?"

"No, just tired. Sorry I'm not more fun tonight."

"It wasn't the naked cooking thing, was it?

"Oh, no. I think that should be a weekly affair. I fully expect you to change back into your cooking costume after we eat."

She chuckled. "So where were you the last two days, if you don't mind me asking?"

"I don't mind." He stopped and put his fork down. The words were trying to form. His throat constricted. How could he start? *I've been a spy for twenty years, stole your secrets, and now my masters will kill my family if I don't ensure the destruction of New Washington. That I've been a selfish asshole, thinking I was so smart that I could worm myself out this treachery without hurting myself and everyone else I care about. That I am so brilliant, I could shuffle the deck, pull a great hand, and not pay a price.*

She was gazing at him. Her eyes kind and inviting, filled with hope. *How will she look at me once she knows, I've betrayed her? When the Brodie she thought she knew becomes nothing but a disappointment?*

"I went for a hike. Sometimes I need time alone to think. I walked almost to the Graham area, and it started to get dark. It was easier to sleep under the stars than navigate my way home. Next time, I'll plan it better."

"Next time, take me with you. I would love to do some hiking."

He returned a smile that he prayed wasn't sad. "I would love to take you on a hike. You have no idea how much."

# 41. The Test

Manny and Dee finished dressing in their space gear. They didn't have the luxury of a master of suits when on earth. Dee turned to Manny and twisted his helmet to verify it was seated properly. Her hands strolled along his arms and legs to ensure the integrity of his spacesuit.

Victor and his copilot, a bearded, young man from France, were on the other side of the hanger making the same preparations. Manny watched them. He scowled at Victor through the protective screen of his helmet. *Unlikely Victor will notice my challenge through the reflective visor,* Manny laughed to himself. *Victor is probably doing the same thing to me right now.*

The next three days would decide who would be selected to command the Enterprise, now in high earth orbit, and then later, the other two destroyers. Picking leaders for what was named The Earth Guard was no easy matter. In any normal organization, leaders rose to the top by holding positions of increasing responsibility demonstrating their competence at every level, but without a starting point for a chain of command, pilot trainees began on an equal footing. Each pilot was given an opportunity to strut their stuff and through trial and training, the best of them were identified. Those that had previous flight experience, most naturally assumed the lead.

The only exception to the experience rule was a gangly kid from Louisiana named Mark. He didn't possess the maturity to be an admiral or captain, but he was clearly the best pilot. How he'd acquired such amazing flight skill playing only video games with friends from his small enclave was an open question. Margo searched for the game that Mark claimed, "Made him a pilot," and provided a copy to every pilot trainee who owned a gaming device. So far, the game had not produced one iota of repeated success. Mark was considered a fluke, but no matter how young and fluke-like he might be, Mark had earned a spot in the final four.

Dee pulled Manny away from his ruminations and "mano a mano" posing. "Earth to Manny. Are we ready for this?"

"I am," he said through his communicator. Using Ardinian matter reorganizing technology that still felt like magic, Manny flipped the switch and his face plate disappeared. "The more important question might be, is Tammy ready?"

An announcement reverberated from hanger speakers. "Ladies and Gentlemen, please move to your wasps. Your order of departure, decided by a random drawing is as follows: Team Amanda, Team Victor, Team Manny, and Team Mark. Once you have boarded your spacecraft, standby for flight departure instructions from the tower."

Each team consisted of five wasps, for a total of twenty spacecraft. Team leaders with their pilots and copilots shuffled out of the crew hanger onto the airfield. Washington skies were crystalline blue as the pilots made their way through a cheering crowd. Mount Rainier in all its splendor consumed the eastern horizon with silver, gleaming peaks and white, frosting-topped pinnacles.

A congregation of envious pilot trainees, flight staff, engineers, and almost everyone else who worked at the airfield gathered to support their favorite team and wish the competitors well. All the participants, except Victor, garnered some level of enthusiasm--Manny as the only New Washington native, Mark for his youth and contagious smile, and Amanda because of her soft spoken, professionalism. Victor's unflappable, scowling bearing didn't easily draw supporters, and he couldn't have cared less. He believed firmly in the Russian proverb that "All that glitters are not gold."

Dee gave a vocal command, "Tammy, open the hatch." In a heartbeat, an opening appeared on the dark, sleek surface of the wasp.

"Welcome Team Manny. I am very excited to crush the bones of our competitors today."

"We're not interested in crushing their bones, Tammy. Merely, performing our best and winning," Manny replied while lodging himself in the cramped compartment and beginning his pre-flight checks.

"A figure of speech, my human team leader. I have completed the checks, but I welcome your verification. All systems are online and fully operational."

Dee heard a trace of sarcasm from Tammy. Most of the AI's idiosyncrasies had been fleshed out over the weeks of training, with most being the operative word. "Tammy, I know we've talked about this, but one last reminder. Whatever happens, you must keep your eye on the prize. We can't stop to develop a health screening module or attempt to revamp flight control systems while in flight."

"Yes, Dee," Tammy said in her breathless, sexual manner. "I have learned my lessons well. I am leaning into today's tasks with my entire processor. And if I may add, I expect our performance to be totally awesome."

"Alrighty then," Manny mumbled. He waited and watched the first two teams depart, their wasps shaking the ground with ear-splitting power as they soared into the sky.

"Team Manny, ground control. You are a go for liftoff. Good luck and good flying."

"Let's do this!" Manny roared. "Tammy, heading is established. Take us out."

They hovered for a moment just above the concrete and then screeched into the air, G-forces pressing them against the gel padded seats. The four other wasps comprising Team Manny followed.

* * *

A viewing screen covered the top half of one wall. Below, a computer-generated, test simulation mockup identified the four different teams by color. Statistics regarding speed to enemy contact, simulated kills, and time to mission completion scrolled on data pads available to each of the judges.

Shakete stood in a corner using a holographic screen, his hands clasped behind his back, nodding each time an action or reaction of one of the participants resulted in additional information. Karen's eyes were communicating confusion to Thomas. They were sitting together at a table trying to make sense of streaming data.

Mike was seated at the corner of the that same table, nearly quaking in fascination of everything Ardinian. From his first step on Delamie after

Shakete had invited Mike to participate as a judge, he'd peppered Shakete and Maleta with specific questions regarding the matter reorganizing technology and how it created the energy to power a huge ship. This line of inquiry was quickly followed by a barrage of questions about gravity within the ship and 3D manufacturing printers. Shakete finally said, "Maleta, could you please find our lead engineer and ask her to walk with Mike to assist with his enlightenment. She is much better at synthesizing complex science into layman's terms than I."

Mike' eyes flitted from his data pad to the viewing video. He commented to Karen and Thomas in response to their musings, "No, the column on the left is tallying kill shots The column in the center shows how many resources, by type, it took to make the kill. Watch the wasp actions on the viewing window and then correlate it to the data. That should help."

"Uh huh," Karen said as she and Thomas shared a wide-eyed look, not at all certain that would help. Rappel, the final judge, was sitting at the head of the table, his whiskers twitching in a random fashion giving no indication whatsoever if he was having the same difficulty as Thomas and Karen or if he fully grasped the intricacies of the lightning fast engagements, like Mike.

Mike yelled and pounded his fist on the table. "Did you see what that kid Mark just did? I've never seen anything quite like it. He must visualize the whole battlefield at once to respond that rapidly. Too bad he missed the opportunity to capitalize on his advantage by aligning his team in a supporting pattern."

"Yes, Mike." Shakete added. "Mark has an almost supernatural ability to be in the right place at the right time. He is not, however, strategically as adept in team maneuvers as Victor or Manny."

"Or Amanda," Mike said. "She does show some real genius when outnumbered. Perhaps her skill is more attuned to defensive capability than offensive operations. I think that could be a matter of experience."

"You may be right, but possibly, a tendency to accentuate defense is the result of temperament. We Ardinians suffer from the same natural tendency to avoid offensive risk, choosing instead to hedge our wagers. That reticence is helpful to survival, but counterproductive to ultimate conquest."

"Interesting insight, Shakete." Mike responded. The Mike-and-Shakete-show continued until the end of the day's exercises. Pilots and their wasps were beginning onboarding procedures to land on the Ardinian ship. They would dine, rest, and begin again the next day.

Thomas pushed back his chair and rubbed his eyes. "I'm starting to get the hang of it. Earth bound battles are similar. They're three dimensional in that you must consider ground based maneuvers and overlay them with any air capability. I had to pull the ground part out. Space pilots must be aware of offense and defense from a truly 3D perspective. How about you, Karen?"

"Getting there. I hope the plan is to take the scores and overlay a holistic approach to final decisions."

Rappel spoke for the first time, "My thought exactly."

Mike and Shakete were already heading out of the room. Thomas laughed in his always raucous manner at the sight of the animated pair. "I do declare. I believe Mike and Shakete have found new BFFs. I'm a tiny bit hurt."

"I know. Who would have guessed?" Karen mused.

Dinner was an elaborate affair in the ship's gathering place. The solar system of the Ardinians' home world glistened overhead, spinning slowly on its axis and showering the room with sparling multi-colored lights like a classy disco ball. Freshly showered, but weary faced pilots were directed by Maleta to the table of honor as the hoots of appreciative Ardinian diners grew in intensity.

Manny turned to Dee and whispered, "I would have preferred take-out in our sleeping quarters tonight. Then I wouldn't have to look at Victor's pompous smirking. I think he's winning."

"Shush. They want to honor us, and we still have another two days of tests. Don't be so negative. Also, they'll most likely serve that special Mermot ale."

"Yes, the ale. That alone is worth the effort."

Karen seated next to Shakete, stood and began to clap. Shakete and Maleta, having knowledge of this earth custom, did likewise. One by one, the Ardinian and Mermot guests followed suit, until their awkward, prayer like clapping and accompanying hooting shook the tables. Shakete nodded to Karen and Mike. He held his hands high in a gesture of quiet.

"Friends," he started. "Today is a momentous day. It is an affirmation of the partnership we have forged with our human friends. Brave earth pilots are willingly testing their newly acquired skills to prepare them for victory against the aggressive and evil Huntas." Because the assembled aliens were united in their hatred of the Huntas, more hoots blossomed through the dining chamber.

"We are extremely proud of our pilots. The day after tomorrow, the judges will select three worthy individuals to command the vanguard of our defense, the destroyer class ships. As most of you know, the Ardinian people are not known for making quick decisions. We prefer to conference, study, and deliberate. That very nature is one of the reasons we have asked humans to lead our fleet and fly the spaceships Mermots have built with Ardinian technology. Together, we form a strong alliance, buttressing the strengths and weaknesses of each of our three species.

"Today, I will take a cue from what I have learned from my human friends and do something different. Today, I will draw from what my friend Karen calls her gut, that place inside each of us that knows something beyond what the conscious processor allows us to see. A knowledge that springs from fact and emotion, after a millennium of inherited experience. You see, what we need most of all is a leader, an admiral to lead The Earth Guard who is both wise and brilliant. I have found that leader in my gut.

"I propose that Mike McCollough serve as the Admiral of the fleet."

The audience was nearly silent. All eyes peered at Mike, who sat stone still, his jaws clenched, his skin turning a mild color of red, which clashed with Shakete's darkening gold.

The Ardinians, a homogenous lot who trusted Shakete in all things, commenced a hooting frenzy. Mike, as the first human to appreciate the inherent strength of the Mermot production capability and put them to work, was well respected by their clan. Rappel was whisker twitching in agreement or, at least, what looked like agreement. Only Victor glared from seat, his posture stiff and erect.

Karen grabbed her husband's hand and refused to let go. She pressed her hand over his. *Damn, but Shakete is right about Mike. He wouldn't want the responsibility, and I wouldn't want him to take it for fear of losing him to some wild-assed, space battle. Mike also couldn't walk away if he was needed, any more than I can run from a necessary fight. Shakete had probably been playing them all along. Like a puppet master pulling the strings, they had all come readily to this place, Shakete's place. That asshole, can't make quick decisions, my butt,* Karen fumed to herself. For all she knew, Shakete had been watching Mike via the dogs for a very long time and had already picked him as their leader using Karen as his pawn. It was after all Shakete's suggestion that Mike visit the ship and be one of the judges.

If Shakete hadn't been right about absolutely everything thus far, other than some significant technical snafus, she would walk right now. But he was right, about Mike, about her, about the Mermots, and about hijacking her beloved husband. She sighed as she witnessed a softening in Mike's features, the siren's call of being needed too powerful to oppose.

Mike nodded at Shakete. "I am very flattered, but I need a day to consider your offer."

Shakete gave Mike an Ardinian smile in return. Karen thought it looked something like a snake sneaking up on a defenseless mouse. Whatever, Mike was never defenseless. He would see through Shakete's pretend fickleness soon enough. She also knew Mike would take the job and that she would see less of her husband. She would support him, and he would do the same for her. It was the way of a their hundred-year-old marriage.

* * *

A small ceremony was held in the cavernous landing platform to award command positions to the tested pilots. Mike, as the admiral of the fleet, was presenting. Completely at ease in his new role, he made a short speech thanking each of them for their commendable effort.

"Victor, if you will step forward and please bring your team with you," Mike directed.

Head held high, shoulders back, and an indifferent expression in place, Victor strode forward and came to attention in front of the new admiral. "You have been selected by a team of judges to command the Enterprise. You and your team will stay on the Delamie to be shuttled to with your new spaceship. I promote you now to the rank of Captain in The Earth Guard. I recognize you were once a general and hope you will honor me with your advice and experienced council as we begin our shared mission to protect our home."

Victor stayed at attention as Mike placed hastily designed epaulets on his shoulders. He gave the briefest of smiles and returned to his position. Manny was up next, also promoted to Captain with the promise of the next ship. Amanda came last. She beamed when Mike placed the too large epaulets on her smaller frame. Mike grinned at her, "We'll have them sized later."

Last in line was Mark. The disappointment registered in his normally happy face. Mike studied the amazing young man. "Mark, you may be the best natural pilot the world has ever seen. We were all impressed with your skill and daring. In honor of your achievements, you are promoted to the rank of Major. You will lead the wasp fleet until such time they are assigned to a destroyer. We need people of your ilk in the pilot's seat. You are one of our most valuable weapons."

Mark stood straighter and let out a yell. "Thank you, Admiral. I will do you proud. Someday I'll be standing where you are today."

"Of that I have no doubt," Mike responded.

Still in shock, Karen watched the proceedings. Shakete, standing next to her, was quiet. "So, how long have you known, Shakete?" she asked without moving her eyes in his direction.

"Know what, Karen?"

"Don't pretend."

"Not easy to pull the wool over your vision, Karen. You are speaking of my recommendation to encourage Mike to assume command of the fleet and accept the rank of Admiral."

Karen's eyes narrowed, "Eyes, not vision."

"Ah, yes. That sounds more satisfactory. More than a few years and less than one hundred."

Karen was mad and wanted to laugh at the same time. "I knew it!"

Shakete shifted his body closer without turning to face Karen. "I am sorry. I have grown accustomed to keeping my motives hidden from others. The burden of holding the weight of my people for so long has changed me. I alone have been the custodian of my race, and it is a very lonely place. I hope you will forgive me my shenanigans. My heart is in my chest."

## 42. Thomas Strafes the Airfield

Thomas kicked the boot of a sleeping sentry and waited. She rolled over, readjusted the gear she was using as a headrest, and muttered incoherently about someone named Stan. Thomas seethed as he took in the dark-haired beauty that was supposed to be ensuring the safety of the airfield. Unhooking the water container on his utility belt and twisting the lid, Thomas leaned over the softly snoring guard. As the liquid hit her face, she screeched as if struck by a bolt of lightning and scrambled to her feet. Her wake-up call was an angry dark face, and an immense man who drew an even bigger sun-blocking shadow.

She trembled at the realization she was caught in the act of napping by the big kahuna. "What's your name, soldier?"

"Deb," she stuttered and then thought to add, "Sir."

"When's the last time you saw your Sergeant of the guard?"

"This morning, Sir. When I first went on shift."

"Has anyone checked since?"

"No, Sir."

"Do you know the penalty for sleeping at your post?"

"No, Sir," the tall, thin woman squeaked back.

"Death by hanging. You have endangered the lives of fellow soldier, pilots, everyone by your failure to do your duty." Her eyes were so wide there were white rings around the irises. Glistening promised the onset of tears.

Thomas allowed his scowl to deepen as he studied the negligent guard. "I know you are new. Hear me now, this is your one chance. If I ever catch you sleeping again or even get a whiff that you have shirked your responsibility, you will feel the full wrath of my indignation. Are we clear?"

With large drops streaming down her face, she stammered, "Yes, Sir."

Thomas moved quickly to his ATV, yelling over his shoulder, "Do your job!" leaving the poor woman paralyzed in fear.

"This is a cluster fuck," Thomas said to himself as he drove away. That woman wouldn't make the same mistake again. A little one-on-one fear of god went a long way in this business, but that technique would never replace overall discipline and consistency. Someone had to check these folks, and they were strained at the seams finding enough trusted and qualified people to manage airfield security.

No way around it, he had to move most of the force to Jed's airfield. He could leave a few personnel in town to round up the frequently rowdy, town drunks and ne'er-do-wells. Everyone else should be here, to include him. There was too much at stake. He would talk to Chrystel as soon as he returned to town.

Thomas sped down the frontage road toward Margo's operations hanger. Accustomed to his master's outbursts, Ghost was sleeping peacefully in the back seat. Thomas pulled into the open hanger and braked, his ATV sliding on the smooth concrete.

Animatedly instructing a heavily tattooed man about some unknown task, Margo held a notebook in one hand. She stopped and whipped her head in Thomas' direction upon hearing the ATV screech to a halt and skid. Thomas leaped out of the vehicle, and Margo headed in his direction. Like two bulls suddenly aware of the immediate need to protect their turf, horns were locked and low, ready to charge into battle.

"What the hell, Thomas!" Margo spit, stopping far enough away to mitigate Thomas' height advantage. "You could have hurt somebody speeding in the hanger like that. What were you thinking?!"

Thomas' voice was a low growl. "I was thinking since you couldn't kill us all with artillery, you would do the next best thing and ensure our destruction through neglect of the security of this facility."

Margo covered her mouth with her hand to stop a scream. It didn't matter that she was working twenty-hour days, skipping meals, and giving every ounce of herself to this mission. The Mermots and walk-ons accepted her; the Washingtonians didn't. She had seen them eye her suspiciously. Given her part in the North Dakota attack, it was astounding they had given her this chance. Still, it might be years before she was fully accepted as one of their own. Margo calmed herself. Thomas was an asshole, but he was right. All that she had accomplished for the sake of earth's protection would be a footnote in history if the airfield was compromised.

"I don't know what you're talking about, Thomas."

Margo's change in demeanor helped take Thomas' fury down a notch. "I found one of your guards peacefully slumbering in the middle of the day. I can't even imagine how much rest they get during the night. This place is a ticking time bomb. People come and go without being challenged, it doesn't appear anyone is checking the laser positions, and the wasps are gone. A blind, deaf man and his younger brother would have a decent chance of overwhelming us. That's what I am talking about."

Margo felt defeated, and her shoulders slumped. "I don't know what to do Thomas. I simply don't have the people. I've done as asked and kept the walk-ons away from security details, just in case they are here for the wrong reasons. It doesn't leave me enough people to do the job."

"You could have talked to me, Margo." Thomas held his hand in a phone position at his ear. "Called me and said, "Hello Thomas, we're screwed if I don't get some help here.'"

God, he's an asshole, Margo thought. "You're right. I should have called. As you say, shoulda, woulda, coulda, except that given my history, I was afraid you would make sure they removed me from this position. And whether you believe it or not, I'm good at orchestrating this beast. You need me here doing what I'm doing, and Thomas, we're screwed if I don't get some help."

"That's music to my ears. And, Margo, whether you believe it or not, my priority is always to the welfare of this enclave and our mission. I don't care about your history, only that we get the job done. Capiche?"

"Understood."

"So, when will the wasps be back?"

"Day after tomorrow."

"Henceforth, leave two here at all times. One in the air to respond to any threats."

"That pushes training a bit, but OK. Anything else?"

"Do you know if Rainier received the Ardinian smart missiles?"

"I know that was supposed to happen, but I'm not sure. Jed would know."

"Okay, I'll check. Chew the guard sergeant's ass off. I was told by Sleeping Beauty no one had checked the guards all day, and I don't have time to do it myself. Someone must check guards and laser positions at least every two hours at intermittent times, starting yesterday. I'm going back to the enclave and inform our mayor that I'm moving most of my force here. Reshuffling will take at least two days to accomplish. I'll try to send a couple of force sergeants before then. Can you handle security in the interim?"

"Yes, Thomas."

"Excellent. See you soon." Thomas pivoted and jogged back to his ATV.

Margo whispered, "Asshole," as Thomas' back moved away.

Thomas pressed his foot to the gas and said to his fast friend, "Ghost, sometimes I'm a jerk. A necessary jerk, but a jerk nonetheless." Ghost agreed but remained silent in the back seat. Thomas watched the blur of Mermots moving from one task to another as he drove. He wondered if it were possible that there were more of them. It seemed like their numbers had doubled in the scant months since landing on earth. Mermots had assumed most of the heavy lifting when it came to work. If they weren't such a cooperative, happy species, he would have added Mermots to his list of worries. They could easily overtake humans on this world in a year.

He pulled in front of Jed's building. It was a hive of activity too, the only major difference being scientists moved in groups, spending as much time talking as accomplishing anything. He supposed the arguments over scientific theories were important. Most concerning, there was no one checking who entered the building. He stopped at the door waiting for anyone to question his presence. A young woman lingering near the entry, her hair pulled tightly in a bun, lifted her hand in a wave and said, "Hey."

"Good Lord, save us all," he muttered. Thomas strode down a highly-lit hallway, passing a large workshop where three scientists were engaged in a heated discussion over something Thomas didn't have a hope of understanding.

He entered Jed's lair, announcing his presence by a booming hello. Focused on information scrolling across a computer screen, Jed tore his eyes from the data and waved back. "Hi Thomas. To what do I owe the pleasure?"

"Security, or should I say, lack of anything resembling security. Jed, protection of the airfield is nonexistent. As soon as I leave here, I'm going to the enclave to inform Chrystel that I'm moving the force here. You are completely vulnerable, especially since the wasps are practicing in space."

"That bad?"

"Yes, that bad. I have a couple of questions for you. Did Rainier receive the missiles, and I'm betting I know the answer to this next one, are there any guards at the station?"

"Yes and no. Yes, the missiles have arrived, and no, we don't have any guards at Rainier. The normal three-person team is onsite. Do you think we need guards?"

"I do. Could you please contact them and ensure they're on high alert? I will get someone up there as soon as I can."

Jed stuttered, "Of course, but do you really have such grave concerns? This time of year, it's difficult to navigate the roads to their location. They are often snowed in."

"I'll send an airship with a crew as soon as weather permits," Thomas replied.

"What has precipitated this sudden concern?"

"Amelia told Karen about one of her visions before her first trip to the Ardinian ship--that there would be some form of bloody slaughter. I've been so busy getting North Dakotans settled, and the daily protests at the jail, I haven't visited the airfield to double check security. I was told it was handled, but it isn't."

Jed's face went white. "I didn't realize. Also, the Ardinian ship is leaving soon to return to the Mermot moon."

Thomas shook his head, a frown of consternation on his face. "Well, now we do know. No point wasting energy fretting. We need action to fix our vulnerabilities, and we need that action ASAP!"

## 43. Tweet gets a Seat at the Table

Wide-eyed, Judy stared at the slamming door with her mouth open. "What was that?"

Across from Judy, still sitting at her desk, Chrystel grimaced. "That was a tornado named Thomas. For a guy that normally takes things in stride and moves forward with an action plan, I'm not sure I've ever seen him so. . ."

"Freakishly spun up?" Judy asked.

Chrystel sighed. "I suppose that might be an apt description, but rightfully so. Like everyone else around here, Thomas is overwhelmed. Everywhere I look, we have poorly implemented, half-assed plans strung together with baling wire, gum, and prayers. Between keeping the enclave running, housing prisoners, resettling North Dakotans, managing daily protests, monitoring walk-ons, ensuring Mermots aren't accidentally hunted as vermin, and building a space fleet to save us from technologically superior, aggressive aliens, well, it barely leaves time to breath." Chrystel rubbed her hand over her eyes.

A light tapping on the office door saved the two women from sinking into a more profound funk. Tweet poked her head in. "May I enter, Mayor?"

"Of course, Tweet. Please, I called you."

Tweet was wearing a particularly mesmerizing outfit. She had adapted an Ardinian formal robe into a pleated dress in a shimmering, light mint color. The dress hung on Tweet's rat-like body in a way that made her visage almost human. If not for the hair on her legs, arms and face, at a distance, she might be mistaken for a well-dressed Washingtonian. Almost, Chrystel thought.

Another Mermot followed Tweet into the office. Brown shorts and a grey work shirt signaled a male. "This is my brother, Noah. He was born on earth."

"Pleased to meet you, Mayor Chrystel," the young male Mermot spoke into the minds of the humans. His whiskers were twitching in the way that Mermots greeted each other. After spending so much time with Tweet, Chrystel had begun to realize the whisker twitching was a form of non-verbal communication for Mermots. If you watched closely, their spiky, grey facial hair moved in different directions and speeds, based on various emotions. When they were happy, whiskers moved up and twitched rapidly in a circular motion.

"My brother will be assuming responsibility for assisting with crowd control during demonstrations. We were hesitant at first to perform any kind of police type actions, believing humans might resent the intrusion. However, what we can do is insert Mermots into demonstrations to talk with people and act as emotional facilitators. We have found great success in calming human alarm."

"Interesting idea," Chrystel replied. "You're ahead of me here, Tweet. I called you in to ask if Mermots could help with some missions that we've purposely kept as a human domain. We are stretched too thin. Besides the demonstrations, we need support securing the enclave and, more importantly, the airfield. Do you think you have enough Mermots to take on additional tasks?"

"Absolutely, Mayor. Our population has tripled, and I have imparted human historical behavior and methods to my people."

"I don't know how you've accomplished that feat, but I'm glad. What concerns me is that Mermots will feel like they're being overused or taken advantage of. Will you tell me if that happens?"

"Of course," Tweets whiskers twitched in happiness. "The fact that you would consider our feelings demonstrates an acceptance of Mermots that makes me want to sing. Our people want to be considered one of you. We will always be different, so we must be necessary."

Chrystel pulled open her desk drawer and withdrew a certificate. "Last night, during the council meeting, it was decided in a unanimous vote, that you Tweet, will become our first Mermot council representative. We will announce it formally at the next town hall meeting, but I wanted you to know. Your people will have a seat at the table."

Tweet's rat eyes grew as wide as a Mermot could open lidless eyes. Normally, Tweet was always moving. It was the first time Chrystel had seen her completely still. "I am too honored for human words." In the Mermot language, Tweet began singing a song into their minds, swaying to the cheerful melody.

"Beautiful," Chrystel whispered. "What's that song about?"

"It's a true story about how Mermots forged a friendship with the Ardinians. When they arrived on our planet, the Ardinians were not as you see them now. They had lost so many of their species during

414

the long journey to find a home, Ardinians had forgotten how to have hope. Shakete arrived at the Mermot clan gathering cave, morose and sullen, certain our people would reject his pleas for sanctuary. A distant ancestor of mine was a great leader of the combined clans. He peered into Shakete's heart, which isn't easy given the Ardinians are not a completely biological species." Tweet gazed meaningfully at Chrystel trying to share some profound insight.

"I'm not sure I get what you're driving at, Tweet," Chrystel responded. "But please, continue."

"I was trying to describe the amazing powers of my ancestor. Shakete is older than we know. His android assisted memories encompass everything that has happened to him and his people. Our great leader possessed the ability to look beyond those memories to capture Shakete's inner moral code. He found Shakete to be arrogant, slightly full of himself, thinking he was godlike, but kind and just. At least, that's what he told the clans when he welcomed the Ardinians. Shakete in turn, pledged the undying loyalty of Ardinians to the welfare of Mermots. Shakete said, and I quote, 'Our people are your people. Your people are our people. We shall be more than brothers and sisters from this day forward.' As far as I know, this partnership between alien species is the first ever of its kind.

"And now, by your act of including me as a council representative, I feel we may move forward with humans in the same way." Tweet's whiskers were happily circling as she concluded her song explanation.

"Very interesting, Tweet. Thank you for sharing. Your story makes me more curious about Ardinians, but we don't have time today to explore my questions." Chrystel wondered about Shakete's age and the android business. She also wondered if the all-knowing Mermot clan leader might have realized the Ardinians were so technically sophisticated, the Mermots could be squashed like bugs and thought it best to play along, offering up the Mermot world in a bargain. Regardless, the loyalty of the two species to each other appeared real. It would take a cold heart, indeed, to direct any cruelty to the loveable Mermots. They thrived by helping others. They rejoiced in service. Perhaps, Ardinians had learned something of immeasurable value from Mermots, and with any luck at all, human's might as well

"I wish we had time for more stories, Tweet. Why don't you give Noah a chance tonight to see his impact in the crowd and we'll see how it goes. Please, make sure he remains neutral. We'll assess the outcome in the next few days. I'm sure I'll get an earful if clavers feel at all put upon by his presence.

"Right now, we need to go to the airfield. Thomas just stopped by and had a hissy fit about the lax security there."

"Yes, Mayor," Tweet and her brother said in unison.

"Perhaps Mermots can quickly shore up the gaps in the airfield perimeter. And by the way Judy, have you seen Brodie today? I don't know where that man has gotten off to. He seems to vanish regularly these days."

416

"No, sorry. I'll try to reach him. Want me to have him meet you at the airfield?"

"Don't worry about it. I'll get him on my new phone on the way there. What a joy to have these new reliable phones. Are we ready?"

Tilley and Tweet filed behind Chrystel's rapid stride.

## 44. The Mountain

The members of the latest Rainier Station crew were almost done with their tour on the mountain. For Becky, the Chief Science Officer and a communications expert, replacement day couldn't come soon enough. It wasn't that she didn't love the wilds of Mount Rainier, because she did. The majesty of a mountain that rose from sea level to over 14,000 feet inspired awe. Covered on the northeast flank by a great glacier, there was nothing quite as spectacular as the view from their little missile station clinging to the side of Rainier.

That was the problem. Clear day views had been few and far between. Weather ranged from frigid to nightmarishly cold since Becky replaced the last crew at the tail end of winter. One storm after another buffeted the compact building, making it difficult to enjoy the sights and even harder to maintain outside equipment. Becky busied herself with work and recorded movies inside, doing her best to ignore Greg, a man with utterly no sense of boundaries or personal hygiene skills. Becky eyed Greg over the top of her computer screen. He was singing along in his off-tone, screeching voice to *Stayin Alive* by the Bee Gees. If that wasn't bad enough, Becky thought she could smell his body odor wafting in her direction.

Becky was alone with Greg for the time being. Jed had called to notify the crew that their security posture was upgraded to Level 1. That meant they had to take shifts outside in another raging storm to guard the station against invaders. Jon was outside now, and Becky was set to replace him in the numbing cold in thirty minutes. Jed had promised reinforcements in twenty-four hours, but until then, it was up to the normal three-person crew to make sure the station remained safe in New Washington hands.

"Staying alive, Staying alive. Uh, uh, uh, uh, Staying Ali...va..ah."

"Enough already, Greg!" Becky shouted, gesturing wildly to his headphones.

He smiled broadly as he uncovered his ears. "I love this song."

"Obviously. Unfortunately, it doesn't love you. Greg, could you please run outside and check on Jon? He hasn't responded to my last status check."

"He probably just forgot because he was so cold. But, yep, can do. It major league sucks out there."

Slipping into his parka, Greg zipped the massive coat all the way up. He shouldered his assault rifle and appeared anything but comfortable with the fit of the weapon slung over his arm. "I wish they had provided more weapons training," he mused to Becky. "I never really thought we would go to Level 1. Think it's real, Beckster?"

"I can't say. I only know Jed sounded truly concerned, and I doubt they would be sending reinforcements up here by airship unless they had good reason. Best to treat it like the real thing. And, Greg, please don't call me Beckster."

"Want to borrow my tunes?"

"Thank you, no. Get going. I'm getting worried about Jon. Send me a text when you find him."

Before he charged out the door into gale force winds, Greg said, "These new phones are totally cool. I helped Jed with the tech."

The temperature in the station dropped a few degrees from the momentary blast of air that heralded Greg's departure. A chill shook Becky's spine. She picked up the lightweight, Ardinian laser gun to be sure it was set to safe. A resupply team had delivered a full complement of missiles, along with the new laser technology. After the team had completed installation of the missiles, their techie advisor spent an hour with the Rainier crew demonstrating how to aim and shoot the laser. They practiced on nearby boulders, disintegrating the rocks into fiery blobs. Practice was fun and a distraction from the tedium of their daily jobs, but Becky never imagined she might need to use the new weapon to protect the station.

Reviewing the settings on the side of the narrow grip and trigger housing, Becky was glad someone had the foresight to mark the weapon in clear English, rather than alien symbols. There was a button switch for short or long range. The fast-talking techie had said, "Use long range for aircraft and short range for people or aliens. The other setting was hi, medium and low—low meaning the gun would stun but not kill, and high ignited anything it touched." No one explained what medium would do. The distance between practical results of hi and low settings was so great, it was a gamble to choose medium. Nevertheless, surmising medium would kill while possibly not incinerating the station, she set the switch to the big "M" and went back to worrying.

They were woefully ill-equipped if anyone would decide to take the station, even given Becky had a nifty laser gun. But who would, and why now? Getting here was incredibly challenging. Before the Great Dying, hundred-year-old roads had been maintained as access, but they were nearly impassible this time of year. Getting an air ship to the site in a storm was equally difficult. The only way to arrive at the Rainier Station on a night like tonight was to climb on foot. Becky couldn't imagine anyone attempting to do so.

Another gust shook the station. Greg's stench was almost gone in the ten minutes that passed since he left the building. Still no word from him or Jon. Becky was beginning to get spooked. She slung her weapon too, just in case, and wished they had brought a dog along to the station with them. Her fingers drummed against the metal of the old-style desk, counting time.

Becky lifted the phone to call Jed and put it down again, worried she would seem like a panicky coward. She didn't know if she should head out into the night to look for her unreachable crewmates or stay inside to guard the missile launch systems. "Probably, stay inside to guard," she muttered an answer to herself. Fear had wormed its way into Becky's gut.

"Cover, I need cover," she whispered. If the wrong person entered that door, she, Becky, a lowly scientist, would be the last line of defense to protect the missiles. *I need to find a place in this room to establish a safe hold to forestall any intruders from entering. But where?*

She glanced around the simple square room. A supply closet resided in one back corner and a small bathroom in the other. The bathroom had two windows. Someone could shoot her in the back from that location. The supply closet was the only option—three walls and a door. If she removed the door to increase visibility and stacked a couple of the standing metal filing cabinets in front of the closet and maybe a desk on its side in front of that, the combined pile of office furniture should provide enough cover for any individual weapons.

*But what if they use gas or a flash grenade?* "We've got some protective masks around here somewhere, and Greg uses noise cancelling headphones that he left on his desk," Becky said out loud to the empty station. As she was searching for a protective mask, Becky picked up the phone and dialed Jon and then Greg. Still no answer. Beginning to sweat even in the cool room, Becky felt her heart hammering and knew she needed to talk herself down. "Becky, you are probably a little off your rocker from hanging out at this lonely station with that infuriating Greg. After you build yourself a firing position, Greg and Jon will walk back in and get the biggest laugh of their lives at your expense. You'd better come up with a good story as to why building a fortress is a part of Security Level 1 procedures."

Becky found a protective mask in the supply closet. A flack vest lay underneath, but she decided to wait on the heavy vest until she honest to God needed protection. She yanked the pins from the door and levered it out of the frame. Attempting to push the heavy wood object to the side, she realized the door itself would provide good cover. She set it lengthwise on the outside of the supply closet. Next, she roughly tipped a five-foot filing cabinet on its side, causing a tremendous explosive sound that made her jump. Dragging the cabinet into position made even more noise as the metal beast squealed along the linoleum floor, catching on every corner where the linoleum didn't lie flat. On a roll now and breathing deeply, Becky manhandled another file cabinet, heaved it on top of the first, then flung a desk over, and dragged it to her pile.

Placing Greg's headphones around her neck, she stuffed the phone into a pocket, shouldered her laser again, and threw a folding chair over the pile into the closet to help with a targeting position. She tried to get Jed on the shortwave before she entered her cave. "Becky from Rainier Station, calling anyone at the Boeing Airfield. Do you read me over?"

"Becky, Jed is out of the office. What do you need?"

"I need to speak to Jed ASAP. My teammates, Jon and Greg, are outside the station in accordance with directives regarding Security Level 1. I haven't been able to reach either of them in over fifteen minutes. I decided it was up to me to protect the station in the event someone bad is outside, and I've built a covered firing position inside the station. I hope this is all a big screw-up, and my colleagues are safe, but I didn't want to take any chances. Can you get anyone up here, like right now!"

"It sounds as if you have taken reasonable precautions. As to getting someone to the station immediately, I'm not sure that can be done. Please assume your safe position and wait out further guidance. I will search for Jed and have him call you on your microwave phone."

"Please tell him its urgent."

"I believe you have adequately explained the urgency."

"Shit!!" Becky screamed as she climbed over office equipment to the closet interior. Her hands were shaking as she tried again to reach Jon and Greg.

* * *

Outside, Greg was following the sound of a phone ringing in the distance. Somehow, he had managed to lose his phone between where he was now and the station. He had backtracked twice, looking for the phone rather than Jon because he knew Becky would be worried by now. She would have his scalp when he returned, of that he had no doubt. She didn't seem to like him anyway.

He could barely see. Squinting into snow, the only thing visible was rock shadows poking out of white crusted terrain. Between low cloud cover and windblown precipitation, he was nearly blind. *Where the hell could Jon have gone?*

The ringing stopped. He thought it had come from a rock formation at a somewhat higher elevation. Climbing into the wind, he headed to the last place he heard the sound. The hair on the back of his neck stood at attention. The ringing had to be Jon's phone. He hadn't climbed in this direction.

Greg watched his feet to keep from slipping. *I should have taken the time to put on snow shoes.* "Is that blood?" Greg gasped. He crouched and poked his gloved fingers in the snow. Bringing the darkened snow close to eyes, and rubbing the snowy droplet between his fingers, he studied the color. The liquid in the snow was red; it was most definitely blood.

Greg's head whipped around in all directions. He jumped up and began moving more quickly following the bloody trail. He passed an outcropping and turned in the direction of the blood trail. Greg heard a huff behind him just before a sharp pain enclosed his neck. He couldn't breathe. He grabbed with both hands at the cord cutting off his air, twisting and struggling with every ounce of strength. His last thought after he realized he couldn't win this fight was fear for Becky.

\* \* \*

Still waiting for Jed's call, Becky sat on a folding chair, knees pressed against the blocking door and elbows propped on the top file cabinet. She held the laser weapon tightly in shaking hands. She was certain now that she was in deep shit. One of the guys would have called or come back by now if there was nothing wrong.

The phone finally rang, and she fumbled to get it out of her pocket, keeping her eyes glued to the door and the front of the station. Her eyes scanned the three windows for any hint of shapes or shadows.

"Jed, here. Is this Becky?"

"Yes, Jed. Thank God. Greg and Jon haven't come back. I've lost track of how long they've been gone but at least forty-five minutes without contact. I'm in our supply closet. I've barricaded the closet entry to provide cover. I have the laser gun, a protective mask, and noise cancelling head phones with me too. Do you have any additional guidance? Is someone on their way here now to help me?"

Jed gave a moment's consideration to bending the truth. He wanted to assure Becky help was on the way. They had tried to get an airship to the mountain, but an ongoing storm had turned them around before they were close. If the wasps weren't in space, those ships would have a much better shot at reaching Rainier and landing safely. At a minimum, wasps could provide aerial support. Jed sent a message to the Delamie asking for immediate assistance, but with the distance, time delay, and flight time to earth, it wasn't possible a wasp could arrive quickly.

"Becky, we can't get an airship there now in this storm. You're doing a remarkable job, and we're all very proud of you."

"Cut the shit, Jed. You could get an airship here, but it's too risky. Seems to me it's even riskier to let someone take over this station."

Jed bit his lip in frustration. "You're right Becky, on both counts. An airship would likely crash in any rescue attempt, and we can't allow anyone access to our missiles. I don't have to explain that to you.

426

All wasps are off-world. We're waiting for one to arrive and assist, but I don't know when that'll be.

"That leaves you, Becky. We need you to do your utmost to stop intruders from taking the station. If you can't resist, we humbly ask that you destroy the station. Most important is the missile interface equipment. If anyone was to gain access and hack the codes, our entire enclave and airfield would be subject to destruction by our own missiles."

"You know what you're asking, right?" Becky whispered.

"I do. And I'm terribly sorry," Jed responded, his voice cracking.

There was silence on the line. Becky took a deep breath. "I'll do my best. Please tell my mom and dad I love them. Also, my little brother. I never thought this job would end like this."

Silence again. Finally, Becky came back again, her voice quivering. "Jed, the power just went out. Someone has cut the power."

"Have the back-up generators kicked in?"

"Give it a moment. Yep, the yellow lights just came on. I'm afraid."

"I know, Becky. You have every right to be afraid. But we need you to be brave now. The whole enclave and everyone you care about is depending on you to do your best. I wish there was another way, but you can't allow anyone to access the missile interface."

"Can't you control them, the missile firing systems, from your end?"

"I can, and I have. Right now, the missiles are set to lockdown. Unfortunately, anyone with electronics know how will most likely be able to route around my lockout."

"Damn," Becky said, tears in her voice. She drew in a large breath. "Okay, I'm Okay. Just tell my family, Jed. And Jed, we endure." Jed heard an explosion in the background, and Becky's last words, "The party is starting. Can't talk."

The door blasted open. Becky let loose on medium setting with the laser. Two figures in white snow gear pushed through the entry, yelped, and then sizzled in a flash of color from laser fire, falling to the ground in a heap. Becky quickly donned the protective mask and placed the headphones over her ears. Her shout of "Bring it on, mother fuckers," was muffled by the gas mask covering her face.

Another white clad invader broke out a front window. Becky saw an arm preparing to throw something, probably a flash grenade. Closing her eyes, she huddled and covered the headphones with her hands. "Those are some awesome headphones," Becky yelled. There was a slight ringing in her ears, but she was still going.

Recovering, Becky aimed her laser at the grenade thrower now trying to climb in the window, and then at another assailant giving the front door a second try. They sizzled and popped, dropping like stiff timber. "Gotcha! Bet you didn't see that coming!"

After an intense minute or two of battle, everything went still. Becky wasn't sure how long she had been protecting the station, but it seemed like hours instead of minutes. *They're probably trying to regroup. Doubt they have much experience with an alien laser gun.* Becky smiled.

*They'll probably try tear gas next.* "Go for it, assholes," Becky shouted and snickered maniacally as she kept her gas mask clad head up and watchful.

True to her prediction, a hand appeared in the same broken window, flinging the next grenade. Becky aimed low at a body she couldn't see, guessing where it would be behind the wall. A direct hit. The grenade dropped to the ground outside the window to give the bad guys a whiff of tear gas. The laser had cut right through the wall into the man behind it. "That medium laser setting was a good choice," Becky said to herself, then giggled in a mad, desperate kind of way.

*What next?* She heard glass breaking in the bathroom. "Uh, oh," Becky sighed. Didn't think to wall off the bathroom. Trying to keep people out from the front and the side bathroom entry at the same time was going to be a bit more challenging. Particularly since it was hard to see around the closet doorframe to the restroom entry.

Becky had an idea. The bad guys were most likely here to use our own missiles against us. If I take out the interface now, the intruders won't have any need to take the station. Without the technology to control a missile launch, they are just big dumb bombs unlikely to kill anyone other than any jackasses trying to remove them from their nearby launching locations. Jed and his group of scientists had done one thing right. The missiles were protected by a hidden dead man's switch. Without the codes, trying to move a missile would light up the entire top of Mount Rainier. As they said around the station, "Goodbye glacier," if one missile explosion cascaded to each of the other eleven missiles.

Becky flipped the laser switch from "M" to "H". *Once I rid the station of the missile controller equipment and the server rack, what then for me?* In 20/20 hindsight, the closet was a worthy place to defend the station, but it sucked in terms of any avenue of escape. She had set herself up for a suicide mission without even knowing it.

A gun barrel and then a baklava clad head peaked out from the bathroom entry. When they saw Becky leaning out over her mound of office furnishings, aiming an unusual weapon in their direction, the head disappeared from whence it came. With her alien death ray set on high, Becky fired in the general direction of that hat covered enemy. She heard an electric crackle, a scream, and then saw of whoosh of flames blown outward from the bathroom door. The flames were quickly sucked back into the bathroom, most likely because of the open windows in the room. Billowing dark smoke indicated the restroom was out of order, permanently. One less thing to worry about.

A silhouette passed in front of a side window. Becky didn't have any idea how many assholes were left outside in the snow, but if she was a betting woman, she would bet their next attempt wouldn't be subtle. *If I were them, I would focus everything I had in one spot and charge me, hoping there would be a someone left standing at the end of the engagement.* "No time like the present," Becky sighed sadly as she stood and began to decimate the computer interface equipment and server rack. She swung her laser back and forth across the room, lighting on each terminal and giving the servers a two-second blast.

What could catch fire was in flames. Becky scrambled over the pile of junk, heat and smoke already overtaking the station. The protective mask she was wearing would protect her lungs from smoky fumes, but not for long. She beat a path to the front access, skirting ensuing flames. The phone in her pocket was ringing, probably Jed. *No time to chat, Jed.*

Only three long strides to the door, but a figure appeared blocking Becky's escape. In motion, she raised the laser and pressed the trigger. The parka clad gunman, as surprised by Becky as she was with him, raised a rifle almost simultaneously. He fired a three-round burst into Becky's chest just before his weapon and arms burst into flames. Becky dropped to the ground. The unarmed assailant screamed and thrashed, stepping forward and falling on top of the brave scientist. As a raging fire took the station, the only thing left standing in a vast field of ice and snow was a brick shell of what had once been New Washington's first line of defense.

## 45. The Vision

"I'm tired, Trent," Amelia said, studying her partner with a satisfied smile. "We did good today, didn't we?"

"Good? No, Amelia you were spectacular today. Do you realize we walked for nearly a half mile down the road before we had to turn around and at dusk no less?"

"It is getting easier, but I still feel entirely worn out when I return. I'm not sure how I can ever thank you for all you've done for me. For my family."

Trent reached his long sinewy arm across the table and tenderly placed his fingers under Amelia's chin. "Amelia, I was a lost man for a very long time. When my wife and kids were killed by that demented psychopath in Colorado, I existed in a haze of anger and hate, so bent on revenge I forgot to live my life. When I couldn't find him and extract justice, I gave up just as surely as if I'd swallowed a bullet. The man I was, the one living on the outskirts of your enclave was no man at all, just a shell of a being devoid of feeling and purpose. It was you, Amelia, that gave me back my life. I owe you."

Amelia got up from the table, walked behind Trent, and placed her arms around his chest. She leaned in and nuzzled her chin on his shoulder. "What wonders the world must hold if two lonely, broken people like us can find each other." She kissed his head. "I have a little headache. I need to lie down for a bit."

"Are you OK? Aren't you going to finish your dinner?"

"I'll get a snack when I get up, and I'm fine. Just a little headache."

"If you don't mind, I think I'll take a run out to your folks while you're napping. Mike is working on a new beer recipe, and I've been helping him."

"I thought my parents were still on the Ardinian ship, judging the pilot competition."

"Nope. The Ardinians sent a shuttle back yesterday to drop them off. The pilots are staying for more training, but Mike said he needed time to think about something. He didn't say what."

"That's curious. You like him, my dad?"

"What's not to like? He's smart, practical, and an all-around good guy. And, your mom keeps me laughing. No wonder you're so special."

Amelia rubbed Trent's hair. "You must be vying for a little action tonight."

"A guy has got to do what a guy has got to do," Trent grinned.

"Can you do me a favor? Leave Lionheart here. His presence is helpful when I have a headache. Also, he's quite the chatterbox when we're alone. He keeps me from missing you."

"Of course, milady. I shall return to your side with the greatest haste!"

Amelia walked Trent to the door. They embraced, and her eyes stayed on his back until he was out of sight. She grabbed her head as she closed the door to the night. Not wanting Trent to worry, Amelia had withheld the extent of her headache and overall malaise. Something was wrong. She could feel the wrongness in her toes and fingers, and it was expanding up her legs and arms.

433

"Come, Lionheart," she called and walked into her comfortable, cozy bedroom, a place that always felt safe. She laid her head on the pillows. Lionheart jumped up alongside, plopping his muzzle on his paws, his eyes lingering on Amelia.

"Amelia, hurt?" Lionheart asked in a sympathetic whine.

"I'll be fine," she whispered and shut her eyes. Lionheart watched the movement under the woman's eyelids until he too drifted into dreams.

*What is that noise? Where am I? Amelia was standing on a vast concrete sheet. She had never seen so much cement in one place. That noise was back. Gauzy apparitions appeared and then solidified into people and large rats. They were all running, scampering in every direction, yelling at one another. She glanced up to determine the source of the thundering sound pounding her ears and saw an object streak across the heavens. That must be what I've seen in my books. It's a jet!*

*Amelia watched the jet perform a turning loop and then fly back in her direction, lower this time. A flash from the wings of the jet sent a white plume plunging to the ground. She could feel the explosion in her feet and only a second later, the concussion of the blast hit her face. A horrible pressing tormented her ears.*

*There was more than one jet and more than one explosion. People were crying. Amelia saw a body, or what was left of one, lying torn and prostate at her feet.*

*She wanted so much to flee. "Please, God. Let me leave!" Amelia moaned. Her head swiveled on her body even though her feet wouldn't move. In this direction, Amelia could see wide, grey topped buildings. A red-haired woman ran out of large open doors, purposeful, a weapon on her shoulder. It was her daughter—Chrystel!*

*"No baby, no. Go back, Chrystel!" Amelia tried to shout, but not a peep came out of her throat. A man in a green and black striped watch cap and wearing a sweatshirt emblazoned with a blue and green sports logo appeared from behind a truck. Seahawks was written above the logo. The man drew his rifle and followed Chrystel's running figure. Amelia could tell her daughter didn't know the man was there. She was too preoccupied with the jets. Chrystel took a knee and placed a bulky, tube like gun on her shoulder. It looked like she was aiming at an aircraft and was ready to fire. Amelia yelled again and strained to move, either to protect her daughter or stop the man. If only she could budge from this spot where she was frozen, immobile and useless. Then, the hatted man targeting Chrystel fired. He shot Amelia's daughter in the face.*

Amelia bolted upright in bed, her eyes open in horror. Her breathing was shallow, and blood was rushing to her head. The room was dark and cold. It was only a moment before she realized the predictable throes of a full-blown panic attack.

"NOO!" she screamed. Lionheart, awakened by the frightening outburst, sprang to his haunches growling, preparing to fight and defend against whoever should try to hurt this dear woman. He sniffed the air for predators. What he smelled was only Amelia's fear and mania.

Lionheart lowered himself again to the bed, placed his head on her lap, and began to talk.

435

"Whatever is this fear, I help. I Lionheart. Slow breathing. Lionheart here. My courage is your courage. Take courage from Lionheart." Lionheart began to inhale and exhale, just as he was asking Amelia to do. Her eyes watched him, and soon, her breathing was matching Lionheart's regular rhythms.

Amelia's voice was a keening plea, "Not again. I can't lose someone I love again, not when I have the power to stop it."

"Lionheart help," he said flatly.

Amelia pulled her feet off the side of the bed and stood. Wobbly and shaking, she grabbed the edge of the bed with one hand to steady herself. She crept in the dark to the light switch and turned it on. Nothing happened. She tried a dresser lamp with the same result. "I don't like this, Lionheart. The power must be out."

Lionheart, now standing by Amelia's side, leaned his body close as support while they moved in darkness from the bedroom to the kitchen phone. The phone was shaking in her hand as she pressed it to her ear. "It's dead! The phone is dead. Something is very wrong."

"Sit," Lionheart ordered. "Think what to do."

Amelia nearly tipped the chair over as she dropped into it. "I know what I have to do, Lionheart. I must contact Chrystel and tell her to watch out for the man with the striped hat! I must leave the house and walk down the road to town. Now, before it's too late."

"Rest first," Lionheart pleaded.

"Go get me my boots and my jacket." Amelia was rifling through kitchen cabinets, searching for a flashlight when Lionheart returned, her boots stuffed in his mouth. Since she never went outside alone in the dark, Amelia never needed a flashlight except for power outages. "Where would Trent have hidden the flashlight?" Amelia asked as Lionheart dropped the boots on the floor.

"I know," Lionheart answered.

He used his claws to open a cabinet, stuck his nose inside, and grabbed a flashlight in his jaws. Dropping the metal object at Amelia's feet, he clamored out of the kitchen to find Amelia's coat.

Amelia tightened her grip on Lionheart's ruff as she stood and peered out at the darkness. Her pulse was racing. A coyote yipped in the distance. Amelia bowed her head and asked the universe to help her save her beautiful daughter.

*Relax, breathe, loosen your shoulders,"* she said repeatedly in her mind. *"You can do this. What's the difference between a half mile down the street and three miles to Geronimo's house? It's the same activity. Lionheart will keep you safe. There is nothing out there to fear..."*

Her stomach was already twisting and turning. She walked several steps toward the road and thought again about sending Lionheart alone. The heat behind her ears was growing. *"Lionheart can get there faster. He can bring Geronimo back to me."*

Amelia answered herself out loud to reinforce the need to go. "You can't leave it to Lionheart because Geronimo might not be home. Or Lionheart will pass the information about the man with the striped hat, but Geronimo won't understand the urgency. Lionheart is a dog, and they don't always get things right—even smart ones like him. Are you willing to take that chance, Amelia? The chance that because you are so afraid of the out of doors, you will once again fail to save your family?

"If you walk fast, it's only forty-five minutes to Geronimo's house. Forty-five minutes of effort to know you've done everything within your power to save Chrystel. And, as Mom has reminded me so often, in the end that's all any of us can do. No one has control over outcomes, even a seer like me."

Lionheart stared up at Amelia during her self-speech. He wasn't sure what it all meant other than the two of them needed to travel to Geronimo's house as fast as possible. He gave a short bark to get her attention. "Let's go!"

Determined, Amelia nodded and said, "Yes, let's."

The first two miles were better than Amelia could have imagined. She didn't look around to become frightened by the foreboding night. Keeping her mind focused on moving, she watched her feet and the area illuminated by the flashlight directly to her front. She walled off her mind from any thought about where she was. Amelia counted steps and calculated travel distance in her head. When her concentration waned, she pictured Trent or Chrystel and started counting again.

It all fell apart at about the beginning of the third mile. A loathsome ranger stealthily glided onto the side of the road. Amelia saw the mangy creature at the perimeter of her flashlight beam and stopped, only uttering a quizzical, "Oh."

For the first time, Lionheart left Amelia's side and darted forward, his head low, his fur raised,

438

and his tail straight out. He growled the most threatening growl Amelia had ever heard. Her pulse rocketed from its walking exertion high to stratospheric heights. She was so terrified, her body quivered, and her breathing stopped. It felt impossible to pull air into her lungs. She was gasping and wheezing as she considered the awful possibility, the ranger's pack was waiting on the sidelines in the woods.

Amelia coughed and then a fountain of what was left of dinner blasted from her mouth. She wiped her face on her sleeve and yelled, "Don't faint, Amelia. Don't you dare!"

The ranger and Lionheart were circling, like wrestlers trying to get the best advantage to attack. The ranger darted forward, and Lionheart met the charge. From a faraway place, Amelia heard the awful snarling and teeth gnashing. Her knees felt like they were going to buckle as she swayed on her feet.

Amelia would never know where the will to act came from, someplace deep inside where her conscious mind never traveled, but as she looked down at the heavy flashlight in her hand, her body took control of her flagging mind. She moved quickly to the writhing animals, directed her thoughts to the ranger's head, and began to whack him with the flashlight every time the feral animal turned his snout in her direction. After the third good hit with her club, good in terms of surprise effect rather than maiming, the ranger yelped and ran back into the woods. If he had friends with him, they left with their humiliated alpha. One crazy woman and one brave dog together, had stared down the danger in the woods.

She checked Lionheart for injuries and found a couple of bloody patches that didn't appear serious. He licked her arm in thanks as she stroked the fur along his haunches.

Confident Lionheart was good to go, Amelia sighed as she looked up at the shadows of towering firs and then slowly curled to knees. Her entire body felt like it was convulsing. She puked acidic bile on the road, her stomach tightening into a knot as her gut turned itself inside out once again.

Lionheart licked her face and began to breathe in the way he had seen Trent do so often whenever Amelia started to fall apart. She stared into his soulful eyes and followed the pattern. "I don't think I can get up, Lionheart," Amelia cried, tears streaming down her cheeks.

"Then walk on four legs, like me," he answered.

"You mean crawl?"

Lionheart stared at his female master, his eyes suddenly piercing and insistent. Amelia put her hands on the ground and moved. As she crept forward on her hands and her knees, she started counting again. She crawled until her knees were scraped and bloody and her hands hurt with every movement. Amelia didn't know how long she crawled, only that Lionheart never left her side. Finally, able to stand and walk the final distance to Geronimo's home, Amelia was so exhausted, she crumbled to the ground on Geronimo's lawn.

Lionheart didn't stop to consider Amelia. He beat a path to Geronimo's door and barked the bark of dogs determined to gain the attention of humans. Geronimo arrived at the front entry scratching his head at the sight of Lionheart's frantic barking. The dog spun twice and jumped up, landing his scratchy paws on Geronimo's chest.

"No need for hysterics. What is it, boy?" he inquired. Candy smelled Amelia, glided around Geronimo, and dashed to Amelia's prone figure lying face down in the grass. "Oh, my God!" Geronimo shouted. "It's Amelia!"

Geronimo raced to her side, dropping to the ground and felt for a pulse.

She turned her head. "We have an important message to get to Chrystel."

"How in the world did you get here?"

"I walked, and then I crawled, and then I walked again."

"What in the world, Amelia? Why?"

"A vision. Do you still have a shortwave?"

"I do. And, one of those new phones. The landlines are down though."

"I know. Very shortly, we will be under attack at the Boeing Airfield. You must contact Chrystel now. Tell her a man in a black and green striped watch cap, wearing a sports jersey with a blue and green bird across the front, will try to kill her. It has the word Seahawks written on it. He will come from behind a truck on the concrete. Tell her, Geronimo. Reach her now and tell her!"

"We're going to be under attack? By who?"

"I don't know. They have jets, and they're going to bomb everyone. Now, Geronimo. There isn't a moment to waste."

"That explains the telephone and power outage. Someone is trying to disable communication."

Geronimo jumped up to run to the house and then stopped and turned. "Are you okay, Amelia? Do you need immediate medical assistance?"

"I'm fine for now, but I need to get inside soon. Make your calls. Chrystel first!"

"Candy, Lionheart, see to her. I'll be right back." Geronimo limped to the door as quickly as he could move, muttering to himself and trying to organize the list of people he needed to alert."

Lionheart stood protectively near Amelia and nuzzled her shoulder. He whispered to Candy, Geronimo's most trusted canine companion, "Have you ever seen a human walk on four legs?"

"I heard that," Amelia giggled.

# 46. No Good News

Arriving at the Boeing Airfield, Chrystel sought out Margo and found her surrounded by a gaggle of guards ready for their next shift. Margo glanced at Chrystel and then went back to her speech. She reinforced the absolute importance of maintaining discipline and remaining aware. The rag tag group of guards listened halfheartedly. Chrystel thought when time allowed, a uniform might help to instill a sense of comradery that appeared to be missing from their disinterested faces. One young man was wearing a bright orange sweat shirt, the hood covering his head and flip flops adorning his feet. Not exactly attire conducive to remaining concealed to hostiles or making a hasty exit if needed, Chrystel mused. No wonder Thomas was so concerned.

Margo freed herself from the circle and strode to Chrystel. "To what do I owe the pleasure, Mayor?" She nodded at Tweet and Tilley standing to Chrystel's left side.

"Thomas said he was concerned about airfield security, and I wanted to see if there was anything I could do to help."

"I appreciate the sentiment Chrystel, but unless you can clone a couple dozen more trained guards, I'm not sure what that would be."

"Tweet, could you please explain to Margo how you can help."

Tweet stepped forward and bent slightly in a Mermot gesture of respect. "Yes, Miss Margo, I am confident the Mermots can assist. We have been breeding rapidly and have greatly increased our numbers. With your permission, I can arrange for a hundred or more Mermots to perform duties at key facilities, weapons placements. and along the perimeter where you might fear our defenses are weak."

"But, I thought we had decided not to use Mermots in that capacity?"

Ready to interject, Chrystel's phone buzzed. She yanked the bulky receiver off her belt and looked at the caller. "It's Geronimo. He probably wants to pump me for information. I'll call him back later. As I was about to say, I think given everything, we need to be flexible. The Mermots are truly our only option for shoring up security gaps. They are ready and willing."

"Sending a bunch of extras to do guard duty without coordination or____"

Chrystel's phone was ringing again. She looked at the caller identification. "Geronimo," she said and rolled her eyes. Chrystel hit the button on the phone to decline the call. "Please continue, Margo."

"In essence, I'm worried untrained guards won't help. More bodies won't solve my problem."

"I don't mean to be impertinent," Tweet added. "I have imparted security information to twenty recent Mermot litters. In total, that's two-hundred Mermots. They understand guard responsibilities, how to maintain and operate related equipment, and have expert qualifications on all weapons systems used in defense at the airfield. That includes the Ardinian laser weapon."

Now, Margo's phone was ringing. She raised her finger in a pausing gesture. "Hello, Jed. Chrystel's here with Tweet offering up some trained Mermot guards." Margo's expression changed. "Uh huh." She listened, her face getting pale. "Oh, no. When will the wasps arrive?" Margo turned her back to Chrystel, her shoulders slumped in defeat as she continued to listen to Jed's call.

Chrystel and Tweet shared a concerned look.

"I hear you, Jed. We'll do the best we can. If Becky couldn't hold them off, I just hope the failsafe on the missiles is as a good as you say. Otherwise, we're doomed."

Margo turned to face her guests. "Bad news. The worst. Jed believes the Rainier Station was likely attacked. He can't reach anyone at the site and doesn't know what happened."

"Why does he 'believe' the station was attacked? Why doesn't he know?" Chrystel huffed.

"Nearly an hour ago, Becky, the lead scientist at the station, called Jed concerned because the she couldn't contact the other two members of her team. They were outside the station performing defense. The power went out while she was talking to Jed. It was the last time he heard from her. This Becky was convinced someone was preparing to take the station. Jed reminded her whatever happened, she couldn't let anyone obtain the missile controller systems."

"I'm not sure I understand why the station was left vulnerable with only three scientists to defend against intruders, but I suppose it's the same issue we have here, limited qualified people for the multitude of necessary missions." Chrystel shook her head. "I hardly know what to say. If someone has gained control of our missiles, it's all over but the crying. Has Jed been able to get anyone up to Rainier to check? Is someone on the way?"

"He sent an airship when she first called, but a storm on the mountain prevented them from landing. A crew armed with lasers is on their way now, and they'll try again to land. He also contacted the Delamie. Pilots and wasps are in space now making their way back to earth. It'll take some time for them to arrive."

"I'm afraid to ask how long." Chrystel said.

"Jed didn't say. You can ask him yourself. He wants you to call him."

"Do you realize, Margo, without the Rainier Station we have no long-range radars? We're nearly blind. We won't have much warning in the event of an attack from the air. Who could it possibly be?"

"I know," Margo frowned. "There's one tiny bit of good news. Jed tells me the missiles are armed with a dead man's switch. They, whoever they are, won't be able to carry them off. He believes the scientist at the station, Becky, did the right thing and destroyed the missile interface. Worst case, it would take some time for even an expert to get through the multiple fire walls to arm missiles and send them our way. Let's hope we get some support up the mountain soon."

"I'd feel better if instead of thinking or believing, Jed knew something for certain. Nothing for us to do about the missiles. We must get this place secured now. Tweet, I need you to-----" Chrystel's phone shook in her hand. "Let me get that. Geronimo again."

"Yes, Geronimo. What's up?" Geronimo was talking fast, screaming hysterically into Chrystel's ear. He led with Amelia's vision and her amazing walk to his house and closed with information about the power and phone outages at the enclave. Geronimo was in full outrage mode because Chrystel had ignored his previous calls when she interrupted. "Geronimo, tell my mother, I love her and thank you. I will give you ample opportunity to chew me out later, but right now, I gotta go."

"Well, where was I? Tweet, one question. Your people are first and foremost cooperative. I've never seen any aggression at all from a Mermot. Are you sure they're capable of performing defense and wounding or killing another being if the need presents itself?"

"Mayor, that is an excellent question. You are correct. Aggression is foreign to our species. There is one important exception, we will gladly do whatever the situation requires to defend our home. Mermots survived and thrived on a planet filled with vicious carnivores. The teeth of a Mermot can cut rock. I will allow your imagination to determine what those teeth may do to flesh. And, of course, as you have witnessed, our species is quicker and faster than earthbound mammals. I have read about the cheetah. This earth animal may come close to matching our speed in the short run, but I have no way to test the comparison. In any event, please allow that one worry to be extracted from your mind."

"Good enough for me," Chrystel replied. She paused for a moment to consider what would happen if humans ever decided to cast out the Mermots. They already considered earth to be their home; therefore, they would not likely vacate the premises willingly. Not that Chrystel could see any reason to send them packing, just the opposite. *Something to think about when I have more time.* "Margo, how much do you trust your guards on an individual basis, that they are not a plant from another enclave?"

Margo grimaced. "That cuts close to the bone, Chrystel. The short answer is mostly, but not completely. They're comprised of New Washington natives and a handful of North Dakotans that I trust implicitly. Certainly, some folks from my original enclave in North Dakota infiltrated New Washington, so the possibility exists, another enclave might have also inserted spies."

"Just as I thought. Tweet, go retrieve your Mermot guards. Place one Mermot in each of the human teams already manning established defensive positions. Work with Margo to determine the best use of the remainder. Bring any weapons Mermots have hidden in their hidey holes." The fact that Tweet did not correct Chrystel when she mentioned hidden weapons was a clear sign to Chrystel, they did indeed keep some for their own defense.

Chrystel scratched her chin thinking. "Oh, and Margo, don't we have some of the old world's shoulder mounted, anti-aircraft weapons around here somewhere?"

448

"Yes, but I'm not at all sure they still work or that anyone knows how to use them. There's a crate of them stored in the ammo facility."

Tweet spoke up. "We included those human defense weapons in our data transfer. Also, how to perform maintenance checks."

"Of course, you did," Chrystel marveled at Mermot awesomeness. "Get a team of Mermots to crack the crate open and have them check if they're still usable. Place them in advantageous positions around the airfield if they find any that still work. I'm assuming Mermots are also familiarized with identification of New Washington and Ardinian aircraft. Wouldn't want to shoot one of our own."

"Of course, they are familiar with aircraft identification. That goes without saying Mayor," Tweet replied in that matter-of-fact, yet humble, way, characteristic of all things Mermot.

"One last thing, well two actually. Geronimo called to inform me that my mother had a vision about my death. It seems a man in a green and black striped watch cap, wearing a Seahawks jersey, plans to shoot me. If you see anyone like that you have two choices, kill him or call me. My mother is always right. Please don't spread a BOLO. If he hears we're looking for him through word of mouth, he might change his outfit, and I'll have no means to identify my assailant." Chrystel saw worried faces from the group. "Chill, ladies. Now that I know about him, he won't get the drop on me. "The second item is far more troubling, but not unexpected. Amelia saw aircraft attacking the airfield. It's coming. I've taken up way more of your time than we can afford, already. Get going and get serious."

Chrystel saw a blur as Tweet entered the closest Mermot hole. "Bye, Tweet," she murmured to her already departed friend. "That woman, girl, or rat alien Mermot, however you want to name her, may be the nicest and most capable being I have ever met."

"I second that," Margo answered. "In the evolutionary sweepstakes, the Mermots won the mega jackpot, even though their hairless tails still kind of gross me out. I don't know what I'd do without Tweet's help."

Chrystel shook her head and smiled. "We need to get to work, Margo. Keep me updated. I need to find Jed, and I'll be back as soon as I can. Tilley, you're with me." Sitting on her muscular backside, the spotted, purple henka and ever watchful companion to the Mayor, stood up, shook off her lounging stasis, and smiled a frightening, tooth-filled grin at her charge.

## 47. Brodie's Burden

Brodie waited at Geronimo's door. He had spent most of the day in useless activity trying to contact Harvetta, his official handler at the Capital Enclave. When no one answered, he drove to the outskirts of the airfield looking for any signs of an imminent attack. Sneaking beyond the fence line, Brodie climbed over and around long deserted buildings in areas which he believed would be the mostly likely routes to mount an offensive action against the airfield. He found signs of travelers--old campfires, discarded food wrappers, a forgotten pair of trousers, but nothing that spoke to an organized presence. When Karen's plea for pilots had been broadcast to the world, hopeful candidates infiltrated through these same overgrown ruins. Signs of human activity were probably from them.

He climbed a leafless oak growing on the crest of the best elevation he could find and gazed into the distance for inspiration. The futility of this search was Brodie's only inspiration. A Capital Enclave inserted army could be anywhere. He didn't have the time or the wherewithal to find them. If what Harvetta said about the militarization of Capital was true, and its leaders believed for every day they waited the chances of a successful attack diminished, they would be here now or very soon.

Capital had cut him out of the final plan, of that he was certain. He had unwittingly given them all the information they needed to create a plan—the Rainier Station, the physical layout of the airfield and its security, information about alien technology. Even the leadership of New Washington and how it functioned was provided to his masters. He had been supplanted by more loyal spies. Spies posing as pilots and ambitious young men and women who wanted to help in the defense of earth. After twenty years as part of New Washington, they were right to guess that Brodie had been compromised and that reliance on him was too risky.

Brodie climbed down from the tree. There was nothing else he could do to stop an attack. He had been a fool and a lackey for too long. He should have known that the leadership in Capital could change over time, that providing stolen technology and information might provide an incentive for something other than a than a peaceful approach to bringing New Washington into the fold. Brodie thought his worst sin among many, might be naïve idealism. That and, of course, his own arrogance.

The walk had cleared his head. He gave a brief thought to strolling into the wilderness in a self-imposed exile, washing his hands of both versions of Washington, the east and the west. If not for Chrystel, that option might be possible. He knew exactly what he had to do. He couldn't stop Capital now, and he couldn't save his father or his family. If Harvetta hadn't been able to get out, she might be doomed as well. The only people he could help were those people who had become his family. Related not by blood, but by caring.

That's how Brodie ended up on Geronimo's doorstep. He couldn't tell Chrystel. He couldn't fathom seeing the hurt that he had caused by his deception, and it was unlikely she would ever forgive him. Mike, on the other hand, was as pragmatic as anyone in the enclave. He might hate Brodie, even want to kill him, but he would listen and chose the best possible action. Brodie no longer cared what happened to him after he told his story, not anymore.

No one was home at Mike's home. No one was home at Amelia's house either, which was a frightening prospect. Geronimo's place was his third try. When Geronimo saw Brodie on the doorstop, he waved him in and said, "Brodie, Chrystel's been looking for you. Everyone's in the kitchen."

Grim faces greeted Brodie's arrival. "Grab a seat," Geronimo offered. Karen had a phone in her ear, and Mike was listening to her conversation. Trent and Amelia sat quietly drinking tea, Tent's arm lying protectively over the back of her chair.

"Brodie," Amelia exclaimed, "I thought you would be at the airfield."

"No, I was there earlier. A far better question is why are you here?"

"Long story," she answered with an innocent smile.

"She walked by herself," Trent announced proudly.

Brodie's eyebrows shot up. "I'm impressed! Uh, Mike, I need to talk to you."

"Can it wait, Brodie? Karen is getting information on the status of a possible incursion on Boeing Field, and we need to decide what we can do to assist."

All color drained from Brodie's face. He was probably too late. He was too late to warn them.

They might know more than him already, but he had once piece of information that could make a difference over the long run. "No, Mike. Now, if you can."

Mike picked up his beer and asked, "Do you want one, Brodie?"

"No thanks. This isn't a beer holding conversation."

Mike's eyes narrowed, and he gestured to the door. The two men leaned on the back-porch railings as Brodie took a deep breath. "Best I just get started. I only ask that you listen to my whole story and try not to throttle me until I finish."

Mike, aware now Brodie had done something very wrong, willed his face to be impassive and ready to listen. "Twenty years ago, I was sent to New Washington as a spy. I was sent by the Capital Enclave to keep tabs on your progress, steal technology when possible, and provide pertinent information about Jed's activities. My father was a CIA operative back in the day. Since I was gifted, the Capital leadership felt my father could train me for a mission as a deep plant, like the Russians did with operatives in the United States during the cold war.

"I was led to believe the mission was to ensure that Capital technology kept pace with New Washington so that at some unnamed advantageous point in the future, they might approach you to form a partnership. In hindsight, what they really wanted was a consolidated North America, with Capital in charge. I won't ask you to forgive what I did, but I was young, full of myself, and impressionable. I loved my father and believed

454

what we were doing was for a good cause. My father did as well.

"As could have been expected, the leadership in Capital changed over the years. During the last election, a reprehensible man led a divisive campaign and convinced enough voters that New Washington was a threat to the stability of the Capital Enclave and its allies. Since his election, he has solidified his power base through intimidation and force. He jails anyone who questions the wisdom of his policies, including my father.

"During my latest covert meeting with another agent and family friend, she informed me of Capital's concerns about New Washington's collaboration with aliens. They believe Capital is the rightful recipient of any alien alliance and began making plans to destroy New Washington to curry favor for themselves with the Ardinians. They thought the longer they waited, the more difficult the prospect of a successful attack would become."

Brodie took another deep breath. "I know. The premise is as absurd as the one the North Dakotans used as justification for their failed takeover attempt."

Mike's face changed several times as Brodie talked. Shock, anger, disgust, and even sadness passed in subtle waves as he processed what Brodie was saying. "So, why tell us now, Brodie? Why in the name of God did you wait so long to tell someone? What kind of man sits on his hands until it's too late to do anything?"

Brodie glared at Mike. He knew Mike was right. Only the worst kind of man, deceives the people he loves and then tries to claw his way out the mess he created by deceiving himself. "Does it matter? I'm a worthless piece of shit—does that help, Mike?"

The two men glared at each other. "What do you want from me Brodie?" Mike asked.

"Nothing. I expect nothing from you, nor do I deserve anything. Please, just hear me out, there's more. Before I left Capital, I became aware of a weapons program that started soon after the Great Dying. While your enclave invested precious people power in a communications satellite, a defensive missile system, and Geronimo's historical archive, Capital had grander plans. They set their sights on an offensive weapons capability.

"Among the weapons systems they gathered and restored is a stealth bomber, F/A 18 Hornets, and a ballistic nuclear missile silo. I don't know whether the silo is functional now, but I do know where it's located. I also know the locations of important facilities, such as the airbase they use, leaders' offices, and a pretty good guess on where they would keep the nuclear launch interface. Whatever happens, someone must disable the missile silo. I can't tell you what to do, but even if you succeed in repelling an eminent attack, they'll be back. They may even use a nuke!"

Mike stared at Brodie. "I need everything you know written down. Also, maps."

"Already done." Brodie pulled folded sheets of paper from the inside of his shirt and handed them to Mike. The shame in Brodie's face caused Mike to wince. Mike opened the folded papers and scanned the sheets as he leafed through the pages.

"You have to send them a sign, Mike. It's the only option to make sure Capital gets the message that any effort to take New Washington will result in their destruction. I don't think there's any wiggle room or compromise here."

"You're probably right. Wait, how are they getting these restored Hornets here? I thought they were parked on ships, destroyers."

"They have one of those too. It's probably sitting somewhere now off the coast in the Pacific Ocean. They replaced the engines with one of Jed's thorium generators. Last I knew, it's a leaky hulk, but good enough to remain afloat and move. Many of the onboard systems don't work. All they really needed was a seaworthy ship to carry aircraft and provide a launching platform."

"How did they do all this? The equipment you mentioned is a hundred years old and more."

"The same way you launched a satellite into space. People are crafty and resilient. It all depends on your priorities. Also, Capital started out with more people. When the Great Dying occurred, many survivors headed to the nation's capital for answers. The local population was always deeply involved in government and defense anyway; ergo, the founders were more likely to have knowledge of the military and unfortunately, weapons."

"What have you told Capital about us? What do they know?"

"They know about the Mount Rainier Station. Obviously, they know you're training pilots to fly alien designed spaceships. Karen broadcast that bit of news to the world. I bought or stole most of the technology Jed's folks have produced over the last hundred years, like the new microwave vector phone technology, and gave it to Capital. The only thing I couldn't obtain was the thorium generator specs. Jed either keeps the drawings in his head or has the design well hidden. He even compartmentalizes production of the generator, so no one person has enough information to replicate the generator.

"As to recent events, a few months ago, I quit funneling information to my old enclave. That's probably why Capital got suspicious and cut me out entirely. I don't even know the names of anyone who may have infiltrated with pilot walk-ons. I tried unsuccessfully to contact spies at the airfield and was told by my handlers I would get that information when I needed it."

Brodie rubbed his eyes. "I thought I could act as a double agent, make it work out so that Capital stood down, but I was kidding myself. In the end, I'm a shitty spy too."

"Ok, I've heard enough. I need to coordinate a battle plan with the Ardinians, Margo, Chrystel, and Thomas. The nuclear weapons silo must be our priority. We should have known someone would get the bright idea to find those nukes and use them. I just wish our chain of command wasn't so loosey goosey. It needs to be sorted out. Another task I can't fix today. You wait out here."

"What are you going to do with me Mike?"

"Have you arrested. I'll get Thomas to send someone over to take you to jail. You'll be tried, just like everyone else that has broken the law." Mike paused and glared at Brodie. "You know this will break Chrystel's heart, right?"

Brodie looked down at the ground and then back at Mike. "Please, just tell Chrystel no matter what she thinks, what we had was real." His voiced cracked as he continued. "Tell her she shouldn't use my deceit as an excuse never to trust anyone again. It was all on me, not her. She deserves far better."

"Damn it, Brodie." Mike heaved a sigh. "Why do people do such stupid things?" he mumbled to himself as he walked back into the house, slamming the door.

Just leave, he thought to himself. He was halfway to the road and stopped. *Why has Mike given me a chance to bolt? To run? A test? Or more likely, to have one less problem to deal with later.* Brodie returned to the back porch. He stayed and waited for someone to take him to jail. The only reason he could fathom for staying was that he didn't want to leave.

# 48. Chaos

Margo was at the northeast corner of the airfield checking a guard post when the first explosion rocked her world. Flames and debris swirled above a crater where her operations center hanger, merely seconds before, had been the hub of activity for an expanding space defense force.

She was frozen. One moment she was explaining to a guard where the terrain might hide an approaching enemy, and the next, her ears were ringing from the concussive power of an explosion so large, she could never have imagined such destruction. Margo's heart raced as adrenaline surged, and her brain struggled to make sense of a new reality. Her head turned as two more powerful blasts lit the night sky in the direction of the pilot barracks. "What's happening?" she whispered to herself before finally regaining some semblance of coherent thought.

She barked orders to the shocked and frightened guards, "Stay under cover. Once they finish this initial bombing run, expect more localized action and perhaps ground forces. You're as safe as you can be right here. Hunker down until this bombing stops and be ready when there's a pause."

These bombs were bigger than artillery, significantly bigger. Margo knew about artillery and the damage it could cause. With heightened senses, she listened intently for the sound of aircraft between horrific explosions. She scoured the sky for visual cues as to the nature of the threat, but there was nothing except the damnable force of carnage.

Her first instinct was to run back to the operations center and help anyone who was injured, to dig through the rubble and find her people. At the same time, she knew the instinct to protect could be fatal. Until this initial madness was over, it would be suicide to attempt a run to a strategic target. Instead, she huddled with the guards, feeling an overwhelming powerlessness as she watched all that she had helped build go up in flames.

The bombing run only lasted for three minutes, even though it seemed a lifetime. Margo waited an additional minute after a deafening silence and shouted at the guards, "Eyes open and be alert. Watch for low flying aircraft and use your laser to take them down. Fire at will if you see any ground forces in your area of responsibility." Margo hadn't meant to yell. She felt like she was underwater. The blast concussions had done something weird to her ears. Jumping into her tiny, airfield golf car, she pressed the accelerator to the floor, hightailing it back to the operations center.

Pandemonium. Anyone who hadn't been unlucky enough to be in one of the bomb targets was streaming onto the airfield. They needed to stay in their positions to defend against the next attack phase, which would shortly be upon them. Margo switched on her microphone. "Attention, Attention! Move back to your designated positions and prepare to defend against a ground and air assault! Those individuals who've been designated as medical support, should split into three-person teams and evacuate the injured to the old ammunition bunker area. I say again, more people will die if you don't get your asses back into position!"

Her screeching reverberated through an airfield intercom system and appeared to have had the desired effect. Margo saw confused people take note of someone, anyone giving them a direction. The panicked scurrying of fearful individuals was replaced by a more purposeful energy.

On the far side of the maintenance facility, Margo saw the recognizable blur of Mermots scrambling from an underground access tunnel to the surface. It was as if they had practiced for years on a choreographed marching band performance, except they performed their movements at exponentially greater speed. Columns of Mermots flowed with precision along the perimeter, positioning themselves at regular intervals. Most carried weapons strung around their necks and carried on the slick fur of their back.

A train of Mermots buzzed by Margo's cart as she drove toward the guard post area she had just left. In an amazing feat of timing and speed, Tweet appeared in the passenger seat of her moving cart. Margo blinked twice to ensure she wasn't suffering from a hallucination. "It's me, Miss Margo, Tweet. I regret that I surprised you, but I am pressed for time."

"We all are, Tweet."

"I wanted to inform you that based on my study of human warfare, a main attack will follow shortly. As such, I have deployed all available Mermot assets, except for mothers about to give birth or nursing just born litters. We will do our utmost to repel an attack, but I must advise you, we are not optimistic if weapons such as those recently used against us are utilized in the next phase."

"Do your best, Tweet, and thank you. Do you know if Chrystel and Jed are okay?"

"The last I knew of Chrystel, she was with Mermots sorting through the crate of anti-aircraft shoulder weapons. That building has not been destroyed. I have no knowledge of Jed's fate."

Margo stepped on the brakes and listened. "Aircraft!" she screamed.

"I must go. May the earth keep you in her embrace, whether in this physical world or the next existence."

Sadness washed over Margo as she gazed at the empty seat where Tweet had been sitting. She pushed her cart as fast as it would go to find cover for the next onslaught.

# 49. Forewarned

The new ammunition storage building at the airfield was one of the last buildings standing. The reinforced structure's survival was dumb luck. A dud bomb from the first attack landed on the roof, penetrated the ceiling, and dropped to the floor inside. It lay nose side buried in the floor, completely missing the ammunition stored within the building. The busy Mermots were, likewise, unscathed.

Mermots scampered over Stinger Antiaircraft Weapons. Carefully unpacked from a storage crate, stingers lay in segregated rows on the concrete floor. Chrystel watched them work, amazed as always with the tenacity of these peaceful beings. Even while the first bombardment commenced, the sides of the storage building shaking with each impact, the Mermots continued their task in an orderly manner, checking each weapon for operability. So far, there were only a handful that were determined to be "probably useable".

Tired of feeling helpless, Chrystel debated where she could have the most impact. She had stepped outside immediately after the initial bombing raid looking to help gather the wounded. Relief washed over her as Margo's strident voice boomed over the airfield speaker system telling everyone to get back into position. At least, Margo was still safe and capable of organizing the defense.

Teams were digging through the rubble in the vain hope anyone was alive. Chrystel stopped to speak to the first medic she saw, identified by a band with a red cross worn on his sleeve. "Excuse me, what can I do to help?" she asked.

He rubbed his hand over a crew cut, an uncommon hairstyle in the new world, and at first seemed irritated for even a minor interruption to continuing his mission. Then recognition dawned. "You're that mayor, aren't you?"

"I am. Please call me Chrystel. What can I do to help?"

His harried face turned toward the devastation and smoking crater to his front, then back to Chrystel. "Sorry, ma'am, but there isn't much anyone can do. People or Mermots inside the blast range of facilities that were hit, well, the best description is they were incinerated. Luckily, there weren't a bunch of folks out and about to catch flying debris. The major injury we're seeing is ear problems from the noise and concussions."

Chrystel swallowed. *Those poor lost souls.* "I understand. I'll be over in that building over there," Chrystel pointed, "if you can think of anywhere I can lend a hand."

"Yes ma'am, I mean, Chrystel. Will do. I'd better keep at it."

"You're doing great work. Thank you."

Chrystel turned to leave, chilled and shaking with anger at whoever was responsible for this carnage. Her phone began to chirp. "Chrystel here."

"Thank God, you're safe." Jed's voice trembled. "I wanted you to know I'm okay. The initial attack missed our primary facility. I can see a gigantic hole a hundred meters to the south from my window that was meant for us. Other than broken windows and some shell-shocked scientists, we got lucky. I'm leaving on an airship to fly to Wyoming to help disarm a nuclear missile or two as soon as wasp escorts arrive. The Ardinians have even deemed it necessary to assist with disassembling the nuclear missiles and are sending their shuttle to meet me at the site."

"A what!? Slow down Jed."

"You heard me right, nuclear weapons. Also, your grandfather called worried sick about you and to share some distressing news. Apparently, this is an attack by the Capital Enclave. They have a ship floating off the coast in the Pacific. There's an expectation of FA 18, Hornets in the next wave. They're splitting off a team of wasps to attack the Capital Enclave in retaliation and to send a strong message this aggression will not be tolerated."

"But, but, how did my granddad know? A nuclear weapon? And when are the wasps going to be here?"

Jed hesitated. He wasn't about to share Brodie's involvement in spying with Chrystel--not now. "Uh, uh, I'm not really sure how Mike obtained the info. I let Margo know about the hornets. Chrystel, whatever you can do to shore up our ability to stop the hornets, that's the most important mission to undertake at this moment. The wasps headed for our airfield will be there anytime."

"Roger, Jed." Out of the corner of her eyes, Chrystel thought she saw someone in a green watch cap running around a corner of a grounds maintenance shed. The hatted man was so far away she wasn't sure.

"You still there, Chrystel?"

"I am. Just thought I saw someone. What about our enclave? Who's protecting them?"

"Thomas is doing his best and will remain for the duration to protect the home front. Pretty much everyone has a weapon and is ready for an attack. Capital chose not to target our town in the initial bombardment. Who knows, maybe they don't want to kill civilians willy-nilly."

"Thanks, Jed. Seems like there's plenty of willy-nilly civilian killing here, but great news they haven't hit the enclave proper. By the way, have you heard anything from Brodie? I've been trying to call him but there's no answer. I'm worried."

"I believe your dad said Brodie was with him earlier," Jed stated, glad he didn't have to lie. Brodie was with Mike before they carted him off to jail.

"That's a relief. Tell everyone I'm good. Gotta go. Be safe and make sure you do what's necessary to disable those nukes."

"Be safe yourself," Jed answered and hung up.

Chrystel was debating whether to go hunt for her possible nemesis when Tilley whined. The next second, she heard the thunder of something powerful in the sky. Chrystel had never heard a jet powered engine before. The first air attack had not been presaged with any noise, and their own airships, using thorium power generators, ran mostly quiet. The small part of Chrystel's brain, the one involved with instinct, recognized the sound and her decision was made. She sprinted to the ammunition building with Tilley in tow. "Tilley, get my attention if you see a man in green and black striped hat. That's your only job."

Chrystel was already yelling as she pounded through the open doors. "Grab a working Stinger and get to good firing positions, NOW!" Chrystel barely slowed as she grabbed a weapon from the good pile with a sprinting stop and launched her herself in the direction of the battle upon them. The Mermots sprang into action, passing Chrystel in a blur as she headed outside to do her best.

A man in a hat watched the redhead dash into the ammunition building. Finally, someone he knew for sure was in charge. The stunning redhead was easy to identify and hard to miss. Since the first bombardment, he had scurried around the airfield in search of any New Washington officials. That was his job—to identify important people and eliminate them. The message he received from Capital yesterday was very clear--*be prepared to seek out all New Washington leaders and kill them. The more leaders missing after the stealth bombing and following hornet attack, the easier it will be for Capital ground forces to assume control of the airfield.*

He would have been set up earlier except for the initial bombing. How in the heck was he supposed to do his job when hell on earth rained down around him? He had done like everyone else, huddled as low as possible and prayed it would end soon. Now, he didn't have much time. When the redheaded mayor ran into the ammunition building, there wasn't an opportunity to get a good shot. She was running with a purpose. That meant, she would probably be coming out soon, and if his luck held, she wouldn't be paying attention to her immediate surroundings.

The man eyed the ATV configured as a truck sitting unharmed only 50 yards in front of ammunition storage area doors. *Perfect!* Excited from the hunt, he took a pot shot at a passing Mermot rat but missed when it ducked out of sight in the nick of time. Fast little bastards. The red-head mayor wasn't nearly so quick. He would take his time with her; she wouldn't live to see tomorrow.

Flashing trails of orange yellow light, surrounded by a purplish haze, blinked in an out, indicating the lasers were being fired at approaching jets. Lasers travelled at the speed of light and would be invisible if not for the deadly beam's reflection when it passed through clouds and condensation. The first hornet in the enemy formation flew from the north along the eastern edge of the airfield, strafing the Mermots standing guard against an enemy ground force. The Mermots, carrying conventional weapons and not lasers, tried valiantly to shoot down the marauding aircraft with little success. They were cut down like ants, as if sprayed from above by a noxious insecticide. The flares of their weapons glowed along the perimeter and winked out as the hornet passed.

Chrystel ran between the supply center loading ramp and double stacked metal cubes used for additional storage. The spot gave her good cover, but not enough visibility. She examined the sky, trying to picture in her mind where the hornets would attack next. On the northern horizon, a bright blast signaled at least one of the hornets was hit. "Tilley, I think I know where we need to go. Follow me."

Another hornet fell from the heavens, but a second craft slipped through the laser defense, passing the airfield border unharmed. As she was running, Chrystel glanced back and up in the sky and realized the low flying hornet was heading in the direction of Jed's science center. Desperate to stop this jet from doing harm, she hesitated in place with a clear line of sight to the approaching aircraft and dropped to one knee. Pulling the M4 off her left shoulder to more aptly aim the Stinger, she placed the weapon on the ground beside her.

Chrystel felt Tilley's nose nudge her back. "Not now, Tilley," she scolded as she settled the stinger on her right shoulder, flipping the view finder up. Harder now, Tilley kicked her back with a sharp hoof like paw. *"The man in the green and black hat!"* Chrystel's mind screamed as she threw herself to the ground and rolled over her M4, grabbing it as she turned. A bullet splatted the pavement where she had just seconds before been kneeling.

Tilley screamed her immobilizing scream. The man in the hat took no notice. He came prepared with hearing protection. He assumed bomb blasts would be extremely loud and had stolen headphones from the pilots' barracks. Drawing a bead on Chrystel, he stepped forward from his position behind a truck to be certain the next shot wouldn't miss.

Tilley charged. She leapt at least twenty feet into the air. The hatted man fired, and Tilley jerked, but the force of momentum carried her the final distance. Tilley's legs hit first, striking the Seahawks emblem in the center of his chest. He

spiraled backwards as the remainder of her body
plowed into him and forced him to his back like a
felled tree. Stunned for a moment and grimacing
with pain, the hatted man tried to regain his wind.
Then he began to grunt as he wriggled and pushed,
trying to free himself from Tilley's over 200-pound
girth.

Chrystel was disoriented from Tilley's scream.
If not for the fact that the pounding noise all around
had dampened the intensity of Tilley's immobilizing
shriek, Chrystel would have been out cold for two
or three minutes. She willed herself to stand. Her
legs felt weak and wobbly, like they were made of
pliable rubber and had been wrapped in heavy
weights. Heaving and clenching her teeth, she
pushed with all her might to move. She could see
Tilley's body like deadweight on the man. Rage that
someone would hurt the henka sent blood pulsating
to Chrystel's limbs.

Slowly, Chrystel rose, breathing in large gasps
of air as the man gained leverage and twisted.
Tilley's still body slid to the side enough that the
hatted man could free himself.

Chrystel crawled on hands and knees, her
arms and legs trembling as she struggled to defend
herself. The M4 sling, still hanging from her
shoulder, meant her weapon was near but dragging
the ground as she crept forward. She stopped,
lifted her hands, and while kneeling with spastic
hands, strained to grasp the M4.

The green and black striped hat was half off
the man's head from wrestling with the henka's
weight. He was drawing his weapon as a kneeling
Chrystel tried in vain to position her M4 for a shot.

Tilley's purple blood had soaked the man's sports jersey. *It hurts,* Tilley cried to herself. She knew the man was going to harm her charge and companion if she didn't do something, but it was so hard to breathe. Tilley tensed her back leg. With all the life she had left, she kicked the standing man's ankle.

He tottered and nearly fell from the impact of Tilley's thrust at his leg. His shot when wide. A bullet hole appeared in his forehead before he had a chance to fire again. The man and his hat dropped face forward on the tarmac.

"Tilley! No, Tilley!" Chrystel stumbled to her protector's side.

# 50. Revenge

After receiving a message from several earth sources, every piloted wasp burped out of launch tunnels from the Delamie. Manny and Dee were burning through the atmosphere, willing their ship to go faster. Dee had pleaded with Tammy to ignore safety concerns and take them in quicker, to which she had locked them out of the controls and said in that infuriating calm, sexual voice, "I can't allow your demise or my own by ignoring the science of reentry. Rest assured that our flight path is the most expeditious possible without getting us all killed."

"We really need to reprogram your attitude, Tammy," Manny fumed.

"On the contrary, Manny. I believe it is your emotional state that has resulted in fragmented judgement. If it is possible to recalibrate human judgement, that would be my recommendation. Nevertheless, you have a message from the Delamie. I will open a channel."

Manny heard Oneleg, his call sign. "This is Delamie control. Please be aware there is a high-altitude aircraft, called a stealth bomber, which must be engaged and destroyed before proceeding to the airfield. Tammy is already scanning for this aircraft to provide a targeting solution. Also, please be advised only your team will provide support to the Boeing Field. The other teams have been given new missions."

"What missions?" Manny asked.

"A ship in the Pacific, important infrastructure on the East Coast in what was the capital of the United States, and a nuclear weapons silo."

"You've got to be kidding me!" Manny shouted.

Tammy interrupted. "Manny, I have located the stealth aircraft and have a targeting solution. Not very stealthy if you ask me, and it has no shields, so one missile will be sufficient."

"Fire at will, Tammy." Dee responded.

Manny yelled, "Take that!" when he saw the missile fire from the wasp's lower aft tube, burning through the clouds. It was the first time they had used any of their weapon's capability in earth's atmosphere.

"Reentry is complete, Manny. As soon as I verify that the not-so-stealthy aircraft is destroyed, you may fly like the wind, all guns blazing, to destroy the so-called aviation assets now bombarding your world."

Manny didn't know whether to laugh or cry. "Target neutralized. They went down like a rock," Tammy cooed.

Manny pushed a button to set maximum speed. "Heading to objective. Delamie, are you still there?"

"Yes, Manny. To be more precise, the other mission is defensive support to a human airship and the Ardinian shuttle. They will be traveling to disarm a nuclear missile silo in Montana."

"Oh shit," Dee breathed.

"Yes, it was an unexpected development. Please notify Delamie control when you have neutralized the remaining threat at your home airfield."

"Roger, out," Manny answered.

"Tammy, please provide situational information on our next objective."

"Yes, Manny. It should be like shooting ducks in a pond. The enclave ground forces have disabled or destroyed six of the ten F/A 18 aircraft, known as Hornets. Interesting, isn't it, that we're named wasps and they're named hornets. There is a great deal of confusion regarding the difference between a wasp and a hornet as it is often believed they are different names for the same thing."

"Tammy! Focus, please."

"We have the time for my insect discussion, Manny, but as you wish. The hornets have an array of weaponry, but they have no chance to penetrate our shields. I am already tracking the four remaining hornets and will have a targeting solution in fifty-seven seconds. I recommend using lasers this time to avoid small bits of these ships raining down on the airfield. One big crash is better, I think."

"Tammy, just so you know, since you insist on inserting as many idioms as possible into your language, it's fish in a barrel, not ducks in a pond," Dee growled. "Also, when we get back, we need to discuss appropriate tone when people are being slaughtered."

"I am sorry," Tammy sighed. "Given the gravity of the situation, I thought keeping it light would do the trick. Firing solution locked."

Dee's frustration with Tammy took second seat to her greater worry about the fate of the airfield. She still couldn't see with her own eyes what kind of destruction awaited them or the hornets they were about to destroy. The range and accuracy of the wasp was beyond anything mankind had so far created. If humans hadn't died to near extinction a hundred years in the past, perhaps they would have produced a spaceship as capable as the wasp. But then again, a wasp-like ship would have only provided humanity a greater means to kill each other.

"Fire," Manny ordered.

"All targets destroyed," Tammy replied only ten seconds later.

Dee gasped as the wasp zipped below cloud cover and hovered over the airfield searching for a good place to land. The destruction was nearly impossible to grasp. Smoking, pitted craters pockmarked the land below. Where hangers filled with training equipment had once stood, nothing but swirling debris remained. Even the pilots' barracks were decimated. Bodies strewn along the edges of the airfield were a testament to brave defenders who had ultimately given their lives to protect humanity from the Huntas. Just seconds before, Manny, Dee, and Tammy had removed the last threat, the remaining hornets, hopeful their actions had made a difference. Even Tammy was speechless.

Tears welled in Dee's eyes. "We're too late," she moaned.

"I am so sorry for your loss," Tammy replied in a sad voice. "I know you need time to grieve, but there is one last action you and your squad of wasps must undertake. My sensors indicate a ground force approaching in two columns from the north and the west. If we act quickly, we can neutralize the threat before they arrive to complete their loathsome mission."

Manny was angry, as angry as he had ever been in his life. "This is senseless. Totally fucking senseless!" he heaved.

"Their strategy must have been to launch an attack while the wasps were off-earth, believing when you returned, a defeated New Washington would have no choice but to align with the conquering invaders. We can thwart that strategy, Manny, and vanquish the aggressors, but there's little time. You must act quickly," Tammy prodded.

"Right. Open a channel." Manny spoke to the three other wasps in his squad, currently hovering in formation around Manny's ship. "Tigger, Pooh, and Blackfish, this is Oneleg. There's a ground force ten minutes out from the airfield. We're going to smash them to smithereens. Tammy is sending location data. Tigger, you're with me heading to the northern sector. Pooh and Blackfish, you hit the eastern flank. Leave no one alive. Lead ship lights them up along the column and trail bird follows at a two-minute interval with a reinforcing pass to catch any stragglers. Are we clear?"

"Crystal clear," Pooh shouted back.

"Let's get them!!" another angry pilot named Blackfish signaled.

Tigger was the last to respond, "I'm with you, Oneleg."

"Tammy, please proceed."

The wasps accelerated so fast, airfield stragglers were left head scratching over the quick departure of their saviors. Manny saw the lead enemy vehicle in his viewfinder. They appeared as an assortment of ATVs, both large and small, with automatic weapons affixed to their hardened tops. Infantry were spread, walking alongside the vehicle convoy, but close enough the heat of explosive lasers would take them easily.

"Slow down for our pass, Tammy."

"Roger, Manny," she responded. "We are within range."

"Fire," Dee ordered.

Bolts of lightning struck the first ATV and lifted it off the ground in a fiery ball. As Manny's wasp traveled the length of the column, nothing remained except burning hulks and the struggle of soldiers on fire, scrambling to douse flames. Dee thought the first pass was sufficient, but in the thrall of his outrage, Manny didn't call off Tigger's sequential pass.

* * *

Without direction, Tammy set course back to the airfield after they had completed the firing traverse of the length of the enemy column. She sensed something different in her pilots. The emotion in Manny's and Dee's physical being was more than a state of the mind. It manifested itself as real pain. She wanted to anesthetize them from this horrible burden, but after calculating the odds, she determined Manny and Dee would be unappreciative of her involvement. She landed the craft on the airfield unassisted as her humans remained silent.

The physiological status program she had written on her first test flight with these pilots revealed a complex chemical reaction to stress. Tammy had been unable to determine conclusively whether human stress reactions were helpful or counterproductive to the mission, but now, their response to loss was an even greater analytical challenge. Did human beings require this intense pain resulting from loss to achieve some end? What the goal might be remained elusive.

Chrystel ran to meet the wasp arrival. Purple spatters, the color of henka blood, covered her shirt. She was shouting and waving before Dee could finish climbing the three steps to the tarmac. "Tilley's been shot. She's in grave condition, and the medics here don't know what to do for her. They don't know anything about her alien physiology. Can you take her back to the Delamie for treatment? Please," she begged.

Dee shot a look at Manny. "Actually, the Delamie is in close orbit now to render assistance. A medical shuttle is on the way to assist with injuries. If you can gather the most grievously wounded, the Delamie will provide medical support."

"Do you know how long?" Chrystel beseeched.

Dee yelled back to the wasp. "Tammy, how far out is the medical shuttle?"

"Two minutes and thirty-two seconds," a voice without form responded.

"Oh, thank God. Have the shuttle land near the old ammo storage bunker. Don't worry, there's no ammunition there anymore. We've set up an aid station nearby. I know you guys are most likely exhausted, but all able-bodied individuals are tasked to help the injured. Got anything left in you to help?" Chrystel asked.

His eyes half closed, Manny wobbled on his feet, trying to hold in the emotion threatening to overtake him. "I'd like that. I need something productive to do."

"Me too," Dee added, tears forming again. "Just tell me where to go."

Chrystel stood next to Dee and placed an arm around her shoulder. "I know you got here as soon as you could. If you hadn't taken out the last hornets, Jed's research facility could have been lost and far more people too. I heard you destroyed their ground force. We had no means left to defend ourselves after the stealth bombing and hornet attack. You did good. Don't blame yourselves."

Dee turned into Chrystel and began to weep. Chrystel held her and let her cry, not allowing herself the same release. She nudged Dee gently and released one arm to point to the southern end of the field. "You can start over there. We have other teams on the northern side already. Introduce yourself to the medic responsible for the south side and ask for direction. Wait, what's that?"

A clutch of Mermots was making their way slowly over the pocked concrete from the barracks area. They were singing a song that traveled the distance into every mind. It was so mournful, so final, the only thing that came to mind was the playing of taps at funerals.

Chrystel and the pilots stood transfixed as the Mermots continued their journey across the airfield toward their access tunnels. A crowd began to gather around the pilots to watch the somber procession. Mermot voices from around the airfield joined in the singing, the music flowing in a swirling breeze, coalescing the spirit of listeners in a communal embrace. The song reached a crescendo and then diminished into a sad humming refrain before a deafening silence. In the center of the circle of Mermots, two Mermots carried one of their own over their heads. A half missing tail was hanging from the dead being, still wet with blood.

"No, please no," Chrystel whispered. They kept coming and paused close enough that Chrystel could see it was Tweet. The little warrior outfit she had worn at the onset of the attack was shredded and dirty. Tweet's sweet face was unharmed and looked to be only sleeping peacefully.

Chrystel began to shake, and then large drops of tears ran free. A Mermot representative scurried to a grief stricken Chrystel. "Mayor, the Mermots request a formal burial for our leader. We ask that you be present to honor our courageous song teller. Will you say a few words for her?"

Barely able to breathe or see through the tears, Chrystel gathered herself enough to respond. "Now?"

"No, Mayor. As soon as you are able. We will prepare her body to return to the earth, her new home that she loved with all her heart. Our way is to bury our dead at sunset. She would have very much have liked for your people to be with her as she travels to the next plane."

"I will be there. My Uncle Geronimo was a dear friend too. I'll make sure he comes."

"Anyone who wishes to say farewell is welcome." the Mermot responded and then ran to

481

catch up with the Mermot circle respectfully carrying Tweet to their burrow.

Chrystel swallowed and squeezed her fists. "*Not now, Chrystel. You need to hold it together just a little while longer,*" she reminded herself. She saw the Ardinian shuttle craft flying overhead in the direction of the aid station. "I've got to go," she said to Manny and Dee. "I need to be there for Tilley. I need to make sure she gets onto the shuttle to the Delamie."

Brodie lay face up staring at the dark ceiling of his jail cell. When Mike had left him outside Geronimo's house, it was a photo finish on whether he would stay and face his accusers or make a hasty departure. During the half hour wait, before Thomas came to retrieve him to take him to jail, Brodie had turned to leave more than once. Leaving was the smart move. Nothing could be gained by allowing himself to bear the burden of the enclave's rage at Capital's unwarranted aggression.

As he shifted from foot to foot and then paced Geronimo's groomed yard waiting for Thomas, Brodie didn't know whether Capital or New Washington would prevail. He pictured himself a resistance leader, staying by Chrystel's side to thwart ruthless Capital, earning back her respect by fearless loyalty. He had to laugh at himself for childish dreams. Either way, New Washington or Capital, trust wasn't something he'd earned from his current enclave or his old, and it was better to just go.

Brodie could make his way into the center of the continent, even south to a warmer climate and reestablish himself with a new group of folks, live a normal life. People in the new world made that choice all the time.

So why did he stay? He'd asked himself that question over and over as rumors leached into his cell of demonstrations calling for his execution. There were too many dead, too much destruction for banishment to be a suitable punishment. It didn't matter that he had been a pawn in a larger game, or that he had too late tried to stop the carnage. Brodie couldn't blame anyone for wanting him dead.

It wasn't until Mike visited, his only visitor during a six-week incarceration, that it became clear why he hadn't taken the opportunity Mike provided. Why he hadn't bolted when Mike left him unguarded outside for a full thirty minutes. Brodie didn't want to leave these people. He didn't want to go somewhere else and wonder for the remainder of his long life what had happened to them, regretting for an eternity his part in their pain. If he left, traitor would be his epitaph, his name synonymous with deceit. His name, Brodie Morgen, might even supplant Benedict Arnold as the preferred moniker to describe a betrayer. If he stayed, he would still be a traitor, but at least he might be an honorable one. At a trial, he would have an opportunity to explain and apologize for a young man's zeal. Brodie, the turncoat who stood to face the consequences.

It was the time of night when he couldn't sleep, ruminating over past mistakes as the riff of "what ifs" began circling the drain. It was then that he thought of Chrystel, not what she would think of him now, but a shared moment to relive and savor. He ran through a remembered scene from beginning to end, replaying the best parts more than once. He might have finally drifted into sleep, but the sound of scratching penetrated a foggy dream. Feeling a sense of stumbling, he bolted awake.

Brodie sat up and listened. Definitely scratching. Swinging his legs off the cot to the floor, fully alert, he waited. Brodie had the gift of extraordinary hearing, and he knew the sound might only be a noise from outside the jail. No concern to him. But the scratching was on glass. He pictured the only window open to the outside. It was on the back wall of the hallway just past the room where he was held.

Nothing good could come of someone breaking into his prison. Brodie was a notorious prisoner. So much so, the enclave had converted a small house to hold him. The guard stayed in the front living area, and a door segregated his cell from whatever the guards did to keep themselves busy. There was another door in the room that led to hallway. Brodie was housed in a locked bathroom that had been excised of all its porcelain features except the toilet. Both doors leading into his cell were reinforced.

Brodie's heart began to pound, certain some enraged claver or several, bent on revenge and maybe drunk, were here to take matters into their own hands. There was nothing in his prison cell he could use to defend himself. Even the toilet lid and seat had been removed to ensure they couldn't be weaponized.

The scratching stopped. Brodie stood, his back against the wall next to the hall door waiting to surprise anyone who entered. A feeble attempt to defend himself, but the only advantage that came to mind. He heard feet landing in the hallway, just barely. Whoever it was, they were quiet. Brodie waited for footsteps when a note slid under the door. Exhaling air held in his lungs, he recognized Chrystel's handwriting. *Stand back. Follow me when we cut the door, quietly, and climb out the hall window.*

Brodie watched a tool burn the reinforced door, creating an outline in the wood. He wondered what Chrystel was using to make the incision, for it left no burning odor. Maybe some weird alien laser. Working his fingers under the edge of the cut panel and pulling the wood sheet inside his jail cell, he crawled through. Chrystel wasn't in the hall, but her smell lingered. He tiptoed to the window, hefted himself through the frame, and jumped to the ground.

"Over here!" Chrystel whispered from the tree line behind the house. The night sky was cloudless. A waning gibbous moon was so bright, he could see his shadow stalking ahead. Not the best night for a jailbreak, Brodie thought to himself. He scrambled through wild, prickly blackberry bushes, and there she was. Trent was standing behind her.

Wanting to wrap his arms around her and hold her for as long as she would allow, Brodie rushed to Chrystel. As he was close and reaching his arms to enfold her lovely body, she held up her hand and said, "Don't!"

"What? Why did you break me out?" he stopped, seeing an expression on Chrystel's face that was different from any that he'd known before.

"You are to be made a martyr for the devastation reeked by your enclave, and I can't allow that."

"But Capital isn't my enclave. New Washington is my home. Capital is the place I was born."

Chrystel studied Brodie's face. "Perhaps. My grandfather told me everything you confessed to him. That's not why I'm here, Brodie, to talk about us. There is no us, not anymore."

Brodie straightened as if he'd been slapped. It wasn't that he hadn't expected this reaction, but knowing it could happen and actually feeling Chrystel's iciness cut to the core. "I'm confused, Chrystel. Then, what is the point?"

"The point of letting you go is to make New Washington what we dream it can become, an example for the new world. If vengeful voices win the day, you'll be hanged from gallows built especially for you in Founders Park. Our enclave will be just like any other, allowing our worst instincts to control us. We'll have become everything that we don't want to be. My grandfather had it right in so many ways when he gave the North Dakotans a chance at redemption. Don't worry, when clavers learn of your escape, there'll be a big, hub bub for a while, but then the people will forget."

"I don't want to go."

"What? Even knowing you'll probably be hanged?"

"Even then. I think hanging would be more honorable than running."

Not wanting to listen to this conversation, Trent folded into the vegetation. Chrystel couldn't believe what she was hearing. Her green eyes glowed in the moonlight as her mind raced. This conversation hadn't gone to according to plan. She wondered whether anything ever did. She couldn't reconcile how this man in front of her, the one that had betrayed her as surely as placing a knife in her back, could still hold her heart. Every part of her wanted to go back in time to give Brodie a second chance.

"Brodie, I can understand how you felt trapped. How you arrived here believing you had good reasons for spying, even though you didn't, and recognized your mistake far too late. I'm thankful you gave Mike information that may have saved us all at great risk to yourself. It was a noble act. What I can't forgive is that you didn't trust me. I thought you knew me. Believed in our future. If you had, you would have let me in on the great burden you carried and allowed me to help. Instead, you treated me as a child, assuming you knew what was best for me and kept your secrets. That isn't what I wanted or expected from you. Without trust, there's nothing—no us." Brodie looked away.

"If you have no other reason to leave, leave for me. I can't officiate as mayor while your dead body swings on a scaffolding. Please, don't make me live through that!"

Tears welled in Brodie's eyes as he nodded, his mouth a slash of grief.

"Trent has some supplies for you, everything you'll need and a recommended route to avoid capture. There's grid coordinates printed on the inside of the pack. It's a secret location in Idaho where we sent Mermots and one human representative to produce weapons for defeating the Huntas. You could be helpful there. I'm certain you can keep a secret. I told the human rep you might join them. If you choose to go somewhere else, that's fine, just don't come back here. Trent will stay with you until you pass the border of New Washington to ensure you make a clean getaway. He knows the area. Now go, please."

"Thomas wouldn't approve of what you're doing."

"No, probably not, but he'll never know about this," she smiled wistfully. "Mike asked me to tell you that after we sent a strong message to Capital, bombed the heck out of them, someone released all the political prisoners. Mike checked, your dad was among them."

Brodie reached out to touch Chrystel's cheek. "Thank you. And I'm so very sorry," he whispered. Unable to speak, Chrystel bit her lip and nodded. She watched him and Trent until they were out of sight. Brodie turned once and raised a hand in a sad goodbye.

\* \* \*

Karen opened her door to her granddaughter. Chrystel took two steps inside and fell to her knees. Karen dipped to the floor next to her grandbaby, smothering her in her arms. "I'm here," she cried as she held this precious, red-headed, strong-willed girl. They stayed on the floor, Chrystel seeking her grandmother as the safe place to rest as she wept until there were no tears left.

## 52. New Washington Historical Notes, Part VII

On May the 7, 2122, a refurbished, old world stealth bomber conducted a raid on the New Washington Enclave's facility for scientific research and the adjoining airfield, the hope for humanity's effort to defeat an alien species named the Hunta. The bomber run was followed by a hornet assault, another old-world technology that was brought back to life curtesy of the Washington Capital Enclave. The hornet attack aircraft were carried by ship around the tip of South America, north along the Pacific Coast to the Northwest Territories on the USS Abraham Lincoln.

Ground assaults from the north and the east were expected to be the final prong in Capital's battle strategy. Fortunately, in the nick of time, New Washington's own far superior spaceships, named wasps for their appearance, returned from outer space where they had been conducting competitions and training exercises.

I must pause for a moment to say it's still odd to speak of spaceships and aliens. This history recitation above sounds like some sort of science fiction, space opera. Not that long ago, such things weren't even in the realm of possibility. As a historian, I should never be surprised at how quickly fates can change, and yet, I am.

All told, even though New Washington won the day, their losses were extensive (as is often the case in war). Current accounting of personnel losses indicates 372 humans killed and 982 injured, including many pilot trainees. The Mermots lost 432 of their species and another 1,144 were injured.

The wasp training and operations facility was decimated along with flight simulators housed in an adjoining building. Pilots' barracks were destroyed. Many support facilities, manufacturing printers provided by Ardinians, and supply facilities, gone. Only the scientific research center survived totally intact.

We, earthlings and our partners, the Ardinians and Mermots, had as little as two years to prepare for the arrival of the evil Hunta. Nearly everything we built to survive this onslaught for all of humanity was laid waste by the Capital Enclave and their futile effort to replace New Washingtonians as the leading human contingent in our part of the world.

First the North Dakotans attacked New Washington under the guise they were starving, and their only option was forcibly to take a more prosperous piece of land. Then another incursion by the Capital Enclave, an arrogant lot, whose founders believed their once great history as the capital of the United States entitled them to a claim of supremacy. Will these senseless wars never stop? There are so few of us, and even now as we stand on the precipice of extinction, humans persist in fighting each other for power, control, and resources.

If not for Brodie Morgan, the Capital spy and my niece Chrystel's prior love interest, I may not be here to write this history. He provided information to my grandfather that Capital held an ICBM in reserve with New Washington's name on it. We destroyed the missile before it was launched. Somehow, Brodie escaped from the prison where he was held to be tried for high treason. Wild speculation abounds on possible culprits with the audacity to set him free. I know I have my own suspicions. Thomas conducted a thorough investigation and couldn't find a trace of evidence to identify a guilty party. I would say it's mostly for the best that someone sprang Brodie from captivity. The spectacle of a hanging, especially the hanging of a man that I knew and respected, is an unseemly prospect.

In meetings after our near destruction, the New Washington government decided enough was enough. Concerned that no one would want to send more pilot trainees to an enclave that was attacked every other week, a worldwide message was released. It stated any further disruptions would surely doom our chances (if they hadn't already) to defend against the Huntas. The message warned that any enclave choosing to attack New Washington would be destroyed, period. Of course, the message contained photos of wasps in action, the awesome power of lasers and so forth, but the communique was strikingly clear. Somehow, in only one hundred years, humanity has arrived back at the place where they started, in an agonizing game of mutually assured destruction.

Now, for the rest of the story. I attended the funeral for my amazing and gifted Mermot friend, Tweet. I cried like a baby. As much as I loved her, I was surprised by how many other people and Mermots had been touched by her heart and wisdom. The ceremony was held outside as the sun set. Nearly everyone in the enclave, humans and Mermots alike, were in attendance. Shakete, Maleta, and Rappel stood next to my parents and

Mayor Chrystel to show their respects. Our orchestra played music to accompany Mermot singing, and the result was a feat of nature, a mingling of species more magnificent than I have words to describe. Chrystel's tribute to Tweet was moving. Tweet was a very special individual, a once in a lifetime friend, and I will always miss her.

On a brighter note, as I take a moment to dab my wet eyes, my sister Amelia and Trent were married this week in a small ceremony attended by close friends and family. The wedding was also held in the out of doors. What an achievement for Amelia. When she arrived at my house after an arduous journey down a three-mile road, she was nearly comatose from stress. She left home alone (except for Lionheart) ignoring her agoraphobia to deliver news of a vision that could save Chrystel. Her bravery in the face of a panic disorder was no minor accomplishment. Even though she told me she still has an occasional panic attack, for the most part, Amelia is now able to live a normal life. Chrystel was Amelia's maid of honor. My mother Karen beamed when she saw them together in front of well-wishers during the marriage vows and whispered to me, "For all the shit, at least we have this."

Becky from the Rainier Station survived an attack on the mountain. At the last minute, she found a Kevlar vest in the supply closet and put it on before she made a dash out of the burning building. She suffered broken ribs, but she's on the mend. She will be awarded the enclave's first medal of bravery when she is well enough to attend a ceremony.

Mike has agreed to assume command of The Earth Guard Space Force that is at present, more a dream than a reality. Every time someone calls him Admiral, my dad laughs. He shared with me the reason he had agreed to Shakete's proposal. "I don't know anything about space or spaceships. Fortunately, there are others that do, and what I don't know, I can learn. But if Shakete and Karen and you have faith that I'm the right person, I'll figure it out. Anyway, I honestly don't know anyone else that's willing to take the job other than Victor. I once lived in a world where no one trusted the Russians, and I can't totally trust one now." Always understating his ability, that's my father.

In the play of life, we all get our shot to perform a leading role in a tragedy--illness, addiction, death, betrayal, take your pick. Some poor souls seem to be well suited for the part and either by happenstance or temperament, spend a lifetime cleaving to misfortune. The difference in people is not whether tragedy strikes, for it will, but rather how the tragedy remakes them.

I've known the bitter, the crazies, the angry, the hopeless, and some combination of each, and I've known a few like my niece, Chrystel. Chrystel is one of those people who somehow turns tragedy inside out to make it her most valuable experience. Since her betrayal by Brodie, the only man she ever truly cared for, and the loss of her friend Tweet, she is different in a good way. Always confident, her confidence now seems to come from a deeper place, one born of loss and the knowledge that people can survive and grow from adversity.

The other day, she stopped by the library to get some information about sewage treatment plants. We were sitting at a work table as she perused diagrams when she stopped and squinted her eyes at me. "Why are you looking at me that way?" she asked.

I responded, "I wasn't looking at you any kind of way, specifically."

"Yes, you were. Why does everyone look at me like they're waiting for me to explode or breakdown? As if I'm going to develop a panic disorder like my mom."

"We're just concerned. We all know your feelings for Brodie. His loss and betrayal had to be very painful."

Chrystel started laughing and rubbing her eyes. "Yep, painful for sure. Here's the thing, Uncle Geronimo, betrayal sits right at the top of my list of hurtful experiences. Even given that, I would do it all again. I feel more alive now than I've ever felt. I loved him. I still do. My body aches from missing him. I hang on to the fact that his escape means he's still out there alive, somewhere, and he's still with me in here," Chrystel pounded her chest. "I would rather have that than nothing at all inside. He made some mistakes for sure, but we have long lives. Perhaps, someday I'll see him again and forgive him, like I did with Mom. Until then, I'll go on with the knowledge that I can be loved, and I'm capable of giving it back. Now, can you leave me alone, so I can finish what I was doing?"

I chuckled to myself. I should have expected no less from our amazing family redhead. Chrystel no longer spends much time at the courthouse. She is out with the people, listening and learning, doing what needs to be done to improve their lives and secure the future. That unusual manner she had with people, indifferent and pushy at the same time, has moderated and is now overlaid with a genuine warmth. I am very proud of the person our Chrystel has become. She is doing a fine job as mayor, and that bodes well for the next few, critical years.

Luckily, Chrystel's pal, Tilley survived. My mom confided that the Tilley that came back to earth from the Delamie healed may be a replicated version. Apparently, the Ardinians possess the ability to download a consciousness, memories included, into a new body. Who knew and how interesting. Regardless, they are inseparable, and Chrystel is none the wiser about whether Tilley is an original or a newly minted copy.

Amelia and Chrystel have forged a relationship out of the ruins of another tragic drama. I think It helped Chrystel to know that Amelia had struck out on her own with Lionheart in the dead of night to warn her. They are still mother and daughter, so on occasion I hear them quibbling with each other, and that's as it should be.

When I gaze over the history of New Washington since the Great Dying, I can't help but believe our people have had a pretty good run of it--from Jed's thorium generator to decent people trying to do the right thing, to the temperate weather in New Washington. At least, good until now. Perhaps, our luck has run its course. My dad gave me the grave news yesterday that the Ardinians now believe the Huntas may be here sooner than expected, as early as six months. If that's the case, we won't have time to build a proper defense. We'll be left to the mercy of our fate. I'll close for now with our new, old motto (after the attack on the airfield, Karen's optimistic motto version was struck down in a landslide vote and replaced with the original), We Endure.

    Geronimo M.

# Epilogue

Brodie slipped out of the forest to a clearing. The trip to Idaho had taken far longer than he expected. He frequently stopped along the way to enjoy the scenery and to think. It was a cleansing process. He longed for Chrystel. To know that he might never see her again or have a chance to say goodbye to his old dog left him empty, bereft. As he had gotten closer to Idaho, a new feeling crept in to fill a small part of that void—freedom. Freedom from carrying the burden of his lies. It was done—the truth was released. He pledged to himself with every step never to live a lie again.

He jogged the rest of the way up a hill and swept his eyes across the landscape. Down below, Brodie saw a man hefting boxes from the back of an ATV, stacking them alongside a cinderblock building. The man must have sensed him. He stopped, placed the box he was carrying on the ground, and looked up in Brodie's direction.

*Oh my God. That's not a man, that's a Bigfoot!* Brodie had never seen a Bigfoot before in person, but he had seen Karen's paintings of Uh Huh. That bony ridge over the eyes, the wide neck, and the hair covering his arms and a good portion of his face could only mean one thing—he was screwed if he didn't run for his life.

The Bigfoot opened his mouth as if to yell, but he didn't seem to make a sound. Before Brodie's eyes more Bigfoots appeared from inside the block building, the cab of the ATV, and even slipping out of the surrounding scenery, there all along but unseen. Brodie knew two things for certain; they didn't look happy, and he was well and utterly screwed. He turned and took a deep breath, making ready to run for his life back into the forest. Hopefully, they were too busy to make chase.

From the corner of his eyes, Brodie saw the flash of a Mermot, scurrying to meet the unhappy band of Bigfoots. Brodie couldn't help himself. He stopped to watch what happened next. The whole tableau was so surreal he couldn't turn away.

Stopping in front of the Bigfoot that had moments before been stacking boxes, the Mermot raised on his back legs and tail, whiskers in motion, to mind meld something into the Bigfoot's brain. At least, that's what it looked like to Brodie from this distance. The Bigfoot shrugged and picked up his box while the Mermot, in a blur, headed in Brodie's direction.

Stopping on a dime, the large Mermot raised from the ground to meet Brodie's surprised gaze. "I am Rappel. We have not been formally introduced, but I was told that a human might join us. You are Brodie, is that correct?"

"Yes, I'm Brodie." He reached out to shake the Mermot hand extended for a human greeting. "Bigfoots? How? Why?"

"It is a wonderful story I will sing to you later. It is a song for the ages. They are quite shy, but tremendous workers and loyal friends. A large group of Bigfoots was living here in this wilderness. They live in clans, much as my people. Because I could talk with them, we formed a partnership. They also want to participate in the defense of their home. They were more cooperative after Mermots demonstrated good faith by helping their clan to build better shelters for their comfort. Come, join us. I only recommend you show no aggression. They are a nervous lot. And whatever you do, don't refer to them Bigfoots. They call themselves Earthers."

Brodie gave Rappel a long stare. He gave more thought to starting a life somewhere else, a place where there were no Ardinians, Mermots, or Bigfoots, aka Earthers, and the only other unworldly creatures for miles around would be talking dogs. He wished for a moment he was the kind of man who could forget about the coming threat of the Huntas. Then he shrugged like the first Bigfoot he had ever seen and headed into the strange encampment.

I hope you enjoyed Beyond the Great Dying. If you could take a moment and leave a review on Kindle, I'd be greatly appreciative. For most Indie writers, those reviews are especially important.

If you're interested in sending me specific feedback or would like to ask a question, my website is https://www.nsaustinwrites.com

Rogerios Pond
Cleaning Service

Made in the USA
Las Vegas, NV
24 May 2021

23589333R00291